SNOWFLAKES, CAKES AND ROYAL MISTAKES

By

Elizabeth Heathly

ISBN: 979-8-9916624-0-6

For my grandmother, who loved baking. And for anyone who wishes they could write a Happily Ever After for those who matter most to them.

Thank you for reading ❤.

Chapter One

"It's time to get married, Lana."

The Queen Consort's words echoed in Lana's mind as she strode down the hallway, passing dozens of portraits of ancestors who stared out at her from their gilded frames.

At first, Lana had thought—*hoped*—the conversation was a pain-induced hallucination caused by the intricate wooden swirl digging into her back. There was *no way* the Council could be so short-sighted. So callous.

So she'd sat in that horrible, overdecorated chair, frozen in disbelief except for the tiny muscle in her eyelid that twitched frantically as if begging her to find an impossible solution. But as her father had continued to say *nothing* and the curtains had finally stopped swaying from the Economic Minister's dramatic exit the moment before, Lana had realized there wasn't another option.

Despite years of hard work and taking on additional responsibilities so her father could step down the following autumn, Lana's fate had been decided before she even knew it had been up for debate. It had been decided long before the Economic Minister started dancing around his "mysterious solution" to solving a critical problem for New Bravaria's failing economy. Before her genial, ever-at-ease father started shifting in his own uncomfortably ornate chair.

How can a wedding solve New Bravaria's economic problems better than a logical trade policy?

Lana hadn't posed the only question worth asking because she already knew the answer: it couldn't. And her parents refused to see it. Jakob II might be king, but he was as optimistic as her Queen Consort mother, Givera, was determined.

And then, although Lana hadn't thought it was possible, the meeting had taken a turn for the worse.

Givera had *sighed*. She'd always been able to kindle every one of Lana's insecurities with a single exhale. That guilt-evoking sigh asked the questions that kept Lana up at night when her other worries took a rare vacation. It asked why Lana wasn't better, why she had the nerve to propose alternatives to the ideas of people who'd earned their places instead of being born into them, and why she'd been gifted so much privilege and had still let down the family—no, the entire *kingdom*—out of laziness and selfishness like their Old Bravarian neighbors.

As Lana approached the map at the end of the corridor, she could still see Givera waiting with her hands clasped in her lap, expression cool as if she could see past Lana's twitching eye to the guarded panic beneath. Every detail of Givera's appearance had been firmly in its place, from the evenly spaced highlights that added shine to her mousy brown hair to the matching pantsuit—this one was a hazy pale blue—that refused to wrinkle even when she sat.

The twitching in Lana's eye had grown faster as she'd tried to imagine how to undo the damage that this ridiculous precedent would set. She'd been beyond stunned. She was—

"You'll need to announce and introduce your fiancé at the Winter Solstice Ball to ensure that the festivities coincide with the festival dates this summer," Givera had said as Lana's thoughts spiraled. *This* was her kingdom's solution to a crippling trade deficit that had been growing for decades? Scheduling a once-in-her-lifetime wedding to coincide with the Alpine Film Festival so its board would delay relocating to a more convenient location by just one year? "You can choose whomever you'd like."

Givera had placed what could only be a thick packet of men into Lana's hand, which was still tingling. Lana had made some polite reply about selecting a candidate after her upcoming trip and left the room before she made the situation even worse by revealing that the personal implications of this ambush would be just as painful as the political ones.

Skin hot, Lana paused at the map and scanned Bravaria's region out of habit, noting the jagged mountain borders separating Bravaria from the neighboring countries of Switzerland, Austria, and Italy. Bravaria always seemed so small compared to its neighbors, and its stubborn politicians seemed determined to further shrink its influence. As Lana's gaze snagged on the border that had split the constitutional monarchy into New and Old Bravaria a century earlier—yet another stubborn decision that made Bravaria seem so, so small—the packet slipped out of her now-unfeeling fingers.

–numb. Numb was the word she'd been looking for in the drawing room. She was completely, entirely numb.

❄

Lana made it to the famed Reading Room (where the legendary Svetlana Eaton had written all six volumes of *Peace in the Mountains*) before her parents caught up with her. She walked to the embroidered window seat where she'd spent countless hours reading as a child, fearlessly exploring worlds of science fiction and fantasy while steam from the river below danced toward the window panes. But for the first time, exploring didn't feel like it would be enough. Lana wanted to escape into another world. She'd even take the idyllic cottage life Ms. Eaton had detailed so beautifully if it were her only option!

It had never been so tempting to wish she were someone else. Someone whose parents hadn't blind-sided her—hadn't served up her marriage on a gold-plated platter for the Economic Minister to use as he pleased. Someone who hadn't just realized that she was going to drown in the guilt of hating, just the tiniest bit, one more sacrifice she should have been happy to make for Bravaria.

Someone who could feel her hands, preferably. And appreciate the world-renowned scene below without eye twitches disrupting her view. Lana's ever-present stress was usually a subtle undercurrent in her mind, but when it flared unexpectedly, it became physically impossible to ignore.

Lana's father squeezed her shoulder, then sat beside Givera, who placed the fallen spreadsheet on the low table by the window seat. Lana eyed it with distaste.

"Lana, are you all right?" her father asked, massaging his temple. Did he get eye twitches, too? She'd never noticed. "We didn't mean to upset you."

Lana always had a reply ready during Council debates. Devising alternative solutions and creative workarounds was one of her favorite parts of her role, even if some of the Councilors she had to negotiate with could be infuriating. But for the second time that day, Lana was at a loss for words. Her parents had demanded she marry, instead of hinting at it by inviting marriageable candidates to tea like she imagined normal parents did. And to have gone behind her back with the Council...well, with the rest of the Council, since Lana had held the honorary (and silent) thirteenth Council seat since graduating from university...

Lana was generally an unemotional person. In fact, two of her failed college coffee dates had cited that exact quality when explaining why they didn't want to go on a second date. But the taste of betrayal—not to mention the surprise that came along with it—was sharp. Hard to think around.

"You've always said you would marry for your country," Givera chimed in. "It's the responsible thing to do. And with your coronation next year...Your father wouldn't be comfortable stepping down so early if you aren't ready for it." She brushed at an invisible speck of dust on her cuff. "We didn't think you'd be upset."

"I'm not upset," Lana insisted, hating her lie. She didn't deserve to be upset. Her first bite of solid food had been delivered on a silver spoon, and she'd lived in luxury ever since. She'd had opportunities others couldn't even dream of, which was further proof that doing everything she possibly could for Bravaria was always the right thing to do. Lana had no right to be upset because some rogue part of her might've—she could barely stomach thinking it—wanted *feelings* to factor into the mix, either on her side or her parents' side. Besides, Lana had always said exactly what her mother claimed: it was her job to marry and provide New Bravaria with heirs. "I'm just surprised that Councilor Merrick told me."

Givera pursed her lips. Lana clashed with the Economic Minister on a near-daily basis since he led the coalition opposing her own party's conciliatory stance on their Old Bravarian rivals. And Councilor Merrick often broke important news. He'd been the first Councilor the Queen Consort had endorsed, and her words had come out of his mouth ever since.

"And I'm surprised that you think a hasty marriage would fix anything." Lana knew her parents wouldn't budge on their stance, but she had to try. "We need lasting change, not a one-off event. Best case scenario, we keep the festival for an extra year. But diverting the resources to do so will set us back in establishing new partnerships that will be more valuable in the future." The Alpine Film Festival was held in both New and Old Bravaria, and the exorbitant border crossing fees and long security checks—both of which had grown as relations between the rivals grew ever frostier over the past forty years—had put an expiration date on the arrangement long ago. Lana hadn't yet convinced the Council that New Bravaria's many tourist attractions and remote resorts were better suited to smaller retreats that could be held throughout the year, and had the potential to generate more lucrative and consistent revenue than the festival. The prestige and guaranteed revenue from the festival was just too tempting, even though it required repeatedly shepherding thousands of people across the border. "Are you sure this is really the best solution?"

"It can't hurt. And there's the other matter…of Michel." Her father shot her mother a meaningful glance.

"Michel wants to marry Kaleb. And because of the Heir First Law, he can't. We've delayed it long enough, honey." The statement was delivered in her mother's Queen Consort Voice—the one that had dominated their conversations since the guilt-evoking sighs arrived, and a voice Michel had likely never heard.

Lana couldn't blame her parents for choosing Michel's happiness over her own, but it still hurt. As she'd learned early on, that seemed to be the difference between being an heir and being a son. Rulers wanted their heirs to successfully fulfill their duties. Parents wanted their sons to be happy. Michel had met Kaleb, the love of his life, at the tender age of seventeen. After four years of dating, it seemed he was ready to permanently secure his happiness. But apparently he couldn't, because of yet another antiquated tradition engraved in the Bravarian Royal Constitution.

"You know this is ridiculous?" Lana asked. "The Heir First Law requires the heir to marry first to ensure that they have a head start on producing their own heir…But it's not like Michel and Kaleb are accidentally going to get pregnant! Can't we just amend the law or make an exception so they can marry?"

"You know we can't do that." Her father sighed. How many times had Lana been told that royalty's stability relied on consistency? That little changes to the rules added up, and that too many changes could leave them with nothing? "And he's been waiting so long. Think of it as killing two birds with one stone."

Lana tried to convince herself to put on her big-girl crown, to remember that it was her duty as heir to provide stability for the family and for the nation. It wasn't best for her or for her country, but Michel would be with the man of his dreams, and Lana would give New Bravaria the heirs and the economic stability it needed to prosper for generations to come.

Lana took the packet of potential grooms from Givera. Her father had likely chosen his bride through a similar process, and although her parents didn't have the burning love of romcoms, they'd gotten the job of producing an heir and a spare well and done. And it wasn't as if Lana were a particularly romantic person herself. She'd dated a bit in college during the glory days when she could try doing what her best friend, Caro, called Normal Person Things since the paparazzi weren't allowed to release photos of royal children until they turned twenty-one. That "dating" had primarily consisted of awkward first dates and a five-date "relationship" with a classmate called Carson. After it culminated in a clumsy, mutually uncomfortable attempt at checking "college hookup" off the Caro-mandated list of Normal Person Things to Accomplish Before Lana's Debut, Lana had stopped sacrificing study time for ill-fated coffee dates. Until someone intrigued her half as much as the latest book she was reading—or even her chemistry homework— what was the point?

Since then, Lana simply hadn't dated. Dating as a princess was complicated, period. Dating as an over-scheduled introvert was about as appealing as skiing through slush. Lana met few people who weren't politicians or subjects (or both), and on the rare occasions when she had met a non-subject, non-politician, they hadn't had the good fortune of caring half as much as she did about Bravaria or her education programs or the latest book on Norse mythology. And anyone who didn't meet those basic requirements was simply not worth the trouble of dating.

Of course, as Lana scanned the cover of the packet, she realized that she'd maintained this belief because she'd subconsciously assumed that someday in the vague future she'd marry a reliable, not-too-obnoxious man who wouldn't hold her back, or even hold her attention long enough to distract her from more important things. Unfortunately, that day had come, and the fact that she had the world's best job security when it came to balancing work with motherhood was looking to be the best part of the situation. Not for the first time, Lana wondered why she'd been born the practical one, while Michel had enough romance in his little finger for the both of them. He was three years younger and already eagerly pursuing marriage, whereas Lana was being dragged to the altar by her crown.

"Why don't we go through this together?" Givera asked, pulling Lana down to her side so the three of them sat in a row to consider the list of potential husbands.

Lana blinked. There were more columns in the spreadsheet than dates she'd been on in her entire life.

"We wanted to give you options, so the list is quite long," Givera began, and went on to walk Lana through columns describing title and nationality, languages spoken, and estimated net worth. "Elegant" men of most sorts had been deemed appropriate, and princes, noblemen, scions, and a few tech entrepreneurs were considered equally acceptable from a political standpoint.

"Mother!" Lana exclaimed, having skimmed through the rest of the columns. She must have missed something. "There aren't even faces on here!"

Givera raised an eyebrow. "Would someone's appearance influence your decision?"

Lana lifted her chin, conceding the point. "No." She couldn't care less what someone looked like. But even dating apps had faces on them; how else were you supposed to imagine the facial expression of your soon-to-be-betrothed while you proposed to them over the phone?

"We can add photos if you'd like," her father cut in. "We did include height so you'd know how they'd fit standing beside you for the annual Solstice photo."

"Either way," Givera continued, "I distinctly remember you telling me that if you were a princess in a fairy tale instead of in real life, your Prince Charming would prove his strength by carrying massive piles of books for you, not by slaying dragons."

"I must've been nine years old when I said that!"

"You were eight, actually." Her mother chucked her under her chin. "But I know my daughter. And that's why, for the very first time in Bravarian history—" she and her husband shared the cheeky glance of coconspirators—"we included these."

Lana's eyes widened as her mother tapped two columns that read "University" and "Grade Point Average."

"And you sorted this by…" Lana couldn't hold back an ambivalent huff of a laugh. Focusing on the humorous was so much better than acknowledging the rest of this ridiculous situation. If she weren't reeling from a sense of familial betrayal and the realization that she was, to her complete dismay, more romantic than she'd realized, she'd appreciate the sorting. It was the exact criteria Caro had attempted to ban Lana from using to select candidates for her semester of failed dates.

"Yes, the best students are at the top," her father assured her with a twinkle in his warm brown eyes. Her eyes. He was young for a soon-to-be-retired man, and slightly tanned skin covered an athletic build that had only started yielding to a softer chin earlier that year. "But please remember that some of us—I like to think myself included—can be excellent human beings even if we didn't get perfect grades. Or attend university at all."

"I know, Dad. But it can't hurt." Being forced to cohabitate and reproduce with somebody who couldn't hold an intelligent conversation was one of Lana's worst nightmares. How someone scored on an exam when they were twenty was hardly an accurate measure, but it wasn't like she had time to meet anyone on the list in person. "At least I'm not running a beauty contest."

Her father patted her hand. "That's what I did."

Her mother elbowed him in the ribs.

"Well, it was a beauty contest and a dowry contest. And look what I got from it all." He winked at her mother, whose face revealed the tiniest sliver of a smile before returning to its stern, business set. Lana's maternal grandfather's family was wealthy, but the real value had been in their connections—and, of course, the fact that Givera Bassano was a taskmaster and natural politician with the fierce work ethic that had been bred out of the royal family generations earlier. From the day Givera became Queen Consort, everything the royals did was more. More appearances for the press, more charities sponsored, more meetings attended, more initiatives led, more positive popularity ratings, and more rules.

Givera closed the packet. "Lana, you said you'll decide after your trip to Grandma's. But if you decide today, your fiancé could go with you, and you could have a seven-day courting period before announcing your engagement at Solstice. It would be appropriate. It's what your father did with me."

Royal courting periods could last up to a month, but shorter courtships had become common toward the end of the twentieth century. It wasn't lost on Lana that an abbreviated courting period was her only option—if she'd have one at all. And now they wanted her to choose in mere hours?

"What do you think? You have all the information you need right here. Why wait?" Givera patted the packet of doom.

Lana couldn't do it.

And she needed a week away from everything—from everyone—to convince herself that she could.

"I need this trip, Mother," Lana insisted. "It's my one week of vacation every year. My one week of true privacy. Let me not choose for just one week, and when I come back, I'll have my decision ready. I promise."

She could compartmentalize. She *would* compartmentalize. Ninety-nine-point-five percent of Lana would focus on doing some much-needed relaxing when she wasn't industriously panicking about the other most important deadline of her life, and just a tiny amount of brain space would worry about choosing her future life partner.

"Of course, my dear," her father said. "You deserve to have a wonderful time. If only I could go with you."

Givera shot him a withering glare.

"Taking a husband doesn't greatly change who you are, Lana, or how you have to spend your days." He winked again at her mother, who ignored it. "It just enables you to welcome the next generation of New Bravarians, who in turn will keep our country strong and proud."

He made to get up, but her mother put a hand on his knee before delivering what she clearly saw as important motherly advice. "In that case, we should make sure everything is ready for your meetings with your fiancé upon your return. And we should book a waxing appointment for when you get back. Just to…smooth the way." She gave Lana a meaningful look. "We'll definitely want to clean up your eyebrows."

Those eyebrows furrowed at her.

"Don't do that, Lana. You already know you're going to get early wrinkles on your forehead."

Lana took a deep breath and tried to smooth both her nerves and her expression. As long as she wasn't subjected to another sigh, she could remain calm. She could.

"We'll touch up your lip, and probably the rest of you, too…" Givera waved a hand. "I'll have Vera arrange it. You should really look into laser so we don't have to keep talking about this."

"Mom, no!" Lana usually addressed Givera as "Mother", but extreme circumstances called for extreme measures. Her father was blushing, furtively looking for ways to escape his wife's grip on his thigh, and Lana was desperately trying not to envision how her mother had prepared for her own courting period back in the day. "Absolutely not! No way am I doing… anything to my body to please some man whom, may I remind you, I haven't chosen yet! And the last thing on their mind will be…" She couldn't make herself say it, but she was mortified both for herself and her father, who'd finally escaped the window seat and seemed to be in the process of dashing off to his private quarters and staying there for a while.

"Lana. Are you really going to argue about this?"

Lana ran a hand over her straight-blown hair, which was safer than rubbing her makeup-laden face. She took a deep breath, suddenly feeling more composed after one of the most unnerving conversations of her life. "No, I'm not. Because this isn't up for discussion. Please don't book me anything. I've never been unpresentable a day in my life."

Givera nodded.

"I'll submit my decision to the Council when I return. If you'll excuse me, I need to add…this"—Lana brandished the twenty-five most ridiculous pieces of paper she'd ever seen —"to my packing list."

❄

When Lana retired to her chambers that evening and saw the carefully stacked piles of clothes covering her enormous bed, she couldn't help but laugh. If she hadn't already known that Vera took her job *very* seriously, the packing preparation would've been a dead giveaway.

Lana's grandmother, Esmelda, lived in Havos, one of the world's safest villages—so safe, so isolated, and so carefully vetted by a discreet but thorough security team before Lana's annual arrival that it was the one place she could go and just…be. Without bodyguards, without Vera, without her parents or brother. And she loved it.

For her assistant, however, the event was probably hives-inducing. Vera was a flutter of energy and paid attention to *every* minute detail. Preparing Lana for a trip for which there was no formal itinerary was likely her version of a professional nightmare.

"Vera, are you still here?" Lana called loudly, knowing her voice would carry to whichever section of her closet or bathroom Vera was currently digging through.

"Yes, Lana!" All five feet ten inches of Vera's tan, slender frame skidded into the room. Her black hair was styled in a high ponytail, and she *owned* her fitted black suit—to the extent that Lana still secretly wondered if Vera had ever worked as a model.

Getting Vera to call her Lana instead of Princess Svetlana had been a massive accomplishment, valid only in private. They were still working on the part of their relationship where Vera followed Lana's packing list. The current mountain range of clothing piled on the bed was evidence of their progress. Vera prepared the piles and Lana reviewed them before they went into a hefty suitcase. Unfortunately, it seemed like Vera had embellished the packing list.

"What's that?" Lana eyed a cord trailing from whichever mysterious device Vera was hiding behind her back.

"A blow-dryer." She brandished it proudly. "So you don't catch cold."

"That wasn't on the list," Lana said, gently taking the blow-dryer from her overeager assistant and looking blankly around the spacious bathroom. There were two sinks, six cabinets, and ten drawers. Where did it go? She'd never used it by choice. "I'm sure my grandmother has one in case I need it," she added to spare Vera's feelings.

Vera begrudgingly returned the blow-dryer to the second cabinet from the left, then went back for the wayward hair straightener that had been hidden behind a pile of sweaters.

"Are you looking forward to your week off?" Lana asked as she started washing the makeup off her face. Cleanser and makeup remover were the two cosmetic items she could *always* find in her bathroom.

"Yes, but..." Vera clasped her hands behind her back. "Are you going to be okay out there by yourself? With no one to...help you?"

Lana patted her face dry and smiled. This was Vera's first Solstice in the royal family's employ. "I will be fine. I have my grandmother there, and my friends, and if it makes you feel any better..." Vera met her eyes when she paused. "You should know that I survived living in a college dormitory. For three years. And it was full of college students."

Vera laughed and Lana returned to surveying the piles on the bed. Lana was proud of the fact that she packed light (for a royal), and she always liked her bags to be ready a few days before leaving so she could add anything she'd forgotten. Minus the attempted smuggling in of beauty equipment, Vera had followed her list with great attention to detail. Lana's most sparkly winter clothing, extra boots, gloves, and scarves, the worn copies of more favorite books than she'd have time to reread, and a makeup bag that she let slide in the name of Choosing Her Battles covered the bed, along with two copies of the husband packet: one in a binder, and one loose.

"You made copies!" she asked Vera, alarmed.

"Just one! It's so important, I figured you wouldn't want to lose it…"

"Do you have a boyfriend, Vera?" Lana asked as she tossed the paper packet onto her desk.

"No. I'm focused on…other things at the moment," Vera assured her.

"So was I." Lana glared at the second packet, which was safely—*anonymously*—concealed in an unmarked binder. It was thoughtful of Vera to disguise it. Lana wouldn't look at it until the drive back, but she'd have to bring it with her because she'd feel guilty otherwise. "It was nice not having a boyfriend. But I'll be engaged to a stranger in less than two weeks."

"If you want me to do any further research on your options, let me know. The Council ran background and credit checks, but I can pull photos or stalk past girlfriends or make some calls if you want a clearer picture of anyone."

Even one picture would be nice, Lana thought to herself, trying not to snort. It wasn't Vera's fault that she was in a terrible mood.

❄

Lana's silver nails glittered as she adjusted the settings on the centrifuge the following evening, reflecting sparks of light onto the bland wall. Normally the evidence that she'd managed to slip a tiny sparkle of rebellion into her otherwise perfectly coiffed appearance would've made her smile. But tonight, that victory paled in comparison with the larger thrill of being in the lab—a victory made all the more dear by the sheer panic and frustration caused by a certain deadline that she *was not thinking about*, unlike the other far more important deadline that she was.

Caro rushed back into the lab as the centrifuge finished its cycle, and they grinned at each other. It wasn't the playlist running in the background (which they'd designed to correspond to the run and rest times for their full test cycle). It wasn't the thrill of being the only souls in the building, since the regular workday had ended hours before. It wasn't even the fact that this was it—the final round of tests they needed to run before submitting their application for what they'd starting calling The Most Important Grant in the World—or the fact that if they were caught, there would be *consequences*, because using the government-funded lab for private research was against its policy. No, they were grinning like children on Solstice morning because these moments, experienced almost entirely while sleep-deprived, stressed beyond measure, and in tedious, repetitive situations like the fourteenth iteration of a very monotonous protocol, were precious. They were *fun*. They were *chosen*. If even they came with a price.

But Lana was good at compartmentalizing and temporarily ignoring that price. She simply didn't have the brain space to do her part in the lab, agonize over the possibility of getting caught, worry about her duties, torment herself about an unwanted fiancé, and be exhausted at the same time. That is—until she reached a good stopping point. The moment she paused, the endless concerns came rushing right back.

Lana shook her head, pushing aside all thoughts of tomorrow's tiredness as she watched Caro work in a whirlwind of arms, pipettes, and test tube stands. Not for the first time, Lana marveled at her friend's seemingly endless energy, which displayed itself in stark contrast to her own growing fatigue. Lana frowned. She couldn't actually remember the last time she wasn't at least a little bit tired. *Is this the price of keeping secrets?* she wondered. *Or do I get an extra-special dose of tiredness just for fun? Is it* karma?

"I need to run in a few minutes," Lana admitted once Caro had snapped the lid onto the final test tube. The next step was simple but involved a long wait time, and Lana felt terrible for not being able to complete what she'd started. "I'm so sorry I couldn't help more."

"Lana, it's okay!" Her friend's forest-green eyes were bright and far more awake-looking than Lana's brown ones, despite the fact that it was eleven thirty at night and Caro often pulled twelve hour days in the lab. "You've been here for hours, and I know the King of Spain won't make it any easier for you to stay awake at that eight a.m. public breakfast tomorrow," Caro insisted. "Seriously, who would schedule such a thing?"

Lana shrugged and burst out laughing before she could stop herself. Her filters melted like so much snow when she was tired. "Wouldn't it make more sense for King Alfonso and I to discuss the history of the wool trade and pose for pictures in our dressing gowns? At least then the paparazzi could watch us fall back asleep as we bore each other to tears."

As well-versed as she was in the role publicity played to generate interest in tourism and lend legitimacy to the New Bravarian constitutional monarchy, Lana still struggled to understand how some of her duties were helpful. Take tomorrow, for instance: what could people possibly get from a live broadcast of a formal breakfast and discussion about the sixty-fifth anniversary of an important trade deal? Wouldn't a private breakfast and brief speech be more effective (and less draining for a certain royal introvert)?

And the King of Spain was famously dull: at seventy-two, he had startlingly long ear hair, a penchant for wearing waistcoats with too many buttons, and a fondness for the mouflon sheep that the Bravarian region was famous for. His jostled appearance contrasted starkly with the demands of Lana's styling team, who wanted her fully conscious and at their mercy by six. Lana's healthy figure and heart-shaped face ensured that it didn't take too much to make her presentable, but her thick hair was just on the curly-and-frizzy side of wavy, and her Bravarian-fair skin made her dark circles painfully obvious, so the styling chair was an unavoidable part of her daily routine. And Lana needed more than the five and a half hours of sleep she was going to get to stay awake for the meeting itself. Just that morning, Vera had reminded her that a maximum of three cups of tea in a two-hour meeting period was considered acceptable. A part of her had wilted at the thought. Boring, she could handle. Boring and supported by limited quantities of caffeine? Questionable.

"It's okay, Lana," Caro repeated, and pulled her into a tight hug. "I've got this. I'll run the rest of the protocol and email the results to you and Erik—with plenty of time to download before you reach Havos's dead zone!"

She did a happy little jig at that last bit, blonde curls bouncing, which made Lana smile again. Caro was a joyful person, but the silly jigs were solely for Lana's benefit. Ever since learning Lana's royal secret, Caro had made it her personal mission to ensure that Lana didn't give up on all of her dreams and conform to *everything* the Council wanted. So even if Caro's dancing did damage to one's eyeballs (coordination was not one of her natural gifts), it was the thought that counted.

"I can't wait," Lana admitted, squeezing Caro's hand before grabbing her coat. Since they'd become friends in college, Caro had come and spent a week at Lana's grandmother's house in the village of Havos before each Solstice. Solstice was a sacred time of year around the beloved national holiday, during which everything in Bravaria more or less stopped while the festivities were underway. In the larger cities, that meant parties, special foods, and reunions with family. In Havos, it meant much the same, but on a more peaceful scale. For someone burnt out and desperate for time out of the spotlight, it was an oasis.

But this year would be different. For the first time, Caro would stay at the Winter Springs Inn, Havos's only hotel, instead of at Esmelda's house. Since this was also the first time that Erik, Lana's good friend—and Caro's boyfriend—would join them, Esmelda had graciously but firmly recommended that the lovebirds stay somewhere that could offer larger than a twin bed.

"Me neither! And it's working out perfectly this year with the grant application deadline falling on December twenty-first. It's a bit rude for them to set a deadline on the morning of the Winter Solstice Ball, but we'll submit early anyway, right?"

Lana nodded. Of course they were submitting early. Lana had never *not* beaten a deadline.

"So our week in Havos is the perfect time for us to finish analyzing the results from these final samples and focus on our application, with no distractions from the internet. Or work. Or your parents. Or the latest season of *Space Pirates: London Fiasco*." Caro counted days on her fingers and then gave a sheepish smile before admitting that the long-awaited penultimate season of the show would start airing halfway through their week in Havos.

"*No*," Lana gasped. The show was as terrible as it sounded, but it was the kind of terrible that made it impossible to look away. Lana was mildly hooked, but Caro was downright addicted. "You can't let yourself fall down that rabbit hole before we get everything ready."

"I won't," Caro promised. "I'm saving it as my Solstice gift to myself. And Erik made me promise not to download any episodes to watch in Havos. On account of it not being 'in the spirit of work and recovery.'" Her voice rose at the end, indignant.

Lana rolled her eyes. Caro's TV addictions were powerful but notoriously selective. If Caro truly convinced herself that something else was more important, she could wait *years*. "As horrible as that sounds, you really won't have to wait very long."

Caro huffed in response.

"It's just one day until we leave! Then one week in Havos, a quick drive back home, and it's you, your couch, and Fernando the one-eyed space pirate for as long as your heart desires."

Caro grinned at her. Fernando was surprisingly compelling for a cyclops-style half-human space-flying vigilante, and he had six seasons of prior conquests Caro would doubtlessly rewatch in preparation for the new season.

Lana grinned back, but for another reason. This was one of the most important projects of her life. If the grant application were approved, the research it funded would be meaningful for the scientific community and life-changing for the Bravarian people.

"One day?" Caro asked as Lana grabbed her coat and pile of outerwear. It had been below freezing when she'd arrived at the lab hours before, and it would be even colder now. "I believe it's two."

Lana pointed her chin at the clock as she zipped her coat. It was just past midnight. "Not anymore."

❄

Stars dotted the sky as Lana began her stealthy walk home. Travel writers often described Baulten as a cross between Aspen, Colorado and a sixteenth-century fairytale; something about the way sleek luxury resorts, shops, and tastefully designed office buildings were interspersed among rows of historic cottages, the original Royal Baths, and the palace complex made first-time visitors gape every time. But the privilege of being able to walk through her city alone, surrounded by centuries-old cobblestones and the gentle glow of streetlights instead of the usual mix of Councilors and security personnel made it even more beautiful.

Lana's parents understood that her friendship with Caro was one of the few concessions necessary to protect her sanity and manage her stress levels, and they respected her routine "girls' nights" in Caro's apartment, which was located in a very safe neighborhood just five blocks from the Winter Palace. Since Lana had never given the security team a reason to worry about her behavior, uniformed officers patrolled those five blocks each "girls' night", and she was spared having a personal bodyguard for the walk itself.

This was also why nobody had realized that biweekly reruns of *Space Pirates* played to Caro's very empty, very well-curtained family room. After arriving at Caro's apartment, Lana would start the show, lock the door behind her, and immediately sneak out the back door of Caro's building to meet her friend at the research center down the street. The ongoing ruse was one of ten thousand reasons why Lana's anxiety levels never dropped below "average," but she refused to feel guilty about it and she refused to accept that secretly burning the candle at both ends could be taking its toll.

It had been bad enough when her parents discovered that she'd double majored in politics and chemistry when they'd framed her diploma. That was the day the Queen Consort voice became a permanent feature of Lana's conversations with her parents. They couldn't disown the heir they were depending on to continue the family line for allowing a "silly distraction" like science to share brain space with her political training, but they could do as much as possible to limit Lana's free time and reduce possible distractions. So they definitely couldn't know that Lana had been moonlighting as a part-time chemist. Especially since the work she and Caro did—preliminary research that pertained to Old Bravaria just as much as New Bravaria—was somewhat illegally conducted in Caro's government-funded lab.

Lana entered the back foyer of the palace complex and a

servant took her coat, hat, scarf, gloves, and boots as if she couldn't remove them herself. But she smiled graciously, thanked the man, and allowed him to carry out the centuries-long tradition of assisting royals with the grand process of undressing.

To be fair, the tradition made sense for much of history, Lana admitted as she eyed the enormous portrait of Princess Svetlana Latticia Haspel Melvin, a princess of Bravaria from the end of the sixteenth century. The weight and layers of the woman's outfit had been impossible to coordinate without assistance (conflicting accounts estimated the weight of Svetlana Latticia's ceremonial dress at both fourteen and nineteen pounds), so Lana didn't fault her for having a famed retinue of eight professional seamstresses to help with daily dressing and undressing. That said, Lana drew the line at the invention of zippers and lightweight fabrics. With the exception of those tricky top buttons at the napes of ballgowns, she would happily believe that the need for all dressing assistance in the twenty-first century was well and truly gone.

As Lana passed portraits of noble ancestors who looked boldly at her from their frames along the staircase, she bit back a tired sigh. Her life was certainly the pinnacle of a first-world problem, especially compared to the struggles her ancestors had overcome to make Bravaria what it was today. Lana had six tiaras, after all. But nobody ever considered the massive amount of pins—uncomfortable, nearly unbearable at times—that were endured to hold those tiaras safely in place. That it was her job to smile even when it felt like her head was going to fall off because she'd been lucky enough to be born into the fairy tale that little girls dreamed of. The myriad of traditions and rules that governed her life felt like those beautiful, surprisingly heavy tiaras. She'd done the math. A slight recasting would reduce the weight and remove the need for twenty-three of the required pins. But when you wore a piece of the nation's heritage on your head, you didn't recast it if it hurt. You held your head higher so others could feel proud.

It helped that Lana adored Bravaria and would do anything for it, pins and all. She loved her father, too, and would never deny him the ability to finally have a well-earned break from the unending duties of a king. That was another reason this Solstice was so important; it was the last Solstice before Jakob II stepped down and Lana became Queen. According to Givera, who'd consistently overworked her support staff of four since establishing and assuming the post of Royal Coordinator, the transitional arrangement was ideal as it gave her two royals for whom to schedule duties instead of one.

Chapter Two

"We shouldn't budge on this, Your Highness," Councilor Aaron said as he followed Lana to the car where her driver, Finn, was waiting. The councilor dragged a hand through the balding ring of still-reddish curls on top of his head. Aside from Lana, he was the youngest member of the Council— and a much-needed, hard-won ally she'd spent eleven months persuading to join the Conciliatory Caucus. It was a disgusting designation, coined by Councilor Merrick's faction, which opposed the progressive stance that mending bridges with Old Bravaria would do more good than harm, but the name had stuck.

The Caucus wasn't as progressive as it sounded, since Lana had quickly discovered that traditionally-minded councilors were far more comfortable taking baby steps than drastically changing their positions over the course of a single vote. And increased support was critical; Lana's honorary position meant she couldn't vote, and not all members of the Caucus supported each initiative. As increasingly drastic trade and border crossing policies regarding Old Bravaria continued to strangle the tourism economy and threaten the tourism-related businesses that had been in eight of the twelve councilors' families for generations, those councilors had become more open-minded.

The only problem was time; New Bravaria's economy had

been on a downward trajectory for decades, and the Council needed to agree to useful action *before* the crisis became irreversible. Not after. Councilor Aaron's support (and consequently that of his family, which ran New Bravaria's second-largest ski resort) had finally come two months earlier, after initial projections for Lana's corporate retreat incentive program pilot had come in. His vote had enabled the Caucus to secure funding for the tourism revenue board to launch that pilot—funding that would, undoubtedly, now be scrapped and repurposed for the royal wedding.

But what was done was done. Once Lana convinced two more councilors to join, the Caucus would be able to free the Council of the gridlock that had nearly paralyzed it for years.

Lana paused in the driveway as she retrieved the revised itinerary she'd planned to discuss with the Conciliatory Caucus at their first meeting of the new year. "I understand where you're coming from," she told the councilor. She really did. The fact that Councilor Merrick, who, as the Economic Minister, served as their proxy (and only) mode of communication with Old Bravaria through his counterpart, had "forgotten" to pass along the update about the Alpine Film Festival until only dramatic measures could be taken— dramatic measures that led to Lana's newly required matrimony—was unforgivable. But trying to remove Councilor Merrick from his position would spook the two councilors Lana needed to recruit: Judge Meyer, who voted with the Caucus about a third of the time and who was the most level-headed person on the Council, and Councilor Lucas. "But we can't do anything dramatic or rash. This is what I was going to propose during our meeting next year." She handed Councilor Aaron the thin folder. "Our economy can't depend on one person's communication skills, but we also need to minimize any potential fallout." Councilor Merrick's rhetoric of blaming Old Bravaria for all of New Bravaria's problems was very attractive to those who prioritized national pride over facts when it came to political decisions. Ousting him would create an uproar among the more traditional voters and politicians. "I suggest that we motion to provide the Economic Minister with an augmented support staff in preparation for the many initiatives that will be happening next year."

Councilor Aaron's jaw ticked, but he nodded. The delayed update about the festival had lost his family's resort an important contract. "I don't like it, but you're right."

"Take a look and let me know your thoughts. This is just a first draft. We should get Judge Meyer's thoughts on the matter, as well."

Councilor Aaron nodded again as he skimmed the proposal.

"Happy Solstice to you and your family, Councilor Aaron," Lana called as she got into the car.

She closed the door once Councilor Aaron had returned his well wishes, the ghost of a smile teasing her lips. There was a lot of work to do, but that conversation wouldn't have been possible even a year ago, when Lana had only tenuously recruited two councilors to join the Caucus. Most days, working with the Council felt like plowing through snow that just kept falling. She just needed to remember that progress *was* possible.

❄

Lana felt like a little girl again as she cracked open the window two hours later, taking a whiff of the snow that coated the mountains surrounding Havos in soft white. She could swear it smelled cleaner, more pure, than in Baulten.

Lana adored her grandmother, but she loved her even more for living in what was clearly the most wonderful place on Earth. Unfortunately—or fortunately, depending on who you asked—nearly nobody knew about it, and Lana had resolved to never expose the village to publicity that would shatter the delicate bubble of privacy that kept it so special.

Havos was a winter wonderland straight out of a fairytale. The entire village had no doubt that the setting of *Peace in the Mountains* was inspired by their home. After all, Ms.

Eaton had noted how the little village was tucked into the side of two great mountains, nestled between an ancient forest and a wildlife sanctuary that predated The Split and contained some of the jagged rural land border between Old and New Bravaria. That forest of spruce and silver fir trees, mossy under layers, and the occasional brave summer flower nearly concealed the village as if to hide it from the passage of time. Ms. Eaton had even noted the distinct lack of modern buildings and the way traditional cottages had been preserved but tactfully updated to conserve heat while letting in more of the precious light that was so limited during the winter.

But since Ms. Eaton's visit, Havos had slipped even further under the radar. A few hundred years earlier, when taking the waters was a popular health trend, many Bravarian hot springs had rivaled those of English bathing towns. If a traveler wanted mild countryside, they went to Bath; if they wanted mountains, they went to Bravaria. With the rise of "active vacationing", big resorts that offered both skiing and hot springs overshadowed the smaller towns, and Havos became the largely forgotten crown jewel of the Bravarian baths. Esmelda had assured a very concerned six-year-old Lana (who'd seen a draft of the New Bravarian government's updated list of "Must Visit Hot Springs" on her father's desk and tried to convince him to include Havos so it would receive the prestige and tourism revenue it deserved) that Havos's largely forgotten status was actually a gift, and that the tightly knit community wanted to keep it that way.

Given Havos's remote location, nearly all winter traffic—which consisted almost entirely of the supply truck's weekly visit and the arrival of the Inn's weekly cohort of guests—went in and out on the same day each week. This quirk was the other reason Lana's security team allowed her to go "unattended"; if everything was clear on the day of their search, no suspicious elements could be added before her arrival.

Lana's shoulders loosened as the car's tires crunched over fresh snow in front of her grandmother's cottage. "Cottage" might be putting it loosely, but Esmelda's Queen Consort daughter had only cooperated with her permanent move to Havos after she agreed to work with an architect to update the inner workings of the place. Of course, one thing had led to another (specifically, the installation of a modern heating system as a "back-up" had led to the discovery of rot in several of the inside walls, necessitating a brand-new floor plan), ensuring that Esmelda's remodeled home was easily the most spacious in town. To the architect's credit, this result had been largely unavoidable, given that Esmelda was the village baker and supplied baked goods for the Inn, the single café, the House of Stories, and individual orders from her state-of-the-art industrial kitchen.

Finn brought Lana's bags to the front porch, which was dominated by a massive, orderly pile of firewood beside a coarse welcome mat. But that was as far as Lana let him help her. It had taken Lana years to realize that she was only capable of letting her guard down when she was with the few people she trusted absolutely. And that "guard" was suddenly the only thing stopping her from having whatever version of a meltdown her usually-very-unemotional self was about to have. Given that she couldn't actually remember ever having a meltdown, she hoped Finn's expediency would spare him from what was bound to be a humiliating experience.

"Are you certain, Princess Lana?" Finn asked, well aware that his duties could flex to bring the bags as far as his charge's rooms if other staff were not available to help. And yes, he'd been her driver since she was a little girl, and he still refused to budge on titles beyond shortening Svetlana to Lana.

"Yes, I'm sure." Lana inclined her head at him. "It's just one suitcase and a backpack. I've skied with a heavier load!"

It wasn't quite true; the most she'd ever skied with was a twenty-pound backpack that had resulted in some very unprincess-like wipeouts, but it reassured Finn, who wished her a good trip before returning to the car.

"Finn, please come in for a moment!" Esmelda called, opening the gleaming wooden door before his could close. "And welcome, my favorite eldest grandchild!" Esmelda exclaimed, waving to Finn and wrapping Lana in a hug. She was wearing a big sweater with an even bigger smile, and stepping into her hug felt like coming home.

Lana held on tightly, closing her eyes as her grandmother's sugary smell, the quiet of the still mountain air, the crispness of clean snow all washed over her. The mix of cold and warmth was settling. Calming. The meltdown decided it might be able to wait.

"Come on, my dear." Esmelda patted her back through several warm winter layers. Esmelda's green eyes—Lana's mother's eyes—crinkled at the corners, and her wavy brown hair was held back from her face by a colorful silk scarf that had been used as a headband. "I know you're an Alpine princess born and bred, but let's get you and your luggage inside. It's where the treats are."

After Finn joined them for a hot drink and some fresh-baked cookies, he was hurried out the door and on his way.

"Just in time," Esmelda murmured as she looked out the bay windows lining the breakfast nook where Lana sat, nibbling on a cookie. It was a traditional light shortbread with anise seeds, and Esmelda always had the refrigerated dough on hand to whip up a batch for visitors.

"In time for what?"

"In time to get home before the storm."

Lana twisted to look out the window behind her. The white velvet curtains were pulled back, revealing fat, fluffy flakes that were falling from the sky, speeding up as she watched. "You're right. There probably *will* be a storm."

"You can always tell when there will be a storm, Lana." Her grandmother shot her an even look. Reading the skies, interpreting clouds, estimating how long until a storm broke out—these were critical life skills that all Bravarian children learned in day school. You couldn't live in mountains known for remote villages and prolific snowfall without them. While Lana had never been in a situation where she'd had to put her theoretical knowledge of survival skills to use, she was usually hyperaware of her surroundings. She should have known there would be a storm the moment she looked out her window in the Winter Palace that morning and saw a blanket of gray clouds covering the sky. And she should have been pushing Finn out the door so he would get home safely—that is, after she pushed him *in* the door, like her grandmother had, to give him food, drink, and a bathroom break before what would certainly be a very long drive home. Instead, Lana's overstressed brain had managed to distract itself by spending the morning reworking the end of the proposal she'd given Councilor Aaron, and then studiously observing snow-covered pine trees blur past for the entire drive to Havos. "Are you okay?"

"I'm okay," Lana insisted, turning back around. She chewed slowly on another bite, half convinced that the biscuit would taste like sawdust in retaliation for her negligence, but it didn't. Her grandmother's baking was just too good. At least she knew that Finn would get home safely; her grandmother never would have let him go otherwise. "I'm just stressed. Can you double check any important decisions I have to make this week to ensure I don't endanger anybody else?" Goodness knew what she'd forget to think about the next time. Maybe she'd forget to get married. *Hah.*

"You didn't *endanger* anybody." Esmelda wrapped an arm around her shoulders. "Finn has been driving in these mountains since before you were born. He can handle himself."

Lana sighed. She'd inherited several personality traits from her grandmother: her sweet tooth, her ability to focus for hours straight, and her patience. If she didn't admit the true source of her worries, Esmelda wouldn't consider it her business to pry. Probably. And if Lana were being entirely honest with herself, she *wanted* her grandmother to know what was bothering her.

"You know the research that Caro and Erik and I have been working on?"

Esmelda nodded. Caro had made an excellent impression the first time Lana had brought her to visit, and Esmelda's esteem for her had only grown over the years.

"Our best chance to get funding for the project—and pass it off to a team that can conduct the next phase of the research—is through a grant. The application is due on Solstice, which is stressful in itself, but Dad has been passing more duties my way and I haven't made as much progress as I'd hoped to prepare our application. That's why Caro and Erik are back this year instead of with their families. Since I haven't been pulling my weight, *they're* here, sacrificing *their* holidays. I feel so guilty."

Lana ran a hand down her French braid. She'd played with it so much that she could swear it had already turned smoother from the oil on her fingers. This was the first time Caro and Erik were spending Solstice season together—their relationship had officially gotten serious enough to rival the time-honored tradition of Caro joining Lana in Havos—and while they'd insisted that being together in Havos was a welcome vacation, she knew they'd have preferred to spend this year's holiday with family.

"You don't need to feel *that* bad for them," Esmelda said. "They get to stay at the Inn during the lead-up to Solstice and escape your millennial internet in one of the most beautiful places on earth!"

"That's true," Lana admitted, and then hurried to get the next words out. "And I need to get married, and my groom submission is due next week." She twirled the end of her braid as if she hadn't just invented an absurd term and dropped a bombshell on their entire conversation.

"What!?" Esmelda put down her mug of tea with such force that it nearly spilled.

"I said I agree with you. Caro and Erik are getting an

excellent vacation out of this."

"I meant the other part, Svetlana Henrietta."

Lana grimaced. Henrietta was one of her fiercest ancestors, and since childhood, she'd only been called by the middle name dedicated to her when she was being naughty. Hearing the name as an adult was no less irksome. In fact, it was irritating to hear *any* of her five names in their full form.

"Oh, yeah. The council made me a packet full of eligible grooms. It's in my bag."

"You have to choose this week? Did you only just find out about all this? That's ridiculous." Esmelda's face displayed all the outrage that Lana couldn't exhibit on her own behalf.

"They told me three days ago. And no, I'm trying not to think about it while I'm here. My decision must be approved and announced by the Solstice Ball, and I refuse to think about it until I have to."

"Why now?" Lana loved her grandmother even more for mentioning nothing about how, at twenty-four, she was the oldest New Bravarian royal in all of history yet to wed. Or how both Esmelda and Givera had been married with a baby by the age of twenty-two.

"They think it will help us keep the Alpine Film Festival."

Esmelda's brows went up, reaching the altitude that her flour supplier had witnessed before he'd given in and agreed to honor the prices he'd offered since the 1990s.

"And Michel wants to get married," Lana added. "He can't until I do. And it's not like I'm waiting for anything in particular, so…" she shrugged. Even if she *had* been waiting for something, she didn't have time anymore.

"I love Michel, but I would've hoped for better from him." Esmelda frowned, but Lana shook her head. She adored her affectionate, sensitive brother. He likely had no idea how his choices would impact her situation, and she half loved, half hated him for it.

"It's okay. Really. I just don't want to think about it any more than I have to."

"All right. But before you leave, missy, we will have

another conversation about this. I might not be royal, but I did have a wonderful marriage for many happy years before your grandpa died." She gave a wistful smile.

"Of course, Grandmother." Lana squeezed her hand. "Just give me a few days, okay?"

"Of course. Now go unpack. And then I need you to help me with some dough for a new order!"

"And tonight? Your special hot chocolate? Do you still have the cup?" Lana hurried to the cabinet that housed her grandmother's eccentric mug collection.

"Of course I have the cup. Now shoo!"

The cottage had two guest bedrooms connected by a shared bathroom. In the past, Caro had taken the guest room at the end of the hall, which was decorated in powder blue and featured two twin beds. Lana's room was about a third the size of her bedroom in the palace, and it felt as warm and toasty as ever, with a full bed, maroon accents, and a cozy chair beside the old-fashioned fireplace. The old family photo of Lana, her mother, and grandmother in the Palace's private summer garden still hung on the far wall, the Bavarian royal crest partly obscured by the frame.

Lana put her backpack in the corner and quickly unpacked before checking on the snow again. It was becoming quite the storm. Flakes were falling heavily, coating the world in a layer of quiet that would become a blizzard the moment the wind picked up. Lana was grateful that Finn would be at least halfway back to Baulten by now and wasn't at risk of getting caught in a whiteout in the rural mountains.

By the time Lana returned to the kitchen, the blizzard had arrived.

"Good news!" her grandmother called from where she was bent over, peering into the oven. "The phone lines aren't down and the power's holding up! I'd say we can safely bake one more round of these without risking a power issue."

"That's great!" Based on the tantalizing aroma of freshly baked anise and shortbread, Esmelda's order must have been for the same biscuits they'd eaten earlier.

"And Carlotta called. Caro and Erik arrived on the shuttle with the Inn's next round of guests. She also passed on a message from Leo and Nico that if this weather continues tomorrow, they'll come by the day after to help catch up. The Inn has enough bread and oats to cover breakfast tomorrow without a delivery."

They eyed the storm, then looked at each other mischievously. Storms were the *best* excuse to have a day of fun. The thrill of a snow day didn't wear off just because you became an adult.

"In that case, is tonight no longer a school night?"

"I suppose not," Esmelda said as she reached into a cabinet above the stove. "Would you like to choose some options for movie night? I ordered new films for you."

She brought down two teacups: one from a hand-painted set featuring six different conifers, and Lana's favorite cup, secretly purchased at the height of her superhero obsession, which read, "What Would Thor Do?". Lana's obsession with mythical heroes had lingered after her teenage years, and there was nothing better than drinking copious quantities of Solstice cinnamon-and-orange tea out of a mug that reminded her to reach for the impossible.

❆

As Esmelda retrieved the ingredients for hot chocolate, Lana turned to the shelves of videotapes that covered the half wall separating the kitchen from the great room. She'd just started pulling out movie options when the phone rang from the office off the industrial kitchen. Esmelda began to pace as she listened to whoever was on the other end, flaunting the incredibly long telephone cord as she did.

When Esmelda's face grew serious, Lana paused to eavesdrop from where she'd scattered no fewer than ten films on the couch.

"Yes, yes, of course," Esmelda murmured. "He can't stay at the doctor's office and if he doesn't need a hospital, nobody needs to do extra driving in this weather. Bring him here."

She put the phone down and immediately began rummaging through cabinets. "Lana, dear, there are extra blankets in the linen closet. Could you get those, please?"

"Of course. What's happened?" Lana called as she disappeared around the corner.

"Felix was on patrol at the wildlife sanctuary and found an unconscious skier. They're bringing him here."

"Oh my goodness. Is the skier okay?" Lana asked as she reemerged. She piled an armful of blankets and pillows on the sofa nearest the fire.

"He doesn't need a hospital, but we can ask Felix more questions when they arrive."

Lana moved the films out of the way and helped pull together an enormous pot of stew to feed however many frozen people would be arriving at any moment. Hospitality was important when you lived in the more isolated mountain regions, and hardy, nutritious stew was a staple.

Lana had just retrieved a simple first aid kit and every bottle of medication she could find when Esmelda opened the door, revealing two villagers struggling to guide a tall, wobbly looking figure up the steps without dropping a battered helmet and a backpack. Felix had the figure's left arm, and Klara, the town doctor, had his right. Both were strong Bravarians—tall, fit from skiing in the winters and hiking in the summers—but between the swirling snow, howling wind, and passive weight of the semiconscious, highly disoriented man, they pitched forward onto the top step.

Esmelda held the door open wider and they reached the large plush rug that acted as a second welcome mat, defending against melting snow as guests removed their shoes. A firm gust of wind and snow slammed the door shut behind them with a white puff, which was blocked by the floating wall—a concession Givera's architect had graciously agreed to to preserve part of the traditional layout of the cottage.

Lana helped remove the man's ski boots as Felix and Klara removed their outer layers. The stranger's body kept trying to flop over when they removed his outerwear, but once they braced him against the wall and held his shoulders, he seemed to be in a more stable position. As Lana hung the coats on pegs near the door, Esmelda raised her eyebrows to Felix in silent question.

"Yes, ma'am. I went through his bag and jacket pockets while he had his tests. We found nothing. Patted down the rest of him, too, and no metal, no tools, no pills. Nothing suspicious," Felix whispered. The tall, brawny man might be a patrol officer at the Lausalle Wildlife Sanctuary, but he also served as a police officer whenever their small village needed one. If Felix said the stranger looked safe, Lana believed him.

Esmelda nodded her appreciation. "Thank you. Let's make sure you talk to him again once he's...himself."

Lana stiffened. She knew her grandmother was trying to balance her need to help others (and her obligation to do so, given her status as a village elder who had the biggest home and was therefore the local default for emergency housing) with her need to look out for Lana. But it didn't feel right to have a semi-conscious man investigated just because she was there.

The man's eyes kept blinking open and closed as he was deposited onto the couch, and Klara made a wall of pillows to prevent him from falling to the floor before enveloping Lana in a warm hug. Felix waited until Klara pulled back, brushing thick, snow-damp blonde hair out of her face and revealing windblown pink cheeks and a worried expression, then launched into a summary of what they'd discovered about the stranger.

"I was actually running a little late on my patrol due to some weird mouflon herd patterns today," Felix began, "which turned out to be a good thing. You saw the weather." They all nodded knowingly, and Lana tried not to feel like a weather-reading fraud, reminding herself that the garage manager had confirmed that Finn had made it safely back to Baulten hours before. "A storm was definitely coming, and I was nearly caught in it. Lucky for this guy, who wasn't having such a good time of it himself. The snow had picked up into a full-on blizzard for about two minutes when I saw a loose ski. I followed the trail and there he was, unconscious after smashing into a tree. Nothing else in sight. He *definitely* shouldn't have been there in the first place, and he's lucky I found him when I did. I'm guessing he'd been skiing in the Queen's Peaks area and got lost before the storm picked up." He paused. "Five more minutes and that ski would've been fully buried." It was a generous way to say that the stranger would've been buried, too, and not found before it was too late.

Lana glanced at the stranger. She dealt with important issues every day, but life-or-death situations were out of her comfort zone. Her comfort zone was working to prevent economic collapse and improve education programs, not physically caring for someone who was very nearly *not with them*, lost out in the middle of nowhere after engaging in goodness-knows-what sort of reckless behavior. She didn't want to judge the stranger, but one didn't just *happen* to find oneself in the back runs of Queen's Peaks in the midst of a blizzard one didn't see coming.

Then again, one usually didn't just *happen* to be ordered to marry at the drop of a hat.

She could afford to be gracious. Empathetic. Life could be unpredictable sometimes.

But the life of the man in front of her had almost been snuffed out, covered by so much beautiful, deadly snow. At least he *had* a life—clearly with enough freedom to get himself into this situation. He deserved to *live* it.

"Anyway, I radioed Doc and scooped this guy up," Felix continued. "He's mumbled a little bit but he's pretty out of it."

"We conducted the usual tests before coming here," Klara

said, picking up the story. All village doctors' offices were fully equipped with CT scanners and a small lab so doctors like Klara could conduct basic tests without sending patients on long, suspenseful journeys to the main hospitals in Baulten or other large cities. "I don't see signs of permanent damage, just a concussion and quite a goose-egg. Painkillers are fine. Don't let him sleep alone or shower for the first twenty-four hours. He should sleep through the night, but if he starts vomiting again, call me. Don't let him overdo it." They all looked at the stranger again. His head was tilted back, angled precariously upon the pile of pillows. He didn't look at risk of overdoing it for a long, long time. "I'll check back in a day or two and we can see how he's holding up. He should start to remember things in the next twenty-four to forty-eight hours, but right now he's got nothing. Not even a name."

"No ID, no wallet, nothing," Felix confirmed.

"Kids these days. Why do they go places without their wallets?" Esmelda shook her head and gestured toward the kitchen. "You all must be starving. Let me get you some Chaland stew."

Both Felix and Klara "mmmed" appreciatively. The traditional Bravarian stew was a hearty treat of thick beef broth, carrots, parsnips, potatoes, beef, and onions—and when Esmelda made it, it came in a fresh-baked bread bowl.

"Can he eat this?" Lana asked Klara.

"I'd recommend broth for tonight. Tomorrow, stew is fine, if he keeps the broth down first. You know," Klara mused as she savored the aroma of the stew Esmelda was ladling, "that kid had a *really* good helmet. It took a beating for him, and left him a lot better off than he could have been. What brand was it?" she asked Felix.

"Jiro, I think."

"Jiro. I'm definitely getting one of those. And some for my kids, too. And my parents," she declared.

After dinner, Klara reiterated the caretaking instructions for the patient, before she and Felix carefully trudged out into the raging storm. It was bone-chillingly cold and the wind had whipped the rapidly falling snow into a frenzy. If ropes hadn't been set up to connect houses to one another in preparation for the storm—another detail Lana had initially overlooked—they would have stayed the night. As it was, they could blindly follow the ropes from house to house until they made it the few blocks home.

❊

Lana turned back to the figure on the couch. The man appeared to be dozing off, still wearing a scarf and powder mask and looking like the world's least talented and snowiest bank robber.

"Do you get a lot of mysterious strangers up here, Grandmother?" Lana asked, surveying their charge with her hands on her hips. Now that she was over the shock of staring at a person who had almost *not been alive*, she found the situation intriguing.

"We don't, actually. You know how quiet it is up in these parts." Lana nodded. It *was* quiet. When it wasn't blizzarding outside, Havos was one of the most peaceful places on earth. If the village weren't such a tight-knit community, it would be lonely, especially in the winters. Aside from the weekly arrival of Inn visitors and the dose of regional gossip Maurizio brought when he visited the café after each supply delivery, few people ever wandered up there, which made the arrival of a stranger so…strange. "But my house *is* the most spacious, so when we do have emergencies, I see them all."

"What do we do with him now?" Lana asked, tilting her head. She'd never even had a pet to care for, much less nursed an unconscious human being back to health. How were things like bathroom visits going to work?

"Let's make him as comfortable as possible, and then try to get him to eat some broth."

Removing the scarf was quick business, and they managed to pull off the powder mask without decapitating their patient. The process left his face half smushed against the back of the sofa, longish blond hair flopping over his forehead, but he didn't so much as stir.

The moment they agreed that the ski pants needed to go, his arm moved, and he groaned. Lana felt a wry sense of relief. They were only removing his ski pants—the long underwear he'd be an idiot to not have on underneath wouldn't be touched—but if a stranger ever removed *her* pants, she'd want to be awake, too. Unfortunately, it seemed that the occasional groan was as alert as he was going to get.

After giving the ski pants a sharp, fruitless tug from the knee area (the most innocent-looking place north of the band of elastic around the ankles), Lana realized she'd forgotten to first open them at the waist.

"This feels wrong," Lana told Esmelda as she eyed what was likely a snap and a zipper. "I don't want to open an unconscious person's pants."

"He's wearing long johns underneath," Esmelda pointed out. "And these are hardly comfortable. You're doing him a favor." A humorous sigh. "Do you want me to do it?"

"No, I can do it." After a surprisingly prolific five seconds of thought, Lana had concluded that if this man did, in fact, come to during this most awkward activity, it would be less alarming to see a woman around his age—she hadn't yet studied his face but he *seemed* like a young man—undoing his pants rather than a lady who could be his grandmother. With that charitable and fortifying thought, Lana took a deep breath, gave a gentle tug at the seam of fabric near where she assumed the snap would be—and froze.

"What is this!?" she exclaimed, caught entirely off guard.

"Lana! You can remove a person's pants without—"

"Oh. My. *Gosh!*" Lana whisper-shouted at her grandmother. She would be *beyond* mortified if this man woke up right now, while her hands were in a compromising position that made it *look like* she was doing whatever scandalous things her grandmother thought she was doing. "I'm talking about this ridiculous knot!"

Esmelda raised an eyebrow, looking positively giddy at Lana's predicament. She then reminded her granddaughter of the basics of knot loosening, and was unsuccessfully smothering a snicker at Lana's dismay over the discovery of not one, but four, snaps beneath the dreaded knot when the young man suddenly woke up.

Lana wasn't sure if it was their hushed conversation, the panicked energy she was definitely sending his way, or the five minutes of accidental bumps around the would-be zipper region (if only he'd had the good grace to *have* a zipper—again, the finest invention known to fashion) that woke the man up. But the second she'd tried to pull off the pants she'd carefully untied, his eyelids fluttered open, and she realized she'd been *oh so wrong*. A pair of rich blue eyes —heavily dilated, disoriented rich blue eyes—gazed up at her in confusion and pain, and she sucked in a breath.

It definitely *would've been more appropriate for Grandmother to undress him*, Lana realized as the unseemliness of the situation hit her. Why had she thought she should do it? It wasn't just embarrassing; it was irresponsible. It was bad enough for some poor guy to wake up to an unknown woman with her hands over his crotch. And regaining consciousness, only to realize a celebrity was putting her hands where they certainly hadn't been invited to go? *He'd probably think he hit his head,* offered a useless part of Lana's brain. *Or go straight to the press.*

"What—what are you doing?" the man croaked, wincing. He tried to lift his neck off the pile of pillows to see what Lana was doing with her hands—hands that had been momentarily frozen in a most unfortunate place on his person, and were now firmly hidden behind her back. The motion must have been as painful as it looked, for he gave up almost immediately.

I'm so sorry. So so so sorry. The thoughts echoed in Lana's head and couldn't find a way out as she gaped at him, her mouth opening and closing like the endangered Bravarian sapphire river fish that never fully closed its mouth in case food decided to fall into it. Lana had done her fair share of sneaking off to Caro's lab over the past two years, but she was always so careful, and so polite in everything else that she'd never actually been caught doing something inappropriate since…she wasn't sure when.

"I'm so sorry," she finally gasped.

Esmelda came to the rescue.

"You're in the village of Havos, my dear," Esmelda told the man, whose eyes had closed again with the strain of his earlier movement. Lana wondered if the light was bothering him, and immediately dimmed the sconces. "You bumped your head, and the doctor has left us with strict instructions to take good care of you."

He squinted up at them, looking confused. "Where am I?" he rasped out.

Lana shot a quick look at her grandmother, trying to sarcastically telepath, *well, that went well,* and failing, as Esmelda indicated that she should grab the glass of water Klara had left out for him.

"You must be thirsty, dear. Here. Take a sip." Esmelda waved at Lana to hold the glass of water to his lips. She did so carefully, and after two sips he sank back into the pillows with a sigh that was nearly a moan.

That done, Lana returned to the man's feet to help finish the debacle they'd started.

"Now, dear," Esmelda coaxed, firmly but kindly. "We need to get your ski pants off so you don't scuff my sofa." She nudged him to lift his hips just the tiniest amount, which was accomplished more by her tilting him first to one side and then the other than by him actually contributing to the effort, chattering on the entire time about how fine Bravarian craftsmen had made the pair of couches in the traditional way, and how if one were ruined by scuff marks, the other would lose its value, too.

Soon he was unconscious again, theoretically more comfortable in his long underwear, and the sofa was spared the pain of devaluation by scuff marks. Lana bit her lip. Her grandmother had made that look so easy.

"How did you do that so quickly?" Lana whispered as they headed to the kitchen to make fresh hot chocolate.

"Do what?"

"Take his pants off."

Esmelda gave her a look. "It's not hard."

"I found it *very* hard!"

"I know you did, my dear." Her grandmother grinned at her, and Lana couldn't help but grin back. She hadn't been this kind of flustered in a while and it was…liberating, somehow. Feeling embarrassed for clumsily helping an injured stranger remove his pants was much better than being blindsided by parents who told the government you were getting married before you knew it yourself.

"Please tell me your skills come from diaper changing and not from a secret habit of undressing semiconscious men."

Esmelda laughed. "I haven't changed a diaper in years."

Lana groaned. The half-serious comment had been a joke, but she *really* didn't want to get into whether her grandmother had been leveraging skills developed with conscious men who'd needed their pants removed for other reasons.

Esmelda stirred the pot of hot chocolate, letting Lana suffer in silence. "There are some skills that you just never forget, Lana. Like riding a bike."

Chapter Three

Lana snuggled into her cocoon of blankets, relishing the soft warmth against her cheek. When she was little, her mother had teased that Lana slept so deeply during snowstorms that she must be part bear. Lana's smile became a huge morning yawn at the memory. She might not be part bear, but there was something so comforting about being tucked safely into a blanket while it snowed outside, knowing you couldn't go anywhere even if you wanted to because traveling in snowstorms was dangerous, and—

Lana shot awake as her hazy morning thoughts reminded her *exactly* how dangerous blizzardy mountains could be. Unsure of the state of their mystery guest—whom she'd volunteered to keep an eye on from the second couch so her grandmother could sleep in her own bed without worrying— she surreptitiously shifted beneath her blanket pile to peek at him. After a great deal of rustling about, she looked directly at the other couch, only to realize he was…gone?

"Oh my goo—" Lana panicked to herself as she tried to get off the couch so quickly that her legs tangled in the layers of blankets, sending her tumbling to the ground with a thump. *Where was he?!* She couldn't have lost the invalid! The wind was still howling outside and the dark grey morning indicated that the blizzard was still alive and well, possibly unlike their guest…

"Are you all right?" a smooth voice asked from

somewhere over her head. Lana twisted around on the rug, tilting her face back to look at the mystery man who was now standing behind her couch. She scrambled to her feet, since she must look *ridiculous* on the floor with fluffy wisps of hair escaping her braid and her legs caught in a nest of blankets—and promptly fell right back down again, startled, as he rounded the couch and came into full view.

The part of Lana's brain that had always secretly worried why she hadn't minded being perpetually single, that wondered if she was actually in denial about having inherited some of the emotional genes that Michel possessed in excess, found the situation hilarious. It was a good thing that she was already on the floor.

The mysterious stranger was…Lana couldn't quite find the word for it. "Beautiful" felt too soft and "dignified" seemed too polished and if she were honest with herself, she supposed that this was what Thor might have looked like if he secretly took piano lessons, cut his hair just under pigtail length, and sported a head wound.

No one had ever accused Lana of being romantic. Feeling attraction, on the other hand…well, people rarely accused her of that either. But she had a pulse. And he had stunning blue eyes, dirty blond hair, and pale, slightly golden skin stretched over what she was sure was an equally intriguing body. One strong hand gripped the back of the couch, revealing long, elegant fingers. His face looked less smooth than the night before, with stubble starting to come in.

Lana blinked at him mutely. Piano-playing, has-a-secret-past Thor was in her grandmother's house looking tall and devastating in the weak morning light and…and he sat down heavily on her sofa, groaning. He was definitely fair-skinned, but Lana's groggy brain finally realized that he looked wan, like his color was off.

"Oh my goodness, how are you feeling?" Lana asked, gingerly sitting beside him in an effort to not jostle the couch cushion. From this angle, she could see the goose-egg on the side of his forehead, looking red and angry and painful in the morning light. She'd been ogling an invalid when he clearly needed help. What was wrong with her?

"You say that a lot," he told her as he covered his eyes with one hand.

"'How are you feeling?' Of course I do! You arrived here more or less unconscious."

"Not that. I meant 'Oh my goodness.'"

"Do I?" Lana laughed, surprised by how easily her usual formal manners had slipped after one good night of sleep. She instantly regretted it when he winced at the sound. "Well, I suppose a lot of surprising things have happened lately. But please tell me. How are you feeling?"

"My head hurts," he replied, still shielding his eyes. "And I was looking for the bathroom just before you fell down..."

"Come with me." Lana carefully took his arm and guided him through her room to the shared bathroom. Once he reemerged, she led him back to his couch and went about heating another bowl of the broth he'd been too out-of-it to drink the night before. She set the bowl and spoon on the end table beside him alongside a glass of water and two painkillers.

"Why are you not freaking out?" she whispered after he made no move for the broth or the water. He was so...calm. Klara had assured them that the man's brain wasn't permanently damaged, but Lana figured he should at least be trying to figure out where he was, not asking about her speaking habits. If she were in his position, she'd be having a full-on panic attack.

"I did freak out," he admitted with a fleeting smile, closing his eyes again as his expression faded. "I woke up in the middle of the night and had no idea where I was, but I could tell I'd hit my head, and that someone"—he blindly gestured in her direction—"was taking care of me. So, thank you. But if I may ask...where are we?"

"My grandmother's house, in Havos." He looked at her blankly, which was fair, given that most people *without* memory loss didn't know about Havos, either. "Drink some broth and take the painkillers. They'll help."

He went to ask more questions, but Lana pushed the bowl an inch closer until he got the hint and started spooning soup into his mouth. Lana was a caretaker at heart; the idea of caring for the Bravarian people, of making life better for them, gave her a sense of purpose. But taking care of another human being? She was so out of her league that it wasn't even funny, so they'd be following Klara's advice to the letter until Esmelda woke up.

The stranger was a dream patient, eating the broth and taking the pills and waiting to fall asleep again until after she'd moved him to the blue double bedroom, despite the considerable pain he must have been in. After lighting a small fire in the guest room's fireplace, Lana turned to check on him. The man was exactly how she'd left him, sleeping like a log and showing no signs of life beyond the steady rise and fall of his chest. A chest that led to a strong neck and prominent Adam's apple that were on full display due to the tower of pillows propping him up. He swallowed in his sleep, and Lana mentally chastised herself. She shouldn't be ogling Thor the Unconscious Invalid. And she shouldn't be associating him with the world's dreamiest superhero-god. She'd call him Jiro instead. And heaven forbid Jiro recognize her the next time he woke up—since he clearly hadn't recognized her this time—and go on to tell the world how the Princess of New Bravaria drooled over him while he recovered from a head injury.

❄

Lana was on her second cup of cinnamon-spiced tea, reading through the final report Caro had sent, when Esmelda walked into the kitchen.

"Good morning!" Lana sprang up to give her grandmother a hug. Hugs weren't a thing in the palace, but they were definitely a thing in Havos. And Lana made the most of that every year.

"How are you this morning?" Esmelda asked as she patted

Lana's back. "And how—and where—is our patient?"

"Jiro's in the blue room." Lana gave a detailed account of her nursing skills and the care she'd provided that morning, feeling rather pleased with herself.

"Jiro? Wasn't that the brand of his helmet?"

"I didn't have anything else to call him, and he passed out again." Lana shrugged. "The Mysterious Invalid was too long and clunky."

Esmelda gave an indulgent sigh. "Did he remember his real name?"

"No—well, we didn't get to that. I also didn't get to explaining about Havos before he fell back asleep."

"Let's not worry about *Jiro* until he emerges from his nap, and then we can explain everything." She didn't say "again," but they were both wondering when his memory would start to stick. "In the meantime, are you hungry for breakfast?"

After two perfectly poached eggs, a thick slice of fresh, toasted bread, and a third cup of tea, Lana was well into the best morning of her life, or at least her year. She'd remained curled in the breakfast nook, bundled in her robe as she considered the report. She was jotting down a note on one of the scattered pages when Jiro walked in, moving more fluidly than he had earlier.

"Good morning!" She offered too cheerily, irrationally hoping he wouldn't *remember*.

"Good morning to *you*, too." He gave her an amused look.

If Lana hadn't begun etiquette lessons when she was three, she would've snorted. Morning greetings were well and good, but they were going to have to exchange names eventually. That is, if whomever-Jiro-actually-was hadn't already guessed hers.

"Please, sit down." She gestured to the table, realizing that the pages of graphs and equations probably didn't look welcoming. "I'll clean this up in a minute, I promise."

"Don't worry, it's fi—"

"Would you like breakfast? Tea?" she cut him off. Each moment she spent doing something useful was an extra moment she could justify pretending to be…normal. It was strangely exhilarating.

"Yes, please." He didn't even ask what breakfast was. He must be starving. *Or maybe just happy to be alive*, Lana's subconscious pointed out. Both options were equally likely.

Lana poured him a cup of tea, popped a slice of bread in the toaster, and went about frying two eggs. She could reliably fry eggs and order anything else, so there wasn't much point in giving him options.

"So, Jiro, have you remembered anything yet?" Lana asked as she cracked the eggs into a pan.

"Jiro?" he asked, puzzled.

Oops. So much for pretending to be "normal". Normal people didn't spontaneously rename others, did they?

"It's the brand of helmet you were wearing when Felix found you," Lana replied quickly. "I don't *think* it's your real name, unless it's ringing a bell? But we needed something to call you, so…"

Jiro looked down at himself, as if realizing for the first time that he was wearing long underwear. "Was I…skiing, then?"

He frowned, then touched his temple as if the expression had hurt. Lana eyed the shiny red bump and passed him two painkillers.

"Thank you." The rough whisper was barely audible.

"Yes, dear, it looks like you hit a tree in the blizzard." Esmelda had returned to the kitchen in time to prevent Lana's interaction with their mysterious guest from going as poorly as the prior night's ski pants removal. "Do you remember anything? Your name, perhaps?"

The stranger pursed his lips together as if trying to wrack his brain, winced, and shrugged. "I… don't." He gave Esmelda a wide-eyed, moderately horrified glance. "I don't remember anything. Where am I?"

"You're in the village of Havos in New Bravaria," Lana replied. She'd felt so guilty about ignoring Jiro's follow-up questions that she'd prepared an entire spiel for this very moment. Hoping to jog Jiro's memory, Lana told him the date, recounted Felix's theory about his activities, and gave him a refresher course on Bravarian geography as she struggled to reconcile the calm, quiet man beside her with the obvious daredevil who'd decided to ski in the face of a storm. It was maddening that she couldn't ask about it. The urge to shout "what were you thinking!?" was nearly unbearable, but Lana supposed it was even worse for him. "If you really *were* skiing over there, it was a risky situation even without the storm. People don't usually ski the back of the Park on purpose," Lana concluded.

Jiro's expression didn't change despite the judgement she'd failed to keep out of her tone, so Lana continued to the next topic. "As for what this means for getting you 'home'? Since you still don't know who you are, it's a bit of a moot point. Havos doesn't have a lot of transportation access in the winter…" Lana's voice trailed off. She was used to announcing updates and presenting proposals, not admitting that there was nothing she could do to help.

Esmelda shot Lana a *look* as she retrieved ingredients for a new order, and Lana attempted to reassure Jiro, tamping down on her useless frustration.

"Since it's also the run-up to Solstice, we're more isolated up here than usual." She paused. Her reassurance sounded more like a warning than a bit of comfort. "Havos is walkable, so many people here put their cars away for the winter. A trucker drops off perishable supplies each week, but he came yesterday, so you won't be able to get a ride for another six days. And we have landline telephones, but no internet or cell phone service—" at that, he looked wonderingly down at where his pockets would be in regular pants, as if considering his potential cell phone ownership for the first time—"not that you seemed to have a cell phone. Or a wallet, for that matter. So you're more or less stuck here until next week's delivery, or until you remember who you are and can call someone to come pick you up."

"And even if you *did* know where you needed to go, I

wouldn't recommend having somebody drive to come get you in this weather, dear," Esmelda added. "No one will be going anywhere for a few days, us included."

Jiro began to nod in response, then immediately jerked back. He swallowed. "Did you search through my things?"

"No," Lana replied quickly. *Too* quickly. *Of course*, she chastised herself. *You meet the first attractive guy in years and if your hands on his pants didn't make him think you're a creep, this would. Then again*, the rational part of her brain offered in the mental equivalent of a cold shower, *it shouldn't matter if he's handsome. Or thinks you're weird. You're about to get engaged.* "The patrol officer did when he was trying to figure out who to call."

"Do you have them?" he asked, as if unsure what those things might be.

"Yes."

"Will you show them to me?"

After breakfast, Lana reunited Jiro with his backpack and winter gear and returned to her report. Caro had called to say that she and Erik would be staying indoors at the Inn until the storm died down, so they'd divided the prep work for the time being. And most importantly? If this stranger didn't know who she was, there was no reason for Lana to change out of her glitter bathrobe until noon.

❄

Lana spent hours prepping for the work she and her friends would start the next day as Esmelda cracked dozens of eggs, sifted pounds of flour, and started the proving and chilling processes for the variety of bread and biscuit doughs she needed for upcoming orders.

Lana had just reached a stopping point when the smell of baking bread wafted over her. Working in her grandmother's breakfast nook was always surreal. At her back was whipping wind, sub-zero temperatures, a world huddled down to wait out the snow. And all around her was warm air, the crackling of the fire, the smell of fresh yeast and delicious baked goods, and her grandmother, bustling around efficiently even without her helpers, who'd called to say they were waiting out one more day of the storm.

"I'll go check on Jiro," Lana announced once her stomach rumbled a second time. She ought to offer him some leftover stew.

"Does he know his new name?" Esmelda asked, amused.

"I told him earlier, but I cannot guarantee that he'll remember the conversation."

"You can also tell him that if he wants to eat lunch, it'll be ready in ten minutes."

Lana traded her pajamas and glittery robe for real clothes before leaving her room and entering the blue bedroom through the hall door. Walking through the shared bathroom was quicker, but she wasn't ready to advertise the fact that a stranger could bypass the hallway and walk straight into her room. She knocked politely on the open door and looked around. Jiro didn't have much stuff, but what he did have was spread out into little piles with him as the epicenter.

"Hey," Lana said when he looked up and greeted her with a small smile.

"Hey." He sounded tired.

"Find anything useful?"

"Not really. I'm still a mystery." Jiro sounded minorly amused by his predicament.

"What's all this? Food?" She waved at the packets of dried noodles, dehydrated meat, and packages of beans, nuts, and dried fruits. It looked disgusting.

"It looks like it. This is a lot of food for one person, though. It's enough to cover at least ten days, probably more."

"You know your camping food, then."

"I suppose I do," he agreed. "But why would I bring tons of food out to the middle of nowhere, in a blizzard, by myself? This pack doesn't have everything I'd need, either. There's no first aid, no..."

"What's wrong?" Lana asked as he trailed off.

"I'm either really stupid, or I somehow lost a second pack. And given that I was found in a wildlife sanctuary where skiing is illegal, I am really hoping that I'm not as stupid as I'm starting to think I might be." He absently ran a hand along his jaw, and immediately pulled it away as if surprised to have found stubble.

"You're not stupid," Lana assured him. Honestly speaking, she didn't know him well enough to vouch for his intelligence, but he was polite, and that counted for something. "You have a brain injury and you just taught me more than I have ever wanted to know about camping food."

"I also found a sleeping bag and camping pillow, both of which made it all this way without unraveling, which is impressive. They must be good quality." He gave a little laugh.

"Or they were well packed," Lana offered. "The doctor mentioned that your helmet was so good that she's buying Jiro helmets for her entire family." She eyed the black helmet in the corner of the bedroom that was still entirely smooth, except for a slight indentation on the forehead. "Apparently, that saved your life."

"I'm sure it did," he agreed quietly. A muscle in his jaw ticked.

"That's why I figured we could just call you Jiro, you know, until…"

His eyes crinkled as he gave a wry laugh. "Until I remember who I am?"

Lana nodded. "And even then. Jiro's a good name. You might decide to keep it."

"I could become the brand's spokesperson."

"Definitely." Lana looked around the room, then back to the black long johns that he'd been wearing for goodness knew how long. "Did you find any other clothes?"

"Unfortunately not. It doesn't look like packing clothing was my specialty."

"We can't judge you so fast," Lana insisted, tossing his infamous ski pants at him. "These were quite nice. Very reliable. Incredibly well-fastened.”

“Does it always take you so long to remove a man’s pants?” he asked with a grin.

“You remember that!?” The corner of her mouth tried to tilt up. Who *was* she? Why was she smiling?

He grinned wider.

Lana covered her face with her hands and tried not to melt from embarrassment. Not only did he remember, but now he’d upgraded the small smiles that had been *nice* to a full-on *grin*—and wow. That grin catapulted the encounter from humiliating to devastating on all accounts. Plus, Lana had experience removing exactly one other pair of men’s pants, and it had gone about as well as this had.

“I wasn’t entirely awake, but I think it took you so long that I went in and out of consciousness multiple times before I could find my voice and ask what you were doing,” Jiro said. Mercifully, he patted down the pockets of his ski pants as he spoke, sparing Lana the agony of making eye contact.

“In my defense, I have apologized profusely for that, you just might not remember. And the only reason it took so long was that you’d tied them up so strangely that I couldn’t figure out the knot.”

“It’s okay. I forgive you, I promise. I’d never forgive myself if I ruined your grandmother’s sofa after her generosity.” He frowned, his headache clearly reminding him of its presence, and then his eyes widened. “Hey, look at this.”

She was looking, all right. The look of wonder on his face was, unfortunately, wondrous.

He pulled a crumpled tissue and what looked like a damp piece of paper out of one of the ski pants’ pockets. “It looks like some snow got in here and melted, but I had a note!”

Lana picked her way through the piles of camping food to look closer. The paper was disintegrating in places, but from the bleed of color, it was clear that something had been written in blue ink. The first few lines of the note were completely lost to the snow, but most of the end was legible.

Peering over Jiro's shoulder, Lana could just make out the words, "the 18ᵗʰ at noon in the Orange Gallery. L—"

The rest of the words were unclear, but Lana recognized the locale. The Orange Gallery was one of the most famous art galleries in Old Bravaria. Attached to the Summer Palace, it was named after the orangeries that it housed for generations, until a new conservatory was built and the interior was repurposed to showcase some of the royal family's greatest masterpieces. She'd thought the Gallery was closed to the public during Solstice, but she must've been mistaken. And the image of someone waiting for him there, on the cerulean and orange tiled floor, was bittersweet. If this wasn't confirmation that Jiro was Old Bravarian, she didn't know what was.

Jiro carefully held the note in his palm, trying to make out the faded words.

"Maybe we can blow dry it?" Lana asked. "I think my grandmother has one in her bathroom." Why hadn't she listened to Vera's overpacking advice? She wanted to help this beautiful lost man find a clue to his identity.

"Thank you. If she doesn't mind, I'd really appreciate it." He stared at the soggy paper again before wincing.

"Is your head hurting again?"

"Yeah."

"Let's get you some lunch, and then you can top up your painkillers and nap some more. Our expected guests aren't coming today because of the storm, so you shouldn't be disturbed."

"Thank you again…" He frowned, trying to remember her name—a name she hadn't told him yet.

"Lana."

"Lana. Thank you, Lana." He smiled apologetically. "But I want to sort out this paper first. What if it's my only clue to figuring out who I am? I'd hate for it to dissolve before I wake up."

"You're right." Lana mentally chided herself. Had her brain cells gone on vacation, too? "Blow-dryer, then lunch, then nap. Promise?" She gave him a hand to help him stand.

"Promise."

Jiro put his hand in hers, and Lana was so unprepared for how it would feel—when was the last time she'd held someone's hand, much less found it *pleasing*?—that she forgot to brace herself as he pulled, expecting her to pull, too, like most people do when they help someone else up. And Jiro must have been feeling much worse than his friendly demeanor let on, because he didn't go easy on that offered hand. He pulled, and Lana had a flashback to Felix and Klara struggling to guide his semiconscious body through the door as she toppled forward, only stopping herself from reinjuring him by falling half onto one of the twin beds and knocking the air out of her lungs.

"Excuse—me—" they gasped at the same time, Lana as she tried to pull air back into her lungs and Jiro as he tried to avoid bumping into her hip with his forehead. Because of course she'd managed to fall so that her crotch was at eye level.

Lana carefully negotiated herself out of the awkward position, leaning onto her torso to put her weight on the bed and slowly moving one leg, then the other, away from Jiro's broad shoulders until she could stand safely.

"Oh my goodness, I'm so sorry!" Lana hoped he couldn't see her cheeks burning. She'd both groped and literally forced herself upon an invalid in the span of twenty-four hours. It was a PR disaster waiting to happen, not to mention eternally mortifying for anyone. And what on earth would she say to Klara if she'd reinjured Jiro? *Sorry, I knocked him out again with my pubic bone?*

"You really do say that a lot," Jiro said as he pulled himself to standing, using the dresser instead of her hand this time.

"'I'm sorry'? I don't, actually. Women say it far too often, so I make it a point to only use it when the situation warrants it. Which has been a lot lately," Lana informed him, chin high. "And almost concussing you with my pelvis certainly warrants it."

"Well," Jiro gave her a long look. "First, I was referring to you saying 'oh my goodness' at every opportunity." Lana pursed her lips. It was true. "Second, that situation did *not* warrant it. In fact, I was quite comforta—"

"Grandmother's bathroom is this way," Lana interrupted, hurrying out of the room. She was a nearly engaged woman, for heaven's sake! Not that he knew that. And not that her fiancé even had a face to go with his title at this point. And she was nearly certain Jiro was going to say something positively...flirtatious? How dare *he* flirt with *her*? How dare he...make her *want* to flirt with him? And who went from catatonic to flirtatious in less than a day?

It was strange. Lana had never flirted a day in her life, unless she counted the time she tried to charm Erik's lab mate, Sam, only to learn that he was in a happy, long-term relationship with a lovely man named Freddie. Lana was fairly certain that all she'd done to attract her dates in college was to wear the colorful clothes Caro had insisted she buy (the wardrobe she'd been sent with had been best described as "frigid heiress chic") and feign interest when someone explained how to do the chemistry problem sets she'd already solved, and she wasn't keen on dipping into that shameful area of expertise. It didn't reflect well on anyone.

"Grandmother, we're borrowing your blow-dryer!" Lana called as she walked to Esmelda's room. Shoving aside her hyper-awareness of her lack of flirting experience, Lana waited for a very slow Jiro to catch up, then disappeared into her grandmother's bathroom.

"You can sit on the toilet seat cover if you need to," she offered, somewhat surprised when he took her up on it. Coming face to face with the fluffy black leggings that she only wore in private must've really taken it out of him.

Lana dug around beneath the bathroom countertops until she found a drawer stuffed with hair supplies. She carefully took the crumpled note from Jiro, making sure to avoid any excess contact with his ridiculously lovely palm, and laid it on the counter. She'd unloaded half of the hair supplies drawer (the dryer was at the bottom in the back of the drawer, obviously) when she realized there wasn't enough counter space.

"Here," she said, handing Jiro a handful of pink patterned shower caps. And then a half dozen rounded hairbrushes. And finally an overflowing bag of curlers that had to be older than she was. As Lana finally pulled out the hair dryer, she snuck a peek at Jiro and couldn't stop laughing. He shot her an indulgent look when she let out a most unladylike chuckle. The sight of him, knees high from perching on what she now knew was a very low toilet, surrounded by framed cross-stitched patterns of local wildflowers and holding a collection of women's hair products, was just too much.

"Come on," he implored. "Do your blow-drying, before I decide that you need to try out some of these." He jiggled the bag of rollers.

"Okay, okay!" Lana gently pinned down the edges of the sodden note with bottles of bath products, attached a diffuser to the blow-dryer, and turned it to the lowest setting. She slowly waved warm air at the paper, going on her tiptoes to create as much space between the precious note and the dryer as possible.

"What are you doing?" Jiro asked.

"I'm concentrating!" she whisper-shouted back.

"On blow-dryer ballet?"

"On being gentle!"

A moment later, Lana tapped the edge of the paper and shut off the blow-dryer. She'd managed to get it nearly dry without causing any tears.

Success.

The penultimate word of the letter was now visible when she held it up to the light: "Love". But the writer's name was blurred out. Whatever it was, it was short.

The last two words, one clear, one illegible, echoed in Lana's thoughts. Someone—a family member, a friend, a significant other—loved this man, a man who'd nearly thrown everything away in a blizzard, on purpose or no, for reasons that might be lost forever.

Lana felt uneasy with that thought. It was even more unsettling than the knowledge that she herself would soon propose to some diplomat or tech tycoon over the phone for no better reason than that someone asked her to. And would the poor fellow even say yes?

"We're done!" Lana announced, and carefully refilled the drawer before bringing Jiro to the kitchen for lunch, letter in tow.

For the first time, Lana wondered how it felt to have someone love you dearly enough to write a handwritten note. She hoped Jiro would remember before he left and let her know.

❄

That evening, after confirming that Jiro was tucked away in the blue bedroom where noise wouldn't rouse him, Lana and Esmelda finally settled in for their movie night. Armed with the fluffiest of mouflon wool blankets, they could nearly pretend that they had the cottage to themselves as they nursed mugs of hot chocolate and giggled at the 1950s Bravarian telenovela they'd chosen to watch. It was one of Astrid Bauer's classic, traditionally over-the-top films—and like all Astrid Bauer films, it took a true story (that of the romantic love affair that inspired *Peace in the Mountains*) and turned it into an unpredictable, unapologetic adventure featuring a wild shepherdess who discovers she's the long-lost cousin of the king with whom her sister had a torrid love affair. There was something freeing about watching a movie that was so ridiculous. But that was the magic of Havos—of Solstice. It was the one time every year when it was acceptable to find joy in whatever made you happy—even if it was completely ridiculous.

❄

The next morning, Lana woke to a silent world. She pulled

on her robe, peeked through the curtains, and nearly spoiled the magic of the moment by squealing with joy.

Four feet of snow covered the entire village in a silent, pearly blanket. All the bumps of the mountainside had been smoothed over, with only trees and a few homes bravely peeking out through the depthless landscape. Pine branches bowed beneath the weight of the snow, and a half dozen tiny cottages looked as if they'd hunkered down to keep warm, hiding all but a few feet of their walls beneath window-high snow drifts and roofs covered by heavy puffs of white. After days of near-constant wind, the stillness seemed to echo.

Lana braced herself as she flipped the light switch, sighing in relief when warm light flooded the room. New Bravaria's bigger cities had underground electricity cables, but Havos still relied on the old power lines, and it wasn't unusual for them to snap under so much snow. Since the cottage's backup generator only supplied the kitchen (AKA the most important room in the house), Lana had plenty of experience getting dressed in the dark.

Lana tiptoed into the family room, careful not to shatter the magic of the quiet morning by waking anybody up. She'd just set foot on the rug when she heard…was that whispering? Feeling uncharacteristically mischievous, Lana crept forward, grateful that the thick wool muted her footsteps. She'd gone the considerable distance of three steps before a warm baritone called out, "Is that little Lana?"

"Leo!" She rounded the sofa to find Leo and her grandmother seated at the breakfast nook.

He instantly wrapped her in one of his huge, famous hugs and Lana closed her eyes, practically purring. Leo gave the best hugs. Everything about the man was big: his smile, his chest, his laugh, and, of course, his biceps, which was why Esmelda had recruited him to help with the baking eight years ago. The fact that Leo and his two daughters had barely been seen around town for several months after his wife died might have had something to do with it. But Esmelda had never admitted to scheming to breathe life back into that family.

"I always forget you're built like an ox," Lana gasped as Leo upgraded the hug from firm to bone crushing like he always did right before letting go.

"Of course I am! Why else would she keep me around?" He loosed a big, booming laugh with far more energy than should be legal so early in the morning.

"Why are you here so early?" Lana asked once she could breathe again.

"It's nearly nine o'clock," her grandmother whispered conspiratorially.

"*No!*" Lana ran a hand over her face. She hadn't slept so late since…well, last year's visit to Havos. "You made me sleep eleven hours!"

"I didn't *make* you do anything!" Esmelda laughed. "In fact, we've used two different stand mixers already, so if you slept through that, it was despite my best efforts."

"I guess lazy blizzards help me sleep well." *And not having seven a.m. meetings doesn't hurt.*

"Lazy blizzards, huh?" Leo asked. His hazel eyes warmed his ever-tan face, which he attributed to his Sicilian heritage, along with his thick, still-dark hair. Lana, however, wondered whether the quarterly trips Leo and his girls took to visit family in Siracusa played a larger role than genetics in maintaining his complexion.

Lana gestured to the blanket of white outside the window. "Lazy blizzard."

"If you get tired of the whole princess thing, you could always be a weatherwoman, eh?" Leo asked as he pushed back his chair and stood, taking care to not bump the table with what he called his "enthusiastic belly."

"Shh!" Lana hissed. "We're not using the 'p' word."

"The 'p' word?" Leo pursed his lips and looked at her grandmother, who gave a most uncharacteristic giggle. "Only if you say plea—only if you ask nicely."

Lana swatted Leo's arm as he moved to the industrial-sized pantry of baking supplies.

"Did you tell him about…" Lana eyed the hallway, and her grandmother gave her a look. Of course he knew about their visitor. The entire village—including the guests at the Inn—probably knew, because what else was there to do during a sneak attack blizzard besides gossip?

"So," Leo began as he carried a ten-pound sack of flour to the island. "Esmelda tells me the mysterious amnesiac is *very* handsome."

Lana felt her cheeks grow hotter than the cup of tea she wished she were drinking, and shot her grandmother an outraged look.

"Excuse me!?"

Esmelda just gave another of those silly giggles, her eyes dancing with delight.

"Apparently, he's tall and pretty and has great hair—which is why Esmelda guessed that you'd probably describe him as a regular Thor."

Lana shook her head in wonder. Her grandmother knew her too well. It was time to change the subject.

"Do tell me why you decided to sneak over here in the wee hours of the morning, mister," Lana insisted, hands on her hips. They definitely hadn't been baking when she'd left her room.

"We had work to catch up on from yesterday," Leo said, before removing ten loaves of bread and an obscene quantity of buns from the proving drawers in the back of the kitchen. Like any good Bravarian home, the oven was located as centrally as possible to give off extra heat during the long winters. This gave Lana a prime view of their morning's work.

Lana mmhmm-ed, but she wasn't entirely convinced. She knew bakers started early and that her grandmother's leisurely morning the day before was more of a blizzard-enabled treat than a habit. She'd also known Leo forever, and while he'd married late, he was at least ten years younger than her grandmother. She was just projecting her own newly resuscitated romantic hopes on two friendly colleagues.

But still…when Esmelda and Leo started kneading the next batch of dough, Lana quietly went to the front door. She opened it just far enough to confirm her theory: Havos was still a pristine winter wonderland, the roads impassable beneath untouched snow. Except for a crisply shoveled two-foot-wide tunnel that stretched across the street, wound up the walkway of what in summertime was a lovely front garden, and ended on the third step of her grandmother's house, where the porch roof ended.

In addition to helping her grandmother each morning, Leo was the town handyman. He was precise and thorough with his work, and Lana knew the path was his before she spotted his snow shovel propped against the wall. The man was either extremely efficient or highly motivated; there was no doubt that his tunnel went directly from his door to her grandmother's. If Lana had more than eleven dates' worth of personal experience to her name, she would declare that clear path to be a love letter—no, a love *declaration*—written in snow.

Feeling surprisingly hopeful, Lana gave the bakers their privacy. She had an appointment with a book and several mugs of tea.

Chapter Four

Lana was four chapters in when Jiro emerged from the hallway. He was looking approximately twenty percent more attractive than the day before—if that was even possible—despite the heavy stubble that had grown in overnight. Behind it, the color had returned to his cheeks, and the bump on his head was nearly gone. His face broke into a boyish smile when he saw Lana doing her best to impersonate a blanket turtle, with her body huddled beneath the wool blankets and her neck stretched out in a way that would *definitely* give her a headache later. It happened sometimes when she became too engrossed in her reading.

"Hi!" Lana scrambled out of her turtle position and straightened her nearly ever-present robe.

"Hey." His smile grew smaller but sweeter, and Lana wondered if he was another one of those people who genuinely liked mornings.

"How are you feeling?"

"A lot better." Jiro rubbed his jaw like he had the day before, but this time, the stubble created a slight scratching sound.

Lana tried not to stare. The men she encountered on a regular basis were groomed and polished within an inch of their lives. Greeting a sleep-tousled, stubbly Jiro felt like the most intimate moment she'd experienced with a man—more revealing, somehow, than that disastrous fumbling around in the dark with poor Carson. Would Michel be proud or horrified that this milestone involved a man wearing two-day-old (at least) long johns who was temporarily named after a helmet because he had no idea who he was?

"We can get you some new clothes tomorrow," Lana offered, figuring he must be nearly as tired of wearing long johns as she was of looking at them. "Hopefully the roads will be passable."

"Thank you." He looked relieved. "I haven't found any money in my things, but I could do something to help out around the house in the meantime, and later I can—"

The doorbell cut him off. Whoever was there must be hardy, since Caro and Erik had called to say they'd be spending another day at the Inn due to the snow.

"Hi, Lana!" Nico exclaimed once Lana opened the door. Her grandmother's second helper pulled Lana halfway into a hug before abruptly pulling back. A slight blush colored his sharp cheekbones as he examined the neckline of Lana's bathrobe, then yanked his eyes up and away. "Sorry if I got snow on you."

"You're good. Come on in!" Lana brushed a clump of snow off her shoulder and instantly regretted not changing earlier. She was comfortable wearing pajamas around her grandmother and Leo—even Jiro, she realized—but with Nico, it was awkward. He'd broken hearts across the dozens of villages and towns in the region. His movie-star cheekbones and Italian perfume model figure gave him an easy time with the ladies, whom he charmed and promptly forgot about with alarming efficiency. But Lana had known him since she was six and he was four, and was quite possibly the one person he'd never been able to charm. With his mother, Carlotta, being one of Esmelda's best friends, Lana knew him well. But the way Nico gazed at Lana when he thought she wasn't aware had never *not* made her uncomfortable, which was unusual. She'd made being appropriate an art form.

Lana thanked Nico for the extra pair of snow boots he'd

brought for Jiro and gestured to the kitchen. "Everyone's in there. I'll join you shortly."

Safely attired in clothing that Councilor Merrick wouldn't look twice at, Lana found Leo and her grandmother poring over a recipe, Jiro making tea, and Nico staring at him with a mixture of disbelief and suspicion.

"May I have some?" she asked Jiro as she stepped into the space between him and Leo.

"Of course." He slid the Thor cup over to her. "I've been told this one is yours."

Lana picked up the mug and took a scalding sip, maintaining eye contact throughout the painful process. Thor was awesome. Jiro had no right to judge her taste in superheroes.

Jiro had just handed Nico one of the cups when Lana asked if he'd read *The Last Kingdom*.

"I don't know."

His voice was quiet, and Lana winced at her own question. "Sorry," she whispered.

"It's fine. Why don't you tell me what it's about?"

Lana had just opened her mouth to reply when Nico interrupted them. "So, you're the trespasser everyone's talking about?" He went in for a handshake. "I'm Nico."

"Jiro."

"Hero? Did you pick that yourself?" Nico smirked.

"No, I chose it," Lana piped up. "And he was gracious enough to humor me. It's a helmet brand, in case you're wondering." She informed him of the proper spelling.

The rest of Nico's conversation with Jiro went about as well as one could imagine, until Esmelda called her team to attention and they fell into the smooth routine of people who've worked together day in and day out for years. As if an "autopilot" switch was flipped, the kitchen burst into action as ingredients were measured, dough was made, ovens were heated, and wrappings for deliveries were prepared.

Havos was a small village, and Esmelda was an

industrious, prolific baker, but her talents created such demand that assistance was absolutely necessary. Some villagers received weekly bread orders from larger, big-city bakeries, but the majority gave Esmelda their business; she made rolls and biscuits, cakes and cookies for special occasions, and, of course, seasonal specialties in addition to the staples of Bravarian cuisine. Leo assisted with the heavier tasks: coordinating supply deliveries, providing "muscle" for large batches of bread and other orders, and contributing to the kneading and shaping process as needed. Nico was an extra pair of hands most days, making deliveries and preparing bulk orders when he wasn't helping his parents run the Inn.

After confirming that Jiro didn't require a nap or painkillers after the exertion of standing for ten minutes straight, they formed an assembly line to finish up an order of Snow Twists, a seasonal favorite. Named for their unique shape and powdered sugar coating, they were an extra-special treat traditionally offered for only two weeks around Solstice. The cookies were made by cutting a shortbread-like dough into small bits, carefully rolling each portion into a log, twisting the log so it twirled but didn't crack, giving it a quick bake, and then dusting it with powdered sugar in the critical period before it cooled.

Esmelda cut and weighed pieces of dough, which then went to Leo for rolling, Nico for twisting, and Lana for baking and cooling. Jiro assumed Lana's usual honorary position of Chief Sugar Duster and proved talented in covering the treats with sugary snow. In just an hour, they'd made nearly four hundred Snow Twists, enough to fill the orders the Inn and café had placed for the week.

"Could you take a picture of us?" Esmelda asked Jiro before the final batch was finished. "We always like to get a few when Lana comes to visit."

"Of course."

Esmelda used her voice and elbows to direct Jiro to the digital camera she kept in a drawer in her office. "You should have plenty of space on there. I just replaced the memory card," she confirmed, to Leo's and Lana's chuckles. Last time Lana had come to visit, it had taken fifteen minutes to discover that there was no space on the card due to the vast amount of baking and botanical photos Esmelda had taken. Great minds must've thought alike, because Esmelda received not one, but *two* new memory cards as New Year's gifts.

By the time Leo and Nico left to drop off the most urgent orders, it was early evening, and a network of intersecting paths was emerging in the snow, one shovelful at a time.

❄

The next morning, Jiro insisted he was well enough to accompany Lana when she delivered the Inn's order.

"Are you excited to leave the house?" Lana asked as she supervised his bundling up process.

"I am! I'm hoping that a change of scenery might spark a memory or two, you know?" His voice grew muffled as he wrapped a scarf around his neck.

Lana nodded. Klara had suggested that Jiro do "regular" activities to try to inspire the brain version of muscle memory, but it was a tall task for someone who couldn't even remember his own name. "I hope it happens. But you do realize that you're not from around here, right? Somebody would have recognized you." Even if he'd visited the Inn just once before, Carlotta would have remembered him.

Lana felt a mix of frustration and affection for the fact that Havos was one of the few true dead zones left in Europe. The community went out of its way to set up ethernet-connected desktop computers for its smattering of students during term time, but otherwise declined all cell phone and internet service for the region. Every two weeks, Felix made the drive to the police station at Silver Pass to log updates and take care of any critical internet-related things, but his next trip wasn't scheduled until after Solstice. Until Jiro's memory came back or someone magically recognized him, they wouldn't be getting any answers before Lana had to go back to Baulten.

"I know. I just have to hope that I'll remember something. *Before* I meet whomever it is on the eighteenth." He zipped his ski coat and tucked the scarf inside. "You know you don't have to watch me get dressed to go outdoors?"

She'd been watching him like a hawk, as if she expected a young man clearly raised somewhere in Bravaria to have forgotten how to prepare himself to go outside. Her perusal had only revealed that he still remembered how to put on clothes and that his stubble had become even scruffier.

Perhaps it's for the best if he continues to become less attractive, Lana reminded herself. It certainly made it easier to focus on other things, like revising her mental to-do list for the grant application or continuing to tweak the phrasing of her staffing proposal to increase the likelihood that Councilor Merrick's cronies might support it.

"You are recovering! I want to make sure you don't hurt yourself again or get sick." It was true. Lana was surprisingly worried about Jiro going outside. She didn't want him to slip and hit his head again, or get too cold and delay his healing. She liked to finish things—passing proposals, completing reports, even finalizing packing lists —and the fact that she couldn't solve the mystery of this man's identity was starting to gnaw at her. He certainly wouldn't be undoing any of the recovery progress he had made under her watch.

"You realize that even if I'm not from Havos, I'm quite possibly from this region of the world, right? I couldn't say for sure, but I have a feeling I've zipped a winter coat before."

"And how did that go for you?" Lana teased as she slipped on her own boots. It came out snappy. "Passed out in a blizzard last time I checked."

"That was one time! Probably." He grabbed the hand she hadn't yet shoved into a glove. "And I know you wouldn't let anything happen to me."

"Oh?" It was the snarkiest reply she could get out. Was that the lightest stroke of his thumb along her palm? Why was it so—

He gave her hand a squeeze and pulled on his own gloves. "If something happened to me, you'd have to take my pants off again."

A humiliating, strangled sound came out of her mouth as she yanked the door open. "Out." She pointed to the porch. "But *carefully*. And I'll definitely delegate that task to my grandmother next time."

She heard a huffing laugh as she trudged down the stairs, laden with their deliveries. It was still well below freezing, and the air held the extra crisp chill it has when a significant amount of snow has fallen and intends to stay for a while.

If Lana weren't so focused on not sending buns tumbling to the ground as she stepped into Leo's snow tunnel, which had held up in pristine condition overnight—and had apparently set the groundwork for a ramshackle system of tunnels crisscrossing the entire village—she would've found it enchanting. She couldn't see much due to the four-and-a-half-foot-tall walls of snow, but there was evidence of other villagers moving around: a red fluff ball-topped beanie bobbing along; a tweed hunting hat making its slow, somber way across the street; a fashionable fur-trimmed white hat skimming along the snow in near-perfect camouflage. Only Mrs. Berger, who ran the café, was distinguishable from the bobbing of the elaborate peacock-shaped hat that had been in her family for generations.

Lana went first through the narrow tunnels, ensuring that Jiro followed Klara's advice and walked slowly. Her mountain gear and fluffy sweater kept her warm inside her coat, but she'd unwrapped the scarf, letting the icy air sting her cheeks and catch in her lungs as she breathed deeply through a sharp gust of wind. The cold was jarring, but she didn't want to miss a single breath of it. The air here felt so alive, like it was fresh and new, turning stale by the time it blew through the window she cracked open in her room in the Winter Palace.

"Are you doing okay, Jiro?" she asked when they'd crossed the halfway point of their short journey.

"Yes, don't worry about me!" She heard a crunch of snow as he took a step closer, and then a puff of breath warmed her ear. "I'd ask to walk faster, but I'm feeling grateful that you let me out of the house at all."

Lana shivered, and immediately frowned. She was literally the epitome of Bravarian good breeding, and it was an affront to her personal honor that she would appear to shiver at anything warmer than twenty degrees below freezing. And she was certain that as a woman who, as Mrs. Bennet would put it, was "very soon to be engaged," she shouldn't encourage an amnesiac to breathe temptingly anywhere near her ear.

Is tempting breathing even a thing?

Lana wished she could ask Michel, but he'd just laugh at her. So she grasped for something practical to say. "If we didn't get you out of the house, how could we get you new clothes?"

Jiro made a happy sound as they resumed walking, and Lana was glad that she'd been facing away from him for their little chat. This gentle-yet-increasingly-snarky Thor was too easy to please. And too nice. And his stubble was growing in so quickly she felt certain that if beard wigs were a thing, he could be a prolific donor. He'd been nearly clean-shaven when Felix found him, and was clearly irritated by the stubble he seemed to constantly run his hands across.

Lana was debating whether it would be rude to offer to get him a razor at the Village Store when the massive, creaky door of the Inn swung open in welcome. She turned to invite Jiro in herself, but the words died in her throat. She was suddenly even more grateful that she hadn't been looking at him as they walked, because she was now certain that they wouldn't have gotten anywhere.

To say that the outdoors agrees with him is an

understatement, Lana marveled.

The wind had given Jiro's cheekbones a slight flush, and his eyes were happy and almost wild, like being out in the snow had revived him. Lana couldn't help imagining what he must've looked like before his ski trip turned disastrous. If *this* was how Jiro looked after a four hundred step walk, how would he look drunk on the exhilaration he'd feel at the top of a mountain, traveling at breakneck speed? She still couldn't approve of reckless behavior, but if physical evidence were to be taken into account, she could almost understand it. Almost. He was *glowing*, despite being bedridden days before.

"I think it does, too," he murmured as someone greeted them from inside. Lana's cheeks burned as she realized she must have said at least some of her thoughts out loud, but Jiro just smiled at her as if nothing embarrassing had happened, offered her—was that a *wink*??—and smiled at the figure in the doorway.

Lana blinked, then turned forward. If she started narrating her wayward thoughts for all to hear, she would be considered unfit to rule sooner rather than later. It wasn't a piece of history Bravaria wanted to repeat.

❄

"Lana, come in, come in!" Carlotta waved from the door.

"Hello, Carlotta! We come bearing important deliveries!" Lana lifted the bakery boxes in greeting as they went inside.

Carlotta stacked the boxes on a table while they removed their boots—house rules—and changed into the slippers she'd set out for them. Esmelda must've called ahead to say that Lana had company, because beside the pair of size seven women's slippers was a much larger pair waiting for Jiro.

"Do those fit all right?" Carlotta asked as Jiro changed out of Nico's extra pair of boots.

"They fit perfectly. I'm very grateful to Nico for lending them to me," Jiro said solemnly.

Carlotta waved off his thanks and herded Lana into a hug.

"We've missed you, my dear!" she said when she finally let Lana go. Carlotta was tall, her freckled skin marked with laugh lines and crow's feet likely carved by the outrageous adventures she and Esmelda refused to tell anyone about. Her dry hair was dyed a dark brown that matched equally dark eyes—warm eyes that saw kindness in everyone and found a way to help in any situation. There wasn't anyone better suited to running the Inn and the charitable organization that quietly backed it. Those eyes also made it easy to share secrets, which was unfortunate, given that Carlotta was as prone to gossip as she was to permanently lending her scarves to visitors underdressed for the Bravarian winter.

"I missed you, too." Discomfited by the fact that she'd verbally acknowledged an *emotion,* Lana quickly changed the subject, introducing Jiro and admitting that she hadn't yet explained how the Inn and the foundation worked.

"Have you heard of the Health Springs Organization?" Carlotta asked Jiro as she led them to the kitchen. The Winter Springs Inn was rustic, with carved wooden chairs, well-loved leather loveseats, a profuse assortment of traditionally woven mouflon rugs, and large, sometimes wall-wide fireplaces that could be toggled from "electric" to "traditional" settings in the case of a power outage. Coziness was the Inn's chief concern, and nearly every inch of the place welcomed visitors to relax on a sofa, sit on a fluffy floor cushion near the fire, or read one of the books left on the three-hundred-year-old shelves by generations of guests.

Poor guy, Lana thought when Jiro politely replied that he hadn't heard of it. She could safely assume he hadn't heard of *anything* at that point, including her—which was a relief, if a guilty one.

"That's okay," Carlotta said with a wink. "No one has. It's completely separate from the Winter Springs name so that Lana here—" Carlotta shoulder bumped Lana affectionately, even as Lana hoped that she wouldn't say anything about the "p" word—"can stay involved. Which is fitting, given that she started the thing."

"Oh, stop," Lana cut in, turning to Jiro. "I started nothing. Carlotta has been running the Inn for decades—and women in her family have run it for generations. It's the only tourism Havos will tolerate, frankly, because it's for a good cause."

"Havos is full of natural hot springs," Carlotta explained. "They're all over the place. The most easily accessible ones just happen to be right next door, so we've been a natural destination for centuries of visitors coming to take the waters to improve their health."

Lana was nearly thrumming with excitement at Carlotta's description, but stayed quiet. She believed in her research, and if they received funding, it could have incredible impact on the entire village, especially the Health Springs Organization. It could give additional credibility to the natural phenomenon that the entire community had believed in for centuries. But she didn't want to jinx their as-yet unwritten application or raise Carlotta's hopes. Jiro, unfortunately, had picked up on Lana's agitation and gave her a questioning look, but she ignored it.

"Our waters don't do miracles, but they often help," Carlotta continued. "And Lana set up the foundation that provides travel and room-and-board stipends so those who need the waters most can afford to get here."

"That's really cool," Jiro said, looking between the two. "You must be proud that you get to help so many people."

Carlotta wrapped Lana in another hug—honestly, one could say that after hot springs and mouflon sheep, hugs were Havos's most plentiful natural resource—and grinned at Jiro over her head. "We're very proud. Some people, like Lana's friend, Caro, can afford to come here on their own, but our foundation even lets—" her voice dropped to a whisper—"*Old Bravarians* come for free if they need to."

"The Foundation has helped nearly a thousand people over the years," Lana chimed in, steering the conversation away from anything tangentially related to politics. The last thing she needed was a vague reference to border disputes jogging Jiro's memory of a headline about her he'd seen three years ago. "We accept anonymous donations and public ones."

"And my Nico here helps run things at the Inn when it's too busy for George and me." Carlotta beamed at her son before Lana could lose another battle with her emotions over the topic of donations.

"Lana, Jiro, good morning," Nico said. "I'm going to warm up some of these"—he gestured to the box of buns Jiro had carried to the kitchen—"and put them out for our guests. There's a group in the dining room right now if you'd like to meet them."

"I'd love to. Can I help carry anything?" Jiro asked.

"Just help me grab some plates, and you're good." Nico gestured to another alcove off the kitchen. It was covered in cabinets displaying a hodgepodge of cups and plates from different sets of porcelain.

"Are you coming, Lana?" Jiro tilted his head slightly.

"No, I need to chat with Carlotta about a few things and then say hi to my friends. Go meet people! I'll come find you when I'm done."

Lana felt guilty. She rarely told Inn guests that she was involved with the foundation, but she loved talking to them and frequently joined their trips to the pools (the steam did wonders to disguise one's face) when she was in town. But with Jiro around, she wanted to avoid innocent tourists who'd wonder if she really was the princess, or if she was just a lookalike.

"How is this group doing?" Lana asked once Nico and Jiro had gone. "Did everyone handle the blizzard okay?"

"*He's so polite!*" Carlotta whisper-screamed, completely ignoring the question.

"He is," Lana agreed, pursing her lips until Carlotta deigned to have an adult conversation and stop gushing about their surprise guest.

Carlotta rolled her eyes, well acquainted with Lana's

down-to-business face. "Everyone has been great. This set arrived with Caro and Erik. I love them, by the way," Carlotta whispered.

"So do I." Lana grinned. "Caro's probably on her best behavior for you, but trust me: as a suite mate, she's a handful."

"What!?" Carlotta exclaimed. "Impossible. She's so—"

"Sweet?"

"Yes! And considerate."

"She *is* sweet and considerate. But she definitely sleep talks. And sleep… I think she called it dancing, but to me it just looked like she was throwing shoes around."

"She throws shoes in her sleep?" Carlotta asked, probably thinking about the antique herding equipment that was tactfully displayed in the room she'd given Caro and Erik.

"Only flats. Never boots or heels. She's thoughtful like that."

Carlotta nodded.

"But maybe Caro's grown out of it now. I'll have to ask Erik. And if she hasn't, then I'll have more things to tease her about." Lana's eyes sparkled with mischief when a telltale yellow-and-green-striped sweater appeared just beyond the doorway. "Oh, and she snores, too! Loudly!"

The second she saw Caro's playfully outraged face—and Erik, looking like he also wanted to chuckle—her composure shattered, and she and Erik broke out laughing.

"*You*!" Caro screeched, and went in for a hug.

"It's okay, Caro," Lana promised as she patted her back. "You sleep dance, but you don't snore."

"*Much*," she silently mouthed to Erik, whose eyes were nearly filling with tears from laughing. Caro snored something fierce, but nobody would ever tell her that.

"Sleep dancing is actually a very effective way to regulate the nervous system," Caro informed Carlotta, stepping back and adopting the posture she used to present papers at conventions. Lana nodded with the greatest solemnity. She'd heard this speech many times before, often while wondering whether the shoe-shaped impression on her thigh would bruise. "Cardio movement allows the individual to burn through excess energy without fully disrupting the sleep cycle, and, as we all know"—more serious nods—"the mental health benefits of interpretive dance remain a vast and largely unstudied source of healthy expression." Caro concluded her speech while looking up slightly, as if addressing the edge of the ceiling would stop her mouth from twitching.

Finally, she returned her gaze to her audience. "It's just a pity I can't dance!" She gritted out before dissolving into giggles herself.

"It's true," Lana confirmed. "You definitely failed the interpretive dance audition when you tried to impersonate a hat."

"A real shame," Erik cut in, pulling his uncoordinated girlfriend into a side hug. "Just think: you could have been exploring the inner musings of dramatic expression instead of frivolously wasting time on medical research."

"I would've liked to do both, I think," Caro informed Erik, who wisely kept his mouth shut. "We ladies can have it all nowadays, can't we? The antisocial career, the whimsical hobby, the tolerable boyfriend"—a wink at Erik.

Lana grinned. She couldn't remember the last time she'd had time to be with her friends and just *talk*, instead of constantly working toward a deadline. Her smile faltered as she remembered that she'd have even fewer opportunities for fun once her father stepped down. Once she was *married*.

Unless you like *your husband*, an evil little voice suggested. *Then you could have a friend built into your daily schedule.*

Lana wished the voice away. She'd already committed to finding a trainable husband; it was a child's fantasy to think she would find a best friend hidden somewhere in that spreadsheet. She would find trainable, tolerable breeding stock to help her "carry on Bavarian traditions," as her father put it, even if the thought turned her stomach, and then…

"Speaking of 'having it all,' well done, Lana!" Carlotta squeezed her shoulder with a conspiratorial wink.

Lana gave her a confused look, until Carlotta pointed through the open doorway to where Jiro and Nico were drinking what was likely spiced tea with a few guests.

"*Very* good job. He's gorgeous, and clearly likes you. And I appreciate a fine eyebrow myself," Carlotta said wistfully. Lana flushed. Now that she thought about it, his eyebrows *were* excellent.

"Mom, stop!" Nico nearly spilled the small pitcher of milk he'd come in to grab. "You know they aren't actually dating. And even if they were, it couldn't go anywhere."

Lana was surprised how…dreary it felt to hear him say that, even though she knew it was true. Perhaps it was because this was her last chance to pretend that she was dateable. To do something for herself, just one last time.

"Nico's right," she said, giving a casual laugh. "Plus, he might be in a relationship and just can't remember. And nobody should start a relationship when their brain is *in recovery*."

"Even if somebody might want to?" Caro chimed in unhelpfully.

"Even then."

"Even if someone might want to what?" Jiro asked, having come in to help Nico and carry in some empty teacups.

"Nothing," Lana assured him. "Are you alright to stay a little longer? I can give you a tour of the rest of Havos once I finish up with these three." She ignored how Carlotta wiggled her eyebrows at Caro upon hearing her offer.

Jiro nodded and returned to the dining room with a plate of Snow Twists. The second he was out of earshot, Caro turned on her.

"I like him." She'd crossed her arms, ready to do what Lana regarded as completely pointless battle.

"Yes?"

"You should date him."

"Excuse me? Based on what?"

"I like the way he stood beside you. And I know you like his face."

"Flawless reasoning, Caro." The entire conversation was especially rich coming from the most scientific mind Lana knew.

"It's not like you have someone else." Lana nearly wished that were true. "And I want to see you with someone—for you to not be alone for a change."

"This is ridiculous. And it's bad timing anyway." The rest of her life would be bad timing, and she really didn't want to talk about the spreadsheet this week. But Caro's gaze had already sharpened, her protectiveness rising to the forefront.

"What do you mean it's bad timing?"

"Just with the grant application due so soon—and, oh, the fact that he's leaving for Old Bravaria in four days, and, while we're at it, the fact that he doesn't know who he is! Just your typical 'it's not good timing' reasons."

"He clearly doesn't know who you are, either," Caro shot back, her gaze narrowing. Lana wouldn't make such efforts to deceive someone she didn't care about, and Caro knew it.

Fortunately, Caro decided not to press the topic in front of an audience. With the interlude of Lana's nonexistent love life over, Carlotta left Lana, Caro, and Erik to map out their schedule for the week in the Inn's tiny office.

Lana was grabbing her and Jiro's outerwear when she heard an old lady mention how hopeful she was that their visit to Havos would help her Loris with the lingering sickness he'd been fending off for the past few years.

"Even if it doesn't help"—a pause, during which Lana fancifully imagined that Loris was kissing his lady's hand—"I'm having a lovely time here with you."

Lana was still smiling when Jiro emerged from around the corner, wishing the elderly couple a good visit and promising to stop by again if he could.

As they made their way toward the snow tunnels, Lana could swear that Jiro was whistling.

"Did you have a good time visiting with the guests?"

"Oh, I loved it," he said earnestly. "Everyone is so grateful to be here. Even if the springs don't solve their problems, you can see that just being here has given them something to be happy about."

"I know. It's why I started the foundation. And it's selfish, but I love to listen to their stories. If that isn't motivating, I don't know what is."

"Do you think the springs really can help these people heal, or do you think it's the hope?"

Lana paused. "I think it's a bit of both. But I do believe that there is something in these waters that helps people. The sick and injured have come to take the waters in Bravaria for thousands of years. And hope can help you get through almost anything, but it can't make many things go away. And that's what these waters seem to do. Sometimes." Lana ran a hand through her hair. "I'm not making any sense, am I?"

"You're making sense."

"I just... I think there's something here. Even if it's amplified by hope. And that's why I want to research it—to do a proper, statistically significant study on all Bravarian 'healing' hot springs. But they're on both sides of the border, and New and Old Bravaria haven't been able to collaborate on something since The Split. That's why this grant application is so important. With Caro's lab being government-funded—and with all of us having full-time day jobs—we can't take it any further like this. We need funding from a non-Bravarian foundation, and we need a neutral, non-Bravarian team who can do work in both countries without causing a scandal. We've done preliminary studies using samples from a few New Bravarian springs, and we *know* there's a measurable difference in the mineral composition of our waters compared to other healing springs in Europe. But our water systems are connected to Old Bravaria's, and we need access to both to do this study properly and understand if these waters really are special.

This grant is make or break it. And if we make it, think of all the lives this knowledge could improve."

Lana stopped, out of breath and heart racing with the usual trepidation and excitement she felt when thinking about her research.

But this was different. This was the first time she'd ever fully explained her dream to someone and revealed how important this research was to her. Considering that only three people knew she was using her chemistry degree at all, it was incredibly rash to confide in a complete stranger.

"You must think I'm crazy," she whispered as she covered her face with her hands. Why had she gone and admitted her most secret hopes, which felt more essential to whom she wanted to be than the fact that she was a princess?

Warm hands wrapped around her fingers and pulled, forcing her to look Jiro in the eye. She felt so bashful, covered in three layers of clothing with her dreams out on display.

"I think that's amazing," Jiro told her. She couldn't look away. "And it makes so much sense. Why hasn't anyone done this before?"

It was the exactly what she needed to hear.

Chapter Five

Lana had read that fewer muscles were required to smile than to frown, but she'd never believed it until that moment. Princesses smiled. It was part of the job. But frowning (or what *felt* like a neutral face, but what her mother called her resting bitch face) came naturally, and after long days of smiling her most polished smile throughout all manner of social situations, Lana often had to massage the soreness from her face. But in this moment, with the winter sun gleaming and Jiro holding her hands and the realization that he'd *listened* as she confessed her most private dream, the smile washing over her face was a relief.

She didn't care that this man likely knew nothing about science—much less his own name—because he'd *agreed*. His tone had been fierce as he stood where the snow tunnels converged in the village square and voiced his support in broad daylight. And support that wasn't for her policies, but for *her*? From someone who barely knew her but had decided to believe in her anyways? Lana had never experienced anything like it.

It felt like some sort of divine symmetry to discover such happiness *here*, in equal view of the Inn on one side of the square, the House of Stories on the other, and streets of jewel box cottages on the perpendicular.

"No one has done this before because Bravaria has been divided since before most of the equipment we use was invented." Lana grimaced. "If we were one country, this is one of the many things that wouldn't be an issue."

"I agree. But we must look forward, yes? The grant application could take this dream and carry it forward for you."

Lana took a fortifying breath. It was hard to talk about outside the lab. "Yes. This is our last chance. We all have… obligations…to fulfill and it can't go on this way. That's why Caro and Erik are here. The application is due on Solstice, which is a very busy time for everyone, so we need to finish as much as possible this week."

"And those obligations…" Jiro's voice trailed off, as if he'd planned to add "that get in the way of your dreams" and thought better of it.

"Yes?" It was hard to get the word out past the lump in her throat.

"What is your role in your…family's business?"

Lana paled. Apparently he *had* heard Esmelda insisting that her parents had turned her into a workaholic that morning. "I'm in management." There.

She could see Jiro start to roll his eyes but catch himself. "For what kind of business?"

The all or nothing kind. "Does it matter?" The question was addressed to his boots.

"Hey," Jiro replied, startling Lana with the casual address. She gave him a confused look.

"Yes?"

"This is really stressing you out."

"Yes."

"Breathe."

Lana glared at him, but did as he said, focusing on the crisp air and the warmth of his hands, which hadn't let go of hers for a moment. She now realized she'd been holding her fingers as still as stones throughout the conversation.

"People can never tell when I'm nervous," she whispered.

"Then people are terrible listeners," he whispered back, a serious look on his face. Or maybe she just never let her emotions get so close to the surface.

"Do you want to know something about me?"

Lana's eyes grew wide.

Do I want to know something about you? Is there snow in the mountains? "Yes! Jiro, did you remember something?" Any morsel of information, no matter how trivial, was precious.

"You don't need to call me Jiro anymore. Call me Hadi." The relief and warmth in his face echoed hers from moments before.

"Hadi!" she exclaimed, testing out the name. She *loved* it. "Do you know how you remembered it?"

"It wasn't like remembering at all." He dropped her hands and ran his palm along the scruff of his jaw. "Loris shook my hand and introduced himself, and I shook his hand and introduced myself right back. My name just spilled out, like I'd always known it."

"You were right, Hadi." She grinned. Hadi was a much better name for him than Jiro, and the light syllable at the end added something to the character she was painting of him in her mind. Now she knew that her piano-playing Thor held hands with the elderly and had brightness in his name. "Fresh air *definitely* did you some good. And since you're feeling better than ever, you have no excuse: you're getting some new clothes."

He opened his mouth to protest, but she stopped him. "No excuses. My grandmother is tired of seeing your long johns. And it's my firm belief that every grown-up should own at least one normal pair of pants."

Hadi raised an eyebrow at her. "I wasn't going to disagree with you, but now I almost want to." His eyes twinkled. "I was going to remind you that I'll pay you and your grandmother back once I get access to my own finances again. Or maybe find an odd job or two around here..."

"Don't worry about it." Maybe he'd finally concede when he realized his unnecessary sense of chivalry wasn't going to get him anywhere. "A few sets of men's clothing are not going to break the bank." Would he believe her if she told him her personal finances were funded by the central bank?

"Even so, I couldn't impose—"

"We'll figure it out later, okay?" Lana adjusted her hat and started marching through the snow tunnels to a street lined with tiny shops. "This way!"

❋

Lana loved Sheep Dreams, the only clothing shop in Havos. White paint covered the little storefront, and the thick, blown-glass windows were so old that swirls marked most of the panes as originals. A wide entry mat requested that they "stomp on me, please!" and hooks carved like rams' horns waited to hold their coats and scarves. Lana looked back to make sure Hadi ducked as he passed through the low, dark wooden doorway.

"The clothes here are highly seasonal," Lana told Hadi as he hung his coat. "Right now, the options are woolen and festive for Solstice, so at least it'll all be wa—"

"Ah!" Hadi cried, bracing himself with a hand against the polished wooden wall

"What?" Lana looked around, puzzled.

"Why are there sheep everywhere?"

"Are you…okay…with sheep?"

Hadi narrowed his eyes as he surveyed the shop, taking in the decorative stuffed sheep, the sweaters with embroidered sheep on them, the blankets with sheep sewn on, the framed photos of…sheep. Sheep Dreams lived up to its name.

"The sheep are…startling," he finally declared.

"They're mouflon sheep," Lana explained, as if using the proper terminology for something he found inexplicably disturbing would help him think past it.

"Are they? That's lovely."

A string of tiny bells rang as a short, stout man in a toasty-looking sweater and scarf emerged from behind a curtain. He had round, flushed cheeks and bushy black eyebrows that nearly hid his eyes when he saw Lana and smiled.

"Lana, my dear, hello, hello!" He gave her a quick hug. "And you must be the mysterious stranger I've heard so much about!" He hugged Hadi, too, before pulling back and quickly scanning his outfit. "I am Otto. I am to call you Jiro, no?"

"Actually, you can call me Hadi."

Lana was always impressed by how quickly news traveled in Havos. Maybe it was a by-product of living without internet access. The entire village would know Hadi's new name by nightfall.

"Very well." Otto clasped his hands behind his back and stood between Hadi and the rest of his merchandise. "You don't like sheep?"

"It's not exactly that I don't like them, just—"

"I have my flocks of wild sheep. I help raise them from a distance. I make sure the young grow up big and strong, and I make sure the herds are safe," Otto informed him, as if assurance that the sheep lived good lives would overcome Hadi's irrational fear.

Hadi looked to Lana for assistance, but she turned away, hiding a giggle as she examined a pair of fuzzy socks with sheep faces on the outer ankles. *Cute.* She grabbed a pair.

"My sheep are happy sheep, and live good, happy lives and make the softest, warmest, happiest wool—which we gather responsibly, spin traditionally, and use to make the happy clothes you see here. So, you see, the sheep should not make you unhappy." Otto patted Hadi's elbow. "You are wearing ski pants to do errands and it is a balmy eight degrees outside. I think wearing these clothes will make you feel much better. You are clearly not yourself today."

"I agree, sir," Hadi gritted out. His eyes kept darting from one piece of sheep-bedecked merchandise to another. "I will look around." He patted Otto's arm in return and extricated himself.

"Your man has a problem with sheep," Otto told Lana, a somber expression on his face.

"He does," Lana agreed. It was unexpected to see

someone so large and calm cowed by a roomful of sheeply attire and a shiny-faced man.

"He will wear my clothes anyway. Because there are no other options. And they are wonderful."

"He will." They made mischievous eye contact. "And I will, too. Your sweaters are some of my favorites."

"Oh, you honor me!" He went to bow.

"Stop that!" Lana turned frantically to confirm that Hadi hadn't seen the bow. "You know that fuzziness is all that matters when it comes to clothes that I choose for myself. And I found these amazing socks!" Lana held up the pair.

"Ah, yes, my little Gerta made those! They were her first design." Otto beamed, looking as if he could melt from fatherly pride.

"Gerta made these? Isn't she only twelve?"

"Yes, she turned twelve this summer. She's gotten so grown-up—you'll see when she tells a tale during Story Night."

"I can't wait. And I'm going to take a few more of these," Lana said, grabbing several sizes of the sheep socks. "Please tell Gerta I loved them."

A short time later, Lana found Hadi at the other end of the store, wide-eyed and worrying his lower lip with his teeth.

"Everything in this shop is connected to sheep in some way, isn't it?"

Lana nodded.

"So it's either decorated with sheep, pure sheep skin, or it's wool."

"The mouflon is a majestic, prolific animal."

"Mmm. And I'm guessing this means that Otto sells woolen underwear, too?"

Lana pursed her lips, trying not to laugh, and peeked at the underwear section. "Yes. But the clothes here really are some of the best! If you can just forget about the sheep part, you might even like what you find."

"I've forgotten a lot lately, but *that* is not likely."

Lana held up a basket of sheep-covered undershirts. "I'll

even match you."

Hadi raised an eyebrow. "With *everything*?"

Much to Hadi's dismay, Lana replied that she was fully stocked up on woolen underwear, but vowed to buy a few normal items of sheepwear to make him feel better.

Hadi ended up getting an entire mouflon wardrobe: a thick black sweater with an enormous, fluffy sheep covering the chest, a navy blue sweater with tiny rams chasing one another and occasionally butting heads across the bottom hem, two pairs of woolen trousers with nothing more scandalous than the embroidered outline of Otto's family sheep crest on the right side of the front of the waistband, two thin woolen undershirts to give the world a break from his long underwear top, and a few pairs of underwear and socks. Lana, in a delightful show of solidarity, also obtained a heavy sweater with a lamb on the chest and a pair of leggings with fluffy little lambs chasing each other across the ankles.

While Hadi was distracted by a particularly realistic taxidermy sheep he'd found in the corner, Lana quietly arranged for Otto to send her the bill. Locals had accounts in most stores, and like other visitors to Havos, Lana typically paid in cash. But she didn't want Hadi to get up in arms about her paying again. It was ludicrous that a commoner would try so valiantly to reimburse a princess, but Lana supposed it was her own fault.

Since Hadi had remembered his real name, she felt even guiltier about not revealing her own identity. Before, they'd both been more or less anonymous. It had been easy to flatter herself into thinking that she'd magically become a bigger person and fess up the moment his memory started coming back—the moment he became *real*, and not just an amnesic Thor-lookalike she'd met in the mountains. But after today, and after Hadi had given her *that smile*, Lana wondered if she could just… never tell him. Make the absolute most of this gift—a few days of friendship with no worries about duty or ulterior motives—before saying goodbye and never seeing him again. And never admitting who she really was before they parted ways forever.

But would it even work? As Hadi's memories continued to return, could she remain "just Lana," a stressed-out twenty-something-year-old visiting her grandmother as a respite from a controlling, wealthy family, and who didn't need to be reimbursed for the purchase of luxury, hand-woven woolen items? Or would he wake up one day and realize who she was, leave immediately, and take all manner of scandalous, press-worthy confessions with him?

Lana mentally huffed at herself. The thought was ridiculous. She knew he couldn't leave yet due to the snow. And even if something untoward *did* happen, she doubted it would be memorable enough for him to announce it to the press after he noticed her face splashed across the papers, announcing her upcoming engagement to a perfect stranger. A pit opened in Lana's stomach at the thought, even as a sly part of her crooned with pleasure at the idea of *getting away* with whatever it was that might transpire between them. She wasn't sure why she suddenly wanted to be both unmemorable and unforgettable to the same person.

❄

By the time they left Otto's store, tiny snowflakes were spitting down from a sky pale with early afternoon light.

"How are you feeling now?" Lana asked, closing her eyes and savoring a deep breath of fresh mountain air.

"It feels good to own a change of clothes again. Thank you, Lana."

Lana. It sounded nice from his lips. Kind of like how nice "Hadi" felt on her own.

"Mmmhmm," she replied, eyes still closed. *The day has a slightly wild scent to it*, she thought. *Almost damp smelling, which is unusual before the snow starts to melt.*

"Um, Lana?"

She opened her eyes, realizing that Hadi had said her name more than once. "Yes, you're welcome." She waved a hand at him. "Happy?"

"No." He'd gone a little pale. Was he going to faint? "Look behind you."

Lana turned slowly.

"What's—oh, my!"

A wild mouflon sheep stood not five feet away from her, its head poking up above the snow as if summoned from her most wondrous dreams and his worst nightmares.

"Well, he*llo* there!" Lana immediately adopted the voice she used to talk to dogs—the one her mother wished she'd use to talk to babies. "Aren't you the cutest?" The sheep didn't seem full grown, and it was a lady sheep; no horns jutted up from the puff of fluff on her forehead, just an adorable twig that had gotten stuck there. "Are you one of Otto's wild sheep?" she asked it, tentatively stepping onto the main road, which had been shoveled to create a wider, shallower tunnel while they were shopping.

The sheep mirrored her step forward, baaa-ed, and stood still. Lana took another step. The sheep followed.

"I think we've got ourselves a buddy! Come on," she called to Hadi, who was eyeing the animal distrustfully. "Walk on my other side. We should take this poor lady to Felix. She shouldn't be wandering into town alone at this age. That's something only adult mouflons are allowed to do."

If Hadi made a sound of disbelief, she ignored it. The little sheep kept pace with Lana as they walked to the rangers' office. On equal ground, the animal came up to her hips.

"Why do you think it likes me?" Lana asked as she knocked on the snow-flecked wooden door.

"Maybe because the bag you're holding is full of wool from its mother?"

Before Lana could respond, footsteps crunched through snow and Felix appeared from around the snow tunnel's corner.

"Well, hello there, Lana!"

"Hi, Felix."

"And hello there, mysterious trespasser." He eyed Hadi suspiciously, looking more intimidating than usual with his ranger uniform visible beneath his unzipped parka—not that he'd be doing much ranging today with all the snow. "I was just coming to check up on you."

"You chose the right time," Hadi said with a grimace.

"We were actually coming to see you…" Lana trailed off as Felix spotted her white shadow.

"What do we have here?" Felix asked, incredulous. He turned to Hadi. "Did you take this lamb away from its flock?"

"Absolutely not," Hadi replied crisply.

"It came out of nowhere when we left Otto's shop, and I think it's following me," Lana said. She sidestepped to demonstrate, and the sheep copied her.

"Unusual. We don't usually get adolescent sheep in town without the adults."

Lana turned to give Hadi an "I told you so" glare. He returned a puzzled, "what's with this village?" look, and Lana resisted the urge to snicker.

"What do we do with it?" she asked.

"I'll take care of it. I need to try to lead her back to her flock." Felix surveyed the sheep for another moment and then looked back at Hadi. "Are you *sure* you didn't do anything to that sheep?"

"I'm sure—since you found me, at least. If we met before, she would know better than I would." He pointed at the lamb, who baa-ed innocently.

"Mmhmm," Felix grumbled. Lana could almost see the gears in his head turning as he debated whether all the unusual visitors—both human and sheep—in Havos were connected.

"Hadi didn't do anything to lure the sheep, Felix. Honestly, he hates the thing, though I can't imagine why."

"And yet he has two shopping bags filled with mouflon merchandise?"

Hadi coughed. "Believe me, sir, if there had been *any*

other options, I would have chosen them."

Felix gave Lana an amused glance. "Didn't want any like-sized strangers to lend him clothes?" He teasingly puffed out his chest.

Lana blushed. Now that he mentioned it, she realized that Felix was tall and more muscular than Hadi. Any borrowed clothes would've been slightly loose, but they would've fit. "I..." Lana wasn't sure what to say. Hadi occupied such a unique category in her mind that it hadn't occurred to her that someone else might have a body like his—or even a body that was *better* than his, in some people's opinion. "I wanted to make sure Hadi had clothes he didn't need to give back after he leaves on the eighteenth."

Unfortunately, both men looked more amused than convinced.

She touched the forearm of Felix's coat. "But thank you for offering. That would have been very helpful."

"You're welcome..." Felix's voice trailed off. "Wait. Why are you calling him Hadi? I thought he was going by Jiro?"

"Because it's my name. To the best of my knowledge," Hadi said.

"How'd you figure that out? Find an ID?" Felix narrowed his eyes.

"I remembered it a few hours ago."

"Remember anything else?"

"Not yet, unfortunately." Hadi didn't mention the note that implied that he was Old Bravarian, but Lana supposed it didn't really matter, given that they'd found him along the border, which was *definitely* not somewhere that he should have been. Regular people didn't harbor the same animosity they once did, but the New and Old Bavarian governments still hated each other, and trespassing was still trespassing.

"You *do* know that entering the Lausalle Sanctuary is considered trespassing, which is illegal?"

Hadi nodded and shifted the weight of the bags in his hands. "Yes, I do."

"And I'm assuming you know that skiing in a storm like that was incredibly foolish."

"Yes, I do," Hadi repeated.

Lana watched their conversation with a growing sense of discomfort. Whether that discomfort stemmed from Felix's frustration at being unable to properly do his job, or the fact that his questions painted a very different picture of Hadi than the steady, perceptive person Lana was beginning to know, she wasn't sure.

"And who packs a bag like that?" Felix asked, sounding more annoyed than anything. "You clearly know how to choose a helmet, but that packing? Man, if you'd gotten wherever it was you were going, you wouldn't have wanted to stay long. You didn't even have a first aid kit."

"I know. I'm trying to piece things together, too, but I have as little to go on as you do. But I do know how grateful I am that you found me, sir. Thank you for that, even if I was somewhere I shouldn't have been."

"If the roads were open, I'd drive down to Silver Pass to run a search, but everything will need to wait a few days until the roads are cleared. So behave until then." Felix shot Hadi a firm look. He could phone down to Silver Pass to have one of his colleagues look into their strange visitor, but that would draw attention to the fact that Lana made annual "unsupervised" visits to Havos. "And tell me if you remember anything. At the very least, we need to figure out *how* you got here so we can make sure it doesn't happen again."

Lana's left eye was on the verge of twitching by the time Felix started walking. It was painful to watch Hadi try to take responsibility for potential crimes he didn't remember committing. Not for the first time, Lana thanked her lucky stars that she'd been born with a risk tolerance of approximately zero.

After hiding in the rangers' office so that Felix could use a carrot to lure the sheep toward the barn at the edge of town, Lana and Hadi cautiously stepped outside.

"Hold on a second," Hadi said as Lana turned in the direction opposite the barn. "Just crouch a little bit—just a little lower," Hadi instructed as he removed a digital camera from his pocket. Esmelda must have lent it to him. "There we go."

"Are you a sheep photographer now?"

"I'm just photographing the local wildlife," he teased, snapping a second picture just of her. Lana's eyes widened. Jiro had given her kind, indulgent looks, but Hadi…teased?

"In that case, you missed a shot," she informed him, and grabbed the camera, delighted with his playfulness.

She took several photos of Hadi, covertly including the butt of the now-distant sheep before he asked where they were going.

"We're finishing your tour of the village—after our next stop, of course." She gestured for him to go first down one of the narrower snow tunnels.

"And what stop is that?"

"The doctor's."

He paused, and Lana could swear she *felt* his hackles rise. "Ah. Did you schedule my whole day for me like a little kid?"

"No." But he didn't have to act like one. "This is the first time people are out and about since the blizzard, so I figured we should get you checked on just in case. Do you mind?" To be fair, Hadi had only thought they were going to drop off some baked goods and take a tour. But why should he be mad about something that was *for* him? Lana swallowed. Making decisions and telling people what to do was part of what made her good at her job. Was she becoming one of those people who got so used to directing people at work that it bled into their personal lives?

"I don't mind," Hadi assured her. She heard his hand scrape over stubble. "I'm sorry if that came off as rude. I'm just…more than a little frustrated with *me*, right now." He turned around, tapping his temple. "And I feel like I've never said this in my life"—a tiny pause, conveying a silent "as far as I can remember"—"but I love just spending the day walking around with you. Watching you handle dangerous wild animals." He grimaced in mock disgust.

"That's very kind of you." There was definitely a "but" coming.

"But I do feel a lot more lucid today than I did yesterday. And you continuing to take care of me is lovely, and very much appreciated, but I need to stop acting like an invalid."

"I'll keep you in the loop from now on," Lana said quietly, feeling ridiculous. Hadi wasn't a country. He didn't need her to decide things for him. But she still felt somewhat justified. "It's your life—but it's *my* grandmother's roof you're staying under, and *her* feelings you'll hurt if something happens to you under our care." Not to mention whatever PR disaster Lana would face if something bad happened and word got out. "So we're going to the doctor." She raised her chin imperiously.

"Yes, ma'am." He bowed, then gave in to a grin. "Since *you* care so much."

The doctor's visit was quick, but while Hadi was cleared to operate machinery and do normal person things—including visit the hot springs as long as Lana kept an eye on him at all times—Klara still didn't know when he'd regain more of his memory.

It had started to grow dark, and a chill wind had picked up by the time they left Klara's office. Hadi didn't seem to mind the cold—crazy skiing Old Bravarian that he was—but he noticed Lana's wistful expression.

"What's wrong?"

"Oh, nothing." She summoned a polite smile and forced herself to stop looking around. Twilight in the mountains—darkness spreading closer to the rugged skyline like swirls of watercolor paint, and warm lights flickering on behind blown-glass windows—did *not* make her sentimental. It was just the exhaustion catching up to her.

"It's illegal to lie to someone with memory loss," Hadi stepped into her personal space.

"Is it, now?" Then she was so screwed.

"It should be. On the grounds of manipulation."

Oof. Lana tried not to suck in a breath, and said the first excuse that popped into her head. "I just hoped Melinda would be out here."

"Melinda?" Hadi's brow wrinkled.

"The mouflon."

"You named her?" He looked offended.

"What, was I supposed to think of her as 'just another adolescent female mouflon in Havos'?"

"Yes?"

"You're the worst," she scoffed at him.

"For not naming a wild animal I knew for fifteen minutes?"

"For that and for other reasons, which I'm certain will reveal themselves in time." Lana started walking toward the Village Store, which was visible from across the square.

"In that case, I think you should do as the doctor said and not let me out of your sight," Hadi told her, coming to walk beside her and grabbing her hand.

"The doctor didn't mention anything about holding hands!" Lana protested, but left her hand exactly where it was.

"If you want more incriminating memories to resurface, it's in your best interest to do everything you can to prevent any repeat concussions. And given the environment we're in," he gestured at the snow tunnels around them with his other hand, making the Sheep Dreams bags bump against one another, "with icy conditions and wild murder sheep coming out of the woodwork, you can never be too careful."

Lana grinned. She *knew* he was laying on the charm to cheer her out of her secret, twilight-inspired sentimentality, and it didn't even bother her. In fact, she thought she might *adore* it.

"In that case, we must take the greatest care." Lana squeezed his hand. "I have incredibly high expectations for the Secrets of Hadi that will reveal themselves over the next few days."

His eyes dimmed a bit at her mention of leaving Havos, but he didn't drop her hand.

"And speaking of secrets…do you need any toiletries from the Village Store?"

Hadi inspired a great sigh of relief by confirming that he did, indeed, wish for a razor.

Chapter Six

The next morning, Lana frowned at the two swimsuits on her bed. Her favorite one-piece—the one she'd asked Vera to pack—looked red and comfortable and inviting on the maroon bedspread. To its left was a second swimsuit that she *definitely* hadn't asked Vera to pack, since she'd forgotten about the cheeky gifts that had been part of Michel's silent campaign to convince her to go on a tropical vacation. Lana hadn't yet been able to take that vacation, and the matching coverup, rhinestone-encrusted sandals, sun hat, and beach bag had remained untouched in her closet for the past year and a half. Or so she'd thought. Apparently, Vera had found the stringy two-piece and decided that it was a useful thing to bring to Havos, where the average December temperatures ranged from negative five to twenty-five degrees Fahrenheit.

While the hot springs were warm, neon pink-and-blue shimmery polka-dot string bikinis were not the typical fashion choice amongst local villagers or tourists, who primarily came to ease their pain. Plus, the bikini was approximately half the size of anything that even the most daring princess would wear in private. The press would have a field day if they so much as saw it packed in her suitcase.

Lana was still staring at the thing in wonder when her grandmother walked in and joined her in surveying the two options. Esmelda bit her lip, but Lana could sense her amusement.

"What?" she asked, going beet red.

"This is pretty," her grandmother replied, gesturing at the bikini.

"Vera packed it," Lana moaned. "The new Tetra," she clarified. "Every time I give her a packing list, it's an exercise in…something. She packed me lipstick, too."

"How terrible," Esmelda agreed.

Lana shot her a glare. "Look at this thing!" She held up the bottoms, which admittedly glimmered beautifully in the firelight. "It's so skimpy!"

"It's not that bad," Esmelda insisted, peeking at the back. "It's not a thong."

It was halfway between a boyshort and a thong-style bikini, which was to say that the coverage was just scantier than a regular pair of underpants. But Lana refused to be appeased on account of all the strings.

"Michel gave this to me," Lana said, picking up the top, which was also stringy, with triangular patches of fabric covering the necessities and extra-long (extra-sparkly, she noticed with conflicted glee) tie strings designed to criss-cross along her ribcage. She was small chested, and while she'd refused to try on the bikini on principle, she could tell it would look good. Michel's superpower was getting everyone perfect gifts. And finding the love of his life before he could legally drink alcohol in more than eight countries.

"Ah." Her grandmother smiled. "That was sweet of him. You'd never buy something so fun for yourself."

"Excuse me?" Lana asked, indignant. She wouldn't, but she liked to think that she would.

"Are you going to wear it or not?"

"Not a chance."

Such attire lived firmly in the "maybe one day" category, right alongside wearing heels more than three inches high and trying base jumping.

"This one's not ugly," Lana insisted, grabbing the one-piece and stuffing it into a carry bag. "Not that I care," she reminded her grandmother.

"Of course not. Have you phoned Carlotta?"

"She knows we're coming at ten. Are you sure you don't want to join us?" Lana asked as she zipped the shimmery bikini safely away into her suitcase and grabbed a hair clip.

"Oh, I'm sure." Her grandmother gave her a cheeky look.

❄

Hadi appeared outside her door five seconds later, no bag in hand. Honoring her promise to not treat him like a child, Lana held her tongue as she wondered why it was that men would choose to wear swimsuits to and from bathing locations, even if said locations offered world-renowned changing rooms.

"Shall we?" Lana asked, shouldering her bag.

"We shall."

The weather was clear, and their boots crunched on firmly packed snow as they passed through the explosion of new tunnels that seemed to have cropped up overnight.

"So, do you have any vague hot springs memories?" Lana was curious, but not as curious as she was about whether he'd remembered anything else, like what a certain princess looked like.

"I don't know," Hadi admitted as they passed an intersection of eight different tunnels. The good people of Havos had been busy. "I can picture what hot springs look like and imagine how they feel, but I can't tell if it's a hazy memory or something I just know."

"Don't worry. Even if you've been to dozens of hot springs, you've never been to ones like these." Lana headed for the Inn's side entrance, which was closer to the hot springs cave hidden within an outcropping of rock near the edge of the village.

"Changing rooms are through here." Lana gestured to the "Men's" and "Women's" signs beside the doors and explained how the lockers worked. She didn't point out that the men's sign boasted a ram with large curling horns, while the women's showed a female mouflon. The hot springs were meant to be a relaxing experience, after all. "I'll meet you on the other side."

Lana waited just long enough for Hadi to disappear into the men's locker room before dashing into the women's. She felt giddy as happy memories of decades of visits to this space flooded back all at once. Visiting the hot springs was her version of being a kid in a candy store, except that the treat was relaxation. Caro might say it was proof that Lana was an old soul, but where was the problem in that?

Visiting Havos's hot springs was the most luxuriating, spa-like activity Lana could do without feeling guilty. Bravarian hot springs were traditionally free to the public, and while the ones in Havos were especially nice, anyone could use them. Donation boxes supported the facilities' upkeep, which was largely shouldered by the Inn due to its location and the nature of its guests.

As Lana moved farther into the dressing room, she was greeted by a wall of warm air that smelled of winter spices and pine needles. The thick scent always brought painfully fond memories of her parents from when she was too young to come to Havos by herself, before she'd ever heard the Queen Consort voice come out of her mother's mouth or realized that the baby brother she loved so much already had freedoms her eight-year-old self hadn't even dreamed of.

Lana traded her boots for a pair of slippers, noting two other pairs of shoes waiting in the tray. Carlotta had said that the few guests using the pools that morning would be gone by the time Lana arrived. Usually Lana didn't mind meeting people at the springs, but now that she'd...*omitted*... information during her conversations with Hadi, she'd rather avoid an awkward situation if she could. It felt wrong to plot to keep the truth from him, but since nothing could happen between them—or, at least, nothing meaningful or lasting— she figured that pretending for just a few more days wouldn't do any extra harm.

Lana changed efficiently, storing her clothes in the fresh linen bags in an empty locker. She wrapped the plush fabric of a white robe around herself, fully concealing her swimsuit.

Lana clipped her hair up on top of her head, scanning the rich-toned wooden lockers, stone floors heated by spring water piped below, and small changing rooms with chairs for those who needed assistance or privacy. Since there was still no sign of the two bathers, she pulled open the thick wooden door and stepped into the springs' antechamber. The air instantly changed from warm to muggy, and Lana had no doubt that any remnant makeup would've been seeping out of her pores in the humidity if she hadn't been makeup-free for the last five days.

Tucking a thick towel below her elbow, Lana walked to where Hadi was standing at the men's door, looking closely at one of its carvings. The historic doors were regularly treated and resealed to preserve the carvings that adorned every inch with traditional Bravarian symbols of heat, healing, and nature. The men's and women's doors weren't identical, but existed in harmony, with the same swirls and patterns created by slightly different symbols and figures.

"It's beautiful, isn't it?" Lana asked quietly, coming to stand beside him.

"It is," he replied in the same low tone. The misty space felt intimate and almost primeval, like they were in a special, ancient cavern—which they were. Carved sconces glowed warmly, and discreetly positioned air vents kept the air fresh, if muggy. "And I know these symbols, which makes them even more beautiful!"

Lana laughed, then suddenly stopped. "You know *all* of them?"

"Yep. Do you?"

"I do." Lana pointed at a stylized tree near the top of the door. "What does this symbolize?"

"Growth of spirit. It's a birch tree," Hadi replied, giving her a patient look that said, "I know I'll ace this test, and next time you'll believe me, too."

"And this one?" Lana traced the edge of a complicated

swirl. It was a trick question, because the design was very rare, and Old and New Bravarians interpreted it differently.

"It's Shanah's breath, the exhale from when she died and gifted healing of limb to the women of the mountains. Usually I'd say that it symbolizes physical healing, but some people"—he meant New Bravarians—"use it to symbolize the earth's sacrifice, since there isn't healing without energy being diverted from one place to another."

Lana blinked at him, stunned. He was completely correct. She knew those answers because they'd been drilled into her as part of the rigorous history and culture lessons she needed to master to fulfill her role. But the knowledge was incredibly niche, known primarily among specialists and historians.

"How do you know that?" Lana whispered, the condensation-slick wood causing her fingers to slip from the Giving Breath to a symbol of passion and fertility. She snatched her hand away with a smooth, nonchalant motion, but not before Hadi's eyes glinted mischievously. He'd noticed. *Bastard*.

"Really?" Hadi teased.

"Riiight," Lana drew out the word. Of course he didn't know how he knew it.

"School, I'm guessing?" Hadi offered anyway. "Where did *you* learn about these?"

"School." Lana barely tamped down a sharp laugh. If only he knew what an unhelpful answer that was. Her version of schooling had minimal overlap with that of the average Bravarian.

She started down the wide, dimly lit hallway that led to the springs, and Hadi fell into step beside her. The air soon grew heavy with steam, until Lana could only vaguely make out the contours of their surroundings.

"How long have the tunnels been here?" Hadi asked above the squish of their footsteps on the increasingly damp ground.

"The original springs are in a very tall cave with a

hollowed-out bit at the top," Lana replied, and caught the faint echo of chatter coming from around the bend. The two bathers would be walking their way soon. "That's likely why people have been able to use this place for so long—the fumes could filter out through the hole. Today, of course, we also have a top-of-the-line ventilation system, and we expanded the tunnels to be wheelchair accessible."

She cut off as the footsteps grew louder and two robed women emerged from the mist.

"Oh, hello!" one of them called, looking somewhere in between Lana and Hadi as she struggled to make them out through the steam.

"Hiya!" the other lady said. She sounded younger and lent the first woman—possibly her mother—her arm for support.

"Hello!" Lana replied, thankful for the steam. "Did you enjoy the springs?"

"Oh yes," the older lady replied, and a light air current momentarily thinned the fog, revealing a rosy, lined face with a big smile. "This was my first time in, and I can't wait to come back tomorrow. And Linhe, you enjoyed it too, didn't you, my dear?"

"It was wonderful." Linhe beamed at her mother, as if delighted she'd confirmed that she was having a good time.

"I can manage," Linhe's mother assured them when Lana asked if they needed any assistance, and patted her daughter's arm with her free hand. "As long as your arm isn't tired."

Linhe insisted that she was fine and flashed a quick glance at Lana and Hadi. "Plus, we don't want to intrude on these two lovebirds."

Was that a wink Lana spied through the steam? And either Linhe had much better eyesight than Lana did, or…who was she kidding? Even someone with partially functional eyesight would know how attractive Hadi was. Lana hoped the flush in her cheeks would be written off to the heat.

Hadi wished the women well while Lana worried if her vocal cords had permanently shriveled from embarrassment.

When Hadi tucked her arm into his and she failed to protest, he cocked his head, as if tempted to ask that very question. A crisp look convinced him not to, and they made their way to the pool in silence.

❄

"Here we are," Lana announced as the chamber opened up before them.

Stone glistened with moisture the way it doubtlessly had for centuries, and expertly crafted electric lanterns flickered from alcoves carved into the curved walls at even intervals. Two small clusters of white linen-covered benches lined either side of the room for bathers to sit and remove their slippers, and a frosty, sweating pitcher of water sat on a table beside a stack of short glasses. Fresh pine branches and tiny screened boxes of Solstice spices lined the walls and benches, layering a lighter, spicier scent on top of the sulfur and unique mineral smell of the water. Lana could recall her father muttering that one could emerge from the Havos baths smelling like cinnamon pine tea if one wasn't careful. A shining silver bell dangled beside the water; while pulling it would make a loud pealing sound that anyone in the baths or tunnels could hear, the rope also had a digital sensor that would alert somebody in the Inn to come running.

"This is incredible," Hadi said, his voice muted above the gentle roar of water that was soothing and chaotic all at once. Lana watched him take in the room, his face bright with the awe of someone discovering something beautiful and natural and timeless. His gaze traced the edges of the room, then wandered up to where the steam formed a swirling pattern as it drifted toward the hole at the top of the cave. When sunlight struck it just right, a beam of light shot straight into the pool.

"I know," Lana said as she placed her towel on the bench farthest from Hadi. "They're so beautiful, and aside from a few modern alterations, the Havos baths have looked like this for centuries. The smaller ones are nice, too, but this is the one you have to visit first."

"I can see why."

Hadi promptly splashed through a puddle on his way to the bench, and Lana spun around.

"Careful! You don't want to slip and hit your head again."

"I'll be fine." He waved a hand and tossed his towel onto the bench. "But that reminds me: the doctor specified that you had to keep an eye on me the entire time we're here." Lana swallowed. The look on his freshly shaven face, cheekbones stark in the electric firelight, was…naughty. Like he'd remembered how to play a game she'd never learned.

"I'll keep an eye on you," she said, casually turning around to fidget with her towel. "But stop dillydallying and get in the water! Or are you afraid there might be some sheep in there?"

"You have no idea."

The sound of fabric moving, and slippers being kicked off. She wouldn't look. She *couldn't*. She fussed with the tie of her robe. She removed a slipper and then put it back on. Finally, having reached what she was certain Klara would consider the maximum medically responsible length of time to wait before checking on a bather with a head injury, she turned, figuring that even if Hadi wasn't yet fully submerged, the steam would be thick enough to hide any skin so she didn't humiliate herself by ogling.

She was horribly, catastrophically wrong. Hadi hadn't made any progress at all, for which Lana's flustered thoughts could conceive of only one ridiculous justification: for some reason, he *wanted* her to watch. She turned back to the wall.

"You don't want to break your promise to Klara, do you?" Hadi called from across the chamber.

"Right," Lana squeaked out, forcing herself to face him again. She tried to ignore the fine sweat that broke out on her skin as she took in the scene before her: Hadi, with his robe loosely secured by the tie around his waist, eyes hot as he awaited her doctor-prescribed attention. Lana swallowed again, forcing herself to maintain eye contact and pretending she hadn't just realized that Hadi was the perfect specimen of a man who could actually get paid to take off his clothes. His occasional bursts of shyness told her that wasn't the case, but that didn't change the fact that…well…he *could* if he wanted to. Eye contact was becoming increasingly hard to maintain.

Hadi put her out of her misery by turning back to the bench and removing his robe, but it turned out to be a false respite. The long, muscular legs that Lana had agonized over bumping during the ski pants incident were on full display. He'd obviously enjoyed some sunshine in the past few months, since his fair skin still held the ghost of a tan, and broad shoulders and a gorgeously muscled back confirmed that he was as athletic as one should expect an off-piste skier to be.

Hadi turned around and his eyes widened for the briefest moment, as if he were surprised that she was shamelessly gobbling down the sight of him faster than a child with a Snow Twist. But then he grinned, eyes dancing, *delighted*. Lana tried to wrench her gaze away, mortified, but Hadi seemed to enjoy prolonging her torture, reminding her yet again that she'd promised to supervise him, that it would be her fault if he slipped and hurt himself. He moved achingly slowly, turning toward her and…

"Oh my goodness!" Lana squealed.

Hadi paused with one foot on the top stone step of the pool, looking alarmingly like a model posed for a cover shot. A Bravarian underwear model, to be precise. For a brand of underwear that apparently specialized in sheep, courtesy of Otto's shop.

"I didn't realize that's…where the sheep went," Lana gritted out as a puff of steam momentarily blurred Hadi's body and then floated away, leaving him glistening. A droplet of condensation trailed down his chest, down his sculpted stomach, and into the waistband of black wool right above the massive fluffy cartoon-style white sheep patch sewn onto the front.

Lana dragged her gaze up Hadi's body to sheepishly meet his eyes, her own so wide that she was sure she'd only kept them open so long because the steam was compensating for the lack of hydration caused by forgotten blinks.

"Oh my goodness," she said again. She felt like her brain had died, and she was stuck repeating the useless thought going round and round in her head. Hadi quirked an eyebrow at her agitation, and she may or may not have seen that sheep…wiggle…a bit, and that was it. Lana threw her head back and *howled* with laughter, cackling until she gasped for breath and tears streamed out of her eyes, joining the dew on her face from the steam. She laughed until her much less toned abs protested painfully, until she had to refasten her robe, until she forgot about being nervous because Hadi— this veritable Prince Charming of a man who was deathly afraid of sheep—was wearing one on his groin and doing his best not to raise it like the flag of Fulgan after the battle of Lighter's Mountain.

He crossed his arms and faced her full on, sheep once again under control. "There's your favorite phrase again. Surely you've seen a man and a sheep in a hot spring before," he teased.

"Oh, all the time." Lana sank onto the bench as she gasped for breath, not sure if they were actually talking about sheep and definitely not about to tell him that clothing was traditionally optional at the Havos hot springs. She untied her robe. Laughing so hard in a ninety-degrees Fahrenheit room was hard work, and she was starting to sweat. "Just never"—she fluttered her fingers at him—"quite like this!"

She shamelessly regarded the sheep again—he hadn't gone an inch deeper into the water, as if he were taunting her —and had the misfortune of making eye contact with it. A new wave of laughter escaped as her surprise mixed with the adrenaline that came from standing so close to Hadi's nearly naked body. She gave him a helpless look, and he finally took pity on her.

"Do you think it looks like Melinda?" She asked as he splashed into the water.

"It damn well better *not* look like Melinda!"

"I didn't get a chance to look for identifying features!" A hiccup popped out, and then a giggle.

"On the real Melinda or my underwear?"

"Definitely your underwear." The hysteria must have thrown all Lana's caution—or brain cells—to the wind. She hiccuped again. "Does it have horns?"

"It better have horns!" Hadi replied as she stood to remove her robe. "If I have to tolerate one of your beloved mouflon murder sheep on my undergarments, it better be a very manly, horned sheep, not—"

His voice trailed off as Lana made her way to the edge of the pool. She felt a prickle of unease, since she'd never worn a swimsuit while someone looked at her like he was afraid to blink, but the euphoria left over from her laughter served as a marvelous numbing agent. Much better than the cinnamon schnapps she and Caro had opted for in college in preparation for the final party she'd attended before her public debut.

This was a man wearing sheep-covered underwear in a remote mountain hot spring, not someone she could actually *be* with. It wasn't a big deal. And if his attention, the way his eyes carefully trailed from the hair piled on top of her head down to her sparkly silver toenails and back up again, paying decadent but equal attention to every inch of her body made her feel like her knees were suddenly glorious, like her collarbones were the most sensual features on earth, like the knuckles on her hand were beyond photogenic, well, what was the matter with that? Lana nearly forgot she was wearing the one-piece that Caro, Michel, and her grandmother had *all* deemed to lie just on the frumpy side of "cute". She felt like she was naked, clad in head-to-toe Vera Wang, and wearing Michel's sparkly bikini all at once, and was startled to look down and see the worn stretch of maroon overlaid with a red and blue plaid trim.

As her toe entered the hot water of the pool, Lana thanked the universe for this gift. She felt captivating. Enchanting. Under Hadi's intense gaze, she could almost believe that illusion of feeling cherished above all else.

A shiver raced up her spine along with the pool's heat. *It truly* was *a gift,* Lana realized. *To have someone look at you like you're the most amazing thing in the world—to look at you so convincingly that you start to believe it yourself.*

❄

After what was undoubtedly the most thrilling eight-step walk of her life, Lana relaxed into the water with a sigh. For a moment, the water burned her skin (she usually eased in gradually, but with today's company, she'd gone right for the cover of the water), but soon the luxurious burbling and soft natural current of the waters became a sensitized, indulgent experience. Taking the waters *always* felt indulgent, but sensitized…that was new.

Lana opened her eyes as Hadi swam over to the underwater ledge she'd perched on and tipped her head back so her neck rested on the waterproof cushion lining the curve of the pool. He sat beside her, and the current either moved his leg or hers, causing their thighs to bump. Lana pretended not to notice.

"Your swimsuit is much better than mine," Hadi whispered, eyes earnest. A droplet of water clung to his nose and she "booped" it away.

"Only real men wear sheep," Lana murmured back, smiling. A tiny hiccup escaped as he leaned closer, and she laughed, embarrassed. "I forgot that I get the hiccups when I laugh."

"You forgot?"

"I haven't laughed that hard in a long time." She pursed her lips. Why had she felt the need to admit something so pitiful in the middle of what was otherwise the most romantic experience of her life? And the fleeting glance Hadi shot her—a look that was so *sad,* so understanding—

somehow made her feel even worse, like his validation confirmed that she wasn't thinking foolish thoughts. She turned her gaze to the top of the cave.

Hadi pushed a loose tendril of hair behind her ear and when she hiccuped again, he pushed off from the ledge to stand in front of her.

"Lana," he began, a very serious look on his smooth face. *Please don't ask me why my perfect life is so sad*, Lana chanted desperately to herself. She did *not* want to go there —or not go there—with this lovely man to whom she'd resolved to reveal nothing.

"Would you be very much opposed to kissing a man with a sheep on his underpants?"

Captivated—grateful, even—she watched him drift closer, and closer, lulled by such wanting that she didn't even mind when the current buoyed her into him. Or did she drift into his arms, like it was a place she had any right to be?

The next hiccup was jarring, surprising enough that her discomfort broke the spell and Lana's "what if" brain rejoined the scene in a rush.

"I wouldn't be opposed to it on principle," Lana admitted with a small smile, realizing he was holding her, just barely, her legs lightly wrapped around his torso and the current gently pushing her into his chest every few seconds. "But you might have somebody—somebody you don't remember right now, who could actually mean a great deal to you. I couldn't do this to them." She dropped her eyes to his chest, unsure if she was just flattering herself when she added, "Or to you. For when you remember."

Hadi waited for her to meet his eyes again, then held her gaze. "I can't tell you with complete certainty that I don't have someone back wherever I actually come from. And I hate that." She believed him. "But I have the sense that I don't. From what I've learned about myself, I was reckless, and thrill-seeking, maybe attention-seeking, I don't know." One hand held her thigh while the other pushed damp hair out of his face. The contrast between the Hadi he described and the man right in front of her was startling, as if he'd somehow hit the reset button on his life. As if he'd left behind all the chaotic energy that the old Hadi didn't know how to deal with, leaving calm in its wake.

"But I do know that if I was that irresponsible, that careless, I wouldn't be able to have a meaningful romantic attachment—or if I did, there would be a lot of unhealthy issues." He looked sad for a moment, but then his eyes sparkled again, intent. Lana could swear they'd grown shiny, but that was ridiculous. She rarely witnessed people cry, and nothing that had happened today would inspire such emotion. It was far more likely that he was experiencing mild eye irritation from the springs. Perhaps head injuries left men susceptible to inconsistent tear production. "And I know you can't believe me on this, not fully, but I think you *can* trust me, just like I've trusted you, and I *want* you to trust me. I want you to trust me when I say I don't think I've ever felt this way before, even about someone I don't remember, because I think of you and it's *happy* and it's scary and too much and wonderful all at once, and I like to think that if this had happened to me before, my brain would handle it better. But it isn't. It's just happy and sad at the same time, and we have this moment together, and I don't think it's in either of our best interests to let something go just in case something worse exists in a world that I can't remember."

Lana could barely breathe, and it wasn't the steam. Hadi was saying such beautiful words. To *her*. But if he knew the rest of who she was, that *she* was the time bomb ticking on a relationship that hadn't even started yet, he couldn't still mean them. Not to mention that he was clearly a more emotional person than she was if he was already delivering passionate soliloquies after five days of knowing each other.

"Lana, are you with me?" How could his face remain so smooth and patient while he poured out his heart to a woman frozen in place because she was melting and panicking at the same time? "You have a scientific mind. A beautiful mind.

And I don't know who you might have waiting for you, either"—an unconscious blow, a wicked blow, hollow and sharp and right between the ribs to a heart that hadn't been moved by much of anything in years—"but I know that incredible mind of yours would see the waste in giving up something for nothing."

Another tiny hiccup, as if her body was dispelling a remnant bit of resistance, at least for the moment. Something for nothing…that was exactly the future she was in the process of choosing for herself. Nothing. She hadn't even chosen the poor groom-to-be, for goodness' sake. Today, she owed whomever he was *nothing*. And owed herself more than a little bit of *everything*.

"No promises," Lana whispered, entranced by his lips, which had just been deemed kissable. It was her last warning before she gave in, and she didn't even notice that he didn't agree.

Hadi slid a wet, firm hand into the damp hair at the nape of her neck, and slowly, oh-so-slowly, pressed his lips to hers. Lana's eyes fluttered closed in disbelief and breathless celebration, and the spell was unbroken.

But despite the perfection of the moment, the warmth of a kiss gentler than the light current they were in, Hadi drew his head back.

"You don't know everything about me." Lana blinked up at him, more than a little distracted and thoroughly convinced that he was telling her nothing she didn't already know. "*I* don't even know everything about me. And I know I don't know everything about you—but what we do know is good. And we fit, so far. Does anyone really ever have more than that to go on? To take what they know and who they think they are and seek to make the most of it?"

"There are things you don't know," Lana whispered against his lips in a last-ditch effort to assuage her guilt. He had a good point. And, to be honest? She agreed with it.

"You don't say," Hadi murmured as he kissed down from her jaw to her neck. He chuckled. "I know very few things at the moment. But one thing is for certain: I like what I do know." Another little kiss pressed beneath her ear. Her skin had been clammy before, with the water's heat and the steam, but now it was scorching. "Do you?"

"Yes," Lana sighed, and he caught the breath with his lips. Those lips…she'd seen them smile, frown, quirk, and make faces at sheep, but Lana felt like she was only just starting to understand them. She tightened her legs around his torso, pulling herself closer. As if he trusted Lana to hold herself there, Hadi framed her face with both hands and kissed her again.

So this, Lana thought hazily, *was a real kiss*. His lips were gentle and warm, but firm, paving the way and insisting she follow. He tilted his head slightly, pressing tiny kisses to her bottom lip, the corner of her mouth, playing, teasing, until Lana grabbed his face, too, held him steady, and kissed him full on with what might have been a growl.

Hadi gasped in surprised, then moaned, one hand dropping to her back to press her ever closer. That moan was her chance and she went for it, deepening a kiss that spun wildly out of control.

Drunk on his kisses, Lana trailed her fingers across his shoulders, over his chest, down his sides…

And Hadi leaned back slightly, breaking the kiss. He brought his palms back to her thighs, caressing them softly beneath the water even as he pulled away, breathing hard. His pupils were dilated, leaving just a bit of blue visible. His lips shined and his cheekbones were flushed with flags of color. His gaze was happy and wild, a more intense version of how he'd looked outside yesterday, like he'd discovered something unexpected and exhilarating.

Lana pulled her hands back up to his shoulders, and then ran a fingertip across his jaw, over his lower lip, in wonder. *She'd* made him look like that. And she probably looked the same. She looked up at him, suddenly shy despite the fact that she now knew what the inside of his mouth tasted like, how the vibrations of his quiet moans felt beneath her fingertips.

He bit his lip, echoing her shyness, like he wanted to say something but was trying to give her space to say something first. But for the second time that day, Lana didn't have words. She'd read romance novels and watched movies and tried dating, but she was completely unprepared for how her heart was racing, her entire spine tingling and her soul singing with a dizzying mix of contentment and yearning.

Hadi kissed her palm and gave a small, adoring smile. "Was that okay?"

In reply, Lana squeezed with her legs, and suddenly he was wickedly close, and they were touching nearly *everywhere*, and then she wriggled out of his arms to float in the steamy water.

When Hadi paddled up to her and grabbed her around the waist, she squealed, kicking up waves of water and trying to splash him in the face.

"We can't desecrate the bathing waters!" Lana said, breathless from the kisses he was trailing down the back of her neck.

"I hardly think this could be called desecrating," Hadi whispered between kisses. The next kiss came with a nip of teeth, and Lana sucked in a sharp breath. "Considering that some of the runes in here are rivers of Orianah." A thoughtful pause as he lifted his head to scrutinize the etchings on a bit of stone beside the nearest sconce. "Actually, you might be able to argue that we're just being observant."

Lana chuckled and twisted so they faced one another again. He nuzzled her neck below her jaw as she looked at the carving this time. "You're right," she gasped out. "That *is* Orianah's River. I wonder how I never noticed that before. At least they're not common knowledge."

"Do all ancient hot springs in Bravaria have those?"

"No. Most had runes carved near the outside as an ancient marker, but only the ones that have been most used over the centuries are highly decorated. The baths in the capital are far more ornate than these, but I love the style here in Havos."

"I like it, too."

They floated quietly for a while, Lana bobbing on her favorite perch while Hadi explored the cave. She peered at the bottom of the pool, at the pattern of engraved tiles inlaid there, but couldn't quite make them out. Lana could have looked them up, or asked her grandmother or another village elder, but part of her loved the mystery—just as part of her could never resist trying to solve it.

Chapter Seven

When she was rosy cheeked from the heat, Lana toweled herself dry before rewrapping herself in the luxurious bathrobe. Thankfully Hadi had done the same, so she had no temptation to give his sheep a most unladylike once-over as he exited the pool. But her cheeks still burned when she handed him a glass of cool water and caught a gleam of moisture on the column of his neck. It was a nice neck, the skin much softer than she'd originally...

Hadi's polite cough broke her reverie and she blushed further, resisting the urge to burrow back into the fluffy robe like a turtle in its shell. It seemed to be her preferred posture these days. "If you keep looking at me like that, they're going to need to add some new etchings to these walls," he drawled.

Lana snorted. An etching for privacy was more like it. "Let's go before we add winter heat stroke to your list of ailments."

Walking back to the changing rooms with Hadi was strange. Lana usually felt dazed when she left the hot springs, so relaxed that she returned to the rest of the world in the type of foggy exhaustion that comes from letting go of months of stress all at once. But today, she felt like something momentous had shifted. Now that she knew what the firm line of Hadi's obliques felt like against the inside of her thigh, now that *he* knew what *her* neck tasted like...

surely the whole world would be able to tell.

When they passed three fresh-faced guests in the hallway, Lana was so preoccupied with wondering if they would look at her and Hadi and *know* what they'd been up to that she didn't even worry if they might reveal her identity. Hadi wrapped an arm around her as the bathers walked away.

"Did you leave your manners back at the pool?" he murmured teasingly into her ear, so close she could feel his breath. It snapped her out of her daze.

"What!? No, I…I suppose I did." What was wrong with her? Even in Havos, she was a representative of her country, first and foremost. How had she not checked on their fellow bathers? "I should go make sure they're okay." She pulled away, but Hadi grabbed her hand.

"They're fine. And I was just teasing you. You smiled and asked if they were okay like you do with every single person we meet here—which is impressive, but seems like a lot of work, if I'm honest. But you sounded too out of it to resist teasing."

Lana gave an awkward chuckle as they resumed walking.

"You are always so polite and attentive to everyone," Hadi mused when they'd reached their separate doors. "Are you the part-time mayor of this town, or something?"

Lana coughed on the clear air. "No, I'm not the mayor. I'm barely ever here. I can only visit around Solstice now that I'm so…busy with work."

"What do you do?"

It was odd to hear such a normal question. It had been years since Lana had been on a date with someone who didn't know everything the tabloids knew—and this was definitely a date, she decided, if only because she hadn't had one in years and would choose to believe that the kiss had been as monumental for him as it was for her.

Lana pulled back, studying his face. Hadi's gaze was earnest, open, as if he honestly wanted nothing more than to learn how Lana filled her days when she wasn't there. And now, here it was—here it had to be: her first real, flat-out lie to the only man who'd ever inspired her to feel something stronger than a mild *liking*.

"I don't want to talk about it." Lana dropped her eyes to the ground. She really didn't want to, but she should at least *try* to warn him away. "I work with my family, and they… are very demanding. They have a lot of rules, and a lot of influence. And everything I do, except for this one, beautiful week each year, I do for them."

Hadi pursed his lips and nodded. "I understand."

That was sweet of him. Very sweet. Even if it was impossible.

"I still like you, though." His gaze had sharpened, until those deep blue eyes held a clarity far beyond that of a man whose identity and knowledge was lost at sea. Lana wondered if one could drown in such depths, even from the safety of the mountains. "You can try to use your family as an excuse for things that frighten you, Lana. Or you can find a way to honor your family and still live for yourself."

Lana stared at him, hardly breathing. His words of honor, of family, of a fear that she ignored every single day—they cut to the bone. Like he *knew*.

Hadi gave her a smile that was slightly arrogant, but who was she kidding? She *loved* that in some ways, Hadi was bolder than she was. He needed to be. "And if I'm correctly reading between the lines here, you will only give yourself the rest of this week to be happy." He held her gaze as he emphasized that last word. "That can discourage *you*. But it doesn't have to discourage me."

Lana barely recognized her reflection in the changing room mirror a few minutes later. Her entire face was an unflattering bright red—no cute flags of color on sharp cheekbones for her—her eyes looked dazed, her hair was completely wet despite the clip, and…was that a tiny mark where her neck met her shoulder? Alarmed, Lana lunged closer to the mirror for further inspection, only to bang her face into it.

"Ow!" she squeaked, and stepped back, wiping away a

smudge on the mirror that she was going to pretend was mainly water and not sweat.

A quick rinse in lukewarm water did nothing to reduce the incriminating mark, but Lana was relieved to see that it had faded slightly by the time she dried off. She had no idea which particular open-mouthed kiss had left it, but that was the other curse of having fair skin. *Everything* left physical evidence.

Lana had never felt more grateful for an oversized mock turtleneck sweater, though it would raise suspicions if she had to wear it two days in a row. For what felt like the tenth time this trip, Lana grudgingly admitted that perhaps some of Vera's packing suggestions—like concealer—would have been wise to accept.

By the time she and Hadi retrieved the bread blankets from the Inn's kitchens, Lana had regained her composure. Hadi seemed to understand that whatever had happened between them was private, and accompanied her quietly, offering his usual exuberant but polite conversation as they spoke with Carlotta. When Loris and his wife, Doris, poked their heads in to ask Hadi how he'd enjoyed the baths, Carlotta pulled Lana aside.

"How are things with the handsome stranger?" she asked.

Lana instantly flushed. "What do you mean? They're… good. He remembered his name during our visit yesterday, so that's…good." She gave a hopeful look, wishing that her reply would satisfy Carlotta's curiosity.

"Is he a good kisser?" Carlotta asked instead, with a saucy wink.

Lana's jaw dropped and a pit opened in her stomach. "You never told me that you have cameras in the hot springs!" How they could see anything through all that steam was anybody's guess.

Carlotta cackled. "We don't. But I can see the way he's looking at you. Everyone can." She gestured across the room to Doris and Loris, who gave a very enthusiastic, very visible thumbs up.

Lana gave her a tight smile. At least she didn't have to worry about Loris and Doris recognizing her. She still resembled a damp tomato. "Don't tell anyone," she whispered.

"I won't, but you should definitely go for it. I would."

"Carlotta!" Lana would've swatted her arm, but years of etiquette lessons held her in check. Barely.

"What?" Carlotta wiggled her brows beneath her slightly burnt-looking hair, as if she knew about the inner etiquette conflict. "I'm just calling it as I see it. If you need the baths again, call me. Just don't desecrate the waters, if you know what I mean."

Lana's face was never not going to look like a tomato ever again. "If I hear those words *one more time*…"

"I knew it!"

"Bye, Carlotta," Lana called as she exited the room, dragging Hadi with her.

❋

Lana was surprised to find Leo and Esmelda sharing a lunch when they returned, but decided that the layer of flour coating the entire kitchen was ample proof that they hadn't been up to anything nefarious. The realization that a cozy, laughter-filled meal was part of her grandmother's daily routine with the burly baker-who-might-be-more-than-just-a-baker was something to overthink another time.

Caro and Erik arrived promptly at one o'clock and they dove into work, refining their analysis based on the latest round of samples that Lana and Caro had run the week before. As they fell into a rhythm, piecing together the report they'd be submitting as part of the grant application, the other activities of the house faded into the background.

Their working session wore on, punctuated first by a spiced tea break, then a hot chocolate break, and then dinner. Between each refreshment, the smells from the kitchen announced the day's progression: midday's yeasty smell gave way to the rich, warm scent of baking bread, which yielded to the mouthwatering aroma of the thick chicken soup Esmelda was simmering on the stove for dinner.

Lana was sitting on the intricately woven rug, her back braced against the sofa by Caro's knees, when a cup of *something* appeared in her peripheral vision. Caro and Erik were sprawled on separate sofas, taking a "quick nap" that had begun a few hours after Hadi brought them dinner. The naps had lost their "quick" status long ago, and it took Lana a moment to shift her attention from the final page of the report balanced on her thighs to the steaming mug. Long fingers nudged it an inch closer, until it rested just a few inches from the edge of the coffee table. Lana stiffly reached for the mug as Hadi sat down beside her, sinking to the floor with a liquid, athletic grace that made her feel even stiffer.

Lana cupped the mug in her hands and peered at its contents in the flickering firelight. It was a deep red color, with aromatic whispers of cloves, orange, and cinnamon. It smelled delicious, but—

"Is this *mulled wine*?" she hissed, bumping Hadi with her shoulder.

"Careful! You're going to spill it on this gorgeous rug, which is probably made from a saintly, pacific mouflon." His voice was a whisper.

Lana eyed him. "I can't have mulled wine. I'm working." Even if Lana could barely keep her eyes open, she owed it to Caro and Erik to try. She owed them *everything* for this project. They brought professional experience and resources to the table. She contributed a good work ethic and little else.

"One of your friends is napping and the other one is half asleep." He raised a brow. "And you're not much better. Relax. You'll be back at it tomorrow."

But it wouldn't be enough. "But I need to help my grandmother and the rest of the volunteers set up for Story Night tomorrow."

"I'll help them until you finish." A kiss pressed to her forehead, and her eyes shot open. It was tempting. Far more tempting, suddenly, than pursuing what could only turn out to be mediocre work completed by a very tired person.

Yielding to Hadi's suggestion—and also the fact that it was eleven at night and she was a morning person—Lana took a tentative sip of the mulled wine. Rich flavor burst on her tongue. It was decadent, but a mysterious ingredient also made it taste *light*, unlike the heady taste she was used to. She licked her lips. "That's delicious. Did you make it?"

"Your grandmother said you like mulled wine, but since she had more than a couple of mugfuls before she went to bed, I was starting to think that you were just an excuse." Hadi took a sip of his own mulled wine and sighed, resting his head back on the couch.

"We both like it, though some of us need more excuses than others." Lana shot him a mischievous grin. "Which recipe did you use?" She'd never tasted that light flavor before, and it was a game changer.

"I made it the way I've always made it. Perhaps it's a family recipe. Maybe us Old Bravarians make it better, eh?"

"I didn't say it tastes *better*. I said it's delicious."

Hadi winked.

"It's impressive, though. Maybe you're a chef?"

Hadi chuckled. "I don't think so. If anything, maybe I'm a bartender." Lana could see it. His chat was top notch, and he clearly knew how to prepare a good drink. Her brain provided a very unhelpful image of Hadi in a black t-shirt, white bar towel tossed over a shoulder, serving a drink to a faceless woman and leaning intimately over the bar to talk to her. Lana chased away the thought. There was no point in imaging scenarios she found both inexplicably appealing and disconcerting.

He angled his mug toward her and they cheers-ed.

"Well, bartender, thank you for this lovely drink." Lana laid her head on his shoulder. "And for keeping us fed and watered all day."

"You make yourself sound like a horse."

"Thank you for tea-ing and hot-chocolating and soup-ing us all day. Does that sound better?" she teased.

"Much better." His voice was suddenly lower, rougher. Lana pulled her head back.

"You don't mind just chilling out while we work?" *Are you bored? Do you wish you were elsewhere?* Why did those thoughts bother her so much?

"Why would I mind?" he looked scandalized. "I'm grateful you and your grandmother are letting me be here at all! And not that my opinion should matter, but I think what you're doing is cool. If I can help by keeping our genius scientists fueled up and hydrated, then I feel like the world's luckiest sidekick."

He'd barely gotten the last word out before Lana lunged at him. She'd never heard such sexy words come out of a mouth in her entire life. He tasted like red wine and oranges, and she felt him carefully put both mugs onto the coffee table before pulling her onto his lap. If Caro hadn't emitted a shocking snort-snore, after which Lana only somewhat successfully smothered her giggles in Hadi's neck, the mysteriously brewed mulled wine might have gone to waste.

And maybe it was the wine, or maybe it was the strange new sense of serenity settling over her skin like the finest blanket, or the comfort of being surrounded by a loving home, good friends, and a stranger who seemed to care for her like it was his job. But as Lana went to bed that evening, she could almost convince herself that everything was going to be okay. She was too tired to think about the implication —that for the last several years, part of her had been convinced that it wouldn't.

❄

The cheery, high-pitched little bells of the old-fashioned alarm clock pulled Lana out of a deep sleep. It took her a moment to remember where she was, but she'd reached full wakefulness by the time she kissed her grandmother on the cheek and joined her with a cup of tea. Even before she took a sip, Lana felt...was that *energy*—honest to goodness, unhindered energy—coursing through her veins? She sipped her tea in awe. She couldn't remember the last time she'd felt alert before having caffeine.

"How's the application going?" Esmelda asked as Lana gazed out the window, noting the pale blue, cloudless sky that signaled an unseasonably warm day ahead.

It was all the segue Lana needed to tackle her most dreaded task of the day and admit that she wouldn't be able to help at the House of Stories as she'd promised.

"I know," Esmelda replied, not sounding at all surprised. "Hadi told me last night." Lana tilted her head. Esmelda had gone to bed long before Lana had, so Hadi must've volunteered *before* their conversation. "You do what you need to do, my dear. I saw how hard you're all working. Are you sure you're getting enough rest?"

"I slept like the dead last night."

"I mean in general. I know you're a woman on a mission. You always have been, but when you arrived, I could see your exhaustion." A critical sweep of her gaze. "You're not taking care of yourself."

"I am." A dubious look, which Lana tried to ignore. Most people would consider her to be one of the best-kept women in the world; she had excellent, chef-cooked meals, regular (mandated) facials, the nicest bed that money could buy, not that she spent much time in it... "I'm trying. There's just so much I have to do, and there's also so many things I *should* do. They don't often overlap." Her eyes dropped to the worn, loved table, tracing the pattern of nicks and grains that had been etched by nature and decades of use. "This application —if we don't get it, it's over."

Esmelda nodded. "You've been working on it for years."

"And I *know* it can't go on like this. But until that application is submitted, I can't not try." She gave a weak smile. "But don't worry. Caro and I set our schedule weeks ago. We capped the time we'll spend on each section, and we're wrapping up the summary tomorrow."

"What about after?"

"What do you mean?" Lana hadn't thought much about

after—refused to let herself consider what would happen after they did or didn't receive the grant. A faceless husband awaited her, a life of endless meetings and opportunities to hone her ability to get Councilors to compromise, of helping Bravaria claw itself out of the mess it had made over the last few decades, of cheering on whoever took up the mantle of her research from the sidelines, if somebody did so at all.

Her grandmother clasped her hand tightly, halting the endless circle she'd been tracing over a swirl of wood. "What are you going to do to bring joy into your life, or to protect the joys that you already have?"

What an odd question. Lana had been born into a position of automatic authority, significant wealth, and diplomatic immunity in one hundred and forty countries; she owed it to the world to wield that influence efficiently and effectively, not to throw it all at a chase for *joy*. All Lana managed to reply was that it didn't matter.

Esmelda's face sharpened, and she suddenly looked livid and at least twenty years younger. Lana had never seen her look so fierce.

"You're a smart girl, Lana, but also foolish. Even a wildfire will die out when there's no more air or energy to feed it. Did you look around at the baths yesterday? Did you remember to respect the runes the way we taught you? It's been the sacred knowledge of our people to respect the process of healing—not just from injury, but from the wear and tear of daily life. You can't go to the hot springs every day for the rest of your life, but you *must* find something that replenishes your soul, your *joy*, and you must honor it. To fight for it the way you're fighting for this research and for the Bravarian people. If you don't find a way to do that—if you can't find a way to protect yourself—the rest won't matter."

"The grant gives me that joy, Grandmother." Lana's voice sounded small, even to her ears.

"You need more than that, Lana. You need something permanent. You've always been an old soul, but you can't go on like this. You can't be too worried to take risks or prioritize what *you* think is right over what someone else tells you is right. You *must* do something for yourself. Everyone else does, my dear." Esmelda cupped Lana's cheek in her palm. "They'll just wear you down faster if you don't protect yourself."

Lana's vision blurred at her grandmother's words. She'd listened to them, but she didn't know how to heed them. Silently, she turned away from her grandmother's hand and slipped from her seat to retrieve the binder she'd vowed not to look at.

"What's this?" Esmelda asked, skimming the pages and noting the columns with visible distaste.

"I have to pick one." *To marry* was implied. "And I have to present him at Solstice."

"When did you get this?" Esmelda slammed the binder shut.

When Lana explained how her parents had given it to her and pushed her to choose immediately, her grandmother snorted.

"I love your mother, despite our differences. And I love Michel, too. But they shouldn't have done this, Lana, and you shouldn't have let them."

Lana's brows flew up in outrage. Her grandmother had administered doses of tough love on occasion throughout her childhood, but this felt like betrayal. "Excuse me? Let them!?"

Esmelda gestured toward the binder. "Nobody has a spouse chosen for them this way, at least not since the invention of the internet. And a lot of work—a lot of time—went into this. Do you think Michel asked your father for permission to marry last week, and the Council instantly produced this report?"

Lana blanched. She was suddenly too flustered, too angry to admit that she hadn't even thought about it rationally like this. She'd been too overcome with the unexpected onslaught of emotions.

Her grandmother cocked her head. "Exactly. And why didn't you think about this, or even try to be proactive when you considered your future?"

Lana was fumbling through her thoughts. She didn't have a good answer. Why *hadn't* she formed her own plan for how her personal and her public lives would intersect in the most irrevocable way? She had nineteen iterations of the foreign trade proposal she'd been—with exceptional tolerance on her part—coauthoring with one of Councilor Merrick's colleagues in the hopes of driving consensus, but she hadn't made so much as a list of factors to determine when it was time to get married. "My future is *for* this country. My marriage shouldn't be selfish—"

"It's not like your marriage is going to secure land rights or enable a treaty with an enemy. Your marriage is the quality of your personal life for the rest of your years, Lana, and you can't callously accept a husband because of how he ranks on someone else's list! You've let them transform the most important, selfish choice you get to make into a matter of public affairs, and it's not."

Lana was silent, her failures flipping through her mind on repeat. Her lack of foresight where her own future was concerned. Her inability to get a majority of the Council to support mending relations with Old Bravaria. Her inability to let people in, which was so chronic that her twenty-one-year-old brother would've beaten her to the altar if a law weren't blocking him. The slow pace of her research, dragging from months into years because her duties didn't leave her enough time—and poor Caro, who was getting dragged into exhaustion with her. How she questioned Vera at every turn because she was too much of a control freak to admit that she didn't have time to do things like pack a suitcase.

"I know my words sound harsh," Esmelda said as she gave Lana a squeeze. "But it's because I love you, and nobody else will say them." She tilted Lana's chin up with her thumb. "And it's not all bad. Look at the past few days— how you feel, how many times you've laughed. I reckon you've even gotten hiccups once or twice, haven't you?" Lana wiped her eyes and gave a watery laugh. "Your home life could be like this, Lana. In fact, if you want it, there's little reason that it shouldn't be."

Lana met her eyes, startled. Her grandmother's words had pierced the bubble of happiness she'd woken up in, and now she felt so deflated that it felt disgustingly selfish to wish for something so lovely in her life.

"I'm not saying to go and marry Hadi tomorrow, or to force Caro and me to move into the royal apartments with you. But just for fun, think about a life with somebody like him—somebody *you choose* compared to a life with somebody from that list. You don't earn happiness, Lana. It's not frivolous. You, of all people, need it."

❄

Lana's work went slower than planned that morning, likely because she spent much of it sitting on the floor of her room, staring at the fire and wondering if her grandmother was right. She'd gone through the past week feeling like the need to choose a husband had happened *to* her—like her parents and the Council had always had control over the issue. But had she *let* this happen? Had she somehow relinquished control over this most personal of matters because she'd assumed she could just throw it in the "for Bravaria" bucket along with everything else? She'd honestly never thought she would mind choosing her partner for her country instead of for herself. But now…she couldn't unhear Esmelda's words.

Sitting with her thoughts was uncomfortable. Foreign. Lana's days were busy. Too busy, which ensured that she'd been running on autopilot for years, never having extra time, always taking on more responsibility—something she now realized might have been less of a noble sacrifice for her country and more of a way to avoid seeing the forest through the trees. To consider what she was doing, and why. But now, Lana wondered if she hadn't been ignoring it as well as she thought she had. Had the ever-present stress, the annoying eye-twitches, the constant fear of inadequacy that followed her like a cloak been signs she'd refused to acknowledge?

Lana pulled her robe more tightly around herself, making sure the collar covered the faint traces left of the mark on her neck. She hadn't realized the worth of what she'd been giving away, but how could she? Until now, Lana hadn't known how vitalizing it was to feel adored. *Wanted.* Hadi was a revelation, or a means to one, but he couldn't be the partner her grandmother was talking about. Lana needed someone familiar with her world, so that living with the endless pressure and rules wouldn't change them.

The logs on the fire sparked and popped suddenly, and Lana blinked. Could she find someone on the spreadsheet who could make her feel the way her grandmother described? Someone like Hadi but...not? With over a thousand options, she was bound to have good chemistry with at least one person, wasn't she?

Lana was still sitting on the sheepskin rug, teetering between hope that she was worthy of such a relationship and the vague hopelessness caused by her lack of progress that morning when light footsteps approached.

Startled, Lana tossed the binder, which had been on her lap, into the far corner. By the time Caro appeared at the door, Lana was back to staring unblinkingly at the flames. In the back of her mind, she thought about how grateful she was that she hadn't put her contacts in yet, since they likely would've popped out or permanently encrusted themselves onto her eyeballs from so much fire-staring. But when she met Caro's gaze, the dryness was replaced by a blur, as if all the normal tears her eyes had forgotten to make that morning rushed out all at once.

Caro immediately dropped to her knees, but she didn't ask if something was wrong. She didn't need to.

"Sorry," Lana said quietly as she rested her head on Caro's shoulder. She noticed, now that her eyes were clearing, that Caro was wearing her usual skinny jeans and a cheerful sweater, striped in lime green and white, with a single shiny yellow heart sewn on near the collar. "This is cute," Lana mumbled, nearly at eye level with the heart.

"I know it is," Caro replied. "We've always had the best fashion sense of our peers."

They'd met by chance, as roommates unable to avoid one another in their Introduction to General Chemistry class their first year. But Lana and Caro had become friends through clothes. Since they were the same size in everything but jeans, Caro introduced Lana to glitter, which had been deemed too flashy for royal attire, and Lana had introduced Caro to the joy of fuzzy clothing.

"Do you remember our second year final exams?" Caro asked. "You showed up decked in my fringed sequined tee shirt, leggings, and Uggs, and I borrowed your cookie monster blue shaggy sweater. And wore it with short shorts." A snort. "We probably burned the retinas of our classmates and threw the curve from that alone."

"At least our clothes were more interesting than their battered jeans and pun-y tee shirts," Lana said, finally sitting up. "Things always go better when you like what you're wearing."

Caro eyed Lana's robe, as if she knew it was hiding plain black sweatpants and a maroon sweatshirt. "It's true. Now tell me, did you bring any clothes in colors revealed during the daylight hours, or are you committed to vampire chic?"

Part of Lana wanted to roll her eyes at her friend's critique —clothing was the least important thing they had to worry about, and Caro knew that—but she appreciated the gesture. Caro stood up and pulled on Lana's hand, trying to get her off the floor to go explore the wardrobe together.

"Caro."

Her friend momentarily stopped pulling.

"I haven't done the analysis for 7A yet. I know I'm supposed to be finished by now, but...I didn't even start it. I'm so sorry." The words felt like a pocketful of stones emptied into a stream, tumbling down, down, down.

Caro started tugging again, widening her stance and putting her full five feet six inches into it. "Don't worry about it."

"But I have to. I've let you—"

"I was hit by a wave of inspiration this morning and knocked out your section. And edited everything. Our summary is pretty much good to go, and right on schedule."

A wave of guilt flooded Lana. Caro was always working too hard, and Lana always added to that.

"Did you know I'd let you down?" she asked quietly.

"You didn't let me down." Caro finally succeeded in hauling Lana to her feet, and tucked her curls back behind her ears. "I actually went to the hot springs super early this morning so I could patter around in there without bothering any of the guests."

Lana did chuckle then; if she liked to impersonate a buoy in the pools, letting the current bob her around as it pleased, Caro was a jet ski, splashing around and changing direction constantly. It was a quirk of nature, that her friend could be flawlessly professional in a work setting and unleash her inner eight-month-old Labrador retriever the moment she was exposed to water.

"And you *know* I believe in the magic"—she twirled her fingers, since the "magic" of the springs and the research they were conducting into the waters' unique composition were one and the same—"but *wow* does it work! I was so hyped up that I did Erik's *and* my work before eight, and figured I'd do yours while I was at it. Especially since no self-respecting princess gets up before nine on vacation."

Lana swatted Caro's arm. "I got up at seven forty-five!" Had she really spent an hour and a half staring at the fire and torturing herself with thoughts of marriage?

Caro just rolled her eyes. "I also thought you might be… busy this morning." Her tone made it clear that moping was not the brand of busyness she'd anticipated.

"What do you mean by busy?"

Caro's eyes flicked to the binder, like she could sense that Lana's melancholy was coming from that corner of the room. "You *do* know that you climbed the hot stranger like a spruce tree six inches away from my leg last night, right?"

Lana flushed, remembering Caro's inopportunely (or perhaps *opportunely*) timed snort-snore. But she was already feeling better from their talk, from knowing Caro had tried to do her a cheeky favor rather than take pity on her. So she gave her friend a quick hug—too quick to be reciprocated, which was for the best as initiating spontaneous hugs was wildly out of character—and put on the smooth expression that she'd used to inform the King of Spain that, no, he actually could not "borrow" a herd of wild mouflon sheep for his niece's eighth birthday party. "I didn't know you were awake."

Caro just lifted an eyebrow, and Lana caved, the words rushing out all at once. "I didn't mean to do it! He just…did you hear the things he said?"

"No. Thank goodness." Caro grimaced.

"They were beautiful things! Very…attractive things." Caro gave her a dubious look, as if unsure whether she should cover her ears. "Things about how he believes in our work, and doesn't mind helping us—I think he called us *geniuses*—and then he made his special mulled wine recipe for my grandmother…" Normal people thought those things were sexy, right?

"Ah, so he's like nerd porn. I see."

"He's not nerdy, though." Lana couldn't keep the disappointment from her voice. She'd always thought she *wanted* nerdy.

"So?" Caro asked. "You've always been way too obsessed with finding the perfect guy. AKA a bookworm who has a quant-heavy job, preferably wears glasses…"

"Being nearsighted is correlated with preferring short-range activities, like reading, when your eyesight develops during childhood."

"Yes, but you don't need to date the guy who has your

dream job and the eyesight to prove it!"

"You're one to talk!" Lana scoffed. "Look at you and Erik!"

"Erik just happened that way. But he wouldn't have met your exacting standards. His favorite genre of literature is *romance*." Lana huffed as Caro continued. "But my standards—before I realized how foolish they were—aren't your standards, so it didn't matter. But Hadi…" Caro wiggled her eyebrows.

"He doesn't check my boxes, Caro. Let's just leave it at that."

Caro sputtered. "Doesn't check your boxes? Excuse me. Looks like Thor," she started ticking off "boxes" on her fingers. "Check. Sexual chemistry. Check. Nice fingers, check."

Lana scowled at her. Nice fingers was one of her particular preferences; if the guy had bad thumbs, how was she supposed to handle it? Those were the thumbs that she'd be looking at for the rest of her life!

Caro went on to commend Hadi's ridiculously caring personality and the puppy-dog-got-into-the-dog-biscuit-jar look he had whenever Lana was within two feet of him.

"That's not one of my boxes," Lana pointed out.

"But 'likes you for *you*' is. Or it should be."

Lana held her tongue. Hadi *would* be a shining example of that, if she hadn't only allowed him to see a very filtered version of herself.

"Plus," Caro concluded, "your pheromones are clearly compatible."

"You forgot a few things, like how he's Old Bravarian, not influential—otherwise we would've heard of him—and how he might not even be single, much less gainfully employed!"

"Who cares? You can afford to splurge for two."

"Um, what about the 'might not be single' part?"

"You can't do anything about that. And he doesn't act like he's in a relationship—except with you, of course."

Lana gave Caro a *look*, because that was not how memory loss worked, but Caro refused to give ground. And when Lana slipped up and added that he'd hardly pass the requirements to be her future fiancé—a phrase she'd *never* used around Caro—Caro simply reminded her that women in the twenty-first century had the freedom to engage in what had become a time-honored tradition of dating for pleasure.

"So you think we should have a fling for the next two days until we both go back to our real lives?"

"It doesn't have to end then."

"It does."

Caro merely waited for Lana to realize she'd been tricked into suggesting that *something* might happen between her and Hadi, then started poking through dresser drawers.

Chapter Eight

A drop from a melting icicle dripped onto Lana's forehead as she and Caro joined the throng of villagers on the porch of the House of Stories. She frowned. It really *was* unseasonably warm. She barely had time to make a mental note to review her emissions limitations proposal before the crowd of eager helpers swept them into the chaos of the House of Stories.

Havos was a small village, but participation in local events was almost legendary. The air was buzzing with excitement, as preparing for Story Night—and the day full of games the village children would enjoy before it—was a beloved tradition.

The House of Stories, located in the historic Town House, could snuggly, and frequently, hold two hundred people. But you wouldn't guess it from the façade, which toed the line between quaint and ornate with two stories of swirled glass windows that seventeenth-century Bravarian glass blowers had warped to look like snowflakes. Wooden beams gleamed black from years of tar and sealant, bowing merrily beneath the weight of years and stone.

Inside, the original floor plan of the House had been transformed from living quarters into three front rooms separated from an expansive great hall by a long hallway. As Havos's only building that was fully heated by underground spring water, the House made the most of the warm floors.

The great hall was divided into sections by small steps up or down in different places—a result of a haphazard seventeenth-century remodel—but it created an ideal venue for floor seating, which was convenient since, following Bravarian tradition, all visitors were required to remove their boots before passing the wind breaker wall by the front door.

They'd just barely reached the hall when Caro burst out laughing.

"What's so..." Lana's gaze landed on Hadi and his sweater, which boasted an enormous sheep on the front—and matched the tiny sheep running around the ankles of her leggings. Lana's eyes watered once again, this time with mirth.

"I need to borrow this," Caro announced, walking up to Hadi and snatching the camera from his hands. "I *need* to capture this moment."

Caro waited until they'd posed awkwardly, then frowned.

"I can't get all the sheep in the shot. Hadi, can you pick her up bridal-carry style, but hold her low enough so we can see—"

"He's recovering from a brain injury! He can't pi—eek!" Lana shrieked, and instinctively wrapped her arm around Hadi's neck as he swooped her up in a single motion.

"He can, actually," Hadi murmured as he looked down at her. "And good morning to you, too, by the way." He winked.

"Good morning, but *please* don't hurt yourself." Hadi huffed a laugh in Lana's ear as she twisted around to glare at Caro, who—who'd walked to the other side of the room and was speaking animatedly with her grandmother. There was no doubt who they were talking about because everyone was making moon eyes at them.

Dang it, Caro! Lana thought, squirming until Hadi put her down.

She took a respectable step back and looked at his sweater. "Have you conquered your fear of sheep?"

"Not in the slightest."

"So the little lambs on my leggings"—she wiggled an ankle—"are frightening."

"Terrifying." Hadi nodded. "I'm trying to look past it."

She commended him on his noble endeavor to tolerate an inanimate fluffy sheep. He rolled his eyes and looked her over again.

"Are you okay?"

"Why does everyone keep asking me that?"

"I just worry. You seem…tired." His fingers brushed against hers, and Lana vainly tried not to blush at his show of affection in such a crowded place. When Hadi held her hand, her blush deepened.

"I was tired. But I'm better now." She *was* feeling better after her talk with Caro, but she also felt drained from the emotional whiplash. Intense emotions were exhausting. How did Michel deal with these on a daily basis? It was like her body had finally relaxed enough from being back in Havos to let down its defenses, and now emotions were striking from all angles. Even the comforting stroke of Hadi's thumb felt emotionally charged.

"We've made a lot of progress," Hadi said as they navigated the ups and downs of the floor to where Esmelda passionately discussed logistics with the Village Council. Caro was wisely maintaining her status as spectator as various Council members took turns debating—with a great deal of arm waving and voice projection—floor cushion distribution strategies.

Caro shot Lana a saucy look as Hadi squeezed her fingers and left to return to his work.

"Where's Erik?" Lana asked quietly, also electing to wait for the debate to end without getting involved. The Havos Council specialized in an argumentative approach to "talking" that seemed like fighting to outsiders; it was amusing to watch her grandmother's colleagues bicker about little details, only to admit that they were in agreement ten minutes later. She certainly didn't get to witness such affectionate nitpicking at the palace.

"Oh, he's having a spa day."

"What?"

Lana knew Erik nearly as well as she knew Caro. She knew the brand of horizontal striped shirts he always wore, knew his thoughts on the qualities of different fictional languages in movies throughout the decades, and knew how many hours he'd spent freaking out before he worked up the courage to ask Caro out on a date. The vocabulary used on spa service menus had him rolling his eyes and cross-checking the whimsically named treatments with Latin, Greek, and homeopathic encyclopedias to predict their effectiveness based on their names (he almost always predicted that they'd be useless). Erik Rubin could not be subjected to anything worse than a spa day.

"He was helping Lena, one of the other guests at the Inn— one of the ones here on your sponsorship—"

"It's not *my* sponsorship. It's still anonymously funded." Nobody knew who the generous monthly donations came from, and Lana still counted her lucky stars that she'd been able to establish and run the foundation through a shell company she'd formed the day she'd turned eighteen for "just in case" purposes. It was imperative that nobody know she was involved. She couldn't increase the risk of being discovered by funding the foundation with New Bravarian money (even if it was royal, rather than public, funds) since the foundation was scandalously inclusive, helping Old, New, and non-Bravarians indiscriminately.

"*Sure*," Caro teased. "Anyway, Lena's a masseuse from Linz with more health issues than you can count, and she spilled her pill organizer at breakfast today. When Erik helped pick them up, he was concerned by some of the combinations he saw."

Lana grimaced. Erik had overlapped with them for a few semesters at university, then worked two years in a lab before graduating from medical school at the top of his class. Even before his residency, his research was respected amongst internal medicine specialists. If Erik saw something that worried him, Lena should listen.

"You know how these things go," Caro continued. "You can't make any sudden changes in regimen, but they went through her entire history and active prescriptions. In exchange for his recommendations, she offered to give him a massage."

"Let me guess: he said 'no' and you said 'yes.'"

"You really do know me so well! Erik was ordered to first enjoy the baths, and he's probably in the middle of a very… powerful deep tissue massage right about now." Caro's eyes twinkled, as if the thought of Eric trying to "breathe deep" while politely accepting a firmly placed elbow to the glute gave her great joy.

The afternoon passed quickly, and by the time sandwiches from the café were passed around for a snack, the House's many-leveled floor had been transformed into a colorful patchwork of overlapping rugs and cushions.

❄

"Have you thought about what I said this morning?" Esmelda asked as she and Lana stepped out of the House of Stories into the now-slushy streets. Since Esmelda supplied the baked goods for Story Night, they always had a free pass to leave before set up was complete. Which was just as well; the annual Game Night feast wasn't going to prepare itself.

Unfortunately. Lana nearly said it aloud, but remembered that she wasn't a fourteen-year-old girl and that she loved her grandmother very much. And that she'd been right. Maybe.

Esmelda paused in a slush puddle. "Don't pout at your future. You can plan it—not the way most people can, but to a degree—and make sure you *enjoy* it, too."

Lana toed a chunk of ice with the toe of her boot and forced herself to take a deep breath. "I know. Or, I think I'm starting to." She *wanted* to. Maybe. "It's a hard shift in thinking. That's a bit sad, isn't it?"

"I guess it's a *little* bit sad," Esmelda stretched out the word, taking Lana's arm and leading her to the middle of the road, where the slush was less deep. "But 'poignant' might be the better word. It's part of growing up, dear—understanding the trajectory you're on, deciding if you like what you see, and making changes if you're not happy." Lana winced. Her trajectory currently felt like a cannonball that was gaining velocity and would combust if she didn't do something to stop it. "It's not easy, but we all have to do it at some point."

"I'm twenty-four years old." Lana could almost hear the Queen Consort voice in her head, citing her lack of personal foresight as another example of why she wasn't working hard enough to deserve her title.

"It's never too late." Esmelda patted her hand. "In fact, I believe most men don't get there until their thirties, or perhaps it's their forties these days…"

"So you want me to take charge of my life and find love." Lana nearly couldn't believe the words coming out of her mouth. She stopped in the middle of the road, checking her forehead for a temperature. Perhaps she was going insane. "*How* am I supposed to do that? *Where* am I supposed to do that? *When* am I supposed to do that?" When Esmelda just looked at her like she was a crazy person, Lana shot her an incredulous look. "You want me to try with Hadi."

Esmelda started walking again. "I'm not telling you to marry him. Just be open to him. You're only here for two more days."

"Exactly," Lana panted as she jogged to catch up. "We have two days. It can't go anywhere. No way am I…'being open' to someone—Old Bravarian, at that!—who's so far removed from my world. It would crush him. Plus, he might have a girlfriend at home whom he doesn't remember. Scratch that. He has an entire *life* he doesn't remember!"

And when he does remember, it's not like I'll have been worth it.

"The entire village can tell that he's crazy about you."

"He's not," Lana scoffed. "If anything, he probably has a

savior complex."

Esmelda was silent as they turned onto her street, leaving Lana to attempt to convince herself that her soup-serving, pants-removing, unrefined kissing skills were savvy enough to give someone a complex.

"You think he likes me, but he doesn't even know me," Lana protested. Hadi was an incredibly affectionate person who clearly had feelings to spare, but how substantial could those feelings be?

"He knows what he's learned and observed the last few days. That's all most people have to go on when they meet someone."

"But what he doesn't know is *huge*. Like, deal breaker huge."

Esmelda unlocked the door and disappeared into the house. "If you're so set on believing that's true, then tell him," she called.

"No," Lana called back, following her inside. "If this *thing* between us can't go anywhere, it's not worth the risk."

But what if I tried it anyway? Lana asked herself as she removed her boots. She couldn't dismiss nearly identical advice from two of the most important women in her life without giving it a shot. *I'll give it two days.*

Lana felt ten times lighter as she hung up her coat. Adrenaline raced through her body in defiance of the memo she'd be writing about her future groom in three short days, of the twentieth draft of the trade proposal that she needed to work on—of everything except the thrill of having made this decision.

Now that the agonizing deliberation was over, things could move forward. The only problem was, Lana didn't even know what that looked like. The furthest things had gone with Carson was confessing ideal thesis topics to one another. She'd only known Hadi for six days, but she'd already started to bare her soul.

❄

"How many people are attending Game Night this year?" Lana asked as she and Esmelda put on the special fluffy slippers they reserved for such occasions. Both were pairs of enormous clouds, one with a grumpy face, one with a happy face.

"We'll have eight."

"Eight! That's our largest ever!" And Caro and Erik had canceled, since Erik had been barely coherent after an apparently life-changing massage.

Esmelda winked. "Only because you have a date." Lana grinned. "And because Leo's bringing his daughters. That means extra nibbles—and stew for the girls *only*."

Lana laughed. Havos fare was delicious, but a person unaccustomed to twice daily stew could only consume it with grace for so long before needing a reprieve.

Time passed in a soothing blur as Lana helped her grandmother roll dough, blind-bake bases for mini mushroom and meat pies, prepare winter vegetables for roasting, and shape breadsticks the way she'd been taught during early visits to Havos when she was still a toddler.

Lana's mother, of course, was a natural with the breadsticks, having grown up with Esmelda's baking, even if she didn't love it the way Lana did. But her father…it had been the first time he'd gotten his royal hands covered in flour. He'd stared at them, bemused, before chasing Lana around the kitchen island, pretending to be a snow monster who'd cover her hair in powder until the others joined in and they were all coated in flour, laughing, and gasping for breath. Today, Lana felt flashes of that same joy, that same breathless playfulness, as she remembered that Hadi would be eating some of the beloved food they were making. She'd never wanted to share that story with someone before. She'd have to edit it, of course, but the thought still counted.

Hadi returned just before their guests were due. He was coatless, his sheep sweater on full display.

"Where's your…" Lana's voice trailed off as she took him in: coat in hand, sheep sleeves pushed up, cheeks flushed.

Which is to say, physical exertion *really* seemed to agree with him as much as the great outdoors or kissing did. She flushed, ashamed that her thoughts treated him like her own personal dessert despite the fact that he still had no idea that she'd made…decisions…about their relationship that afternoon.

He seemed to get one quickly, though, given that it took him all of five seconds to push his sleeves up further, revealing muscled forearms, and then stretch outrageously, providing a teasing peak of a delicious abdomen and crisp hair arrowing down.

"Stop it!" Lana spun on her heel and pushed the front door, slamming it closed. Hadi wasn't flirting; he was *preening*, as if he'd done some thinking today, too, and come to the same conclusion—and decided that flaunting every gorgeous tool at his disposal was the most effective course of action.

He'd caught the door, evidently, because it closed softly behind him, and then that low laugh was in her ear. She turned to see the smuggest, most pleased expression on Hadi's face.

Oh, he definitely *knows.* "What are you doing!?"

"I'm barely doing anything." He raised an imperious brow. "You just enjoy the way I look, it seems."

She lifted her brows right back at him. "So?"

"Or maybe you like the way I feel even better?" he murmured—thankfully. Despite their frank conversations, Lana would scarcely be able to look her grandmother in the eye if she overheard such a thing.

"You're ridiculous." Lana slipped out of the sneaky arm that had wound around her waist and started back toward the kitchen, scoundrel in tow.

"We've finished nearly everything at the Town House," Hadi offered by way of explanation for his state of deshabille. "The final task was to move these enormous replicas of…I'm not sure, really, but they looked like goats with wings, and we had to hang them to provide 'upward visual interest' for tomorrow night."

"Ah, the infamous Alpine Gryphon."

Hadi gave Lana a questioning look.

"The Gryphon is an obscure figure from ancient Bravarian mythology. It's even more archaic than the hot spring runes, and Havos is the only place that still tells their stories," Lana explained. "It's an ancient mythological Bravarian version of a gryphon with a unique blend of animal traits. It's mostly goat—probably based on some long-gone Alpine mountain goat—and it has wings like an eagle and a fluffy tail like a mouflon."

Hadi looked horrified. "Just…why? Why did they have to throw a mouflon in the mix?"

Lana's lips quirked, and she tried to ignore the fact that Hadi now seemed transfixed by her mouth. "It *is* weird that they put something so fluffy and innocent on the powerful body of a raptor and a mountain goat. It's not vicious enough to be in such company."

"What's not vicious enough?" Esmelda asked, emerging from the pantry.

"The mouflon being part of the Alpine Gryphon."

"It *is* vicious enough," Hadi insisted. "That thing has the tail puff of doom. All its enemies would know exactly what manner of beast was running off to terrorize its next victim." He crossed his arms over the mouflon on his chest.

Lana shook her head. "I will never understand why you hate those things so much."

"Neither will I, but we have to accept it. Some things just don't have a rational explanation. Like how you ended up being the Princess of Politeness."

Lana didn't know what to say to that. *No, sorry, you misread the map. My kingdom's actually the one full of antiquated rules and engagement dates scheduled by the Economic Minister?*

❄

Their guests arrived to a cottage glowing with warmth. High

flames crackled in the hearth, and the enticing aroma of baked pie underlaid the spicier scents of vanilla, orange, and winter spices from Hadi's secret mulled wine recipe. The kitchen island was overflowing with treats and nibbles for the intense evening of games: bowls of nuts roasted with spices, slices of fresh bread, and jars of seeded breadsticks, roasted root vegetables, olives, and the thick stew reduction villagers spread on bread year round. There were mushroom tarts and tiny meat pies, and little bread bowls ready to be filled with stew for Leo's girls. And, of course, plates of Snow Twists and a wide trivet waiting for the Leona cake to come out of the oven.

As Leo, his daughters, Nico, and Carlotta trickled in and settled on the sofas with full plates and mugs, Lana tried to focus on pleasant it felt to have Hadi sitting beside her—instead of how Leo and her grandmother seemed to mirror her and Hadi's positions exactly.

By the time the girls made a pillow fort and unrolled their sleeping bags near the fire, the adult guests were full and tipsy. The ritual of the evening was warm and familiar, but Hadi's presence made everything feel different. Lana hadn't had a chance to talk to him about their remaining forty hours in Havos, but between plates of food, increasingly heated rounds of charades, and bottomless cups of mulled wine, she found herself distracted by his tiny gestures—which was quite a feat, as Hadi seemed to enjoy serving so much that she wondered if his unknown job was waiting tables.

The moment anyone's mug reached the one-third mark, he was up to ensure it didn't run dry. And he brought a tiny gift for her each time he sat back down. First, it was a roasted walnut, which she snatched off her plate before it could wobble into the seasoned brine left over by an olive. Second, it was the tiniest of the mushroom tarts she'd been moaning over, despite the fact that she'd declared herself too full to have any more (it turned out she wasn't). Third, it was a single lingonberry from the jar of compote that had been set out once the vegetables were finished. It felt like her face was on autopilot, breaking into an unstoppable smile in reaction to a gesture smaller than her pinkie nail.

After that, Hadi brought the compote over to the coffee table and served Lana another lingonberry every time he got up to refill a mug. She wanted to blame the ridiculous grin stuck on her face on the rapidly flowing mulled wine (they'd used one of Esmelda's industrial-sized pots—perhaps more accurately described as a cauldron—and it had proven to be an accurate estimate of demand), but the tiny touches of Hadi's leg against hers and the accidental eye contact were just as heady. She noted with satisfaction that a matching (though unfairly flattering) blush had appeared on Hadi's cheekbones by the time the conversation took a turn for the outrageous.

They were halfway through a round of boisterous, highly ineloquent Taboo when Carlotta drew a card for a word that nobody would ever guess. Descriptions were offered, ranging from "Lana and Hadi, but a week from now" to "how George and I used to be," and it was enough to set Nico to seething, Lana to blushing even redder, and Leo to loosing a booming laugh that set the room off again.

Empowered by the evidence of her audience's entertainment, Carlotta spiraled off into a semi-drunken aside, abandoning all pretense of describing her word and turning to Hadi.

"You're quite the handsome man," she whispered to him, loud enough for the entire room to hear. Lana could swear he looked embarrassed.

"Wouldn't you consider staying with us a while longer?" A sly glance at Lana. "I'm sure New Bravaria would be happy to have you."

Lana was grateful for the mouthwatering scent of honey, chocolate, spices, and fruit that wafted over, announcing that the Leona cake would be done in five minutes.

"I would love to," Hadi replied, and Lana would've startled if his hand hadn't brushed against the small of her back, settling her. "But I have things I need to do back home, wherever it may be."

"Ah, well if you change your mind, there is *always* a place for you at the Inn." A saucy wink—a wink that implied nothing because Carlotta and her husband, George, had one of the most stable and passionate relationships in Havos, and because Carlotta's default mode of conversation was flirting. Nevertheless it seemed to inspire Nico's face, which had darkened further with each of Hadi's eight lingonberry deliveries, to reach a shade of furious purple that was, quite possibly, the only color that didn't look good on him.

"You two are just too cute," Carlotta continued, oblivious to Nico's growing agitation.

Lana smiled sheepishly but didn't deny it. Hadi glanced at her expression and grinned. Esmelda smiled coyly. And Nico looked like he wanted to explode and dissolve into the floor at the same time.

"I'm so happy you finally found someone," Carlotta told Lana.

Esmelda announced that she was in desperate need of more mulled wine before Nico could finally combust, and before anyone noticed that Lana's smile had faltered.

❄

"Nico, could you help me with the Leona cake? It's a heavy one."

Lana could very well handle the tray herself, but she needed to calm Nico down before he slipped up and exposed her identity to Hadi.

Hadi smiled smoothly at her when she got up, but otherwise gave no indication that he'd noticed anything amiss. Which he definitely had. The first time he'd noticed Nico's rising blood pressure, he'd discovered a lock of hair that was at a low-to-moderate risk of falling into Lana's face sometime in the next two hours. After slowly, carefully tucking it back behind her ear, he'd winked at her and redirected the conversation to Nico. Hadi hadn't done anything else to goad him, so Lana let it slide, but she envied

Hadi's people skills. He was able to charm people—when he wanted to—almost effortlessly. What would it be like to be able to win people over so easily, to get compromises reached and policies passed and not feel completely exhausted from the social maneuvering it took to make it happen?

Esmelda made to stand and supervise the cake serving, but Lana's assurances and Leo's broad hand on her arm urging her to sit back and relax—Lana would dissect the proprietary nature of that gesture *later*—convinced her to stay and join the next round of charades.

Lana didn't speak until she'd shrouded both hands in oven mitts and Nico had joined her in the kitchen.

"Is something bothering you, Nico?" Lana asked as she extracted the Leona cake from the oven. It was a traditional Bravarian sharing cake—strings and clumps of gooey yet crispy dough knotted and twined together in an elaborate (some would call it messy) configuration. It was baked in a single enormous round cake pan and was designed to be eaten entirely by hand.

"No," Nico insisted, suddenly flustered. Lana was certain her scalp was sweating from the face full of hot air she'd just gotten from the oven, but Nico's shiny, chiseled cheekbones were giving her sweat glands a run for their money. "Just— is he making you uncomfortable?"

At Lana's confused look, Nico clarified. "Hadi." He said the name like a dirty word.

"Of course I'm not uncomfortable," Lana assured him. "Does he make you feel uncomfortable? Did something happen at the Town House?" Concern tightened her throat. She was drawn to Hadi the way she was drawn to a fresh baked honey bun, but that couldn't supersede her loyalty to her people and her specific love for *these* people, the villagers of Havos who'd probably done more for her wellbeing than all her medical treatments combined, and she'd taken migraine medication for years. They came first. Always.

Lana glanced over to where Hadi was patiently listening to Cora, Leo's older daughter, who'd emerged from the pillow fort and asked quite loudly if Hadi could tell her what Old Bravaria was like, if he *really* was from there like everyone said he was.

"He's just—" Nico *squirmed*, and Lana narrowed her eyes. Was he jealous? "He came from the middle of nowhere and conveniently ended up in your house. And due to the snow, you couldn't get rid of him if you wanted to. Doesn't that seem suspicious to you?"

"It's certainly unusual," Lana allowed as she surveyed the overflowing cake. It had all but exploded out the top of the cake pan, growing enormous but keeping its pattern in a riot of colors and twists and toppings. It was going to be delicious, if only she could extract it without breaking the weave. "But I don't think it's very suspicious. You saw him when he first got here. It took days to even get his name back. If anything, I think he's being very good-natured about being stuck here."

Nico gave a bitter huff of laughter. Lana thought he might have mumbled something about how he'd also be good-natured if he were 'stuck' sleeping eight feet away from her, but Nico just shook his head. "And does he know—" he waved a hand at her. "About *you*?"

At least he didn't say the "p" word out loud.

Lana released the latch on the outside of the cake pan with a sharp snap. "No. And I appreciate you keeping it that way. Coming here—it's a break from all that. The only one I have. And it means the world to me." Her gaze was fierce. Nico was moody and acting like a ridiculous teenager despite the fact that they were almost the same age. If he so much as threatened this fragile, beautiful peace that was *hers*, if he caused the people she loved pain or stress out of jealousy, she would never forgive him.

Nico looked chastened. "Are you going to keep in touch with him after you leave?"

"No," Lana muttered she performed the baker acrobatics

of removing the bloomed cake display from the loosened rim of the pan. Nico came closer to help detach the cake from the baking parchment.

"No, we won't stay in touch," Lana repeated, giving an experimental tug on one side of the parchment. It stuck firmly to the cake. Leona cakes were notoriously tricky to remove from the parchment, but if you pulled the parchment firmly and at the right angle, it usually came right off. "I might need your expert assistance with this."

"I think that's for the best," Nico said as he tested the parchment from various sides. "Can you imagine how difficult that would be to manage, when he doesn't even know his own background? What if he has a record? We already know he was trespassing." He gave a sharp tug, and several inches of parchment fell away from the right side of the cake without dislodging a single crumb.

"I know," Lana assured him, forcing her tone to be cheerful and direct, like when she'd been fourteen and he'd been twelve and Esmelda had teased her for accidentally making a hopeless preteen fall head over heels in puppy love for a princess he barely knew. "But you really don't need to worry about this anymore. I have it all under control."

Nico's triumphant "voilá!"—and the soft plop of a Leona cake falling free of the parchment—sounded behind her as Lana went to "check on something" in her grandmother's office. She closed the door, taking deep lungfuls of air that was ten degrees cooler than the steamy kitchen and trying to remind herself that there was no reason to be upset.

Chapter Nine

"Are you enjoying your time here?" To her annoyance, Lana realized that she could hear Nico's voice clear as a bell through the closed door. She stared fiercely out the window. *Just ignore him.*

"I am." At the sound of Hadi's voice, Lana abandoned all plans to not eavesdrop on what would likely be a train wreck of a conversation. She heard the slosh of mulled wine being ladled into mugs—likely the fourth refills Carlotta and Esmelda had been racing toward. "Have you always lived here?"

Please don't say anything about me, Lana thought, *forcefully,* at Nico. She'd go back out there and play the part of a human insulator for the two of them, but her inner introvert needed a few more moments in the cool quiet of the office to recharge.

"Your thing with Lana—it won't go anywhere."

For goodness' sake!

Lana had never wanted to throttle anyone more, probably because Nico was telling the truth. And she *deserved* for Hadi to hear it.

"Lana is…" Nico drew out the pause, as if he were impersonating a mob boss from a movie. "…more of a 'look, don't touch' kind of girl."

Lana's jaw dropped. It was technically true, but it felt wildly inappropriate for Nico to say aloud. She wondered if

Hadi's clearly broadcasted interested had just invited something akin to open season on her previously nonexistent dating life, when she'd been entirely untouchable her whole life.

She waited, tense, but Hadi didn't reply.

"What I mean is, you can't have her," Nico continued. "No one can, so you shouldn't waste your time."

"Hush now, Nico," Esmelda's voice cut in. "Be nice."

Lana emerged from the office when Nico returned to the family room, depositing the still slightly-too-hot Leona cake on the coffee table. She felt a pang of sadness as she sat beside Hadi. She *was* a "look, don't touch" kind of girl. Everything in her life had felt like that. She turned her eyes to Hadi, noting the tenseness of his jaw, the firelight painting flickering shadows on his cheek. *That* was something she wanted to touch. Hadi noticed her staring, and his eyes darkened.

"Nico, honey, are you ever going to call back little Sarah from Hydeland Springs?" Carlotta asked, mercifully changing the subject. "She keeps leaving messages at the Inn asking if you're ignoring her."

Lana could swear she saw steam coming out of Nico's ears when a roar of laughter followed Carlotta's remark. Carlotta had happily roasted each of them in the past, and the truth behind her reprimand made an otherwise uncomfortable situation funnier than it should have been.

"He must've gotten her quite in love with him," Carlotta continued, encouraged by her captivated audience. "She's tried to book a room under four different false names! And she keeps requesting the Olaf Suite, whatever that is."

The tips of Nico's ears turned pink.

"Why is she asking for the Olaf Suite, Nico Olaf Tedesco? Are you claiming to be related to Olaf Bauer again?"

Olaf Bauer was the sexiest actor to come out of Bravaria in forty years. He'd been on the covers of gossip magazines around the world, and while he had a famously insured million-dollar face, he was equally famous for his leaked sex tapes and for winning the Best Abs of Europe competition for five years in a row.

Nico's only reply was to scowl, and Hadi's memory chose the cruelest, most embarrassing moment to do something useful. Only once the room had broken into side musings about Nico's dubious seduction methods did Hadi, in what sounded like a mix of amusement and relief, *howl* with laughter. Lana startled, shocked that such a loud sound could come out of him.

"You must *really* appreciate Nico's charm." It was more of a question than a statement—a safe statement, since Nico had gone to sulk near ten-year-old Cora, who'd laughed to copy the grown-ups despite the fact that the joke had gone over her head.

Hadi's eyes danced. "I know who Olaf Bauer is!" He'd finally gotten a cultural reference, unlike earlier in the evening, when he'd drawn a blank for each pop culture clue. "He holds the record for winning the most Best Abs of Europe contests in a row, right?"

When Lana confirmed that this was still the case, Hadi gave her a dazzling smile. She blinked for a moment and pulled in a deep breath of chocolatey, slightly yeasty air, stunned at the joy in it. She must've stared at him over that mouthwatering cake for too long, because Carlotta caught her all but drooling over the both of them.

"Like I said earlier, Lana, good job. You should *go for him*," Carlotta drawled, swooping in over Hadi's shoulder to grab one of the steaming mugs. "He's no Olaf Bauer," she continued, tipping her glass in Hadi's direction as if he weren't just ten inches away.

Hadi faced her, amused.

"But he's deliciously close. And Lana here is lovely," she told him, hugging Lana around the shoulders.

"Oh, I know."

If eyes could melt panties, Lana's sparkly boy shorts would be a puddle bedazzling the cracks between the floorboards.

"If you two ever want to use the pool again"—Carlotta pointed the finger of one hand and the mug of wine in the other at both of them, and then moved her hands back and forth, nearly spilling the wine and implying *activities*—"give me a shout. Just no desecration."

Carlotta's filters had clearly stopped functioning somewhere between her second and fourth mugs of mulled wine, because she *kept going*, despite Lana's mortification.

"Do you two have enough privacy in this house?" she made the gestures again, and Lana desperately hoped her grandmother wasn't fluent in Carlotta sign language. "Because if not, Esmelda usually comes over for tea at two on Mondays. Or, if you want to stay an extra day, we can make up one of the rooms for you—"

"Not the Olaf Suite, I presume," Hadi cut in.

"I have a feeling that the mythical 'Olaf Suite,'" Carlotta whispered, putting the title in quotes, "is Nico Olaf's bedroom. So you won't have to worry about that. But whichever room you *do* use…well, as long as it's not the Noble Pine or the Molting Sheep, it's yours."

Esmelda announced that it was time to tear into the Leona cake before Hadi could comment on Carlotta's suite naming skills. Even little Talia, who'd been sleeping in the pillow fort, had been roused by the smell of the cake as it finished baking.

Hadi was sent scrambling for the camera as Lana cleared a small orbit of space around the sharing cake so he could capture it in all its glory. Her grandmother had truly outdone herself. Shaped by dozens of logs of dough, the sharing cake formed an intricate bouquet of leaves and yeasty flowers that had bloomed in the oven. The result was a compact, round base with a complex, mushroom-like top of intricately twisted and braided sections of different flavors, each with a slightly different color: there were twists of orange peel and dark chocolate, pistachio and rose, winter spice and tiny chunks of apple, ginger and lemon, and cinnamon and honey. Esmelda had first honors as baker, and then everyone dove in with bare hands, tearing off pieces of the sinfully moist cake of gooey goodness and settling into the contented silence of gourmands enjoying a special treat.

❄

Within five minutes of trying the Leona cake, Leo's girls initiated a fierce, sugar high-fueled pillow fight near the fire. Lana made sure the grate her grandmother had positioned in front of the open flames was secure, then returned her attention to what she considered her second-favorite food group.

The adults savored different sections of the sharing cake, each of which highlighted different ingredients that Bravarians traditionally kept in their cellars throughout the winter. Every now and then, Carlotta made a moan-punctuated claim about exactly how delicious the cake was compared to other delicacies, and they lightly discussed how they could offer baking classes at the Inn. Of course, the discussion went how they often went when Esmelda and Carlotta got into the wine; Carlotta asked if Esmelda would help her and her husband make a sharing cake for their anniversary, since she was fairly certain that it was the most potent baked good in Bravaria—but then Esmelda suggested doing river cakes instead, which the winter spirit Vesper was said to have given to the spring spirit Orianah on the Spring Equinox.

Hadi shot Lana a questioning look when she couldn't prevent an awkward giggle from escaping her mouth.

"Vesper baked Orianah a special delicacy, the river cake," she whispered, barely managing to get the innocent-sounding name out without sputtering. Hadi dipped his head toward her, as if hoping to make her explanation easier by not having to project as far. But Lana's voice simply ended up breathy as she clarified. "They are called river cakes because Vesper's creations were so delicious that…that… streams melted from the winter freeze, and rivers began to flow. Because Orianah's pleasure was so great, or perhaps because in turn Vesper's pleasure came forth—or—you get it," Lana forced out, before dissolving into giggles that sounded suspiciously similar to the sounds coming from Carlotta and her grandmother.

"I didn't know that story."

Lana groaned, nearly wishing she hadn't shared it. Or *giggled* at it. She was too old to laugh at an innuendo-laden dessert. "It's a rare one. Havos has preserved a lot of... *special* mythology over the centuries. It's got to be the baths," Lana mused as she leaned back into the couch—and into the crook of Hadi's arm, which had made its way to rest along the top of it.

"Don't tell me your research is setting out to prove the correlation between the water's mineral composition and the importance of sexy history in the local culture."

Lana laughed, turning slightly to face him. Hadi's hand brushed her shoulder, fingers tangling in her hair, and she shifted an inch closer.

"Seriously, though. What's in these river cakes that makes them so good?"

"They used to be called The Divine Pleasure of Havos"— even Hadi's brows raised at that—"so their yumminess *really* isn't overstated, even if the combination is unusual. They're fairly flat, rounded little cakes with a pattern like lace—or the latticework of snow when it coats something frosty, if you want to be historically accurate about it. But it's more of a shortbread than anything. A light, lemony shortbread filled with marzipan and, if you time the serving just right, a molten center of raspberry liqueur."

Hadi swallowed thickly as Lana explained that the Divine Pleasure was the textbook example of how the right combinations and precise attention to detail could come together so perfectly that it felt like it was formed by celestial hands.

"Vesper knew what he was doing, didn't he?"

"The cakes *were* pleasurable enough to create the first shift in seasons and melt winter snows by allowing spring to tap into her…inner fires. So yes." Lana delicately cleared her throat. "He knew it so well that we've praised his prowess for ages, clearly."

"And your grandmother bakes these river cakes?" Hadi accompanied this safer question with the tiniest brush of his thumb against the fluffy sparkles on her shoulder, and Lana shivered as if he'd stroked bare skin.

"She used to make them, and they truly were as good as they sound. But I haven't had them since I was a child. She stopped making them when my grandfather died."

Lana bit her lip, eyeing her grandmother. Esmelda had adored Lana's grandfather, but still lived with joy and love, especially since she'd asked Leo to assist with the heavy lifting nearly a decade ago. Leo, whose booming laugh and strong hands were surely fierce enough to chase away sad ghosts, to help turn their memories from heavy shards of glass to something holy and bittersweet. Leo, who kept one eye on his girls and another on her grandmother, who leaned into him as she nursed what must be her *fifth* mug (Lana could hardly judge, as she was on her third and was clearly made of less stern stuff) of the evening.

Esmelda's advice that morning suddenly took on new meaning. Esmelda was heeding her own advice, and her happiness was a revelation. Staring the evidence of her grandmother's brave, resilient heart in the face was beautiful. Nearly blinding. And for the first time, Lana realized that she wanted *that* for herself, too. It was just a question of whether she could ever be allowed to have it.

It's good that she's speaking of river cakes again, Lana realized.

"Leo makes her happy," Hadi said, following the gist of Lana's thoughts. Those ridiculous blue eyes were so close, so intent, that Lana wondered if the wine had warped her vision. *They're blue like the mountain lakes fed by those spring rivers*, a very *very* useless part of Lana's brain supplied. *Oh, but Hadi probably doesn't even need river cakes to make someone hot and melting. Not with a soul like that, or with eyes like that, or with lips...* "Who makes you happy, Lana?"

Again, this was it. This was when a mature, responsible princess would tell Hadi the truth, tell him why he couldn't be that person who brought her happiness, even if it was for his own good, and then boldly ask him to have a confidential fling with her for their remaining thirty-six hours in their mountain oasis. And Lana *wanted* to be selfish, to embrace that life with Hadi, even for a day. So she compromised.

"I don't have someone like that. I don't have a Leo in my life. At least, I didn't until I met you." She swallowed. She was bold in negotiations, in Council meetings, in her demands to visiting dignitaries. Just because she had no practice with romance—scratch that, *with Hadi's*, as he clearly inhabited a league of his own—didn't mean she couldn't try being bold here, too. "But it's complicated. My parents want me to get married. They need me to, though I can't tell you why, and they've all but chosen my fiancé. And if I don't accept it by the twenty-first, getting 'disowned' isn't even the start of my problems."

She'd delivered the news to the mouflon on his chest, who'd taken it in stride, just taking calm, big breaths, but now she dragged her gaze up. His brow was furrowed in disbelief but, thankfully, not anger. "That's ridiculous! It's practically medieval!"

Lana snorted. He couldn't possibly know how true that statement was.

"I can't remember which year it is, but I know we're a long way away from *that*."

"I know. I never wanted to do it, but I'd accepted it before I came here—maybe because I didn't see what I was missing out on."

"You were missing out on men with evil sheep pajamas, clearly."

"I know it's not typical. But we both have a deadline: I have to face the music, and you have to go back home and figure out who you are. Is that...okay?"

"I have my date, but I don't know what awaits me, or if I'll ever remember enough to be who I was, if that was even a good person. A person worth being *again*. But I do know that being with you makes me happy. It feels right to me, like we could have a future this way even if I don't have a past."

Lana didn't fight the smile that danced across her face, but she drew on years of practice to keep her surprise hidden. The things he'd said…those weren't lovers' words. They were head-over-heels-in-love-with-you words, words her rational mind would *never* let slip past her lips without collecting exhaustive and extensive research beforehand—the kind of research that was conducted over the course of *years*, not days.

"I don't want to say goodbye in two days. But if you feel that way—and I understand why, even if I don't think it's a good enough reason—I won't push you. For now. But only because I don't want your stubbornness to ruin whatever chance we have until you leave."

My stubbornness!? It was on the tip of Lana's tongue to argue, but she didn't. Instead, she looked into those bottomless blue eyes and felt another piece of her fall into them.

But Lana couldn't tell him about the impossible dream percolating in the back of her mind, a dream that was probably impossible from a legal standpoint.

"It's not something I *want* to do, but it's hard to let down family. Especially when they've done their duty and made sacrifices for this their whole lives. It feels…insufficient, shameful to even dream of not doing the same."

Apparently, it was the right thing to say.

"Obligations are important." Hadi sighed. "I have a growing feeling that until very recently, I shied away from honoring them. But I know how important they are. They keep us going. Waking up here and not knowing who I am, to whom I owe my time and loyalty, what I'm supposed to do in the morning—it's disorienting. But I'm starting to think that obligations keep *you* going a little too much." He tapped her nose when she shot him a dubious look. "Especially because you ignore your duty to yourself. The snow that feeds all streams, right?"

Lana took a large sip of her mulled wine as the Bravarian proverb tumbled around in her mind. It wasn't so different from what her grandmother had said that morning.

"Are you saying my snow is running out?"

"I'm saying you seem to have more snow today than you did a few days ago. You live in Bravaria. You'll never run out of snow unless you want to."

It sounded ridiculous, but it was true. "Do you not think that giving into whatever might be between us could be…an inefficient use of snow?" Lana refused to wince at her clumsily worded question.

"You should know by now…" Hadi trailed off as he shifted, a mischievous grin lighting up his face… "I'm a snow-*maker*."

Lana rolled her eyes, then sputtered as she was covered in a puff of powdered sugar. Hadi had grabbed a Snow Twist, shaken it at her, and shoved most of it into his mouth before she could shake it back at him.

Esmelda said something to him from across the room that made Hadi's bulging cheeks flush, his flirtatiousness giving way to embarrassment. The contrast was adorable.

"How are you still hungry!?" Lana asked him, accepting that dusting powdered sugar off her fluffy sweater was an exercise in futility.

"It's not about hungry," Hadi mumbled around a mouthful of cookie. "It's about deliciousness."

"I second that!" Carlotta called from across the room, brandishing her own Snow Twist and devouring it with nearly the same speed as Hadi.

"Carlotta, that's only going to make your hangover worse tomorrow," Esmelda told her, laughing as Leo waved one in her face.

Lana could swear he murmured, "but they're worth it," to

her grandmother, who took a playful bite. Indulging—or, what was probably more accurately describing as overindulging—was a time-honored tradition during Solstice season. Just as she'd found room for the annual treat that was the sharing cake, Lana found some space for another Snow Twist.

What harm was one more twist? Lana wondered an hour later, one of her last fully conscious thoughts before the combined influences of a sugar coma, mulled wine, and her soft maroon comforter dragged her under.

Chapter Ten

Lana slept poorly despite the idyllic evening. She'd accidentally put herself to bed when the temptation to lie down for a moment overpowered her need to exchange her newly-whitened sweater for a clean pajama top. The final mug of mulled wine had taken effect the moment her slightly powdered-sugary head hit the pillow, and she'd drifted in that semi-awake, in-between state in which tiredness, inebriation, and hope collude to make half-asleep dreams seem real.

Wrapped in the cocoon of her grandmother's house, the lulling chatter of people she loved, and the crackling of a large fire, Lana barely realized she might be dreaming.

A faceless man—whom she knew to be six feet tall, of a minor noble line from Wales, and in possession of a 3.6 GPA from Dartmouth—walked into her room, and the emptiness of his body blew out the fire. Lana gasped awake, or might have dreamt that, too, only to see Hadi sitting in the chair holding the binder of possible fiancés. The firelight flickered across the pages as he asked why she hadn't told him she was a princess, for he didn't date anyone *but* princesses—but only princesses who told the truth.

Lana witnessed dozens of variations of that scene. *This is how it feels*, she realized at one point, *to want and fear something so badly that you torture yourself with dreams of it*. In each variation, the yearning and regret and adrenaline-fueled exhaustion of having the object of such turmoil there in her room jolted her out of bed, heart racing.

By the time she awoke with a calmer pulse, Lana wasn't sure which version of events was real, or if her delight at the thought of Hadi sneaking in to see her was stronger than the dread of realizing that he could've found the binder while she slept.

Where is it? Lana thought groggily, tipping out of bed. There it was, hidden behind the laptop in her backpack, untouched. Undiscovered. She loosed a sigh of relief. Hadi reading it and rejecting her *had* been a dream.

When the earliest mountain birds began chirping, Lana left her room with a groan and a headache. She hadn't drank for fun since her last time in Havos, and her lack of practice felt like it showed. She flicked on the bathroom light, expecting to see dark circles and smudged makeup and perhaps a crumb or two that had managed to stay in her hair overnight.

But there was no makeup to smudge, only faint dark circles, and while those were definitely the spots where frown lines were working to etch themselves onto her forehead, her face looked...smoother than usual. And not just the skin. It was like the stressful, malicious thoughts ricocheting in various patterns through her brain had finally quieted, allowing her space to think about fewer, but more important, things.

But there was no denying that she had the morning breath to prove that she'd unintentionally fallen asleep. After a vigorous brushing and quick change of clothes, Lana tiptoed out of her room, grateful that the fluffy cloud slippers cushioned her footsteps.

Leo's daughters were asleep in the pillow fort, if the little sock-clad feet sticking out were any indication. Nico was gone, but his mother was sprawled out on a couch, taking up an impressive amount of space despite her thin frame. Carlotta wasn't a frequent drinker, and her dramatic drunken sleeping poses made that impossible to forget. But what caught Lana by surprise was stumbling upon Leo, carrying two tall glasses of water and clad only in a pair of sweatpants that he *definitely* hadn't brought with him the night before, heading for her grandmother's bedroom. Lana's eyes flicked to the half-open door and back to where he'd frozen in the hall. Were those…yes, her grandmother had underpants covered in a pine needle pattern, if the pair half-visible on the floor was any indication.

Lana quirked an eyebrow at Leo and crossed her arms. Every part of the encounter felt ridiculous: here she was, she who had ungracefully passed out from mulled wine in the middle of a party, doing her best to level a disapproving big sister glare on the man who was apparently her grandmother's bear of a boyfriend. A *younger* boyfriend, who Lana now realized wasn't nervous about *her* finding out, but about her causing a scene and waking his daughters, who were sleeping ignorantly just across the room. He might as well have been caught with his pants around his ankles.

Leo seemed to decide he'd had enough of her gawking, and gave her a sharp, dismissive nod before disappearing into her grandmother's bedchamber, lightly toeing the door closed behind him. Lana blinked at the door, desperately trying to unsee what could only be half-faded scratch marks running down Leo's back. They definitely didn't have a cat.

❄

Caro and Erik had been over for ten minutes when the lights above the breakfast nook suddenly died. Lana groaned. She'd only just tamed her headache into something manageable, and she wasn't feeling useful enough to start the productivity countdown before their laptop batteries died, too.

Esmelda leapt into action, and Lana tried very hard not to think about what, or who, was powering the spring in her step. That "who" had left an hour ago with his daughters, revealing nothing when Lana narrowed her eyes at him until they were tiny, disapproving slits. The gentleman.

"Power line's probably down," Esmelda called as she began a practiced series of checks, nearly all of which were in the kitchen. "This happens all the time with blizzards. If the storm doesn't get you, the snowmelt does."

At Erik's confused look, Lana explained, always amused when she could teach her brilliant friend, who'd grown up in a far more temperate climate, something new. "When lots of snow builds up and starts to melt, the melting can cause problems. Probably a huge chunk of snow slipped off a tree or building and clipped the power line. But we're good at this. Felix should have it up—"

Lana's voice choked off as Hadi rushed into the room, dripping wet, with nothing but a towel slung around his hips. *Low* on his hips. Caro possessed supernatural powers of concentration, but even the clicking of her keyboard halted. Lana could swear she heard a droplet of water fall to the floor between Hadi's feet.

Her mouth went dry. The clock was ticking. She had twenty-six hours left to make the most of this—*this* being on prime, agonizing display in the middle of the kitchen—and yet her work could not wait.

"I was in the shower and the lights went out. Is everyone okay?" Hadi's words managed to break the spell on the four gawkers in the kitchen.

"Yes, we're great, dear," Esmelda replied for the room. "But if you need to finish your shower, I'm sure Lana here could hold a flashlight for you."

"I can also help with that, if you'd like," Carlotta hollered, poking her head up from behind the couch. "Though I do feel like my head's been hit by a boulder in an avalanche. How are you so perky this morning, Esmelda?" Carlotta fell dramatically back onto a pile of pillows.

"You know me, Carlotta. I just don't get hangovers." Esmelda shrugged happily.

"Maybe I should stop trying to prove you wrong," Carlotta moaned.

"Have you tried drinking a Prairie Oyster?" Hadi called as

he headed back to his room, hopefully to put on clothes. "It's the best hangover cure. I can make you one in a moment—if you'd like."

Four heads turned to Lana once he'd vacated the room, leaving nothing but a puddle and several racing hearts in his wake.

"My offer still stands," Carlotta told Lana as she got up and attempted to straighten her clothes. Her hair was magically perfect. As always. "And while I would gladly let that man spoon feed me whatever he wants, if the power's out for more than just you, I need to help George. He's been manning the Inn solo."

Carlotta kissed them all goodbye, left, and immediately poked her head back in the door to announce that the power was out for the whole village. Dread mixed with relief when Lana heard Felix's voice on the porch relaying news about an avalanche. Apparently it was a small one, with nobody reported injured or missing, but it was large enough to down the region's power lines and block the main roads out of Havos.

Lana's pulse quickened with a tiny whisper of hope. How long had her twenty-six remaining hours with Hadi been extended? Minor as the avalanche had been, there was no chance the roads could be cleared in time to leave the next day as she'd planned.

Lana went to grab something from her bedroom, but found herself slipping through the shared bathroom into Hadi's room instead. He had the curtains open wide and was pulling on a pair of pants when she burst in, surprised him, and sent him hopping, which did very nice things for his abs. Any thoughts of updating him on potential travel schedules dissipated like fog.

"Hey, Lana?" he said, voice husky as he walked up to her. "My eyes are up here."

Lana wasn't sure if it was healthy for a heart to start racing so quickly. Her eyes darted up to his, then back down. One of her hands reached out as if it had a mind of its own, as if to touch one of the lines of muscle that had stolen her ability to speak. She stopped it just in time, about to apologize for trying to grope him while he was just trying to get dressed, but he caught her hand, bringing it the final inch forward.

It's okay, his eyes seemed to say as he pressed her palm against his chest, even as he sucked in a sharp breath and his body tensed beneath surprisingly soft skin.

Lana suddenly felt achy, breathless. *It was okay*. Even if her brain had stopped working, her heart wouldn't be okay ever again. "I..." She leaned in slowly. Hadi's other hand cupped her neck, his body shifting against her hand as he bent his head and brought his lips to hers. The breath she didn't realize she'd been holding stuttered out of her at the first nibble to her bottom lip.

"Lana, we need to do this first!" Caro's voice called from the hallway, as if she *knew* what they were doing. "You can do that after."

Hadi smiled against her lips. "Go on, genius. You can do this after, right?"

Was it possible to *hear* a wink?

Lana gaped at him and fled the room.

❄

Since Esmelda's backup generator powered only the industrial refrigerator, ovens, and a single kitchen light, laptops couldn't be recharged. Lana and her friends worked on their laptops until the batteries died, then switched to pen and paper until their hands cramped. Lana was grateful that she'd printed out the questions for the grant application, but now it was more crucial than ever that she leave Havos in time to re-edit and upload everything when she regained internet access.

After Caro's third hand cramp, she and Erik accepted the limits of nature and went in search of the town's smaller hot springs, which were safe to visit with their motion-activated, solar-powered lights.

Fifteen hand-written paragraphs later, Lana stood and shook out her arms, trying to get her fingers to remember how to unclench. Only one of them so much as wiggled. She shook her arms harder, then decided that jumping jacks might achieve what localized movement could not.

"Lana, dear, are you exercising?" Esmelda called from where she and Hadi sat on the sofa nearest the windows, taking advantage of the natural light.

"Trying—to—get rid of—this—hand cramp," Lana panted between jacks.

"Please don't sprain anything."

"I—shouldn't—it's not like—I'm not—athletic," she gasped out before returning to another round of forearm shaking. Two separate fingers decided to spasm in tandem, so she shook even more fiercely, until she resembled the inflatable men that gas stations use to attract attention. Her audience looked on in concerned bemusement.

Lana gave up once her pinkie returned to its normal state, figuring the rest would follow in their own time. Until then, she simply needed to avoid using her hands.

"I'm working on a pair of baby socks for a friend's new grandchild," Esmelda explained when Lana went over to investigate what they were doing. Two tiny pale yellow socks were nearly finished, the neat purls perfectly ordered. "Hadi here is making me a new drying towel. I desperately need one."

Lana eyed the very short, very uneven lines of his work. "Oh, wow," she offered lamely. It was truly atrocious, made mostly of knots and gaps instead of purls, but she appreciated that he'd done it at all, keeping her grandmother company while Lana deluded herself that she was saving the world via hand cramps. Even more attractive was the fact that he hadn't quit, even when it was apparent to Lana, esteemed knitting veteran who had made a grand total of five —yes, *five*—mittens throughout her entire career, that it didn't come naturally to him.

"Esmelda was telling me that power outages always

inspire her to make something warm for those who are less fortunate." Hadi glanced at his jumble of yarn. "This was going to be a scarf. But we decided that it might end up being more reliable as a rag."

"It will come with practice, my dear. And never get between a baker and her rags."

Lana rubbed her right hand as she peered more closely at Hadi's creation. "I guess you can't be good at everything."

He laughed. "No—not yet, at least. But I have a feeling that I am excellent at hand massages." He eyed her hand, which was giving him a very firm middle finger entirely of its own volition.

"I'm not flipping you off on purpose," Lana whispered, torn between pain and amusement as her poor hand protested its overuse. She supposed she needed to work on her problem with over-gripping pens. It was a telltale sign of her anxiousness.

"At least one part of you is a fan of direct communication," Hadi murmured as he gently began massaging her palm with both thumbs. His strong fingers felt so good that Lana simply "mmm"ed. "The Princess of Politeness draws the line at her fingers, eh?" was all he said as he gently coaxed the muscles in her miserable hand into blissful relaxation.

Every year, the magical transformation of the House of Stories hall took Lana's breath away. This year was no different. In sock-clad feet—Lana was wearing Gerta's design as promised—they joined the crowd of comfortably-dressed people enjoying their beloved tradition (and, perhaps, the warmth of the springs-heated building) despite the power outage.

Electric fairy lights had been strung across the wide expanse of the high-ceilinged space and they glinted, unlit, like crystals of ice in the flickering glow of hundreds of candles safely locked in glass lanterns. Round glass lamps of all sizes hung along the walls, and clear vases filled with clusters of white candles illuminated the Snow Twists, candied fruits, wine, water, and pine needles filling each table. Smaller lanterns were tucked into the corners of each floor platform.

Esmelda drifted over to join her friends at a platform outfitted with chairs "for those whose knees weren't as bendy as they once were," and Lana and Hadi found Caro and Erik. Erik and Hadi piled a platter high with treats while Lana and Caro snagged a platform and made it into a comfortable nest for the evening. By the time Hadi and Erik returned, Gerta had demanded to sit there, too, on account of her, Lana, and Caro wearing matching socks. They posed for Hadi to take a picture.

"The Gryphon up there really steals the show, doesn't it?" Lana asked Greta, pointing at the creature Hadi had spent an afternoon dutifully positioning.

"It's my favorite animal," Greta said very seriously. "I know they're not real, though. But if they were, they would be."

"It's hard to find an animal better than a mouflon," Lana informed Hadi.

"It's impossible," Greta confirmed. "Nothing is as fluffy." She frowned. "Why aren't you wearing your mouflon sweater?"

"I'm wearing it tomorrow," Hadi promised her. "It's so warm in here and that sweater is so toasty that it's too much for tonight."

Greta nodded solemnly. "That is a fair reason."

Conversation tapered off, and then the village elders took turns telling stories from the central platforms as children and adults alike leaned back amongst the pillows, watching the lights glint off the decorations above as they listened.

When it was time tell the story of The Split, Lana tensed, certain that it would spark some memory—or anger—for Hadi, who'd likely grown up hearing a different version of the story. She braced herself for the story of King Jakob I, the kind, beloved leader who unintentionally inspired the conflict that tore Bravaria in two a hundred years before, and the man who became both the first Haspel king and the first king of New Bravaria.

"The noble family of Haspel had been friends with the Bravarian ruling family of Melvin since the nation's founding," Shauna, one of the elders, began. "The Melvins ruled Bravaria through centuries of prosperity, while the Haspels advised them and helped govern. Haspel second sons married Melvin cousins, and vice versa, and the Winter Palace was given to the royal family as part of Princess Svetlana Latticia's dowry. Since they wielded considerable influence of their own, the Haspels had never desired to join their heir with that of Melvin and unite their great families.

But when the last king of Bravaria fell gravely ill and asked Jakob Haspel to take the throne, everything changed. Jakob begged his friend to reconsider, but he refused, so Jakob relented, but insisted on ruling from the Winter Palace, rather than the Summer Palace where the king lived, in the hopes of encouraging him to change his mind.

Over the following years, the old king's bouts of madness grew worse, and knowledge of his condition became public. Jakob I proved to be a fair, effective ruler, and the nation flourished under his care, but Bravarians from the regions closest to the Summer Palace began to doubt whether their king had been in his right mind when he made his decree— especially since he'd also prevented his own young son from inheriting. Bravarians from the regions near the Winter Palace, on the other hand, insisted that the king's word was law, and that Jakob I was therefore the rightful new king. By the time tensions had begun to escalate, physicians had finally found a cure for the old king's madness, and he and Jakob were able to meet in person one last time. They decided to divide the country in two, banning Haspels from what would now be called Old Bravaria and Melvins from entering "New", in the hopes of preventing the tensions from rising to violence. The king's young son would go on to inherit the Old Bravarian crown, and our kingdoms have been separate ever since."

When Hadi didn't react, Lana finally let herself relax and enjoy the rest of the evening. If anything about Story Night was going to jog his memory about Bravarian royalty, it would have been that story. Lulled by the heat coming from the floor below her and the sense of belonging and history suffusing the hall, Lana made it through one more tale before laying her head in Hadi's lap, secretly relishing the feel of his fingers stroking her hair as enthralling voices, including her grandmother's, drifted over her. After the elders shared the eight core stories of Story Night, attention passed from platform to platform as villagers of all ages shared the tales they loved best.

Those soothing fingers only stopped once, during the story Gerta told about the bear goddess Ula and her wolverine sisters, and Lana felt something in her chest unfurl with each stroke. Large social gatherings usually left her feeling depleted, but Story Night never did. Tonight especially. She felt energy coursing through her veins, calm but powerful, like the ceaseless brush of ocean waves against a protected beach—always there, always moving, but, for the moment, quiet.

By the time the villagers hurried home, the night was cold enough to cut glass, and they held their coats around themselves until they reached the heat of their own hearths. Lana looked up as she hurried over the now-frozen slush, overcome with the same wonder she felt every year at how the Bavarian mountains brushed the sky, touching a cold, star-flecked night that had an alien, unfathomable life of its own.

Lana, Esmelda, and Hadi settled onto the matching couches with blankets and cups of tea to rewarm themselves before bed. When Lana decided to rebuild the girls' pillow fort from the night before, Hadi helped her re-create the design down to the number of pillows stacked on either side. Esmelda prepared herself to sleep on the couch—a feat she hadn't attempted in at least six years, she informed them with a grumble.

Fortunately Esmelda proved to be a peaceful sleeper, emitting no more than the occasional snort and looking relaxed in a glorious botanical eye mask with glow-in-the-dark poppies covering each eye.

Situated just a few feet away from the fire, the pillow fort was toasty, with its walls of fluffy mouflon cushions and a thin sheet tented over it keeping the warm air from escaping. The end of the fort opened toward the hearth, and Lana sighed when Hadi pulled her to lie with her head on his shoulder so they could watch the flames together.

❄

"So, we have an extra day," Lana whispered, not wanting to disturb the peace hanging over the room like a blanket.

"*At least* one," Hadi replied in a low voice, squeezing her tightly for a moment.

"I'm sorry you'll miss your appointment." She wondered if the person he was meeting would come back the following day when he didn't show, or if it was a one time opportunity.

"I am, too, but I hope that my mother will understand." Sadness tinged his voice.

"Your mother?" she asked, shocked. With a single word, Hadi suddenly had a *family*.

"The note was signed 'Love, Mom.' I don't want to imagine what will happen when I'm not there tomorrow."

Love, Mom.

The unknown person who'd asked him to meet at the Orange Gallery—who'd sent her love—wasn't a girlfriend, or a fiancée, or even a friend who wanted to be more. It was his mother. And her son wouldn't be there. Lana tried and failed to imagine how it would feel to receive a note like that from Givera. But she knew exactly how it felt to let her down.

Hadi's expression looked pained and lost, as if he were steeling himself to care less about the heartbreaking fact that he was missing a meeting with a mother he could not remember. He looked at Lana wordlessly.

So she loosed a big breath, gazed up at the embroiled top of their pillow fort, and changed the subject. "Did you enjoy Story Night?"

Hadi grabbed the change of topic like a lifeline. "I did. I don't know that I've ever been to something like that. And the part where the children got to share their stories at the end…" She could hear the smile in his voice, but then it seemed to fade. "But when Greta told the Ula story…"

Lana propped herself on an elbow to see his face. "What about it?"

"I have sisters," Hadi said quietly, still staring at the sheet. His beautiful face looked conflicted, as if he could tell he loved these sisters, but felt helpless at not knowing more. "I don't remember their names, but I heard that story, and I knew that I have sisters."

He swallowed, and Lana flipped back onto the blankets, stunned. They had their extra day, of course, but in a way, maybe they didn't. If Hadi's memories—and the sadness that came with them—were coming back now, everything might change. And yet…

"That's wonderful. Would you tell me what you remember about them?"

Do you know who I am? she wanted to ask, but selfish curiosity had no place in this conversation. Now that pieces of Hadi's memory were coming back, she wanted to know *everything*.

"I have two sisters, both younger than me." Hadi's voice was tentative, yearning. "One has the brightest smile, and she's…independent…a little bit wild, but focused." His brow furrowed. "And the other, she's still little, I think, with the cutest blonde ringlets. She's asking questions about more things than she should be at her age."

"You must be close, then." Lana envisioned Hadi hugging his sisters and coddling the littler one, not wanting her to need to grow up too fast. She tried not to compare it to her relationship with Michel, how they'd been raised in different wings of the palace and had only gotten to truly know each other over the past few years.

"I hope so. Family is important," he said, voice breaking, and Lana wondered if that was a lesson he might've once forgotten. *Before* he forgot everything else.

"Do you remember their names?"

"No."

"And your parents? Do you remember anything about them?" She purposefully didn't use the word "mother."

"No. It's…it's like I don't want to, for some reason."

Lana was quiet, pulling one of his hands into hers and tracing lines along his palm. She wondered if any of his past was there, if only she were skilled enough to read it. The silence dragged on as she traced imaginary patterns on his skin.

What could she say to someone who couldn't remember anything—who maybe *didn't want to*—and how could she like a person who had that kind of relationship with his parents? It didn't fit with any of the things Lana had always valued so much in a potential partner. "Has strong family values" was always right up there. But Hadi, who spoke of his sisters with such yearning on his face, who treated her own grandmother with respect and affection…Lana refused to believe that this was a man who didn't care about family.

Something had happened. She knew it had.

"What's your family like?" he asked.

"Well…" Lana took a moment, tracing her fingertip along his knuckles now. "I get along better with my father. He… understands me better than my mother does. And he's the reason I work so hard—so that he can start backing off, eventually retire. He recently turned sixty and discovered that he's quite fond of sleeping in." She laughed. "He'd never had the opportunity before."

She peeked at Hadi, saw that he was still staring at the sheet, and continued. "My mother is tricky. My grandmother is her mother, but we have more of a…professional relationship than a mother-daughter relationship. She's closer with my brother, Michel, who is the exact opposite of me. He's carefree—he's so good with people—and he's a hopeless romantic. He met the love of his life at seventeen and has spent the last four years making him the happiest man in the world."

"You, opposites? You're good with people."

"Oh, yes, and I'm so carefree. And *very* romantic."

A low laugh. "You don't seem *not* romantic. Just... focused."

"I've always been focused. It's my duty to be. I've been given so many opportunities, and if I don't make the most of every single one, then I don't deserve them." Lana only realized her fingers had curled into a fist when Hadi pushed them apart.

"Being born with privilege isn't your fault. But it doesn't make it any easier to convince yourself that you're enough. That you're enough even if you make the conscious decision not to push yourself until you can't do it anymore."

Lana stopped breathing.

Hadi pulled her hand onto his chest, and now it was his strong fingers trailing paths between her own. "And you *are* enough, Lana. Even if all you were physically able to do is care, some days, that's enough."

He turned to his side so that they were face to face. Lana stared at him with huge eyes, as if he'd begun to speak all the words she didn't know she needed to hear. Even if it felt shameful to hear them, like her shield of pride and worthiness was cracking with each syllable. If just caring were enough...she couldn't live with herself if she lived like that everyday. But if she could believe it *some* days...She inhaled a shaky breath.

"And you can't do everything anyway. You just told me Michel is more of a people person than you. Unless you *love* doing the social things that come so naturally to him, why torture yourself with it? Why waste your time doing something he could do better—and with more enjoyment?"

He had a point. But just like with her grandmother's words, hearing and believing something was different from making it happen.

Hadi frowned. "What kind of pressure are you under anyway? Who runs a foundation on the side for fun?"

"It's a very old family. And everything I do is very public. Which is why the foundation is secret. And why this entire grant application is secret. Why what I do with my time here is secret." *Are all the good things in my life secrets?* "An avalanche looks like *nothing* compared to what happens when I break the rules."

At least, Lana thought it would.

"Lana, the Serious," he teased, but it didn't sound light. It sounded solemn. "You feel you owe everyone everything. What do you owe yourself?"

Lana felt a chill skate over her spine and along her arms, raising goosebumps at the question.

I don't owe myself anything. She almost said it. "Not a lot."

A warm finger brushed her cheekbone and tucked a lock of hair behind her ear.

"I don't think your family would agree with that."

My mother would. My people would. She could hear it now, just as she'd heard it at university when students would roll their eyes whenever one of the British royals was in the news for attending yet another impossibly stuffy tea party, or when the playboys of European royalty were involved in yet another sex scandal on a champagne-drenched yacht.

She could hear it in the voices of young girls born with nothing, who had to fight just to get *something*, and then turned on the TV and saw people like her, who'd been subjected to hours of hair styling and makeup application, and been given thousands of dollars of clothing in order to look picture perfect for a twenty-minute discussion on micro-loans for underprivileged women in a field that had been meticulously landscaped before filming.

Worst of all, she could hear it in the voices of her old

classmates—who'd taken exams beside her in university, who'd sat for the same national exams back in high school—who'd always thought they were just people of the same age taking the same tests, never wondering if she'd had the best tutors money could buy, had access to some of the greatest minds in the world, had the privilege of speaking to some of the inventors and scientists they'd only read about.

And, of course, she could hear the Queen Consort voice constantly assigning her and her father more work, endlessly devising new plots and rules to make Bravarian royalty bigger, better, more perfect, more overworked…just *more*. It was a voice that hadn't grown up royal, that knew just how much work Lana should do to be deserving of the fact that she had.

"Have you ever been proud of yourself?"

Lana dragged her mind back to the present.

"Of course. I'm proud of the research Caro, Erik, and I have worked on for so many years, and that we got it to this point. I'm proud of the foundation at the Inn. And some of the tiny things." The things she squeezed in time to work on between the meetings and formalities her mother piled onto her schedule like Jenga blocks. Things like the women's education grant she'd created to encourage young Bravarian students to attend summer camps focused on STEM and entrepreneurship. Or her proposal to reduce tariffs on Old Bravarian goods and services, which had come *so close* to getting the simple majority of Councilors it needed—not enough, this time, to pass the plan into action, but enough to show it might be possible one day. Once the Conciliatory Caucus could actually act like a caucus. And she was proud that she could still look herself in the mirror, even when the perfectly coiffed face staring back at her felt like a stranger.

Hadi quirked a brow at her. "How tiny?"

"*So* tiny." Lana couldn't help but wink.

Hadi rolled his eyes and sighed. "You are worth being proud of." He brushed a tiny kiss to the side of her mouth. "And you *know* it." A tiny kiss to the other side. "You're just suffering from an extreme case of stubbornness."

"I don—" she made to argue with him, but his tongue swept into her mouth instead, ending all argument.

Hadi in the bathing pools was sexy, and hot, and just about more than she could have imagined. Hadi in a pillow fort, offering his body heat and telling her to stop being ridiculous and to evaluate herself with the worth she gave everything else in life—that Hadi was flat-out irresistible.

Her protest turned into a moan, and Lana fisted her hands in Hadi's hair, holding him closer as he tasted her. He was ravenous, entirely focused with his hands, his mouth, his tongue, as if kissing were an Olympic sport and this was his chance for a gold medal. She was hot and cold all at once, and she could swear that Hadi felt the energy, too. He pulled her leg over his hips so their bodies were flush against each other, and Lana found herself moaning again.

A scatterbrained thought about the proximity of her grandmother, glow-in-the-dark poppy eye mask or no, had Lana breaking the kiss and hiding her giggles in Hadi's chest. She'd never had a chance to be a naughty teenager, but she felt like one now. Hadi's hand rested in her hair, firmly enough to convey, leaving no room for doubt, that he would be more than happy to oblige if she decided to continue. When she didn't, that hand loosened its grip and resumed the soothing stroking rhythm from the House of Stories.

By the time Lana drifted off to sleep, she was half convinced that even if she couldn't find a way to love herself today, Hadi could do it for her.

Chapter Eleven

The unmistakable scrape of metal on metal woke Lana the next morning as her grandmother put the tea kettle on the stove. The fire was low, but still flickering, and Lana allowed herself five more minutes of warmth, of enjoying Hadi's arms around her shoulders and waist.

Hadi's arms hadn't moved an inch all night, as if he were afraid that she'd run away. And while Lana had thought that sleeping through the night would be impossible—not because she was sleeping in the arms of someone she'd known for barely a week, but because of the energy crawling beneath her skin—she'd slept. *Well.* A night of using Hadi's arm as a pillow, of hearing his gentle breathing and sensing the flickering of the nearby fire proved to be incredibly restorative.

It was like sleeping was a team sport, better achieved with a partner, and Lana had been going at it alone every other night of her life. She'd shared a room with Caro before, but this was different. She'd somehow managed to convince a complete stranger to be proud of her, to like her enough to hold her subconsciously. And she liked him, too. *Really* liked him.

Lana fought the temptation to stretch as she came to wakefulness, trying to remain oh-so-still so she wouldn't wake Hadi and break the magic. But her forced relaxation might not have been as stealthy as she'd liked, for he stirred a moment later, arms briefly tightening, and she swore she could *feel* his smile as he rolled slightly to nuzzle her neck and promptly drift right back to sleep. Now he was sprawled on his stomach, his head upon her shoulder, one fourth of his body trapping hers and the rest doing an excellent impression of a starfish.

"Good morning," Lana murmured, giving into the childish temptation to hide the fact that she was awake from any "adults" present for as long as possible.

"Good morning." Hadi's voice was scratchy and muffled by her neck.

Empowered by the fact that *she* was now the human pillow, Lana slipped a hand under Hadi's shirt to feel the warm skin of his lower back. He gave a low sound, almost like a purr, and managed to nestle even closer.

"Did you know," Lana asked as she lightly scratched his skin with her nails, "that you talk in your sleep?"

His shoulders had tightened the slightest bit when she started playing with his back, and now they shook in a silent laugh. "I didn't, but now that you mention it, that sounds like me. What did I say?"

His body relaxed again as Lana went back to using her fingertips and she smiled. It was like they were having two conversations at once: one with skin and another with words.

"I only heard what you said right when you got to sleep—and you fall asleep really fast, by the way." Lana was a notoriously bad sleeper, likely on account of all the stress, and felt lucky that she'd managed to sleep at all without her nightly routine of completing Sudokus and rereading comfort books until her tired eyelids beat out her anxiety. "You mumbled something about axes and shifties. And buzz cuts. Do you remember what you were dreaming about?"

He huffed into her neck. "It sounds like I was dreaming about skiing, which makes sense. I mean, have you *seen* my quads?"

He made as if to pull his pants down to show her, so she

tickled the skin she could reach instead. He immediately dissolved into a rolling, howling jumble of giggles.

There goes our ruse, Lana thought as the sound of water being poured for tea paused, then continued, as if her grandmother was onto them and decided to let them continue whatever on earth it was that they were doing.

"Oh my *goodness*, you are ticklish!"

At this point, Hadi had curled into as tight a ball as he could manage, still howling, which meant that Lana was reduced to tickling the back of his neck and the part of his sides that weren't protected by arms and elbows. Even though she barely reached anything, it worked. He howled even louder.

"Look at you! Brought down by just a little—"

Hadi had regrouped, and used the incredibly unfair advantage of his taller body and bigger muscles to pin Lana in a hold probably invented for some martial art. His face was flushed, and tears of laughter streamed out of his eyes. Lana giggled, feeling invincible. Hedging his bets, Hadi released her left hand, but kept the right one pinned. He slowly brought his fingertips to her armpit, where he then launched a full-scale tickle attack. Her armpit, her side, even the back of her knee—nothing was safe. But Lana didn't move. She merely looked up at him, still giggling, as his expression changed from one of playful revenge to frustration.

"What—"

"I'm not ticklish," Lana informed him, praying he'd give up attempting to torture the back of her knee before she proved herself a liar.

"You're not ticklish? What kind of monster are you?"

"I'm—" The sensations were starting to get to her, but she could ignore them for a little while longer. "I'm not a ticklish kind of person."

"No, you're not, are you?" he whispered mischievously, as if he'd felt the tremor that had flashed up her body from her leg and knew she was close to caving in. "*Heaven forbid* you yield to something as *fun* as a tickle fight." His fingers moved faster, and if she weren't starting to sweat from the effort of hiding the growing discomfort of her poor knee, she might've admired the lightness and strength of those fingers and imagined what else they could do.

"Not at all," Lana gasped out. She really should have tried to break out of whatever hold this was, maybe *use* the left arm that he'd discounted. "It's not…proper!"

The last word came out as more of a squeal as Hadi released her right arm and added a dual assault to her stomach just as she was about to cave.

"Nooooooo!" Lana half-moaned, half-laughed, as the full force of Hadi's prolonged tickle attack hit her. She squirmed. She wiggled. She tried to roll over. But he had her caught, and now she was *definitely* sweating, especially in the places he was tickling, as he showed no mercy.

"Not—fair—" she gasped out, and Hadi's eyes gleamed as she realized that she had no hope of regaining control of the situation.

"Hadi!" her grandmother's voice called from a few feet away, and those fingers halted for one merciful moment. "Based on my extensive life experience, I know you are tickling my granddaughter and not doing anything more nefarious. But if either of you makes one more noise like that in my family room, you're sleeping in the House of Stories until you leave."

Lana tried to give Hadi a stern "you deserve it" face, but burst out laughing instead.

"Yes, ma'am," Hadi called back.

He began the process of disengaging from the tickle fight-mussed blankets, and Lana shivered, the echoes of tickles skirting up her nerve endings. She couldn't remember the last time she'd been tickled, or the last time she'd laughed like that, squealing like a pig and wanting it to stop but also loving the…were those endorphins? Or was it dopamine? Whatever it was, maybe tickles did have a place in the world. In moderation. In definite moderation. And primarily administered to other people.

Esmelda looked Lana up and down as she emerged from the pillow fort, eyes laughing. Lana tried to scowl, failed, and ended up snickering instead. She eyed the three steaming cups of tea her grandmother had prepared as Hadi had devastated the back of her knee—and her abs, apparently, which had gotten quite the workout lately.

"I can't believe you did that!" Lana hissed to Hadi as they sat down in their pajamas.

"I can." The arrogant statement was matched with the world's sweetest grin. It wasn't fair. It really wasn't.

"You seemed to take great joy in torturing me."

"I just liked seeing you lose control."

Lana saw red. And a whole lot of exclamation points. Was that normal, to react in punctuation? And how could he say something so suggestive but also so inaccurate? She maintained control over the few elements of her life that she could. And that control was *precious*. Except…except she had yielded it, watched him calmly, in fact, as she ceded the thirty seconds she knew it took for tickles to kick in.

"*Svetlana Henrietta*. Once again you look like a river fish."

At the sound of her grandmother's stern voice, Lana snapped her mouth shut. It had fallen quite far open, she had to admit, upon hearing Hadi say such a thing.

"Svetlana?"

"Long for Lana," she grumbled, barely caring at this point if he had enough of her names to conduct an incriminating internet search when he returned home—which she was decidedly not thinking about. Just as she was not thinking about how they would likely part ways no later than tomorrow.

"Hmm." Hadi sipped his tea.

"Hmm?"

He tapped her chin. "*Svetlana…*" he drew it out, making the syllables sound rich and exotic—quite a feat for an antiquated Bravarian name that had been given to approximately twenty percent of girls born in the year 1908 —and then he smiled. "It sounds like a princess's name."

❄

Oblivious to the fact that he'd just made a bombshell of a comment, Hadi returned to the pillow fort, leaving Lana with her tea.

What do normal people do the day after Story Night? Lana wondered once her heart stopped racing. She always returned home that day, so she didn't actually know what her grandmother usually did before joining her family at the palace in time for the Solstice Ball. And due to the day's worth of buffer built into the schedule she'd agreed on with Caro, there was, for once, nothing that Lana *needed* to do in that moment.

Hadi seemed to be thoroughly enjoying another REM cycle when Esmelda bustled back into the kitchen, saving Lana from the puzzling question of "what to do?" by announcing that they had a big order of Ram's Horns to fill, and that Lana needed to get dressed if she wanted to participate.

Lana returned to find Hadi awake and dressed. Her abs were already sore from the tickle fight, but she couldn't stop herself from giggling painfully when Hadi turned toward her. *Of course* he was wearing the sweater with the massive mouflon on the front for Ram's Horn day. And *of course* they were matching from head to toe.

"That is horrible," Hadi informed her. "Me wearing this thing is bad enough, but having to look at it on *you*?"

"My eyes are up here," Lana informed him sweetly. She felt happy and light, the way she'd felt the first (and so far, only) time she'd convinced Councilor Merrick to support one of her initiatives. She'd even gone so far as to wear the red lipstick that Vera had slipped into her bag, since it matched the fluffy tie at the end of her braid. Lana was grateful the power was back, allowing her to apply lipstick without having to guess where her lips were, but with the power came the phone lines, and the news that roads would be cleared for travel tomorrow.

They had one more day, and it felt like a borrowed lifetime. She was going to make the most of it. And if wearing lipstick was part of that, well…It wasn't the most surprising thing Lana had learned about herself lately.

"What are Ram's Horns?" Hadi asked as Esmelda herded them into the kitchen.

"Only the trickiest pastry known to humankind," Lana replied.

"They're *elaborate*, not tricky," Esmelda corrected before launching into Baker Drill Sergeant Mode.

Producing an unholy amount of puff pastry dough proved to be the easy part. The process was messy, if satisfying, leaving Lana's and Hadi's matching sweaters with a healthy dusting of flour.

"May I finally know why these are called Ram's Horns?" Hadi asked once the dough had finished chilling on the porch.

"Instead of deriving from mythology, these just come from nature," Lana practically chirped at him. This was *fun*. "The horns of the mouflon are small but mighty. Ram's Horns celebrate those horns and decorate them with the symbols of Bravaria."

Hadi rolled his eyes. "You've got to be kidding me."

"She's not. Now pay attention. This is the hardest part," Esmelda explained as she cut a sheet of puff pastry dough into strips and demonstrated how to twist them into the traditional pattern. "The basic Ram's Horn is made by twisting a strip of dough around one of these." She held up a slender metal cone. "Half the order can be basic Ram's Horns, but the other half needs to be more decorative, which is why we have extra dough. By entwining multiple strips, we can form braids and patterns to make the Horns more ornate."

Lana and Hadi watched closely as Esmelda demonstrated the proper technique, winding four strips of dough into a complicated plait that flared at the wide end of the horn.

Lana had been helping make Ram's Horns since she was a child, but the plaits were always tricky. An elaborate decorative ring formed the base of the Horn, and the four strips were plaited into a swirling pattern that climbed to the tip, where it ended in an elegant little arc. She was focusing on her first Ram's Horn, finally getting into the swing of things, when Hadi lightly elbowed her in the ribs.

"Hey!" The elbow had caused her to drop the strips of dough balanced in her hands, and one fell to the counter with a particularly heavy "plop."

"You're going quite slowly." His eyes twinkled at her. She'd rolled out eight balls of pastry dough in the time it had taken him to do two. "I would've thought you'd be faster."

"I *would* be faster, if someone weren't sabotaging my horn!" She elbowed him back. He didn't even grimace.

Stupid obliques of steel.

"Are you having problems with your horn, Lana?" Hadi inclined his head toward her twist, which she'd unconsciously taken in a stranglehold. Dough dropped between her fingers. "Because if you are, I can lend you mine."

It was a good thing Esmelda was in her office, because not only would she have overheard an innuendo that made Lana herself flush, but she would've seen Lana do something worse than flirt with a memory-loss patient. Lana sabotaged her horn, ripping off a piece of dough and flinging it at Hadi's face—a face that apparently didn't need to do *anything* but open its stupidly perfect mouth in order to push her buttons.

The sight of Hadi with half-shaped dough on his face, angled so it looked like a very buttery, very flour-coated worm oozing down his cheek, was enough to crack Lana's scowl with a smile. Or maybe she'd been smiling the entire time.

"I know how to handle a horn perfectly well, thank you very much." She flung a second strip at him. "I'm a natural."

She hoped they were still talking about dough, because getting caught overpromising would be even more embarrassing than getting caught having a food fight with Bravaria's national pastry.

Hadi carefully removed the worm from his face and caught the second one before it slipped from its precarious position on the sleeve of his sweater. Lana was too focused on the streaks of flour that remained to question why Hadi dredged the rescued strips in a pile of flour—until he slashed them across Lana's sweater. *Twice.*

Lana gaped at him.

"A natural wouldn't need to fling flaccid dough strips at me, would she?" Hadi asked as he followed up his dual attack with a pinch of flour. They *definitely* weren't talking about dough anymore.

"Did you just call *dough*—" Lana held one such strip out in front of her, and oh so slowly twisted and pulled it until the center of the strip went taut, growing thinner and thinner —"flaccid?"

It broke, and like two incredibly flaccid...dough strips... became two very droopy, very sad wet blankets.

Hadi winced as the strips swung slightly in the air.

"Besides," Lana said as she attempted to feed new, *clean* strips into her plait, "everyone knows that you have to keep puff pastry dough fresh. If it gets too warmed up, it goes soft, and that's game over. I would have thought that you knew that."

Hadi blinked at her, perhaps in surprise, and his expression said that he was caught somewhere between intrigued and disturbed. "I...suppose I have more personal experience with other types of dough."

"And how many types of dough do you have experience with?" Lana asked before she could stop herself. She cringed. What was she, fourteen? Did she *want* him to realize she knew nothing about...dough? She re-floured her fingers and flicked the extra flour his way.

"All of them. None. I don't know!"

She sputtered at him, then laughed until tears threatened her eyes. The thought of Hadi—flirtatious, affectionate Hadi, who kissed like it was an Olympic sport—being a virgin was just that: laughable. He might not remember having sex, but they both knew he'd certainly known what he was doing in every physical encounter they'd had so far, and had the confidence to go with it.

"Now come closer, you two," Esmelda said as Lana and Hadi made eye contact and burst out laughing once again. "Lana, can you hold your…oh, my goodness, what *is* that? No, hold Hadi's horn instead." Hadi cackled with laughter, and maybe they were both cackling, because Esmelda rolled her eyes as if asking for patience and help with remembering her own silliness when she was young and in love. "Come on, you two. I need more pictures. You might be ridiculous, but you look cute doing it."

Lana turned slightly to face Hadi in between her grandmother's photos. "Do you like the way I'm holding your horn?" she whispered.

Hadi made a choked sound, and put a proprietary hand on her butt in retaliation. He squeezed, smiling for the camera once more and acting like nothing untoward was afoot. The moment Esmelda finished taking candid photos, Lana craned her neck and discovered an enormous white handprint on the black leggings covering her left butt cheek. "*You*—"

"Yes, I do," Hadi said said softly into her ear, his voice warm and sinful and richer than any amount of puff pastry.

Lana's eyes trailed to her hand, still holding the cone. The flush in her cheeks might as well be accepted as permanent, she figured—at least until tomorrow—given the rate at which Hadi did or said audacious things that couldn't help but make her blush.

Holding his horn, for crying out loud. *The guy all but* whimpered *when he saw a sheep in the wild, but give a man a horn and he will give the world jokes for a yea*—

Lana's eyes snagged on the pastry wrapped around Hadi's horn. It was *good*. Better than good. An unhelpful part of

Lana's brain daintily observed that there was no way that any horn associated with Hadi would *not* be incredible. But that handiwork…

"Hadi, this is really good."

She could *feel* him resist the urge to wink and say something suggestive and put on his big boy pants instead.

He gave her a steady look. "Oh?"

Lana looked closer. Hadi hadn't finished his first horn yet either, but the center of the pattern was shaping up to be similar to hers—to the pattern that her grandmother had demonstrated. But the base…

"That's lovely, my dear," her grandmother said, having deemed it safe to reenter the kitchen. "You have very consistent knots and weaving, which is important for an even bake. But that's very complicated—and it's not my pattern." She peered at him.

Hadi's eyes flicked between the two generations of Bassano women studying him and his pastry. It was clear they were expecting a miraculous explanation of where his horn honing skills had come from, but he just shrugged.

"Please continue." Esmelda gestured at the dough. "I want to see how your pattern shapes up."

They ended up with two beautiful but different horns. Lana's followed her grandmother's pattern, which was the traditional pattern made in New Bravarian regions for centuries. It was also the form used for the pastries on the tables at the Solstice Ball each year.

Hadi's pattern was different. Where Lana's was all swirls and loops leading to a graceful arc, his interlocked larger strips of dough with patterns of tiny twists and braids that ended in an intricate knot at the tip of the horn.

Lana and her grandmother blinked nearly in unison, and briefly made eye contact before regarding the horn again. It was a nearly perfect traditional Old Bravarian Ram's Horn design, the way their neighbors baked it for their own annual Solstice celebrations.

"Well, we always knew you were Old Bravarian," Lana

said. "I guess this proves that you're a good one."

"It's a very traditional—which means it's a very *difficult*" —her grandmother winked at him—"Old Bravarian-style Ram's Horn. Good job. Whoever taught you must be very proud."

Hadi pursed his lips at the pastry, frowning slightly, and then shrugged. "If these pastries taste as good as they look, I hope that's true."

Esmelda insisted on taking another picture once they'd completed the Ram's Horns—even adding the Old Bravarian twists into the order on account of the fact that the average person likely wouldn't notice the change in pattern. Hadi snapped one of the two of them, as well, so Esmelda could add it to the collection of family photos on the wall in her office.

❄

Lana excused herself to shower off the flour that she suddenly felt *everywhere*, wondering again at how the human race had evolved to rely on such a messy thing as flirting to ensure the propagation of the species. She'd discovered that when flour got to certain places, it was terribly uncomfortable, and she had the urge to get it off *immediately*. It didn't help that she'd gone a day and a half without bathing due to the power outage.

Lana beelined for the shower, flinging flour-covered clothes as she went. She wasn't usually one to stare at her naked body in the bathroom mirror, but a cursory glance revealed that while she might have been overreacting just a teensy bit, she did indeed have a streak of flour down her spine, and on her collarbone, and neck, and, yes, somehow her underpants had been dusted with white when she yanked them off with her leggings. She was still wondering how Hadi had managed to get flour *there* as she stuck her head under the flow of water and gradually shed the costume of a human doughball.

Lana reveled in the miracle of good water pressure,

turning her back to the shower head and tilting her head back to try to sluice any remaining flour out of her hair. Like any decent individual, she waited until she had two hands full of shampoo-y, bubbly hair to make the mistake of opening her eyes—a mistake that made another one abundantly clear.

As Lana blinked water out of her eyes, the half-open second doorway of the bathroom came into focus. A flicker of movement in the mirror caught her eye—*was that Hadi's shirt flying across the room?*—and Lana finally registered the fact that Hadi was singing (that was new) her favorite song from *Mulan* at the top of his lungs. And she'd forgotten to close the door. He hadn't noticed yet since he was preoccupied with singing and shedding clothing, but the moment Hadi realized what she'd done...well, the pane of glass that acted as a shower curtain for two thirds of the shower-bath offered nothing in the way of privacy. And unfortunately, Lana's fight or flight instinct was proving useless since her muscles were trying to choose the "freeze" option instead.

Heart racing, Lana tried to breathe through the panic and forced herself to scrub viciously at the copious amounts of shampoo on her scalp. She was certain she must resemble a white French poodle based on the amount of bubbles on top of her head, and she couldn't think beyond the need to get it off so she could end this shower and flee before things got awkward. But she was too late, and she couldn't look away from the open doorway, also known as the public-humiliation-that-was-her-life waiting to happen.

Hadi, who was doing his very best to earn a Grammy nomination for his rendition of "I'll Make a Man Out of You," was coming closer, and—

Hadi took one step into the bathroom, letting loose on a lyric about the moon, and seemed to get stuck.

The worst part was that she did, too. Lana still had half the bubbles covering her hair and the side of her face, and she couldn't move. She couldn't tilt her head to wash those burning bubbles out of her eyes. She couldn't take her hands out of her hair and cover herself, couldn't somehow cross her legs the way models do to hide that fact that she absolutely hadn't gotten that waxing appointment her mother insisted on, couldn't so much as turn around or yell at him to look away. *This is my fate*, that useless part of Lana's brain offered. *To be frozen and naked and humiliated by the most perfect-looking man I've ever seen.*

Her piano-playing Thor probably didn't play the piano, but he did sing, and now she was going to ruin it by being soapy and naked and *why couldn't she have closed the door??*

Hadi's mouth had gotten stuck on the "moo" part of "moon," and his vocal chords seemed to get the "freeze" memo later than everything else, so the syllable had been drawn out. He sounded like a cow who'd just gotten an eyeful of some luscious grass. And even worse? As his "moo" slowly ran out of air, he didn't move. He just stood there, stunned, accidentally mooing as his eyes went wide and his cheeks turned bright red and the door, which he'd given a bit of a shove as he walked in, slammed shut behind him.

That broke the moment. Hadi's mouth gaped open from an "oo" to an "oh," and Lana was miraculously liberated from her paralysis. She made a most unladylike sound and started scrambling.

Her hands escaped from her bubbly hair and slammed down, trying to cover what they could. His mouth shut with an audible click. She lurched forward. He reared back. Her momentum made her wobble, and then she was flailing backward, slipping on the wet floor of the bath. Hadi shot forward as she seesawed, catching her by the slippery forearms. Bubbles were everywhere, including in her mouth, and she spat them out, wincing at the stringent taste. And then she realized.

She was buck naked except for the bubbles and Hadi was standing in her shower, hands still gripping her forearms as if she might fall. Lana flushed from her head to her toes. The water was still running, streams of bubbles obscuring her vision, forcing her to close her eyes.

"We can't both be concussed!" Hadi said breathlessly, still not letting go.

Lana pulled her arms away from him and turned around to face the shower again, focusing on finally freeing herself of the shampoo. When she turned back, Hadi hadn't moved a muscle, except perhaps to clench his jaw. He was staring studiously at her feet, blushing furiously as his pants and socks grew completely sodden.

Just in case a few of the capillaries in her cheeks had taken a break from blushing, they resumed their course, and Lana could swear her entire body flushed. She crossed her arms over her chest, sent a silent prayer to the universe that he'd ignore everything else and just look her in the eye, and then gave a pointed cough.

Hadi, bashful gentleman that he was, took her cue and made instant eye contact. From the muscle feathering in his jaw and the fact that he had not moved despite being soaking wet, Lana could tell he wanted to look. But it was like he knew that looking or moving would be crossing a line. A line he hadn't yet been invited to cross.

"What are you *doing* in here?" Lana asked him, and she could swear their cheeks were having a competition to see who could blush more deeply.

"I came in to shower."

Lana's eyes trailed down his now-glistening body, which technically *was* being showered, but she was careful to keep her perusal quick. She didn't want to see everything outlined by woolen pants that suddenly didn't seem very substantial at all.

It was Hadi's turn to cough, and the sound was rough. "Do you usually leave the door open when you shower?"

Lana dragged her eyes back up to his, goosebumps raising on the back of her neck despite the hot water. "No. In fact, this is the first time I've done that."

His gaze turned hotter, stronger, and then he was stepping

forward, wrapping an arm around her waist and dipping his head oh-so-slowly until their faces were inches apart. "Oh?" He pressed a wet kiss beneath her jaw, closing his eyes to the spray of the water.

A second kiss, then a third, trailed their way to her mouth where he hovered, a hair's breadth away, waiting for her to decide.

"And I didn't do it on purpose," Lana whispered against his lips, so softly that he froze. But she didn't give him the chance to back away.

They somehow made it to her bed, damp and clean and aching. His lips were a brand against her neck and she wanted—no, she *needed*—to be closer. If the shudder Hadi gave when she kicked his pants to his ankles was any indication, he felt the same.

Then they were toppling together into the pile of pillows and blankets, but nothing was as warm as the places where their skin touched, hot with the energy of doing something unpredictable, something that the soon-to-be-engaged Lana of next week wouldn't be happy about but that Havos Lana would.

"Um, I...I don't have anything," Lana gasped out. He'd started trailing kisses down her neck and had kept going, and if she didn't say something now, nothing was going to be said.

Hadi paused and tilted his head as he looked up at her in confusion. His breath was hot as it fanned out against her skin. Had she made him breathless?

"*Condoms*. I didn't bring any condoms."

Sense returned to his face, and he pressed another kiss to her sternum. "The entire village knows that I don't have any, either, given that half of your neighbors have seen the contents of my bag." He laughed against her skin, and it felt like dancing in champagne. "And I wish I didn't have to say this, but I honestly don't know if I'm clean."

He turned his face to the side, and the motion would have burned if he hadn't shaved before joining them in the kitchen that morning. As it was, the skin of his cheek was soft with just a little bite. "I didn't even wonder about it until now." His jaw moved against her skin as he spoke.

"It's okay," Lana whispered, stroking a hand through his hair. She couldn't imagine how it must feel, knowing nothing about yourself and not trusting whomever you *were* to take care of your body. It wasn't as if STDs or STIs were rare, but not knowing if you were healthy, even if you thought you were—it somehow felt sadder than the rest of Hadi's forgotten memories, to have another heartbreaking unknown stand in the way once they'd finally moved past all their other excuses.

Lana was quiet as Hadi's breathing gradually slowed. She'd been on birth control for nearly a decade since she had terrible cramps, but it didn't matter. Even if he was clean, it wouldn't matter; she wasn't exactly in a line of work that made it easy to live life without solutions. And backup solutions. They *would not* be having sex. Part of her felt like whining about it, frustrated at the copious amount of want circling through her body. But another part felt settled by the decision, and the fact that, once he'd cleared his head, Hadi had been upfront, even knowing that meant he wouldn't get laid. She admired that, even if she wasn't a fan of the words coming out of his mouth.

"We can do other things, though," Hadi said as he pulled himself up so they were face to face. His hand skimmed her waist, the side of her hip, lower. His eyes met hers. They were dark in the firelight, and his blond hair was darker, too, still damp from the shower. The look would have been enough for her to shuck her undergarments, had she been wearing any. In fact, his pupils were so dilated that only a small ring of blue was visible, and it was mesmerizing. That idle part of Lana's brain wondered whether he'd looked the same when Felix found him. "If you want to," Hadi finished, bringing Lana's scrambled thoughts back into focus.

"I want to." She wrapped her arms around his neck and kissed him.

* * *

❄

It's amazing, Lana thought to herself, *how pleasant air-drying can be.*

Air-drying was not a thing that princesses did. It was too inefficient—why take an unknown amount of time to dry your skin when you could be finished and presented to your stylists in one minute?—and risky. What if your hair dried in a weird way? What if you missed a wet spot on your back and ruined that Chanel gown? Now, of course, air-drying had achieved hedonistic status in Lana's mind. She wasn't sure if she'd ever have the courage—or privacy—to try it again on Vera's watch, but this one instance would live in her mind forever.

She could also confirm that Hadi became an octopus when he was relaxed. They faced one another on her bed where they'd managed to fling her pillows and blankets into a nest-like arrangement. Hadi had one arm behind his head—when she'd asked if it was uncomfortable, he'd replied that it had fallen there and he was too content to move it—and the other draped across her ribs. One of his legs was bent at the knee, and the other was sandwiched between hers, as if he'd been running horizontally and tangled their legs together. As for her own limbs…they were sprawled out. Somewhere. She couldn't give precise locations.

And as they'd alternated between dozing off and…not… the eye contact had felt soft. Intimate.

"What are you thinking about?" Hadi asked.

"What am I thinking about? Aren't I supposed to ask you that, and you're supposed to say, 'nothing'?!"

"But I'm not thinking about nothing! Why would I say that?"

"Because that's what boys do!" Every romcom ever had it on good authority.

Hadi got a coy look on his face and wiggled an eyebrow. "Good thing I'm a man, then."

Lana groaned. She'd fallen right into that one, but didn't

even have the energy to blush.

"Seriously, though, what are you thinking about? I've never seen your face look so relaxed. Those little angry Lana lines are nowhere to be seen." A fingertip ghosted across her forehead.

"Angry Lana lines!?"

"Whoops, they're back!"

Lana gave him her best grumpy look and then gave up, easing back into laziness. It felt *good* to just do nothing for a change, to have someone hold her while she lazed about, and she didn't feel guilty.

Her heartbeat picked up a fraction at the thought.

Is this *what it's all about*? Lana wondered. *What Grandmother was trying to get me to experience? What if part of taking care of myself is having someone I can do nothing with and still have it feel worthwhile, make it feel…* the sated relaxation in her limbs and Hadi's soothing voice lulled her once again into thinking of nothing. Just listening.

"Your little lines are gone again," Hadi informed her, the corners of his mouth tilting up and his eyes so, so warm.

"I can't believe you can make telling a woman that she has wrinkles *romantic*."

"It means you're happy! It's like your personal weather vane."

"Weather vane!?" Why did he compare her face to the least sexy things?

"Yes. It tells me which way the Lana winds are blowing. At least one part of you is a reliable source for broadcasting your emotions."

"Hey!"

"What? I'd be doomed otherwise. For example, *your mouth* seems too shy to respond to simple questions like, 'do you like *this*?' but one glance at your forehead? All becomes clear."

Lana's cheeks finally found the energy to flush. Her "shy mouth" had been occupied making embarrassing noises and spewing compliments like they were bad shrimp she couldn't keep down. She hadn't given it a second thought in the moment, but now? It was mortifying. She'd never done something so undignified in her life.

Lana slapped a hand over her forehead, presenting him with what she hoped was only a pair of very dignified, very unreadable eyes. "So, Hadi, what are you thinking about?"

He smiled smugly. "*Now*, I'm thinking about weather vanes. But a moment ago, I was thinking about how this feels *new*."

"New?"

"Like I haven't done this before."

Lana shot him a dubious look. "Memory loss or no, I think we both know that you knew *exactly* what you were doing." And oh, was she eternally grateful for it. Lana sent a silent "thank you" to the women who'd gotten him to this point.

Carlotta had always made jokes about her own long-ago "courting period" with George, who'd needed lots of "training"—how to hang up his towel after he showered, how to pick up on her emotions when he got home in order to provide the appropriate quantity of hugs, how to remember to cuddle after…*relations*. But Hadi seemed fully trained, at least in this.

Hadi's cheeks turned pleasantly pink, and Lana was struck again by his sweetness. She liked that she could give him a compliment like that and he didn't turn into a smug asshole. Yes, there was happiness and pride in his face, but he was almost bashful about it, like…he wanted to please her, but disliked the thought of bragging about it. Or maybe it had felt like a new experience because he'd managed to keep his muscle memory but nothing else. Or maybe he *did* remember other times, and was blushing for some other reason, and…Lana mentally chided herself. She had no idea how she could do the mental gymnastics to go from lackadaisical to mentally hyper in the span of one minute.

"I meant that *this* part—" he squeezed her tightly—"feels new. Like I've never…wanted to spend this kind of time with someone before."

He'd addressed the last bit of his comment to her neck, specifically the spot where her neck met her shoulder.

Lana felt warm from his words. Too warm. She sought to lighten the conversation. "I know I have a great neck, but what's so interesting about it right now?"

Hadi flushed further, and she could swear she felt a tiny shiver beneath her palms as he leaned in to feather a kiss to the spot that had caught his interest. "I—um—you have a little mark here."

She should be thinking about how to hide that from her stylist when she returned home in eighteen hours, but instead, she'd be damned if that didn't make some parts of her tingle. "Do you like it?"

Was that low, husky sound her voice?

Okay, vixen Lana, she thought to herself, delighted. Who *was she* with him? A slightly bolder Lana, apparently. She *liked* that Lana.

Hadi rolled them so that he was braced above her on his forearms, and Lana wished she could claim that she just looked wholesomely into his eyes, but she couldn't help skimming her hand across that gorgeous stomach, because seriously, when was she ever going to have access to this many abs again? And on somebody she *adored*? His body shuddered with the touch, but he didn't break eye contact. "I do. I like it very much. More than I thought I could."

He bent his head slowly then, always, always giving her a chance to turn away, as if he thought she could, and he kissed her. It was slow, and achingly sweet, and Lana didn't mind that he was trembling, that he welcomed her legs around his hips but seemed intent on worshipping her mouth and doing absolutely nothing else.

It was only a kiss, but by the end, she'd become a wobbly mess, like a jelly that hadn't set yet. Lana wasn't a romantic, but she was fairly certain that Hadi's kiss was his way of wrapping her in a coat of his affection, and it was the best coat she'd ever worn. He always seemed sure and open with his emotions, but something about that jelly-kiss was *more*.

So Lana forced her thoughts back toward nothing. She couldn't acknowledge it. They were leaving tomorrow. This moment was a gift from every mountain spirit that had ever existed, and nothing more.

Chapter Twelve

Esmelda was taking a call from her office when Lana returned to the kitchen to draft the "why" section of the grant application. She'd planned to tackle it from the palace since Caro and Erik were far more comfortable with summarizing and analyzing than they were answering Big Picture Questions. But after the day with Hadi, Lana was itching to do something productive.

It was an exercise in torture from the moment she reread the opening question and felt her brain cells go on strike one by one.

How will receiving this grant change lives?

A straightforward question, with an inspiring, straightforward answer. But every time Lana tried to write a response to this most important question—the answer to which had literally defined her schedule and dreams for two years—her words always felt inadequate.

It could save lives.

Maybe.

It could scientifically strengthen the power of hope.

Hopefully.

It could create a bridge between two countries whose governments hated each other, allowing them to work together by proxy in order to pursue the greater good.

It has the potential to indirectly save my country from economic decline.

But economics never won grants from *this* foundation. If anything, the argument might disqualify their proposal.

At some point between Lana's eighth and twenty-eighth failed attempts to answer Big Picture Question Number One, Hadi had wandered in and enjoyed a delicious Ram's Horn snack—at least, it seemed like it was delicious, based on the noises coming out of his mouth. Lana was saving hers as a reward for completing a first draft of the entire section, and it was looking like she might not get a chance to have it before she left.

Hadi had left Lana to her fruitless drafting, chatting with Esmelda and starting Lana's worn copy of *The Last Kingdom*. But after twenty minutes of what he described as "reading punctuated by excessive huffing and puffing" on Lana's part, he went to investigate.

Lana had sighed a particularly gusty sigh when she looked up and realized she had an audience. Her left eyeball had also started twitching again, sometime between when she'd written the words "for the good of the people" and "to change the face of heritage as we know it" in separate attempts to answer that same question. She couldn't blame the eyeball. It was awful.

"Why are you making dying sheep noises?"

"Because I feel like a dying sheep," Lana mumbled, turning back to the page of questions.

"Because…"

"Because this application is…not cooperating." Lana combined an eye roll with looking up at him so sharply that she gave herself a headache. "Ugh."

Hadi just smirked and raised his brows. "Really? You, defeated by a sentence?"

"It's a hard sentence."

"Show me." He punctuated the demand by tossing *The Last Kingdom* onto the table, and Lana cringed. To have such a masterpiece in the vicinity of her…not masterpiece… well, maybe some of its quality would be absorbed into her submission through osmosis.

Hadi glanced at the sheet of questions for all of two seconds. "Why is your research interesting, Lana?"

She frowned. "That's not the question on the application."

"Tell me anyway."

She did. And she answered his next question. And the ones after that, ignoring the half-empty pen in her hand and reminding Hadi of all the reasons she'd given that day in Havos's main square why she believed in what she was doing, why she'd sacrificed sleep, why Caro had jeopardized her job and why even Erik believed they had a more than fifty percent chance of success.

And then Hadi did the last thing Lana expected: he took her pen, flipped to a new page in her notebook, and helped her draft concise, clear answers to the questions—the questions the way he asked them, with their answers somehow molded into what the grant committee wanted to know.

He guided her through every prompt, crafting opening sentences for each reply and leaving bullet points for the additional topics to cover in the remainder of her answers. By the time Lana's pen ran dry, she was speechless. Hadi hadn't just taken her words and captured them on the page; he'd turned them into something incredible.

"Are you a writer?" Lana asked, staring in shock at the words laid out in front of her.

"I doubt it."

"Did you study literature in school, then?"

"I doubt that I went to university, if that's what you're asking." Hadi's gaze was steady as he spoke, as if he knew Lana's opinions on education and was genuinely curious to watch her reaction.

Her brow furrowed. "Why?"

"It just…doesn't seem familiar to me." He shrugged. "Or compelling."

Lana bit her lip. This truly was a test in logic, or perhaps it was fate, coming to tap her on the shoulder and say, "See?"

The universe had sent her this articulate, emotionally

savvy, talented stranger—someone who impressed her at every turn—who was certain he didn't go to college.

For the first time, Lana realized that her prior "requirements" might not matter so much after all. She could almost hear her father laughing, asking for what must be the fifth time if she was *sure* that GPA and alma mater were qualities worth ranking people on.

Lana was still turning that thought over in her mind as she bit into her Ram's Horn, every mouthful of cream, chocolate, sour cherry compote, and pastry made more delicious by the fact that she had a partly drafted application that might even turn out better than she'd hoped.

❆

Each year, Lana expected it to hurt less when she left Havos, but it never did. This year, she was downright dreading driving away.

The next couple days—full of final dress fittings, event appearances, application submissions, and a proposal by phone if she couldn't get out of it—would be busy. Important. And thinking about them didn't make it any easier to ignore the elephant in the cottage, which had taken the form of a gorgeous stranger whose chest had made a surprisingly comfortable pillow for the previous eight hours.

Hadi's backpack, which now struggled to contain his new mouflon wardrobe, waited beside Lana's bags in the entryway. But they might as well have been miles apart. Hadi himself was leaning casually against the half wall of the kitchen, alternating between studying the floor and glancing Lana's way, saying nothing. Lana knew exactly how that conversation would go, as they'd had it several times.

"Don't you think we have something here? Can I convince you to stay in touch?"

"No. It wouldn't work in the real world."

"Why are you so sure? We work here.*"*

"Just trust me."

Lana looked away and stared out the window instead, idly hoping to see some wildlife as she inhaled the potent cinnamon scent of a final cup of spiced tea. She'd made an extra strong brew today. But her twitching eyelid made it hard to focus on the clearing outside.

Lana was debating leaving the room so she wouldn't have to re-answer Hadi's silent question (and re-convince herself), wouldn't have to remind him that they couldn't work for reasons she still refused to talk about, wouldn't have to remind herself that he was going to hate her once he learned the truth, when the front door burst open and a pair of boots were flung off in someone's haste to get inside.

"Lana!" Caro called in a singsongy voice.

Lana heard a "humph" that sounded a lot like the grunt Erik made when he was used as an impromptu coatrack.

"We're leaving in a few, but I wanted to take one more look at the draft in case I'm struck by inspiration on the drive!" Lana glimpsed an airborne scarf flying Erik's way and tried to wish away her grumpiness. Certain parts of her life were tricky at the moment, but finalizing the application draft was one thing she could definitely do, and do well.

Caro launched herself into the room, bracing her hand on the edge of the wall to fling herself around the bend and nearly dislodging Hadi in the process. She looked so eager, so...*honest* about her excitement with the rosy color in her cheeks drawn out by the pink on her lips that Lana forced a smile despite the sickening feeling in her chest.

"What is it?" The smile must've not been convincing.

"Nothing."

A regal brow lifted and Lana wondered, not for the first time, if Caro had more than a little royal blood running through her veins.

"I'm just sad to leave, like I am every year." Lana kept her voice quiet and mild, well aware that Hadi's powers of perception were about as strong as a dog's sense of smell, which was potentially problematic. She was *fairly* certain that he couldn't hear them, especially as he'd gone to talk to

Erik, but one could never be too careful.

"It'll be okay." Caro squeezed Lana's shoulder and eyed her sweater approvingly. "At least you're wearing sparkles. But you know what would really help?"

Lana gave a long-suffering sigh. If Caro hadn't memorized the cadence of that sigh by now, Lana would eat her own foot. "What?"

"Having a bit more control over your life. Like, I don't know, dating somebody or wearing glitter where other people can actually see it."

Lana refused to wonder when Caro had realized that she only wore glittery nail polish if her public appearances involved gloves. "The latest draft is in the pink folder in my backpack."

"Are you at least going to give him your number?"

Lana crossed her arms over her chest. "It's in the front section of my backpack."

"Or tell him who you really are?"

Would Caro ever drop the subject? "My backpack is by the front door."

Caro shot her a look as she walked toward the backpack, and Lana almost had the decency to feel ashamed of their childish conversation. But…Caro didn't have important things to hide from someone she had feelings for.

Lana had nearly finished her tea before she realized that Caro, who loved traveling as much as she loved actually getting somewhere—and who therefore should've resumed exhibiting high-energy behavior—had been quiet for too long. Even the low hum of Erik's and Hadi's discussion had faded away since Caro returned to the entryway.

"Caro?" Lana called as she put the mug down and made her way over.

She reached the entryway and froze. Caro wasn't holding the application draft Lana had printed out the night before. She was holding the unmarked binder, furiously flipping through pages and pages of names and clutching the spine with fingers that had gone bone white. Evidently, she hadn't said a word as her anger had skyrocketed, and both men were staring at her from the corner.

"What on earth *is* this, Lana?" Caro's tone was mad, madder than when she'd gotten her second choice lab internship her first year of college, and definitely madder than when she'd discovered that Lana had fibbed about being able to sleep past six on the mornings after she worked at the lab.

Lana felt a pang of gratitude that she'd left the mug in the kitchen. Given the fact that her fingers occasionally went numb when she got very stressed—given the fact that she could barely feel her hands at the moment, actually—it was for the best. Her entire body flashed between hot and cold as she glanced at Caro, Erik, and Hadi and failed to come up with a single excuse worth saying to her best friend.

"'Have first draft ready by December nineteenth'?" Caro pulled off the blue stickie note that Vera had stuck to the binder's inside cover.

Lana closed her eyes. "Can we talk about this in there?" She hoped one finger was pointing toward her bedroom, but she wasn't sure.

Caro stomped off, and Lana followed without sparing a glance at the others.

"What's going on, Lana?" The words were out before Lana finished closing the door.

The breath whooshed out of her. "I have to choose a fiancé by Solstice."

"Why?"

Caro's face confirmed that "because my parents said so" sounded even more pathetic out loud than it had in Lana's head. "You're Princess, soon to be Queen, of this country, for goodness' sake. Why do you need to listen to them?"

"It's for Michel, and it's for New Bravaria, and if I could find a way out of it, I would, but I can't, and it's the right thing to do."

Caro gave her a critical look. They'd had this kind of argument before. "Then ask *him*."

"No."

"Why not?"

Lana flung out her hands and threw her head back to the ceiling, exasperated. "Why not? We have absolutely no idea who he is, and he would have to be titled, landed, or famously wealthy, Council-approved, and at least trilingual to make the cut! Oh, and he's obviously Old Bravarian, so that's an immediate 'no'!"

Caro opened her mouth, but Lana kept going. "Oh, and how about 'I could ruin his life!'? You've seen what it is to be me. I have five hundred-year-old jewelry and top of the line bedding and my access to private ski resorts is unparalleled, but I have no privacy, no control, no time to be myself, whoever that even is! Why would I subject somebody else to that? Especially somebody that I care about? The humane thing is to pick someone entirely insufferable so they can simply endure the rest of an already miserable life, and I can at least live with myself because I'm not subjecting a good person to further unhappiness."

Caro threw the binder onto the bed and forced Lana into a hug. It was only after Lana registered the soothing rhythm of Caro's hand on her back that she realized she was crying. She'd cried more in the past few days—been happier, too— than she had in the last six years, and she felt woefully unprepared to deal with the onslaught of endless emotions.

"So this was your last hurrah?" That soothing hand kept going.

"I suppose so."

"Why didn't you tell me?"

Lana allowed herself a final, tiny sob, and then pulled back. "I didn't want to tell anybody. This was my last chance to pretend it wasn't happening."

"And Hadi was just a miraculous stroke of luck?"

"Hadi was the universe taunting me, giving me one final tease of what I can't be."

"Happy?"

Lana nodded. She could agonize later about fate's cruel

sense of humor. Of course she only met the only man she might actually *fit* with after it was impossible for them to ever be together.

Caro bit her lip. "Maybe it wasn't a taunt. Maybe it was a gift."

Lana looked at her quizzically.

"I've never seen you like this before," Caro said. "You giggle. You go easier on yourself. You give yourself room. You've always been driven when you're on a mission, but with Hadi, you're *eager*."

Lana rolled her eyes and immediately regretted it. The movement irritated her blooming headache and may or may not have unleashed a fresh trickle of tears.

"You're more *you* right now than you've been in a long time. And I'm not saying it's because of Hadi. But I think it's because you've finally found a way to give yourself some of the love that you give this country every single day, and that's amazing." *The snow that feeds all streams*. "You sparkle, Lana. And if you don't find a way to take some of this back with you, you're going to lose your shine again."

Lana's heart cracked.

By the time Lana admitted that her parents had pressured her to make her decision immediately, Caro's expression had shifted from earnest to disbelieving. And when Lana again explained how her marriage would make Michel happy, that it wasn't her place to deny her twenty-one-year-old brother the perfect life he so desperately wanted—and that would at least temporarily alleviate some of New Bravaria's problems —Caro went from disbelieving to outraged.

"Do you have to go through with it?"

"What do you mean?"

"If you pick someone from this list, do you have to go through with marrying them?"

Lana paused. She hadn't considered staging an engagement and planning a breakup, just like she hadn't yet seriously considered a single name on the list.

* * *

❄

Neither Hadi nor Erik said a word when Lana and Caro returned to the entryway. Caro had agreed not to tell Erik until they were driving home, but Lana felt ashamed. It was only a matter of hours before Hadi was exposed to the internet. Before he'd learn who she really was, what she was about to do, and all the things she'd left unsaid.

After Lana promised to call the second she submitted the application, Erik and Caro were off. There was no more delaying her final conversation with Hadi. Lana had always thought of herself as someone who didn't avoid things, but perhaps that wasn't true; she'd spent a lifetime avoiding taking responsibility for her personal life, and Hadi was a casualty of that habit.

"I know this is probably unfair to ask," she began, picking up his hand but immediately feeling guilty and putting it down again. "But please don't be mad at me. Not right now, and not later."

Hadi frowned at her. "What are you afraid of, Lana?"

"I told you I wouldn't talk about it here, and I'm holding myself to that. You know how I…feel about you." Her fledgling emotional vocabulary might not have caught up yet, but he was good at reading feelings. "At the risk of further inflating your ego, I've never met anyone like you, and I'm entirely confident that I never will again. I wish we were different people, or that I was a different person—a person who could be with you. But I can't change the responsibilities I was born into. I have loved every minute with you, but it isn't fair for us to stay in touch after you leave."

Any other day, Lana would feel proud of herself for confessing feelings *and* maintaining eye contact with a ridiculously beautiful, engaging pair of eyes drenched in a multitude of feelings that she wanted to deny, including a heavy dose of hurt—hurt that she was causing. But it just felt like she'd won first prize for stabbing someone in the heart.

Hadi didn't look away as he picked up her hand again,

pressed a kiss to the palm, and lowered his arm, resting both their hands in his lap. Lana had seen more of his upfront personality emerge over the past few days, knew he must be exerting an impressive amount of self-control to remain civilized throughout this conversation, especially in the face of potentially wounded pride for a man who lived like his sleeve was the only reasonable place to wear his heart.

"I know you have things going on that are…difficult." It was the understatement of the year. "And I respect that you don't think I could fit into that…difficult world. I don't accept it, but I respect it. But are you certain that there is no place for me *somewhere* in your life?"

Lana opened her mouth to insist that, for his own good, there couldn't be, but some sneaky emotion had slashed her vocal cords to shreds.

"I remember what you said about needing to marry somebody your parents approve of. Obviously, a foreign amnesiac with an unknown background is entirely unqualified. But we could be friends."

Hadi's eyes were so pleading, so sad, that those lingering fears that it was a fluke, that he had some sort of savior complex, resurfaced.

"We can't be friends, Hadi. It's not fair to you."

"Why on earth not? And what about you? The way you talk about your life, Lana, I'm worried about you. Your grandmother and friends are worried, too."

Is his pain only selfless?

"It's my burden to deal with. And if our paths somehow cross again, I'll speak with you. I promise. But you need to be free to discover who you are, who your family is, and reclaim your memories without me complicating everything. And I would."

Hadi pursed his lips and nodded, the emotions clearing remarkably quickly from his face.

Wow. That happened sooner than I thought it would, Lana thought to herself, reeling from emotional whiplash. But she had to force herself to say one more thing.

"Hadi—" she brushed her fingers over his chest, then dropped her hand. "I know I'm not a nice person to have this conversation with. It's not because I don't care about you. It's because I do. And—I—I—I wanted to tell you that I'm proud of you." A flicker of hope, of disbelief, and then his eyes went quiet again. "I know you're going to fill in all the gaps about who you are. Who you *were*. Whoever it is, you are someone I am proud of. And I am certain I am not the only one."

He swallowed and pulled her into one last hug. It was firm and all-encompassing and over all too soon, and Lana returned to her room to avoid seeing him go.

❄

It had been at least a decade since Esmelda drove her home, and Lana had forgotten that she was a speed demon. The return trip to the Winter Palace would take half the time it did with Finn, so Lana tried to focus on the spreadsheet, blocking out her ever-growing kaleidoscope of worries—the grant application, how she'd left things with Hadi, choosing a fiancé, the fading mark on her neck, the realization that her eye was *still twitching*, fear that her application would be rejected and that her proposal would be accepted, getting wrapped around a tree when Esmelda turned too quickly…

Lana had never been heartbroken before, never liked someone enough for it to be a risk. So the notion that she was experiencing heartbreak was unbelievable. She had to flip through the pages a dozen times, fighting to think past the echo of her heartbeat in her ears, before she realized that she actually recognized a few of the names from the numerous diplomatic duties she'd taken on over the last few years. She'd never considered *marrying* one of them, but at least they were familiar.

At one point, Esmelda asked if she'd given their conversation any more thought. Lana merely "mm-hmmed," adding that she had an idea brewing in the back of her mind.

It likely won't work, Lana added silently. *But I have two days. I can give it a try.*

The fact that she had two days was a very good thing. She had a lot of calls to make.

Chapter Thirteen

"Lana, look at this."

Lana sighed. She, her grandmother, and Michel were all sipping hot chocolate in the palace's hot spring-heated conservatory, and Lana was trying to pretend that the outside world didn't exist for a few more hours. Michel had shepherded them there the instant they'd unpacked, and his constant chitchat (he was a nonstop flow of all the news, and by *news*, he meant *gossip*, that she'd missed over the past eight days) wasn't helping.

"What is it? Did another suitor get married?" The moment she'd reached her rooms, Lana had called Felippe Lorenzo, scion of a western Italian family whose official dukedom might've been dissolved in the 1940s, but whose wealth and influence had earned him a place on the spreadsheet. They'd met at an atrociously boring luncheon a few years earlier and had become convenient, if sporadic, friends. As a famously persuasive art dealer and an impressive manifestation of Italian stereotypes, Felippe was one of those rare men who understood feelings, the pressures of family, and getting what you want—a delicate balance that Lana had committed to pursuing as of that morning.

When she'd called him from the privacy of her bathroom's toilet room—keeping a grand total of three closed doors between herself and Vera, who denied that she'd been lurking out in the hallway—Felippe had passionately wished her the best, and then given her the inside scoop: the woman he'd been secretly courting for over a year had just agreed to marry him, and the announcement was hitting the papers that afternoon. And his cousin, who'd also been on the list, was announcing his own engagement the following week. 'Twas the season. If she didn't act fast, Prince Elias VII of Belgium, a forty-three-year-old collector of historic two-horse carriages, would be the best choice left.

"No, it's the prince of Old Bravaria."

Lana snorted, and Michel sent her a glare. Despite the fact that Lana knew it was teasing, the expression was *intense*. Her brother was a walking contradiction, since the universe had decided to pair one of the world's warmest souls with its sharpest face. Even so, Michel's eyes—the same brown as her own—sparkled in his slightly tanned face. He was *much* better about taking those self-care vacations that Lana hadn't gotten around to yet. He was also much better about letting people know he was happy to see them, and Lana's hug-wrinkled sweater proved it.

She wouldn't rescind her snort, though. The prince of Old Bravaria was allowed to be everything Lana was not. He was infamous for rarely grooming the enormous beard that seemed to run in the family (as proven by his ancestors' terrifyingly plush mustaches and sideburns, which were preserved for time immemorial in the royal galleries), doing extreme sports, and appearing exactly zero times at any functions of government since he'd reached his majority. That contrast had fueled Lana's motivation more than once over the years, as she reminded herself that *she* was doing everything she could for the betterment of her country, while the heir of their rivals was not.

"Did you know he's hot?"

"Hot?" Lana asked. Michel already had a gorgeous pretty-much-fiancé. He didn't need to go convincing himself that a man who'd done nothing with his life except grow a bristly beard was attractive.

Michel adjusted the collar of his turtleneck, and Lana

wondered if he was wearing one for the same reason she was. She smirked at him.

"Yeah, like *hot* hot."

Michel pushed his phone at Lana as she took another sip of hot chocolate, which turned out to be a colossal mistake. Half the hot chocolate streamed right back into the cup, and the other half sprayed out of her mouth while she choked, dousing Michel's phone. The cup in Lana's hand was forgotten.

"Can you breathe?" Michel leapt out of his seat and pounded Lana on the back as she sputtered.

Lana barely heard him, grabbing at his phone and quickly wiping the screen against her sweater, not even caring if she ruined it. Esmelda, who'd hurried over as well, took in a sharp breath as Lana cleared the screen.

"Is that—" Lana choked again on the sorry bit of hot chocolate that had managed to maintain its tenuous place in her throat. "How did he—"

Michel rubbed Lana's shoulders and explained in a soothing voice that the Prince of Old Bravaria had shaved, and had posed for his first official photograph in years, according to the press release—a press release that was important because...

That handsome face, the strong column of his neck, those stupidly blue eyes and that just-slightly-too-long hair...It didn't look like Hayden, reclusive prince of Old Bravaria, staring back at her. It was Hadi.

"I'm sorry, *what*?" Lana asked. Michel seemed far away. Her pulse was hammering in her ears, her hands felt tingly, her eye was probably twitching but she couldn't feel it anyway, and was that...she'd dropped a cup of some of the world's finest (read: *thickest*) hot chocolate directly into her lap and let it seep into her clothes and the cushion of the conservatory chair, because *that was Hadi* on the press release, with his face broadcast to the world, and he looked...well, he was *royal*, and he was the heir of the country that New Bravaria would economically doom itself to spite, and *for the love of Orianah*, the heir of their sworn political enemy wasn't a good-for-nothing at all, and he'd seen her naked!

"He's taking over. His coronation is January first."

Panic suddenly set in, and Lana grabbed her grandmother's hand, even though her hands had gone way past "tingly" into "numb" territory and her eyeball was twitching maniacally. Esmelda's gaze was unreadable. "*Shit.*"

"Do you know him?" Michel gasped, likely on account of never having heard Lana say anything as impolite as "shoot" before. He looked back and forth between his sister and his grandmother, who were both suspiciously silent.

Lana's frantic eyes landed on Esmelda's, who squeezed her hand, then returned to her chair. "It's fine. *You're fine.* You clearly just had more in common than you thought."

Lana just gaped as her pounding pulse grew louder. She vaguely registered Esmelda giving Michel a *very* summarized account of the past week as she typed in a quick internet search on Michel's phone.

Hadi was Hayden V? Hadi *was* Hayden? When he'd said his name was Hadi, she'd believed him, hadn't even considered that it could be a nickname. But why hadn't she? It wasn't as if Lana weren't short for Svetlana.

As lukewarm hot chocolate seeped through her leggings, a catalogue of other unpleasant feelings wormed their way into her awareness.

Betrayal—but that wasn't really fair.

Fear—this was literally worse than her worst nightmare.

Pain. Shock. Helplessness.

She felt it all.

Meanwhile, Michel was all but *bouncing*. "Did you know it was *him*?" The conversation had been objectively good for Michel's complexion; whether it was the possibility that his emotionally stunted sister had finally formed an attachment, or the possibility of a scandalous international love affair, he was practically *glowing* with excitement.

Lana looked down at herself in disgust. She was coated in no-longer-hot chocolate, seriously doubting her ability to judge others' character, and couldn't remember feeling more panicked in her entire life. She'd rather re-discover that she had to get married than relive this moment.

"No, we didn't know it was him." Lana finally choked out the words. "*He didn't know it was him. I think.* He isn't even allowed to cross the border. Just like we aren't."

Michel waved his eyebrows. "Forbidden romance. Mmm."

"It's not 'mmm.' It's…a disaster." Her hands were shaking now, Michel's phone at risk of tumbling to the ground.

Michel pressed his hands around hers until they steadied, then gave her a patient look. "Why is this a disaster? You and your boyfriend run in the same circles so you can only meet up during diplomatic visits to Spain, Italy, France, Switzerland, et cetera? Poor you."

He looked so eager, so happy at the idea of Lana having a scandalous love affair with the almost-king of the other half of their country, so…unaware that such a thing was legally impossible, especially given the spreadsheet situation.

"He's not my boyfriend."

Michel's "mmhmm" conveyed more judgement than active listening.

"Neither of us knew who he was until today, and I told him not to stay in touch."

"That's cold."

"It's *practical*. How was I supposed to know he was—" Michel released her hands so she could wave them around— "who he is? And if I did, I definitely wouldn't have talked to him. And now I do know who he is, and it's worse than if I didn't."

That's why her body was in panic mode, right? Because flirting with the literal enemy was firmly in the disaster zone, not because he'd just become both the best and worst possible match she could have imagined.

Michel just rolled his eyes. "At least now you know where he is." He didn't say anything about getting in touch. Direct correspondence between the Bravarian ruling houses had been outlawed since The Split.

"Why would I care about that?"

"So you can apologize?"

Lana must have been doing her impersonation of a river fish again, because Michel tapped her chin, reminding her to close her mouth.

"I don't have anything to apologize for."

"Um, castrating your romance before it could really blossom? Because let's be honest, you probably take a really long time to warm up to somebody."

Lana shifted in her soggy seat. "You're ruthless."

"Am not. You're the ruthless one. That's why you'll be such a good queen." Michel moved to ruffle Lana's hair, but she glared at him. "Really, though, it sounds like you two had a lovely time together. Like you could *be lovely* together. For longer."

Michel made his most effective puppy dog face, which was ironic, given that he was one of the main reasons—or at least one of the main excuses—why there was absolutely no point in doing anything with this new information.

Lana poked his forehead. "Stop doing that with your eyebrows. It makes it look like a caterpillar is crawling across your face."

"Stop avoiding the question, Lana. Why won't you reach out to him?"

"What does it matter?"

Lana could swear Michel's eyes grew sadder as he looked at her, picking up on the frustration and panic beneath her bewilderment. "Because finding someone who makes you happy matters? And you might have finally done that? Did you wear the sparkly bikini?"

She barked out a laugh at the unexpected question. "No! Why did *everybody* ask me if I was going to wear that? Vera tried to sneak it into my suitcase when I wasn't looking. And after I caught her, she managed to sneak it in anyway!"

"It's a lovely swimsuit, dear," Esmelda said, and squeezed Michel's shoulder. "Where did you find it?"

"The Canary Islands," he replied absentmindedly, still watching Lana's face. "Why did you say this doesn't matter?"

"Because I have to select my fiancé from a list of men pre-approved by the Council, and I have to announce it to the world at the Solstice Ball. And he's not on the list."

"What?"

Does Michel really not know?

"Me. Getting married. Soon. For love of country."

Michel frowned. "Why did you decide to get married now?"

For the second time that afternoon, Lana's stomach twisted. Had their parents really not told him? She paused, trying to find the gentlest way to break the news. "Apparently we need some royal...festivities...to support the tourism industry next year. And..." Lana swallowed, wanting him to be aware of the situation but *not* wanting him to feel the guilt she knew was coming. It felt like kicking a puppy. "And I also need to get married so that you're free to move forward with Kaleb."

She watched as Michel froze, his features sharpening further in dismay as he realized that Lana was telling the truth. His lower lip gave the tiniest wobble before he pursed his lips, the same way he would before he'd burst into tears as a toddler. Lana wanted to hug him like she used to when he cried and her parents weren't around to remind her that that was the nanny's job, but she gave him space. This was why nobody told Michel bad news unless they absolutely had to.

"What do you mean you're doing this so I can move forward with Kaleb?" His voice wasn't sad, though. It was *angry*.

Lana blinked. She'd never heard this tone from her affectionate brother before. "Because of the Heir First Law."

Michel just looked at her.

"You can't marry until I do. Due to a misguided logic that by marrying first, I get a head start on making new heirs."

Michel examined the pool of chocolate that had formed on the ground. "I didn't know that."

Lana eyed their grandmother, who'd sat back down and was sipping from her intact cup of hot chocolate.

"It's okay," Lana assured Michel. The situation wasn't his fault; it was their parents' fault. And Councilor Merrick's. And, as she'd recently discovered, *hers*. "I know Kaleb is important to you, and I'm okay with doing this. We always knew that I would, at some point."

"You might have been okay with it before, but you don't have to be okay with it now," Michel insisted.

"Michel." Lana tried to give him a sticky side hug, but ended up patting his shoulder instead when he lurched away from her chocolate-ruined sleeve. "You don't have to take care of me."

"Nobody told me that there would be consequences if Kaleb and I were to marry soon," Michel said, his voice quiet. "I can't believe nobody told me."

"I can't, either. But it's just another silly rule that we have to live with."

"But a silly rule like that shouldn't govern your life. A silly rule shouldn't be the difference between me choosing my *person* and you being…assigned one." He ran a hand anxiously through his hair. "Take your time back, Lana. I don't need to get married right now."

"You do. You're ready for it."

"Clearly, I decided I was ready for it without understanding all of the consequences."

Lana hated the look on Michel's face, like the happiness of two people he cared for dearly—Kaleb's and hers—were incompatible. "How can I choose my happiness in the place of yours?"

"You're not. I love you, Michel, and I want your happiness. It's my happiness, too, and I would hate it if you changed your mind because of me. You and Kaleb have been talking about this for a long time." The thought of Michel suffering so she could be happy made Lana nauseous. Her brother had always been protected by the fact that he'd probably never be king. The freedoms that gave him were precious.

Michel's phone buzzed with a news alert, and Lana nearly dropped the phone. She had to read the alert three times before it registered.

"Michel!"

"What?"

"Unlock your phone!" she thrust it at him, snatching it back the second he'd opened it.

Oh, no.

Lana's body went cold as she watched a video of Hadi standing outside the Orange Gallery in Old Bravaria, exactly where the note had said to go. Linhe and Leah stood beside him as he looked around the atrium, likely searching for his mother. *He still thinks he's just a normal guy*, Lana realized in horror.

Suddenly, a crowd of teenage girls swarmed him, doubtlessly recognizing his now-famous face from the press conference photo. Hadi, Linhe and Leah tried to back up a step, but the wall was behind them.

Lana's hands started shaking again, and Michel helped her hold the phone so they could keep watching.

Hadi's beautiful eyes widened in confusion at the chaos that ensued: girls squealing, begging for autographs, calling him Your Royal Highness, even bowing. He turned back to Linhe and Leah, whose mouths hung open in matching O's, and the video showed Leah do something on her phone, cover her mouth with a gasp, and silently turn the screen to Hadi.

He swallowed. Blinked. Swallowed again. And the passersby kept coming.

Lana could see the moment his muscle memory must've returned, and suddenly she saw the golden, regal smile he'd given in that formal photograph for the press release. The smile was stunning, but none of the girls seemed to notice that Hadi's eyes were too wide, that he'd braced a hand against the wall behind him, that his gaze frantically scanned the square as if looking for an escape.

The video cut off with another squeal—likely the videographer going in for her own Hadi autograph. The press conference was linked beneath the article's headline:

ROYAL RECLUSE EMERGES AT ORANGE GALLERY

Lana couldn't imagine being ambushed like that—to not know where you came from, imagining, perhaps, some average family from an average neighborhood with an average home—and discovering you were royal, just like that. For the first time, she wished she had a way to contact Hadi and make sure he was okay. The Prince Hayden people read about in the press was a party boy, a semi-faceless thrill seeker who was, if anything, emotionally closed off. The Hadi she knew? The man who'd just been ambushed outside a museum? He felt *everything* strongly, even her minimal cues. He would certainly be feeling this like a sledgehammer to the heart.

Michel tapped the link for the press release again. It was dated the previous day.

Yesterday.

Back when Lana had done everything she wanted, letting today become a distant thought drifting in the back of her mind like a hideous tumbleweed she hoped would blow away.

❄

Lana was no stranger to sleeping poorly, but that night might have set a record.

She'd felt off-center ever since leaving the conservatory. It wasn't fair to Hadi, but Lana couldn't help feeling duped. She'd finally done something rash, something selfish, only to realize that she'd unwittingly chosen her royal nemesis as her partner in crime. Her misjudgment was humiliating, and the dried mess of her clothing had added a physical layer of discomfort.

So unease and embarrassment chased each other through Lana's mind as she laid there, somehow already missing Hadi's presence even though she'd only slept beside him twice. There was only one full day before the Solstice Ball. One more day until she presented an unknown solution—be it a man or a plan—to the world. And she needed to be alert enough to submit the application the next morning, which would be impossible if she couldn't ignore the agony roiling in the back of her mind every time she thought about Hadi in that gallery, looking dumbfounded and then somehow finding his public mask and wearing it like a lifeline. She wondered if he could tell that the mask didn't fit right anymore.

At some point before dawn, Lana gave up on sleep, began uploading her final answers for the grant application, and stopped herself just before hitting "submit". Her mind was still frazzled from her sleepless night and the shock of the previous day. And given the fact that even her eyelid had finally stopped twitching—likely out of exhaustion rather than any meaningful amount of calmness—waiting to submit felt like the right decision. The last thing she needed was for a shaky hand or a sudden bout of nerves to have her accidentally submit the file for her updated income tax proposal instead of the latest summary of her research.

So Lana set aside the most important task of her life, and focused on the second-most important one.

❄

Lana's shoulders drooped in relief when her call was answered on the second ring. Several times that morning, she'd picked up the phone to dial someone from the spreadsheet, only to delete the number, toss the phone back onto her bed, and reevaluate her plan.

"Miguel, hello! It's Lana. Yes, from New Bravaria. How

are you?" She initiated the call to the King of Spain's nephew in Spanish out of respect.

"Hello, Lana! A happy early Solstice to you!"

"Miguel, do you remember how your uncle requested a herd of wild mouflon sheep for his niece's birthday party? I believe it was for your sister, Alina?"

"Yes, I do." Conversations with Miguel were always blissfully concise. He was roughly Lana's age, and they got along in the way that two nerds—even incompatible nerds—will always drift toward one another at a dinner party due to a shared aversion to small talk.

"How badly does Alina want those sheep?"

His quick, uncharacteristically enthusiastic reply confirmed Lana's suspicions; Alina was an excuse. Miguel had inherited his uncle's irrational obsession with Bravarian sheep and it seemed that they both wanted a reason to be near some of the fluffiest herd animals in the world.

"I'll tell you what…"

After their conversation ended, Lana went for a ski in the small private resort behind the palace to clear her head. It was the purest illusion of privacy Lana could get, and the steeper runs always calmed her mind. She now had a small flock of sheep she had to bring to an accessible location for the Princess Alina's eight birthday party that summer, but coordinating sheep was the least complicated task ahead of her.

❄

Mind as clear as she could hope to make it—and clock ticking—Lana retreated to her office to submit the application. Technically speaking, it was Helga's office. The head housekeeper had first caught Lana hiding out behind her desk when she'd returned from university to discover that her own official study, which was furnished with showy antiques and more kidney-torturing chairs like those in the drawing room, featured not one, but *three* lockless doors that granted access from various angles. It was impossible to get real work done in her own office, but Helga had guarded Lana's secret vigorously, and nobody had ever disturbed her there.

To be fair, Helga's office wasn't entirely silent, but even that was an advantage. One wall was thick stone—likely a repurposed storage area from the original ancient castle—and entirely soundproof. That wall had a subtle entrance to the "upstairs" section of the palace, where royals and noble guests once resided and which was now a main hallway between the semiformal dining room and the kitchens.

The second door opened into a small sitting area where maids took their tea breaks. Lana usually limited her focus sessions to two hours per afternoon to avoid inconveniencing Helga, and they overlapped, like clockwork, with the tea breaks of two very chatty maids. Lana had never revealed her presence, afraid to expose her secret working place and intending to ignore their innocent chatter. But over the years, ignoring gradually morphed into accidental eavesdropping. It was too late to reveal herself now.

Besides, those maids were a font of information. Without them, Lana never would've known that Michel was so nervous the first time Kaleb slept over at the palace that a sous chef had delivered a legendary pep talk and three doses of TUMS in just two hours. Lana also wouldn't have realized the extent to which her stance on relations with Old Bravaria—which Councilor Merrick's sect had nearly convinced her were irrationally radical—would have widespread popular support. And when Lana experimented with boxing to expel some of the frustration caused by her inability to get Councilor Merrick's colleagues to compromise—and she heard the maids tittering about that, too—not a word made it out to the gossip sites. The chatty maids were her litmus test. Lana hoped she'd find a way to thank them someday without revealing her eavesdropping.

Lana had just logged in to the application portal when she heard two voices outside the door. One voice was familiar—likely one of the usual maids enjoying a lunchtime break, instead of an afternoon one. The other voice was new.

"Did you know," piped the new voice, "that when Princess Lana saw the press release about Prince Hayden, she shat herself? All over the conservatory!"

Lana grimaced. It wasn't exactly normal to spill incredibly thick hot chocolate all over one's pants and then marinate in it for twenty minutes before remembering to change, but still!

"What?" gasped the familiar voice. "No!"

"Yes! During the hot chocolate service, too. Maybe between the shock and the lactose intolerance, it was a double whammy."

Lana didn't have any food allergies, but she was suddenly feeling an intolerance for her own eavesdropping—and inability to wrench open that door and correct the maids without causing even more trouble. She sighed and rubbed her temples. She could drown out *anything* for just a few more minutes, right?

"That poor girl."

Ignore them. Focus on uploading your documents, Lana chanted to herself. *Igno—*

"I know. I should really make sure Cook knows to take hot chocolate off the menu in the future—or at least to get some of that oat milk that's so popular now."

Lana nearly groaned at that. *Not oat milk.* She liked her hot chocolate nice and…dairy-y. And suddenly, she wanted to be back in Havos, the land of hot chocolate that *didn't* spill in her lap or earn her hours of speculation from strangers, where she could spend time with people who made her feel comfortable in her own skin, lactose intolerance or no.

After Lana finally managed to tune out the maids and submit the application, she walked in a daze straight to the kitchen, hit Cook with a blinding smile as she fixed herself a cup of hot chocolate with *whole milk, just because,* and drank it at the large wooden table that kitchen staff used for breaks and meal preparations. As she consumed the drink sip by slow sip, she made a point to chat with *everybody* who walked in, offer them some of the hot chocolate, and generally broadcast to the room that she had consumed lactose and nothing disastrous was occurring with her stomach. Lana left the kitchens after an hour. She wasn't *great* at small talk on a good day, but she'd given it her best shot, and now her brain felt well and truly dead.

❄

Lana had barely stepped into the hallway when a footman ran up to her, his polished boots thumping on the thick rug. Caro was waiting in her rooms—Caro, whom Lana had completely forgotten to call after submitting the application. For better or worse, Lana's guilt was muted by the sheer exhaustion that had accumulated over the past day. Sometimes it was better that way—to be overtired to the point where she felt nothing at all. It was certainly better than feeling like she had the day before.

"You look awful," Caro said by way of greeting. She was sprawled out amongst the eight decorative pillows that a maid expertly rearranged each morning.

Lana would've shot Caro a stink eye, but her eyes were too tired for such antics. So she waved lazily as she walked to her closet, ski pants crinkling. In true Bravarian fashion, she'd discarded her boots and helmet at the door and switched to indoor slippers, but the rest of her gear was kept in her own closet. There hadn't been time to change since she'd gone skiing.

Mmm, we do *have great cushions,* Lana mused as she joined Caro on the bed. She opened her eyes—they must've closed—and realized Caro was looking at her expectantly.

"So? Did you do it? I have Erik on speed dial right here if we need to do an intervention."

"I submitted it. We're done!" Lana squeezed Caro's hand and gave her a grateful smile. "Thank you so much for all your help. It wouldn't have been possible without you."

"Don't thank me." Caro shoved her hand away. "This is

our project, not *yours*. You don't need to thank me. But you *could* have told me you'd submitted our life's work and not, you know, just thrown caution to the wind and gone skiing, risking goodness knows what, before submitting!"

Lana made a tired, guilty face at her.

"Ew. You're resembling Jabba the Hutt again."

Her Jabba face turned menacing. "Sorry. It's been a day."

"Yeah, talk about news! Now that we've gotten the important stuff out of the way…Hadi is Prince Hayden? How on earth!?"

Lana dragged a hand over her face. "I know, I know. I didn't know! He didn't know! This is why I don't do… feelings."

"Because your 'feelings' might lead you to a secret prince? Boo-hoo." The lack of sympathy on Caro's face was insulting.

"*Caro*. Because meeting a guy who can't even remember that he lives in a palace and knowing him for eight days will *never* be worth a political scandal!"

"*He's* not scandalous. Just his bloodline. And his past. And his entire family."

"He *is* his bloodline!" Lana threw up her hands in exasperation. "Havos was nice. It was perfect. But it wasn't real life. It's like Vegas. What happens in Havos stays in Havos."

At that moment, Vera barged in. "Your Royal Highness!" she exclaimed, breathing hard.

Lana frowned. Vera had been so good about calling her "Lana" in private. Something must've rattled her. "Vera, Caro is here. Can we speak later?" Having been duped into…*liking* the crown prince of Old Bravaria was Lana's private shame. The last thing she needed was Vera overhearing their conversation and spreading the news.

"It's quite urgent, Lana," Vera insisted. "You see—"

"Vera, *please*," Lana said, then winced. Princesses didn't plead with their assistants—even those hired by their mothers. "Not right now."

Lana wasn't sure if it was the exhaustion or the desperation in her voice, or the fact that she was definitely looking paler than usual, as confirmed by a regrettable glance in the mirror that morning, but Vera nodded. "Okay. I will come back later. But please, Lana. Check the news, You should see it."

It? What now?

Vera left as quickly as she'd come, silently closing the door behind her as Caro opened her phone.

"Well, those are cute," she stated in an even voice.

What *is cute?*

Lana leaned over Caro's shoulder, and that damn eye started twitching again. Four pictures of Lana in her new black wool sweater with the sheep on it, baking Ram's Horns in her grandmother's house in Havos, had been leaked to the press. Hadi had been in the room—had been beside her for most of it—but he wasn't in any of the shots. It was just her, hair escaping a messy braid, flour on her cheek, and the most unguarded grin she'd ever worn, publicized for all to see as she braided dough and made a complete mess.

Lana's jaw was so tight she thought it might crack, which didn't help the fact that the unwelcome water swirling in her eyes was about to spill over. She was losing the battle on multiple fronts. Maybe if she'd actually gotten a wink of sleep in the past thirty hours, she could've clamped down on her reaction, but she was emotionally and physically drained. That water wanted out, the sob stuck in her throat wanted out, her hands felt so cold they *hurt*…

She didn't look ugly in the photos and she didn't look mean. But they'd been taken in confidence, in the place she felt the safest and most loved in the entire world, in her grandmother's private *home*, and someone had gotten them, someone had seen Lana with her mask down when she didn't know it, and then they'd taken those photos and gone to the press. Lana, who had tiptoed around awkward situations for her entire life to ensure that she *never* disrespected a Bravarian tradition, because the Old and New

Bravarian monarchies were constantly trying to out-Bravarian themselves, was shown *ripping apart* a pastry that symbolized their joint history, and looking happy and messy while doing it. It was the baking equivalent of a drunken party reveal-all where the bride-to-be accidentally goes home with a stripper from her bachelorette party.

But how had this happened? The article said almost nothing, and the photos had only lived on the memory card in her grandmother's camera. Lana read the short article again. It was originally posted by an Old Bravarian publication but had been syndicated to a dozen other websites. A famous Old Bravarian baker was quoted confirming that it was, indeed, a Ram's Horn, and commenting on the New Bravarian pattern she'd been caught both creating and destroying. There was speculation about the origins of Lana's playful sweater, which was so different from *anything* she'd ever been seen wearing that the headline had the nerve to call it pajamas. And beneath the four photos, in small, italicized font, were the photo credits: "Photos courtesy of anonymous Old Bravarian source".

Hadi. He'd somehow *gotten* these photos, and then he'd done one worse: he'd shared them. Even without revealing who she was, Lana had asked him to keep them private, *just in case*, because she wasn't born yesterday. But in the end, it hadn't mattered.

How could I be so stupid?

A life of constant vigilance, even before she was formally presented to the press, had shielded Lana from the majority of scandals that seemed to plague other royals—royals like Hadi. She'd worked hard to maintain that shield. But now, the press had intruded into her private life—and, worse, her *grandmother's* private life. Lana felt violated—not just by Hadi, whose behavior now confirmed all the terrible things she'd thought about him before she met him, but by the press in general. It was an ugly feeling, to feel exposed and presented in a way she wouldn't let herself be seen in any other circumstance.

Caro had been quiet, but evidently decided that enough was enough. She snatched the phone back, locked it, and hid it under some pillows.

Lana let her. Caro had grown up in an upper class family that cared a lot about publicity. It wasn't the same, but it was similar enough that she got it.

"You okay?"

"I just…I'm going to have to deal with it, I guess."

Caro gave her a "really? Is that it?" look, so Lana continued, trying to keep her voice even as she spoke in short sentences with long pauses.

"I don't like it." She could *swear* the corners of Caro's eyes crinkled. Her friend took some sort of sadistic pleasure in getting Lana to reveal her feelings, which was always like pulling teeth because Lana's feelings lived *deep*—so deep that she wasn't even aware of them most of the time.

"It's mean." Now she sounded, and *felt*, like a two-year-old. Caro just kept nodding. They'd been through mini versions of this before.

"I look ridiculous." At that one, she could *feel* Caro praying to the river spirits to give her patience, but she wouldn't laugh. Not when she was feeling so awful. Princesses were supposed to care about how they looked. Princesses were given five-to-six-digit *state budgets* to ensure they had all the uncomfortable and wear-once and frilly things they needed to remain "respectable," even when they wished they didn't have to wear them.

"That was a happy sheep and now it's a sad sheep." And now she was expressing herself through sheep again. Caro was about to lose her battle with a straight face, and Lana wasn't far behind her. She was sad, gosh darn it! She wasn't going to—

A tiny chuckle escaped out the side of Caro's mouth, and that did it. Lana's first giggle came out as more of a wet snort, which of course made Caro laugh even harder, but then, there it was: an endless, abs-will-be-sore tomorrow belly laugh.

"They caught me with flour on my face!" Lana complained. "I look like a floozy!" She couldn't voice her mother's go-to fashion critique with a straight face. Lana, who'd been respectably covered from clavicle to knee for nearly every single minute of the past ten years of her life, was anything but a floozy. Caro had had to show her what a push-up bra was, and even that had been rejected as "too risqué" to be worn beneath a knitted sweater.

"I think Hadi leaked the pictures." It took a moment for Lana to stop hiccuping into the sudden silence.

And it felt like such an enormous confession that it took a moment to register that Caro's first instinct was to ask if he also had nudes.

"Excuse me!? I tell you he did it and your first instinct is to ask if he has nudes? He violated my *trust*!"

"He could violate a lot more than that." Caro didn't back down. "Does he have them?"

"What 'them'!? I've never taken a nude in my life! Oh my goodness!"

Why was that Caro's first question? Were nudes that common? Does Caro *have some? Does* Erik *have nudes of* Caro? Lana felt horrified at the side of the world that she'd just imagined for the first time.

"Good. Then you're fine."

"I'm not *fine*!"

"Well, I know you're not fine fine, but look at the bright side. There's three bright sides, actually: the only pictures of you that have ever been leaked are *adorable*." Caro counted on her fingers. "Even if Hadi *did* leak them, he isn't claiming credit, so even now he's respecting your ridiculous charade."

Lana scowled. A leaked photo was a hell of a way to say, "Hi, I know you didn't want to stay in touch, but there are more where these came from..."

"He doesn't have anything actually incriminating that he can leak later. *And* maybe this will give you some bargaining power for the whole marry-your-life-away thing. You've given your entertainment to the people. They should let you rest. And look, that's four!"

Lana shook her head. "I just can't believe he'd do this. I thought he was different."

"So did he."

Caro had a point. Reconciling sensitive, thoughtful, just-a-bit-playful-and-mischievous Hadi with the reckless and reclusive Prince Hayden required Olympic-level mental gymnastics.

"But it doesn't mean that he consciously tried to hurt you, Lana." Lana wanted to argue, but Caro wasn't having it. "This isn't a good enough excuse for you to shut yourself off from having love in your life forever. It just isn't."

Lana gaped at her. *Yes, it is!*

"It *isn't*," Caro repeated, as if she could hear what was going through Lana's head. "Come on." She got off the bed, pulling Lana along with her. "You're sad, but you're *fine*, and you don't deserve to wallow about this. I'm sorry, but you haven't earned it."

Lana frowned. *Earning things* was her weakness—something she'd been sensitive about since childhood, when she'd realized that she'd done a whole lot of not earning *anything* when it came to the advantages of growing up as a princess. "I think I've earned this."

"Nope," Caro said as she pushed Lana's door open. Vera was literally standing there in the hallway, hands twined behind her back, as if she knew this was an incredibly important thing for an assistant to be around for and had absolutely no idea what to do with herself until Lana agreed to talk to her about it.

"*She* will discuss this further with you," Caro pointed at Vera. "Right?"

Vera nodded eagerly. "Yes, ma'am. Thank you, ma'am."

Right.

Chapter Fourteen

"What do you mean, it's good news?" Lana asked. She was once again in the drawing room, except that this time, *she* was going to be the one making demands. She just had to ease her parents into them.

"People *love* the pictures of you," her mother clarified.

Vera had said the exact same thing, punctuated with several statistics about the royal family's raised approval ratings and the forty-seven fashion and royal blogs that were already positing theories about where Lana's sheep sweater came from. The fact that twenty-two of those blogs were from Australia and the United States also boded well for the tourism industry; an entire PR team in the trade ministry was devoted to projecting such things, and Lana couldn't count the number of reports she'd read correlating the frequency of royal mentions in English-speaking blog posts and tourism revenue. And the projections were *staggering*. Lana hadn't seen such optimistic reports since she'd joined the Council.

"I didn't know our little Lana-Nana still loved mouflon sheep." Her father beamed, reaching over the table to squeeze her hand.

"Of course I do!" She'd almost forgotten that her father famously loved the creatures; the first photograph released of him to the public, which Lana had been shocked to learn had made it onto the cover of a *Sexiest Royals of the Decade* memorabilia catalogue, showed him crouched deep in the mountains with a lamb and its mother.

"Did you get the sweater from that little shop down the street from Esmelda's house?" her father asked, ignoring her mother's agitation, which grew as her comment continue to go unacknowledged.

"I did. And Gerta designed my socks." Lana lifted her pant leg a few inches. "Aren't they cute?"

"Moving on, these pictures are good news, Lana," her mother said.

"I love them," her father whispered.

"I got you a pair," Lana whispered back.

Her mother glared at them, and Lana refocused on the issue at hand. "Do you not care about *how* these photos got out there?" Lana asked. She wasn't going to enlighten them —if she didn't have to confess to knowing *prince Hayden*, she wouldn't—but it felt surreal that nobody seemed to care that photos of her had been leaked.

"It happens." Her mother waved a hand. "Good call on taking them in the first place. It turns out that this is exactly what we needed."

It happens? Lana shot a disbelieving glance first at her father, who was frowning, and then at Vera, who was valiantly trying—and failing—not to worry her lower lip.

"It's not like you smile like this for everyone," her mother continued. "You did great."

Lana closed her eyes for a moment and reminded herself that this was exactly how she'd expected her mother to respond. "Thank you, Mother. That's why I called this meeting." Lana smiled serenely, then nodded at Vera, who deposited printed copies of the PR team's updated projections and Lana's proposal onto the table. "Based on the success"—Lana couldn't believe she managed to get the word out—"of the photos, it's in our best interest to test out a PR and marketing-focused strategy to boost tourism for the next six to nine months, then revisit the marriage idea if we don't see the lift we're expecting."

Lana certainly would never be a British royal, happy for

every moment of her life to be splashed across the tabloids, but if a photograph of her in a handmade Bravarian *sweater* could raise projected second quarter GDP by more than ten percent? New Bravaria's economy wouldn't be fixed, but it would be moving in the right direction. Not to mention that Bravarian exports might have just gotten a new lease on life.

Her mother opened her mouth, and by the cold look in her eye, Lana could tell she wasn't going to like what was coming.

"This changes things." Lana gestured to the projections. "It *makes sense*. This is an objectively better solution than a hasty wedding. It has more potential in the short term and the long term. And if we catch up to the rest of the world's royalty and learn how to *use* publicity to our advantage, it will give the wedding far more impact than it will have if we follow your original plan. Plus, this will give me time to choose the right person from the list."

"But Michel is getting married!" her mother exclaimed, and Lana couldn't pretend that it didn't hurt that her mother continued to prioritize Michel's happiness even in the face of logic. She and Vera had spent hours running the numbers. There was literally no way this proposal didn't make sense—unless she'd missed something.

Lana narrowed her eyes. "He's twenty-one. He can make it to twenty-two."

"Your eggs will die."

"Really?" Lana didn't try to temper her haughty tone.

"I know it's not…appropriate…to say things like that nowadays. But ensuring the future of the line *is* your responsibility." Her mother eyed her father, looking for support—that he gave, for once.

Lana stood. "I *will* marry. Within a year." It was the best compromise she could hope for. "Which means that I'll announce my engagement this spring." Royals announced engagements at least three months in advance—far enough to make it *very, very* clear that no funny business had occurred before vows were exchanged. If possible, six months was ideal to allow tourists to make travel plans. "Support me in this, and I'll spearhead the PR initiative. I'll pose for as many photos as we need, give interviews…I promise we'll have positive results." Lana hated being on display, but for her freedom—for Bravaria—she'd do it.

Lana wanted to smile, but she didn't want to jinx it. She'd finally done it. She'd stood up for herself, for the belief that she could have something better than a mediocre marriage in which she lived in a separate residence form her spouse, and that she could finally do something real her help her country. They couldn't ignore logic now, right?

"Lana. You can't delay your announcement." Her father's words cut through any desire to smile.

"What?"

"Announcements about the wedding date are going out across dozens of publications first thing tomorrow," her father continued. "On six continents. The articles will say that the groom is still a secret, but we wanted to give people the optimal six months to plan."

She stared at her father, horrified.

"Why did you do that?"

His gaze dropped to the floor.

"We would've discussed it together, but you were stuck in Havos with the avalanche and we had to set things in motion," her mother said as she walked to the door. Her father followed.

"How can you continue to ignore the facts?" Lana called after them. How could they continue to ignore *her*, and the things she'd only just realized she needed?

"It's too late, Lana," Givera said from the hallway. "Your energy would be better spent speaking to the candidates on the list."

The proposals her parents had left on the table blurred as Lana's eyes filled with tears. She was *tired* of things being done behind her back, of being made to feel guilty for influence that never seemed to be useful enough, of having her needs always come last. Not all of her ideas were winners, but *some* were decent, and they were rejected anyway. Vera closed the door behind herself, leaving Lana in the empty drawing room.

Watching her country continue to crash and burn was going to eat her alive. What was she going to do?

Chapter Fifteen

Lana was making the most of her oversized bathtub, trying to pretend she was back at the hot springs and ignore the sense of doom that struck every time she remembered that she was expected to present a fiancé at the Solstice Ball in less than eighteen hours, when her phone rang. It was an unknown number.

Carlotta had warned that she'd be receiving a call; apparently the foundation's mysterious donor had decided to reveal themselves, and they'd issued a "chat or bust" ultimatum. Given that nobody knew Lana ran the organization, the call didn't pose a huge risk, but it was unusual.

The stress of it had gotten buried in the other events of yesterday, but the idea that things might be changing with this, too…Well, Lana would do her best to secure future funds from the donor, but it wasn't a guarantee.

Lana wiped the bubbles off one hand and answered. "Hello?"

"Lana, it's Hadi. Before you get mad, will you please give me thirty seconds?"

It was a good thing he'd spoken quickly, because Lana barely avoided dropping the phone in the water. As it was, the phone skidded along the wide lip of the tub, stopping just before it crashed to the floor. She wasn't about to apologize for potentially damaging his eardrums.

"Why should I? You're keeping me from a very important call." Lana couldn't even bring herself to cringe at the snootiness in her voice. He'd hurt her by releasing those photos, and then he'd gotten her number! And had the nerve to call her *now*, while she was waiting for that call! The royal houses of Old and New Bravaria were famously *not* in direct contact with one another, relying only on their respective economic ministers to handle any communications by proxy. The fact that Lana and Hadi had broken a century of official silence—and that Hadi had managed to break it *again*—well, it was groundbreaking. And illegal.

"Thirty seconds, and then hopefully we can have a conversation, Lana. But at least promise me thirty?"

"The second I get another call, I'm hanging up."

"First, Carlotta gave me your phone number, so please don't think I'm stalking you."

She needed to have a talk with Carlotta about giving her number to random strangers.

"And I'd never share it with anybody. I promise. Which brings me to the second thing: I didn't leak those photos of you. I didn't even know you were *you*, which is crazy, and I'm upset you didn't tell me, but I get why you didn't, and if you're still with me, I've got one more thing to tell you, and I think you'll want to hear it."

"Your time's almost up, and I really do have to go." Even if he *hadn't* leaked those photos, she wasn't recovered from the imagined betrayal of it. And a call from the anonymous donor trumped a call with Hadi anyway, whether she liked it or not.

"You don't, though."

Lana's eyebrows almost shot above the lining of her shower cap at the *nerve* in that statement. Maybe she really didn't know this man at all.

"You don't, because you're waiting to talk to me." That was Lana's cue to get out of the bath. Any attempt at relaxation was ruined by the anger coursing through her veins at Hadi's presumptuousness.

"Excuse me?"

"You know the mysterious donor you're always talking about for the Health Springs Organization?"

Lana couldn't speak. If he'd managed to ruin that, too…

"It's me. I'm the anonymous donor you were talking about. I've been donating to the Health Springs Organization for six years. Enough for ten people from anywhere in the world to visit each mo—"

The phone slipped from her fingers again and fell straight into a puddle of bathwater.

❄

Static spurted from the phone's speakers, and then it shut off.

"No!" Lana grabbed the phone with shaking fingers. She needed to call Hadi back.

Lana flung open her bathroom cabinets, trying to remember where Vera had stashed the hair dryer she'd refused to bring to Havos. She found it in the second cabinet and made a mental note to *really* give that woman a raise.

Lana removed her phone from its case and attempted to dry it using the hair dryer's "cool air" setting. A bowl of rice was supposed to be best, but she was still dripping wet in a towel, and begging the kitchen staff to guide her to rice so she could talk to her secret prince-slash-secret-donor-ex-but-not-ex-boyfriend who'd apparently *not* leaked pictures of her wasn't an option. Lana replayed Hadi's words in her mind as she waved the hair dryer at her phone. She had more questions than ever, but hearing his voice had been…nice. It was still warm and calm, but he sounded more self-assured than he had back in Havos.

Hadi is the mysterious donor, Lana repeated to herself as she paced in her bedroom, forcing herself to wait before turning the phone back on. *Prince Hayden* had been powering the foundation that kept her motivated even on bad days. *He'd* given her a way to help people even when the

Council refused to pass her reforms. She had no idea how Hadi had found her foundation, or why he'd gone looking in the first place, but this again challenged everything she thought she knew about him.

The immature, mindless Prince Hayden who'd reportedly spent the last however many years throwing away time and opportunities had sponsored hope for hundreds of people. He'd used his own funds, which Lana was certain were as heavily scrutinized as hers, to help people in a way she couldn't. What else had he done that she'd never given him credit for doing?

Fortunately, Lana's phone turned back on and she shut herself in the toilet room to call Hadi back.

He answered on the first ring. "Lana? Are you okay?"

"I dropped my phone in water, but it's working for now."

"Did you hear what I said? About the—"

"Yes." She didn't even care if her voice wobbled. "Is that really true?"

"I wouldn't lie about this." She heard the firmness in his voice, as if he'd learned some things in the last day or two that he *had* lied about, once upon a time. It was so different from the innocent earnestness she'd learned to appreciate in Havos that her heart ached.

"How did you find out?" She and Carlotta had never been able to track down their anonymous donor.

"I've been going through my emails, and my medical records, and my bank statements…everything to try to piece together the details I couldn't remember. My sister helped me, and as we talked, my memories began to come back." She heard the discomfort in his voice. It didn't sound like he'd missed most of his memories all that much. "I found recurring payments to a shell company that I apparently own, and I followed those, which get paid through a company credit card. I haven't actually found the card, but it's mine."

"Wow." Lana remembered the joy on Hadi's face when he'd learned that somewhere out there, a wonderful person enabled the hope and healing he'd witnessed at the Inn. How had it felt for him to regain his memories and discover that he was his own hero?

"I know. And after all the things I've learned in the past couple of days, I couldn't let that opportunity go to waste. I had to make the most of it to try to get you to talk to me."

"How did you do it, though? I would've done the same thing, but my finances are so regulated. I'm lucky I've gotten away with running it without the Council finding out."

"I think we both know that my risk tolerance was extremely high." His tone was wry. "It felt worth it to me. And I spent money so carelessly that if someone did notice, they probably figured it was better to look the other way." She heard him swallow.

"But you're not like that now." It was almost a question.

"No. You saw me. You *know* me."

"It's very different, Hadi. I know the tabloids exaggerate everything, but you can't make all of it up."

"I think—I think part of the reason it took me so long to get my memories back was that I didn't want to. I didn't like who I was. I still don't. I did some good things, like the donations, but the rest..." He sounded hoarse, and Lana wished she could give him a hug. What did it feel like to regain your memories and realize you weren't a good person? To feel ashamed when you remembered who you were?

"I was terrified of my responsibilities. I...well, you know I have two sisters."

Lana bit her lip. One sister was still too young to have had her debut, but the other...Lana's throat tightened as she remembered seeing the report a few years earlier, and how she'd *smugly* informed her mother that the spare heir of Old Bravaria had illegally crossed the border and led some sort of protest. Lana knew her mother had judged the situation harshly, but now that she thought about it, she realized Givera hadn't said a thing, merely raised a brow as Lana all but monologued about their rivals' poor choices and propensity to cause scandals. The Princess Sabrina had been removed from the line of succession immediately, and the first headline about Prince Hayden's indiscretions appeared the next day…and based on the general sense of dread twisting her stomach, Lana was starting to think it wasn't the worst thing in the world that she'd decided to have this conversation on a toilet.

"I'd always planned to abdicate to Sabrina when it was time for me to take the throne," Hadi was saying. Lana could see where this was going. She wanted to sob for Hadi, for his sister, for how foolish she'd been not so long ago. "She was always so smart, so diligent, so dedicated—a lot like you, in many ways. She would be better for Bravaria than I ever could." Hadi swallowed. "I've always struggled to sit still, to make important decisions. But then Sabrina's rebellious streak kicked in. I handled my excess energy by using my body—skiing, hiking, normal things—but Sabrina went and organized one of the largest animal protection protests of the decade. The protest was already making international news as it marched through Old Bravaria, but the moment she led it over the border, it was game over. She was disinherited within a day, and my plans were for nothing. I finally accepted that I was going to have to step up eventually— Elena's too young—but *I didn't want it*. And I didn't want Sabrina to suffer more than she already had. She'd already lost our family's—well, our parents'—official support. She didn't need to be villainized further. So I sort of…lost it. And I made sure everyone saw it. I didn't care if they dragged my name through the dirt. I *wanted* them to. Better me than her. But then I let myself get sucked in." His voice sounded desperate, as if he wasn't sure Lana would believe him. "I was just so *angry*, Lana, and it escalated. I got into more extreme activities. My family didn't trust me, didn't think I was ready for the things they needed—*need*—me to do. And they were right. I wasn't ready. I'm *not* ready. But I didn't realize how lost in it I'd become, how bad it had gotten until I forgot everything and had to learn it all over again." His voice broke. "I didn't know how to handle any of this before. But I was given a clean slate. I still don't know how to handle the stress, how to sit with my emotions, how to find a way to live with this and do what I need to do."

Lana's cheeks burned with shame. Hearing memory-back Hadi confirm the sentiments that Havos-Hadi had voiced to her two days before should've been a relief. Because it meant the other things he'd said remained valid, too. But it wasn't. It made her regret judging him and his entire family back when she knew *nothing,* and it made her regret not trusting him when he said he understood his own feelings, when he wanted to focus on *how* he'd act rather than *who* he'd been before losing his memories. She hadn't considered that he'd remember his life from before and not choose it. "Are you okay?"

"I don't know. I don't know if I can do this by myself."

Lana's heart cracked. Strong, confident Hadi—Hadi, who helped others even when he self-sabotaged, who wanted her happiness, who *listened* and tore down her barriers before he knew who she was *and* after, didn't know if he was okay. She knew he loved his sisters, but families were complicated, and she couldn't begin to imagine the quality of the "friends" he'd cultivated over the past few years. And even if Lana *did* find a rare pocket of free time in her regular schedule that she could use to *be his friend*, she couldn't even legally cross the border. "Do you have someone, Hadi?"

"Lana, I loved you when we met in Havos. And I wanted you in my life, even though I didn't know what that life was. I still feel that way. But I think that now, I also need you."

She'd never had a phone call with a crying man before, but she was certain his voice sounded wet. She wanted to help him. But what could she do? She was scheduled to announce her engagement that night. Hadi needed a savior— and for once, ironically, she didn't fit the bill. She hadn't even been able to save herself.

"Lana? You don't have to reply. I just wanted you to know." His voice was shaky. "I wanted you to know that you *know me*, the *real me*, even if you didn't think that you did. And I wanted you to know that knowing all of who you are now, I feel the same way. More intensely, even. Because I understand some of your…eccentricities better now."

"My eccentricities?" She could almost feel his mood shift slightly, like a glimmer of sunlight peeking through a crack in a cave.

"How did you keep yourself from laughing when I called you the Princess of Politeness?"

"It was more painful than funny," she admitted, eager to distract Hadi from his problems for just a little longer. "It was like you were daring me to tell you when I'd promised myself I wouldn't."

"Thank you for talking to me. And for calling me back."

Lana could talk to him forever, but she shouldn't, she realized. She had too many terrible things to do today. Starting now.

"Hadi, I'm certain you've seen it by now, but I really am getting married."

He paused, and for a moment she thought he was going to hang up. "I know. I didn't want to make this about that, but I had to let you know *before*…"

"I don't even know who it is." She told him about the spreadsheet. "And I have to choose someone in the next few hours. It ranks everyone by GPA, for goodness' sake, and I knew it was ridiculous before, but now, it's worse, and…" She realized tears had started streaking down her cheeks at some point, carrying a mixture of sadness and relief. It was a relief to finally confess everything to Hadi, even though he was the last person who should have to hear about her problems.

"If we were just normal people—if we were Nico and Sarah—" Lana snorted as he said Nico's name with distaste, "would you be with me?"

"Yes." Her answer slipped out before she could second-guess it.

"Would you be with me now, if you could?"

Lana didn't answer. It felt too dangerous to dream about out loud.

"Because I would. If you found a way to want it, and to choose it."

"Do you mean that?" Lana whispered, heart pounding.

"Sheep and all." His laugh was choked.

"Did you ever figure out why you hate sheep so much?"

"No. It's probably recent."

Lana frowned. "What do you mean?"

"The doctor said that I likely won't remember the last three months or so, since those memories haven't come back at all."

"I'm sorry."

"On the bright side, in case you were wondering, I'm clean."

Lana sputtered out a laugh.

"Well, that's good to know, I guess…Did you dig up an old doctor's record?"

"I made them test me for everything. I don't want to know how I occupied my time since my last doctor's appointment, but at least I don't have to worry about *that* anymore." His voice trailed off, and Lana could nearly feel his revulsion through the phone.

But she loved him, she realized. Even if he'd learned some things about who he'd been that weren't so pleasant. Never in her life had she wanted to help somebody learn to love themselves as badly as she wanted to be that person for him. To be *with* him, so they could both have a constant reminder of how good this world could be. Of the better people *they* could be.

"Hadi, I have to go. I think I might…call you later, if that's okay, but now I have to go."

Hadi didn't think he could do this by himself. It had taken all of Lana's self control to not admit that she didn't think she could do it by herself, either. But what if they *could* do it

—together?

✳

Lana made one more call before leaving her bathroom sanctuary.

"You okay?" Caro sounded breathless.

"Are you…exercising?"

"I'm working off my stress."

Lana pursed her lips. Caro wasn't the world's most athletic person, but she read her medical journals and forced herself to achieve the bare minimum recommended weekly activity. Her exercise activities could generously be considered mildly hazardous. "Your stress?"

"About the application." Caro's voice grew louder, like the endorphins were kicking in as they spoke. "It's silly, I know, especially since we won't hear back for at least a month."

Shame settled in Lana's gut. Caro was such a strong, positive force in Lana's life, and she hadn't even registered that Caro had been stressed the past day—perhaps even the past few months. "I think we'll be okay."

"Of course we'll be okay, but what do you mean?"

"I think that even if we don't get the grant, there might be a way—complicated, but a way—for us to assemble a team to do joint research in New *and* Old Bravaria. Communications with our rivals has…opened up."

"You talked to Hadi!"

Lana hoped Caro couldn't hear her blush through the phone. "He called me."

"*And*?"

"He didn't leak the pictures."

Lana swore she could *hear* the fist pump over the phone.

"And he more or less confessed passionate, undying love. Again." She tried not to sound nauseated.

Caro snorted. "You sound like someone replaced your mineral sample with table salt."

"It doesn't matter, though, because of that ridiculous

spreadsheet," Lana insisted.

"I'm calling it the spreadshit from now on, for all the good it's done you."

Lana's lips twitched. It was actually a good idea. "Anyway, I just wanted to call and tell you you were right. Especially about how I handled the situation with the pictures. Thank you for being so wonderful."

"Aw, Lana, I know I was right. I'm *always* right. But I'm glad you're feeling happier."

Lana was about to hang up when she heard Esmelda's voice in the background.

"Grandmother?" She heard the muffled sound of voices and Caro's front door closing. What was her grandmother doing at Caro's apartment?

Caro must've put the call on speakerphone, because the too-loud sound of Esmelda's voice soon echoed off the tiles in the bathroom. "If what I heard is true," she called into the phone, "pull your head out of the ridiculous royal sand and *choose him*. Just add him to the damn spreadshit, Lana!"

❆

Lana had always been careful about what she let Vera overhear, given that she'd been hired by Givera. But great challenges required great accommodations, and Lana needed someone trustworthy and knowledgeable by her side. It was time to take a leap of faith and trust her assistant.

"How much do you know about Bravarian law?" Lana asked. It was probably the first time she'd had a conversation in the small sitting area in the corner of her bedroom—but that was the benefit of speaking *with* your number-one eavesdropper instead of hiding from her.

"I don't have a law degree, but I studied public policy and history before working for two years as a paralegal."

Lana nodded.

"Despite my lack of formal training, I take this job and the opportunity to work here very seriously. I have attended or read the minutes from every Council meeting in the past two years. I also know the affiliations and backgrounds of each Councilor and the top one hundred ranking members of government."

Lana was impressed. Vera had never let her down, but her commitment to *everything*, including things like styling appointments and the sparkly bikini, had caused Lana to underestimate her. "And how up to date are you on my marriage situation?"

"Quite."

Lana gestured for her to go on.

"I wasn't aware that your parents and the Council were preparing the list or setting the deadline, but I did some research while you were gone."

"Oh?" Lana's brows had taken a nice walk up her forehead. She hadn't thought about what Vera had done while she was in Havos, and none of Vera's predecessors had been proactive enough to work on things without being asked.

Vera's face gave nothing away, though Lana noticed she was sitting up straighter than usual. "If I can be of any assistance, Lana, please let me know."

What did she mean by assistance? Vera's enthusiasm made it hard to tell whose side she was on—and the fact that Lana felt, for the first time, that there *were* sides wasn't heartening. Lana was going to have to be direct first.

"The order that I choose a husband blindsided me," Lana began. "Marrying for New Bravaria was always a given, but I wasn't prepared for the immediate request, and I certainly didn't have an intended in mind." Even if she should have.

"Of course not." Vera gave a curt nod. "How could you expect it? Especially without a Writ of Intent."

"A Writ of Intent?" Writs of Intent were required whenever the country needed to introduce new legislation or negotiate a new agreement. They served to officially kick off the project, but Lana wasn't sure how it applied to something as personal as marriage.

"From a legal standpoint, the monarch and Council are

required to deliver a Writ of Intent in advance of a request that an heir marry. It's one of the protections put in place when New Bravaria became a constitutional monarchy."

Of course it was. Lana was equally frustrated that she hadn't thought of it and that her parents hadn't mentioned it, though she shouldn't be surprised.

"Is the accepted time period the same as for everything else?"

Vera nodded. "The thirty day commencement period is the same, unless it's deemed urgent by the monarch."

"I suppose that's the case here. Is it reasonable to assume that, given the apparent urgency, there's nothing I can do to delay or reschedule or..." Lana's voice trailed off. These were just synonyms. "...convince the Council otherwise?"

"You need a Letter of Request." The second mandatory document, after a Writ of Intent.

"I need to write one?"

"You need to *receive* one."

Lana cocked her head. "And if I don't receive one, it's... canceled?" She had to ask.

"Realistically I don't think your parents would let you get away with that. But the Council hasn't written one for a royal marriage in twenty-six years and they've had nearly complete turnover during that time. I don't believe one has been prepared, so if you demand the Letter and they write it quickly, they might miss something—something you could take advantage of. The document is supposed to be prepared ahead of time, so nothing would legally stop you from creating your own deadline when you demand your copy. They would have to comply with whatever timeline you set."

Lana tried to temper the hope rising in her chest. "So there is nothing stopping me from setting an aggressive deadline —of, say, thirty minutes from receipt of request—to see if we can pressure them and find some wiggle room in the official wording?"

"There isn't. Would you like me to request the documentation from Judge Meyer right now? I can be quite…intimidating, and something written under stress is *much* better than the alternative."

While Vera pursued Judge Meyer, Lana made another half dozen calls from Helga's office. She really needed to do something nice for the housekeeper, whom she'd more or less deprived of an office for several days. Perhaps she could offer to fund Helga's granddaughter's college education or book her a trip to a museum where she could view the Ancient Greek artifacts that inspired the tiny replicas on her shelf.

By the time Lana returned to her own rooms, the tea-drinking maids had confirmed that Lana was once again lactose-tolerant—and Lana had nearly managed to chase away the pang of unease she felt at her plan. Judge Meyer was the Councilor she most respected. Despite not yet being part of the Caucus, Judge Meyer had mentored her, agreeing to debate various aspects of her proposals before her presentations and helping proactively identify inconsistencies and potential weaknesses to strengthen Lana's arguments. Hoping he made a mistake didn't feel right, but it was her best shot.

❄

"How by the book are you, Lana?"

Lana ticked an item off her list with more vigor than was necessary.

For years, I did everything by the book. And look how that turned out. "As much as I have to be." It felt good to say. "And no more."

"Because we are allowed to request an update…" Vera shuffled the papers in her hand—likely the Letter of Request—before seeming to catch herself.

"What do you mean?" Lana took a deep breath, trying to brush away fantasies of adding an entire year to the deadline in the Letter of Request that Judge Meyer had hastily typed up for Vera. He'd been required to attach the infamous spreadsheet to the email request *and* print it out, because *tradition.*

"I understand that you might want to…add somebody to the list. Is that right?"

"Are you in cahoots with Caro and my grandmother, too?"

"No, Lana. I have eyes and a brain. And ears," Vera added as an afterthought.

Lana winced. She knew all about those ears. Perhaps Vera could've been better employed as a spy.

"The Council was in such a hurry to finalize the spreadsheet that it seems that a great deal of thought did not go into restricting who could theoretically be included on this list. Even better, the Queen Consort presented the list as exhaustive, but the Letter of Request describes it as a 'guide'."

Lana's eyes widened. Judge Meyer *hadn't*…That would mean she could add a candidate of her own choosing. The Council simply had to approve it.

"Judge Meyer has the modified document," Vera announced several spreadsheet versions later. "Along with your assurances that the Council should be pleased, changes were minor, and delayed approval for the updated list will deride New Bravaria on the world stage for becoming the most recent constitutional monarchy to crumble into history."

Lana blinked. "Thank you." It was amazing what could come out of somebody's mouth—or fingers—when they weren't bending over backward to make everybody happy. "In that case, I need to start meeting with the Caucus immediately."

"Not yet. Let me follow up in person with Judge Meyer first. You need this signed. *Then* you can do your thing."

Lana could swear she heard the pert click of Vera's heels through the plush carpets on her floors. "Vera?"

"Yes?"

Impatience was a new, if relatable, tone from her assistant. "Why are you helping me?"

Vera looked at Lana like she'd grown a second head. "It's

my job."

Lana waved a hand. "*Everyone* is doing their jobs. You already *were* doing your job."

Vera stared at her for a minute longer, then sighed. "I care about this country. My family cares about this country. I think you will be an effective, important leader—especially if you can boost yourself up, because there are a lot of things that need to change and it's not going to be easy."

Lana allowed herself a single heartbeat of shock—and a moment of gratitude for the fact that Bravaria stopped imprisoning people for this brand of treasonous speech generations ago—before ensuring that her face was serene. She was struggling to reconcile makeup-loving Vera with moderately revolutionary Vera.

"The exact extent of my duties is quite flexible," Vera continued. "You're just allowing me to embrace more of them now."

"Did you say that in your job interviews?"

"Of course not. Aren't you glad I didn't?" Vera left without waiting to hear Lana's agreement and returned moments later, signed document in hand.

The rest of the day passed in a blur, and if Vera hadn't magically been able to juggle her regular duties with her new semi-legal alter ego, Lana was fairly certain that she would've forgotten to submit herself to the styling team to get ready for the ball. As it was, she was grateful that the men attending four of the most critical meetings of her life pretended that her over-filled schedule didn't require that she lead those meetings with her hair in curlers.

Chapter Sixteen

Lana twisted as Michel swept into her room, puffs of white tulle swishing as she turned her gaze from the stylists packing their kits to her brother. His snow-colored tuxedo celebrated his princely status and exquisite taste, but his face was solemn.

"What's wrong?" Lana carefully perched on her bed beside him, skirts flaring out around her in every direction. She'd been told to sit no longer than five minutes at a time to avoid crushing her dress.

Michel fiddled with the gauzy, shimmering overlay of her skirts before meeting her eyes. "You look so beautiful."

Of course she did; he'd helped her choose each detail of the dress, and Solstice colors happened to suit her. She'd yet to look in the mirror, but according to the stylists, the fluffy, delicate white coaxed warmth from her complexion, and her hair gleamed against the rich blue draped over her shoulder. Seeing his success should've made Michel glow with pride. "Then why do you look so sad?"

Michel laced his fingers in his lap. "I've told our parents —and Kaleb—that I'm not marrying him. Yet."

Lana's heart stuttered in pain. "*Michel*." She squeezed his hands firmly, as if she could force comfort and reassurance into him through that simple touch. Lana wanted to promise that she'd make sure he got everything he needed, but she was about to shatter from the stress of so many unknowns, so many moving pieces, so many people potentially hurt. She had a plan and she had to trust it. "You shouldn't sacrifice *anything*."

"I don't know if it will help you," Michel admitted, his eyes going watery. "With everything the press has already been told, it might be too late. But I tried, and I am so sorry that I failed you."

"You didn't fail me. You haven't failed anyone!" Lana tried to hug him, but it became more laughter than hug given how far she had to extend her arms to reach past her enormous dress.

"I think I might've failed *myself*," he continued, ignoring her disagreement. "You know how much I need to please people."

Lana nodded. Michel was an absolute sweetheart, and as one of the most reliable people pleasers she knew, it was a good thing that he focused on New Bravarian charities—with a budget that *someone else* controlled—rather than politics. He didn't have much practice looking out for himself. Over the past week, Lana had started to wonder if she didn't, either.

"And I was worried that Kaleb would leave me if I didn't please him in this."

Lana didn't know Kaleb well—something she was now ashamed to admit—but he'd always seemed besotted with her brother. "What do you mean? He loves you."

"I've never said 'no' to him, Lana."

She thought of the countless times she'd disagreed with Hadi, how difficult it became to deny someone once feelings —once *empathy*—was involved.

"Not revealing my identity when we met was the closest I'd come, and that was a doozy"—Michel shuddered—"but unavoidable. But it never occurred to me to tell him that I might not be ready to get married yet. And I know our parents have coddled me. You've coddled me. I'm grateful for it, if I'm being honest. I'm not fierce like you." He gave her a proud smile. "But I had no idea marrying Kaleb would have consequences for others, and once I understood that, I realized I've been coasting along blindly in so many ways."

Lana loosed a shaky breath. The feeling was all too familiar. How had they never talked about it until now? "But you're staying together, right?" Being a rule breaker was new—and apparently something she might end up being good at. But being a *relationship ruiner*? That was a line she wouldn't cross.

"Yes. I will marry that man. There's no doubt in my mind." He looked so calm, so sure. "But I don't need to be married yet. We're waiting. And next time, *I'm* going to propose."

The thought of her little brother on one knee was nearly enough to make her cry. "I'm so proud of you."

"Oh my gosh, Lana, don't!"

She froze. "What?"

"Don't cry!" He magically produced a tissue, then carefully stepped into the halo of her dress, held her chin, and expertly dabbed a folded corner of the tissue beneath her eye. "Don't ruin your makeup. But also"—he stepped back, surveying her tear-free face—"don't be afraid to *try*, Lana."

She shot him a questioning glance.

"I can tell you have a plan." When had she become so transparent? "I want you to go for it, Lana. You don't always have to protect me."

She made to protest, but he cut her off.

"I know this probably isn't enough, but I just wanted to make sure you knew that I see it now. What you've been doing for me, for this country. And this isn't enough, but this is me trying to do something for *you*. Because *you* deserve to be taken care of, too."

He caught the next wave of tears before they finished escaping her eyes. "Though I am curious to see how this emotional awakening—"

"*Emotional awakening*!?" The words finally freed Lana from the devastating impact of Michel's words. Words she had never even imagined she'd need to hear. "Don't you dare."

"This *whatever*." He winked at her. "Is going to go for you."

Lana wasn't about to admit a word of her plan unless it worked, but she didn't want to leave Michel with nothing. "Thank you, Michel." She brushed a hand down her dress, and he nodded. "See you there?"

❄

Lana double-checked the contents of the sleek bag that Vera would carry for her because princesses still couldn't wear purses to balls, then took a deep breath. She could *see* the pulse fluttering at her neck in her reflection.

Svetlana doesn't do nervous, Lana reminded herself. *And neither does Henrietta.* She took a deep breath and forced herself to see beyond the nerves, beyond the names, to the woman looking back at her from the mirror.

Lana blinked. And stared.

She had to hand it to Michel; she looked like the face of her country, proud and strong and shining. The pale winter beauty of Bravaria was in her dress, in the full skirts and tight bodice that shimmered like frosted snow. The sumptuous amount of fabric was feminine and powerful, white for the snow that would fall ever more thickly after Solstice, and which, like clockwork, always started by midnight. The vibrant rivers that snow would feed come spring, the lifeblood of her country powered by purity and patience and light, were there too, in a sash of luxurious deep blue silk—cerulean as the purest sky—draped over one shoulder. The sash covered half her bodice at a diagonal and tied in the back in a large bow. Complete with white gloves, a head full of waves and braids, and the joyful knowledge that this was the one time each year that she could glitter in public, Lana was the perfect canvas for her jewels.

A single row of dangling teardrop pearls, one per strand, dripped from chains of tiny diamonds on the Glacier Tiara— one of the four Solstice tiaras. Pale sapphires rimmed the swirls at the top. The asymmetrical neckline of her dress left no room for a necklace, but the Heir's Brooch, a swirling cascade of platinum and diamonds that echoed the Ram's Horn's swirling pattern, was fitted firmly onto the white side of the bodice. The tiara, of course, was secured with the regular forty pins. It would hurt later, but for now, Lana felt glorious.

❄

As the royal family passed a portrait of King Hayden III on their paparazzi-laden way to the ballroom, Lana was grateful that her corseted bodice kept her facing forward. The famous king, whose portrait she'd grown up with, was considered one of the most impressively mustachioed monarchs of all time—and he was Hadi's ancestor. Lana refused to let her gaze drift over any of the potentially incriminating portraits, especially since her mother had been eyeing her suspiciously for the past hour.

Vera rejoined the royal family after they were presented to the ballroom, and when Lana eyed the bag in Vera's hand, her nerves simply decided they'd had enough. As if from a distance, she felt them snap as one. It was a strange kind of relief.

When her mother whispered in her ear, asking for the fifth time that day whom Lana had chosen to marry, Lana merely repeated that she would see. When Lana identified all twelve Councilors scattered across the ballroom—and noticed two of them flinch when Vera made eye contact—she nodded politely and held her head high. And when her grandmother briefly squeezed her hand, her gaze kind but unreadable, Lana simply braced herself.

Lana made small talk with guests, graciously refused to reveal her fiancé, and politely clapped for the dignitaries who took turns on the dance floor, glad that she wouldn't be expected to dance until after midnight.

Usually, the gilded spectacle of the Solstice Ball Ball took her breath away, allowing Lana to ignore the paparazzi in the excitement of everything else, but tonight, she was highly attuned to their every move, grateful they'd be there to live broadcast the evening. The paparazzi would make or break her plan, providing either legitimacy or fodder for a scandal in the making.

Each year on Solstice, the monarch addressed the nation just before the midnight bells chimed, announcing a moment of silence for the learnings and gratitude of the year before, and hope for the year to come. And then with a crash of fireworks, the celebrations would begin in earnest. In light of the big announcement for this year, King Jakob II had begun his remarks ten minutes before midnight. Lana wryly thought of how Old Bravaria's queen (Hadi's *mother*) was likely doing her own version of the exact same thing.

Her father gave her a quick smile, his cue that he was nearly done speaking from his place on the central balcony overlooking the ballroom. Vera, standing several yards to the right of the balcony, gave Lana a nod, a rare excitement in her gaze. From the other side of the balcony, where she stood amongst two of Lana's least favorite Councilors—the two who'd often led Lana on a wild goose chase for compromises they had no intention of making—Esmelda gave the tiniest wink, shifting her hands, and…was that a cane? Esmelda didn't use—

Lana's father turned toward her, cutting off her desperately distracted thoughts as he concluded his final Solstice speech as monarch. Miraculously, Lana's numbness prevented her from exhibiting a single eye twitch on international television.

Lana gracefully switched places with her father and surveyed the ballroom. *This* was the easy part. It was what would happen next—what had already begun—that was the gamble.

Lana schooled her face into a slightly more reserved version of that messy baker who'd been so charismatic in the leaked photos, making eye contact with Councilors, guests, and the cameras (never had she been so grateful that royals never formally addressed one another during speeches), keeping her voice even and clear, and flawlessly delivering the speech she'd written that morning in Helga's office. She wished blessings upon her people, shared her dreams for a stronger, forward-looking Bravaria in the years to come, and announced the extent of her gratitude and joy to present to them the partner who had spent two weeks in the traditional courting period wooing her with his mind, his spirit, his love of the Bravarian people, and his openness to love and grow together.

❄

"Your Majesty, if you would, please." She curtsied and took her father's arm after bestowing her final request. The cameras hadn't stopped rolling or flashing since she'd opened her mouth and now, in anticipation of the official reveal, guests were starting to sneak out their phones. Gasps broke out even before the doors opened.

"Please accept"—and those feelings all rushed in at once as Lana saw a pair of polished boots step through the doorway, because avoiding eye contact was the only way she could do this—"my choice, the Prince Hayden Henri Tobias Maximilian David Gotthard Melvin of Old Bravaria."

There was silence, except for the clicks of cameras, then a moment of deafening sound as several things seemed to happen in slow motion and all at once.

Hadi was there—he was really, truly there—and Lana worried for a brief moment that this wasn't what he'd wanted, wasn't what he'd meant, before reminding herself that he was an adult and had only made the journey because he wanted to.

The fluttering of camera shutters continued along with the hush of broadcasters urgently gesturing at their crews to pan their camera angles and show the royal choice. Then the broadcasters, too, went quiet, putting their hands to their earpieces as one while their correspondents from HQ informed them of what was happening on the internet: those forty-seven mouflon sweater-loving blogs were posting more baking photos of Lana—this time with Hadi in his matching jumper. The same two photos had been circulated: one of Hadi and Lana throwing dough at one another, and another with them both smiling, each holding the Ram's Horn pattern of their country. Every publication had been given an exclusive "juicy" detail: they fell in love in the Bravarian mountains, one of their first dates was at a hot spring, they were both good at traditional pastry, they both had a sweet tooth, both of them considered the mouflon to be their favorite animal (that had been added in a moment of hysterical panic).

It was agonizing, silent torture as Hadi walked toward Lana and her father. Only when his boots were a foot away did Lana will herself to look into his eyes.

When he'd asked her to choose him, she hadn't had time to clarify, so she'd put into action the only scenario that made sense—that she could live with: add Hadi to the list, like her grandmother had said, and choose him. Lana had passed Hadi's contact details to Vera, who'd organized nearly everything while Lana met with Councilor upon Councilor, securing special signatures and drafting the innocuous facts to spread to the blogs she'd identified to lend legitimacy to their announcement. In the chaos of it all, Lana hadn't wavered, but now, she realized that she'd more or less—definitely *more*—proposed to Hadi in the most public way possible. And he could refuse.

But Hadi's gaze was steady when they shared a brief glance before he acknowledged her father with the slight but purposeful bow that princes used to greet kings of other nations. Hadi kept his hands calmly at his sides and regarded her father with his strong chin held high. As King Jakob II scrutinized him right back, Lana took in Hadi's dirty-blonde hair, which gleamed like burnished gold above a freshly shaven face. He was clad in traditional tight breeches of shimmery white that matched her dress and a regal navy-blue jacket, streaked with its own sash of white and the

Heir's Brooch of Old Bravaria on his breast.

Lana had avoided looking at her father, dreading his reaction to her public betrayal—even if that betrayal was for the greater good. But she looked at him now. Beneath the tiny smile he'd managed to keep in place for their audience, his jaw was as firm as Hadi's. Lana refused to look at her mother.

The king gave the slightest incline of his head—barely a millimeter, more a change of angle than anything—to avoid prolonging the moment, as some of the crowd had started to pick up on the fact that something was wrong. The instant he moved, sound crashed through the silence as fireworks burst across the sky, illuminating the ballroom through the floor-to-ceiling windows lining the sides.

Prince Hayden's reveal had accidentally overlapped with the annual moment of silence, and the burst of celebration coinciding with King Jakob II's nod was taken by the public to convey the approval of King and Council. Lana had hoped to manipulate the media storm that her parents so often yielded to by making the reveal as dramatic as possible, but she hadn't realized that Hadi would enter at the pinnacle of the drama.

After the formal exchange with her father, Hadi stood by her side, his fingers brushing lightly against the outermost layer of her gown in chaste acknowledgement.

The king called for the dancing to begin, urging the cameras to focus on that instead, until the entire balcony section was cleared of everyone but the royal family, Hadi, Vera, the Councilors, and their guards. As the orchestra started up again, masking the sound of their conversation, the second trial of the evening began.

"Lana, what is this?" Lana knew her father's mild tone was a mask.

"This is my choice, Father. I honestly believe it is best for the kingdom, and for me."

"You cannot marry an Old Bravarian," insisted Councilor Merrick.

"Actually, sir, I can." Lana nodded to Vera, who firmly clasped the shiny leather bag that she'd kept with her the entire evening.

"We have written confirmation from a simple majority of the Council approving the addition of Prince Hayden's candidacy to the list of possible grooms."

Councilor Merrick's face started to go ruddy. "How can this be?"

"I approved it," announced Judge Meyer. Lana couldn't help but think that the rest of the Councilors looked like piranhas as they pushed further into the ring forming around the royal family. "I provided written approval this morning," he continued. "I figured that approving such a strategic addition was the least we could do given that we failed to submit a Writ of Intent, *as required by this country's law*."

Judge Meyer delivered his final sentence with a hard look to Councilor Merrick, who scoffed, not so easily deterred. "But he can't legally be here. He should be arrested for trespassing on New Bravarian land! This violates the Treaty of Baulten."

Lana's mother's eyes sharpened. "I agree. His very presence is threatening to this realm." She glanced briefly at one of the guards near the door.

"Arrest him." Lana was so *tired* of her mother's words coming out of Councilor Merrick's mouth.

"You can't." Vera's chirpy voice was confident as Councilor Merrick's complexion surpassed ruddiness and began approaching purple. "You need a warrant to make an arrest. And we have a special permit allowing his presence." She pulled a thick document emblazoned with the Chief Justice's seal from her bag. Judge Meyer, who rarely mentioned his second title, said nothing as cheers of "ay" and hearty applause from the social dance below cut through their group's silent disbelief.

"But he is threatening the future stability of this realm,"

Lana's mother hissed. "And a marriage to him, a soon-to-be king of our rivals? His authority as King trumps hers as Princess. He will *subvert* this kingdom."

"A united Bravaria is a stronger Bravaria," Lana insisted. "We've been in steady decline since The Split, and we're not as different as we think. This could let us *fix* things."

"But your speech," her father cut in quietly, turning Lana slightly to the side. He spoke so quietly that the clapping from the dancers below nearly drowned out his voice. "You said you know this man, that he courted you. You didn't take a courting period, Lana. Why are you making this up?"

His brown eyes were disappointed. It hurt that her father thought she'd purposefully lied about this, too, even if she hadn't been completely transparent about the last week and a half.

"It wasn't a courting period in the formal sense, but I do know him."

"How on earth did you meet him?" Her father's hand shot out, signet ring gleaming, to point an accusatory finger at Hadi. "Because you've been given an enormous amount of trust every Solstice season for your little visits to Havos, and I know for a fact that this man has never legally passed into New Bravaria before today."

Lana swallowed. "I met *this man* in Havos. At Grandmother's house."

Her father's eyes widened in surprise, and he shot Esmelda a critical look.

Lana's mother moved closer. "You met him at Grandma's house?" She looked at Esmelda. "Mom, what did you do?"

"I didn't do anything beyond display the Bravarian hospitality expected of me." Esmelda crossed her arms, completely ignoring her cane, which tapped Councilor Merrick on the calf.

"Prince Hayden was rescued during a snowstorm and we took him in. We didn't even know who he was until two days ago," Lana explained.

"*What?*" Lana's mother screeched, and Lana was fairly

sure her father was on his way to sending himself to an even earlier retirement with how the vein in his neck had started pulsing. "You let a strange man sleep in the same house as my daughter?"

The Councilors were bristling now, as if starting to second guess the wisdom of letting Lana and Vera strong-arm them into pledging their support a few hours before.

"Everything was safe. Really." Lana cut in, providing an abbreviated account that might have slightly exaggerated the extent of Hadi's injury-driven incapacitation. "When I saw the press release a couple of days ago, I realized who he was. And realized that my one reason for saying no was no longer valid. So here we are," Lana concluded.

"So he *did* violate our treaty by coming over," Lana's mother insisted. "You have a permit now, but he didn't have one back in Havos."

Lana swallowed, scrambling for a reply. Vera beat her to it. "Prince Hayden didn't enter New Bravaria willingly. He was unconscious, and a wildlife ranger spotted him from across the border and brought him in."

Apparently Vera had worked with Felix to get the coordinates of where Hadi was found. She was getting a raise the moment Solstice season was over.

"This doesn't solve the authority issue. This union would sacrifice our independence—everything we've worked so hard for for over a century. You cannot do this," Lana's mother pleaded to the Council, and Lana could swear that her grandmother had accessorized with a cane for exactly this moment. A tiny tap at their heels, and the Councilors she'd spent the afternoon speaking to admitted their support one by one.

Councilor Aaron and three other Conciliatory Caucus members whose family businesses would see the largest immediate benefit of improved relations with Old Bravaria had been surprisingly enthusiastic about Lana's proposal. Two others had gradually come around when Lana promised to put protections in place to look after New Bravarian interests through a transition period to a fully joint government—a transition that would be sealed by the birth and coronation of an heir raised to advocate equally for both sides.

Judge Meyer had been the seventh vote. He'd been the hardest to convince, but had conceded once the ten-year transition period was extended to a twenty-year one. It was a good thing, too, since they hadn't been able to trick him into blindly approving the modified list.

Now, Judge Meyer relayed the protections that the Caucus required to support the transition, and Vera produced a printed list of Lana's own demands. Councilor Merrick and Lana's mother both seemed to be in shock as they looked around and saw the remaining Councilors nodding stiffly. Even Lana's father had grabbed Vera's list, muttering to himself as he skimmed it.

"I'm confident this arrangement will work and benefit all parties," Lana said. "And I know you don't like to update things once they've gone out to the press, so I will say this now: let us wait to marry until after my coronation. If we are forced to marry in six months' time, a king will marry a princess. If we both marry as regents, we marry as equals." Lana's parents said nothing. "Give us a year-long engagement."

Lana only hoped Hadi wouldn't change his mind.

❄

"I knew it!" Michel exclaimed a few moments later, brushing past Councilor Merrick to wrap Lana, then Hadi, in a careful hug.

"Knew what?" Their mother's voice was thick with frustration.

Michel ignored her. Apparently he hadn't yet forgiven his parents for forcing Lana into this situation. "You couldn't agree that he was that hot and do nothing about it!"

Lana dragged her eyes to the ceiling to beg for patience.

Hadi said nothing. In fact, he hadn't said a word since

entering the country, as far as Lana knew.

"That wasn't the reason," Lana said quietly, mindful of the fact that twelve middle-age male Councilors were listening to every word, "but I'm pleased that you approve."

And she meant it. Michel was a good, if too forgiving, judge of character.

"We will discuss this tomorrow," Lana's mother snapped, turning to head down the stairs.

"We need to discuss this further," Lana's father whispered into her ear as he went to follow his wife, "but for the record, I think it's brilliant. Heartbreaking"—Lana wondered if the hint of betrayal in her father's eyes would ever fade—"but brilliant."

I'm sorry. She almost said it, but stopped herself. She couldn't give Givera a reason to think she felt even an inkling of doubt.

Out of the corner of her eye, Lana saw her grandmother saddle a grumbling Councilor Merrick with the cane before walking over to plant a kiss on her cheek.

You're okay. Esmelda didn't say that, either. "I'm proud of you."

Lana was blinking back the moisture in her eyes when Hadi finally spoke. "May I have the next dance?" His tone was so formal, his deep bow and outstretched hand so rigid, that Lana startled. *If* he didn't change his mind, *if* things went the way she thought she wanted them, would that formality be the signature of their marriage?

Lana slipped her hand into his and nodded. "You may."

Prince Hayden tucked her arm around his elbow and whisked her away from the twelve Councilors chattering rapidly amongst themselves, from Michel and Kaleb, whose first official argument seemed to have supercharged their relationship with a frisky chemistry, and from Vera, who was murmuring something about press audiences into her phone.

❊

Dancing with Hadi…some part of Lana had always thought it would be incredible. But it wasn't. It was torture.

Waltzes were formal enough by nature, but between her gown's corset, which suddenly felt like a cage, and the potent concoction of adrenaline and dread coursing through her system, Lana couldn't have relaxed if she tried. Fortunately, she had muscle memory to fall back on as Hadi —*as her fiancé*—pulled her seamlessly onto the dance floor.

Despite the dozens of other dancing pairs, all eyes were on the Bravarian heirs' first dance as a couple, which is to say that while their bodies flawlessly executed a waltz, the smooth expressions and silence between them became increasingly intolerable. Lana had no chance to ask if Hadi was okay with what she'd done. Having given up on feeling most of her body parts the moment she'd felt Hadi's spine straighten for the dance, Lana focused instead on trying to unlock her tingling jaw.

I should probably propose properly, Lana realized as Hadi maneuvered them past another couple to the middle of the floor, as far from the spectators lining the ballroom as possible. A quick glance away from Hadi's shoulder—to which she'd given her undivided attention to avoid risking eye contact—revealed that they'd come within alarming proximity of her parents. As they spun away, Lana corrected her gaze just a moment too late, and found herself making eye contact with her father. It was an impressive feat, given that it felt like Hadi was moving in the opposite direction. But her father was an impressive dancer, matching Hadi's rotations long enough to send Lana a smile and a wink.

And then he turned slightly, just enough that Lana couldn't help making accidental eye contact with her mother. And Givera's face…something that was almost *approval* flashed there when she met Lana's gaze. Lana's mouth dropped open in surprise, causing her mother's eyes to narrow, that whisper of pride gone so quickly that Lana wondered if she'd imagined it.

That pride helped bring feeling back into Lana's hands,

and she noticed the fineness of the fabric beneath her left hand, the warmth of Hadi's fingers around her right. Lana took her first steady breath of the evening.

Buoyed by a new sense of hope, Lana began dragging her gaze the interminable distance from Hadi's shoulder to his face when she thought she saw... *Was that Leo?*

Lana was immensely grateful that Hadi was a good lead—a nearly telepathic one—as he used the momentum of a last-minute turn to give her a clear view of her grandmother, whose purely decorative cane was likely still in the hands of a befuddled Councilor Merrick, and whose laughter pealed out across the dance floor as Leo spun her around.

"I *knew* it!" Lana muttered under her breath, giving Hadi a stunned smile.

And with that look, the dance truly did become incredible.

It felt like they were standing still, though the whip of air against her skin, the swirl of her skirts against her legs, assured her that Hadi continued to guide them flawlessly across the floor. But once Lana met his gaze, she couldn't look away, trusting him to lead her safely, as he had for the entire dance—as he had since the moment she'd tumbled off the couch at the sight of him.

Lana swallowed, the smile that had sprung so easily to her lips fading. He'd kept her safe again, this time from scorn, by coming to New Bravaria to follow her harebrained plan, by showing up when she announced him, by standing (however silently) at her side as she, Vera, and Judge Meyer faced the wrath of her parents and the rest of the Council. But did he want to be there?

Lana's pulse fluttered. They were *engaged*. The entire planet thought they were in love and wanted to get married, uniting their nations in the process. Hadi's limitless blue gaze held her captive as her thoughts spiraled.

What if it wasn't true? Lana was starting to panic. *What if I misunderstood everything, and he just wanted a friend, not a fiancée—a fiancée whose baggage included another country, for goodness' sake!*

The spinning was coming faster now, chasing away her frantic thoughts. The room was spinning, the couples were spinning, and she had never felt so out of contro—

The spinning stopped, and they moved smoothly again, perfectly in step with everyone else. Lana blinked, realizing that *they* had been spinning, perhaps in an effort from Hadi to break her free from her thoughts. It worked.

"I'm sor—"

The slightest shake of his head, almost imperceptible, cut her off.

Not here.

She swallowed again, returning her gaze to his shoulder. It would be much more polite for him to reject her in private instead of under the watchful gaze of the entire court and countless cameras. How could she have thought to do this, to *trick* her country into accepting him, to trick *him* into accepting *her*? And she had to wait until this interminable dance was finally over to hear him confirm her fears.

Spinning cut off her thoughts once again until she met Hadi's eyes, and…they were happy. *Glowing.* And the smile stretching across his face…it was so broad that *dimples* were popping out on his cheeks.

Lana blinked, nearly blinded by his happiness. Could she have done that? Made him so happy that staring into his face felt like looking into the sun?

A smile slipped across her own lips, shaky, unsure, until the skin around his eyes crinkled, until she saw *him* swallow as his eyes flicked over her dress and back to her face, that grin returning instantly.

The dance ended, and Lana's skirts brushed against Hadi's legs as she curtsied and he bowed, an intimate caress of fabric in a formal gesture that had stood the test of time. Lana wondered if they would, too. They had certainly stood the test of memory.

❄

Lana smoothed her expression as new couples took the floor

for the next dance. Hadi mimicked her, consciously or no, and she led him on a slow, meandering path to one of the balconies jutting off the ballroom. The doors closed behind them—Vera's doing, if the flash of a black bag was any indication—offering a thin screen of privacy from the revelers.

The contrast in temperature between the ballroom and the fresh air fogged the glass doors, but despite her bare arms, Lana wasn't cold; spring water heated the marble floor of the balcony from below, and she was Bravarian through and through. The cold would feel refreshing for at least five minutes of long-awaited privacy.

Hadi stepped into the space delineated by Lana's skirts, and the rich smell of jasmine wafted up to clash with the crisp scent of new snow. Lana looked down, realizing that this was one of the Tropics Balconies. A long-ago Queen had created the tiny, whimsical pleasure gardens by recessing low planters into the heated flooring. Carefully tended star jasmine bloomed year round in the pockets of warmth that lined the carved stone railings. The fabric of Lana's skirts brushed against the planters, which were still dry despite the fat flakes of snow that had started drifting down at midnight.

Hadi had remained silent, waiting as she looked around. That uncharacteristic silence worried her.

"Why are you so quiet?" Lana asked in a soft voice. The only light came from the steamy windows and her shimmery dress, which seemed to glow from within.

Hadi gave an awkward laugh, his hands clasped behind his back. "Believe it or not, I haven't had the best track record with this kind of event."

So he *had* recovered his memories of some of the infamous debauchery he'd been known for in the past. Lana took a fortifying breath.

"By 'this kind of event,' do you mean a proposal"—his nostrils flared on a sharp intake of breath—"or a ball?" She looked up at him innocently.

Hadi flushed at her words before a shy, wondrous smile teased his lips. He cleared his throat. "The ball, certainly. I intend to have a perfect track record when it comes to proposals."

She grinned back at him, so wide that she could barely get the words out. "You *intend* to? It was my understanding that you are already spoken for." Would he change his answer if she asked properly?

"Oh, I am." His eyes gleamed. "But I suppose a confirmation wouldn't hurt."

Was he trying to torment her? The teasing note in his voice didn't sound wicked. It sounded…nervous. Longing. The way he'd sounded when he couldn't remember his family but desperately wanted to. She had to do this, for both of them.

"Hadi," she began, reaching for his hand. A snowflake fell into his palm, and she watched it melt as she spoke. "Or do you prefer Hayden now?"

He flipped their hands, so her palm faced up to catch the next flake. "What do you think, Svetlana?"

Lana groaned, closing her fist around a shard of cold. "*Never* call me that. Ever…*Henri.*"

"Henrietta."

"Maximilian."

"Adelaide."

Lana wished the snow had accumulated into a pile she could throw at him.

Hadi laughed. "Our names are ridiculous. I was dismayed to relearn mine."

"I don't blame you for forgetting them."

"Lana."

"Yes?" she whispered.

"Are you growing cold?" His warm hands rubbed her arms, brushing off the flakes of snow that had begun falling in earnest.

"No."

His hands paused.

"But please keep going."

His hands assumed a more leisurely pace, trailing fingers across skin in a delicate caress that left goosebumps where the snow could not.

This could be the rest of my life.

The thought was liberating. Shocking. Lana had never wanted anything so dearly. "Hadi, I'm sorry I didn't listen to you in Havos."

He tilted his head, as if half amused and half surprised that this was what she'd been attempting to apologize for for fifteen minutes. But it was only the start of what she needed to say.

"But I've listened to you since then…especially when you said that if I could find a way to choose you, you'd choose me, too. I believed every word, and I hope you will believe mine." Lana took a deep breath, worried her corset would pop with the strain, yet grateful it was continuing to prop her up in the face of her words and those achingly gentle, endlessly reassuring thumbs, which hadn't stropped stroking her skin for a single second. She realized they'd stepped closer at some point, her skirts creating a bubble around the both of them. "I—I love you. I probably loved you since you gave me a lingonberry, but I *definitely* love you now, and I think you're right. We could be good for each other, every day. We could *do good* together. And thinking of my life without you in it, even though your being part of it is all so new…I want to be with you, with the incredible person you are, and the even better one you will become. I know you basically said yes in there, but if you say no now, I can make it all go away, I promise. Will you marry me?"

"*Yes.*"

Hadi's arms were around her in an instant, wrapping her in his warmth and squeezing so tightly that she could feel his Heir's brooch pressing into her right shoulder. Two brooches, two heirs, two countries…a sob might've come out of her during that embrace, or maybe it came from him. *They could do it. They could unite two peoples, together.*

Still holding on tight, Lana tilted her head back to look at him. His eyes were wet.

"I love you."

They might've both said it, a breathless gasp as they had this priceless gift, this rare private moment amongst the snow and the stars. It was difficult to kiss when too much joy made it all teeth and smiles and mouths with too many words to say, and suddenly none at all.

Lana buried her hands in his hair, barely registering that his hands had floated up to do the same, only to touch her tiara and trail down to grip her waist instead. She didn't even mind when a telltale flash announced that a photographer who looked suspiciously like Vera had just secured the photograph of a lifetime.

He tasted like moonlight and freedom.

And for once, when she thought of the years ahead, she felt joy.

❄❄❄

ABOUT THE AUTHOR

Elizabeth Heathly channels her expert worrying skills into writing happily ever afters for fictional people. Although she currently lives in Manhattan, her time living in San Francisco, Denver, Chicago, London, and Cambridge provides endless inspiration for her novels. Elizabeth's oldest couple crush is—fittingly—Elizabeth Bennet and Fitzwilliam Darcy, and she aims to bring a lighthearted version of their quick banter and reluctant romance into a modern romcom setting. When she isn't writing, Elizabeth loves to eat chocolate (the darker, the better), plan adventures to new places, and dream about the black labs she'll have one day.

To keep up to date on future Elizabeth Heathly novels and bonus content (including the recipes for river cakes and Bravarian sharing cakes!), follow along at @elizabethheathly on Instagram, Facebook or TikTok.